A FAREWAY THROUGH HEAVEN

MARY FISCHER

Lucky Bat Books

A Lucky Bat Book

A Fareway Through Heaven
Copyright 2016 by Mary Fischer

Cover Design by Brandon Swann

ISBN 978-1-943588-41-1

Published by
Lucky Bat Books
LuckyBatBooks.com
10 9 8 7 6 5 4 3 2

Welcome in *A Fareway to Heaven*, to a transpersonal journey of Inspiration!

Leon Buist, Ph.D.
Author and Lecturer

A Fareway Through Heaven shows the difference we make in peoples' lives through our acts of kindness, and presence; and that these qualities are significant. The connection between the living and the deceased is portrayed, and the idea that this connection is everlasting. These ideas bring comfort. *A Fareway Through Heaven* is a delightful, sensitive, and humorous story, which will uplift the spirit of its readers.

Rev. Catherine Linesch
Unitarian Universalist minister and
Bereavement Counselor

Random Acts Of Kindness…we never know how far they reach. This inspirational novel will make the reader consider how the good we do in this life can have repercussions in the next. A must read!!!

Audrey Cournia
Author

Dedicated to Tom—
A friend to all

PROLOGUE

NOW ON THE first tee, Tom Malone from Red Rock, Nevada."

This is it; this is what it's like to be in a pro tournament. Keep cool. Keep it under control. Tom took an easy practice swing, then addressed the ball and swung. He estimated he hit the ball about 260 yards. The ball landed dead center in the middle of the fairway before it rolled another twenty yards or so. *Not the longest, but it's in the fairway and I can still be on the green in regulation.*

As he walked downhill towards his ball, Tom took in his surroundings, mainly to be aware of any obstacles to his next shot. A creek ran along the left side of the fairway and mature oak trees lined the right. *Trees, I hadn't thought about trees; there are so few in the desert. Shouldn't be a problem though. I learned the game playing on courses with trees.*

Late spring in the Midwest, and the air had a touch of humidity to it. Not stifling, but enough for Tom to know his palms would be sweaty and he'd need more than one glove throughout the round to help keep a grip on his clubs. Fortunately, he'd remembered to bring a spare.

Continuing down the fairway, Tom saw several geese crossing to the creek as if they owned the fairway. He wondered how much of a problem they would be. On one of the courses back home, there was a 'course' dog that ran alongside the assistant's cart to try to keep geese off the fairways and greens and keep the geese from becoming a real nuisance to the players.

For his second shot, he just needed a nice, easy swing and that's what he hit. He loved the sound of the club head striking the ball, its crack echoing through the trees. His ball landed exactly where he wanted. His third shot on the par five hole would be directly onto the green, with no trees blocking the way, no sand hazards or water to clear.

His third shot reached the green, but landed further from the hole than he wanted.

On the way to the green, Tom glanced to his right where a few spectators had gathered. The gallery of about fifty people consisted mostly of employees from the tournament's sponsor. Family and friends of the players made up the rest of the crowd.

His wife, Liz, waved from the gallery and he waved back with a smile. *Always wanted to wave from inside the ropes.*

He was glad the number of observers was small. Liz, as he kidded her, was vertically challenged, being only five foot, two. If the crowd had been large, he knew she wouldn't be one to push her way to the front where she was now. But it was always easy to pick Liz out because of her red hair.

Tom tapped in his third putt, bogeying the first hole of the tournament.

As he retrieved the ball from the hole, he felt a little dizzy, but he welcomed the huge sense of relief. *Not too bad a showing. No whiffs, no duck hooks. I didn't hit a shot killing someone in the gallery. Maybe I can relax now.*

He handed his putter to his caddie, Deb. She placed the putter in his bag and threw the bag over her shoulder. He'd felt uncomfortable not carrying the clubs himself, but his concern had eased when he'd found out carts could be used by the amateurs and their caddies.

Tom had known Deb about a year or so through phone conversations and the quarterly business trips she made to his office. She participated in many sports: skiing, softball, running. She had a very athletic body, and although she was vertically challenged, like Liz, she had no problem handling his bag. He'd probably want to ride in the cart before she did as the round proceeded, but for now he was enjoying the walk.

While Tom, Deb, the other players in the group, and some of the spectators proceeded to the second hole, radiance illuminated the area, as if the sun had suddenly burst through a thick cloud cover. But there hadn't been a cloud in the sky when he'd teed off minutes earlier and no clouds had developed.

What the—? Where'd that light come from?

While players and caddies recorded scores and selected clubs for the second hole, a man stepped from the shadows of the second fairway and walked up to Deb. He wore traditional weekend amateur golfer garb: khaki knee-length shorts, a white shirt, white socks, two-toned golf shoes. The man could have passed as Tom's twin. His white golf hat had "GA" embroidered on the front and he wore a caddy vest with Tom's last name embroidered in gold thread on the back of his vest and on the back of his cap as well.

Tom couldn't help but be impressed. *WOW! This is really a first class tournament.*

"I have it from here," the man said as he took Tom's bag from Deb. "There has been a change in venue."

3

❧❧ ❧❧ ❧❧

SECTION ONE

A CHANGE IN VENUE

❧❧ ❧❧ ❧❧

Chapter 1

THE SECOND HOLE

TOM WAS CURIOUS. More than curious, actually. He was confused and very suspicious. "Why the change in venue?"

The new caddy admitted he did not know any specific details and explained there had been some mix-up in the schedule.

"What course are we playing?" Tom asked.

"You probably have not heard of the course but it consistently gets rave reviews. From what I understand it is unlike any course on Earth."

Tom and his new caddy walked over to the second hole. Tom shook the caddy's hand firmly. "I'm Tom. Sorry, I didn't catch your name."

"I hoped you would recognize me. We met years ago. My name is Ralph."

"Hmm, Ralph." Tom racked his brain. "I hate to admit it, but I'm not good at remembering names and faces. But glad to meet you. A great day for golf. Like they say, the worst day on the golf course is better than the best day in the office, right?"

"So I hear," Ralph adjusted the golf bag's strap on his shoulder and gave Tom a grin.

The comment puzzled Tom. "Sounds like you don't play much golf?"

"No. Mainly, I observe. I called for transportation to the course you are to play today." Ralph pointed to a bench off the second hole. "While we wait, why not relax on that bench over in the shade?"

Tom walked over to the bench and sat down. Ralph sat beside him. Tom watched from the side bench as the other players, their caddies, and the gallery headed to the tees for the second hole.

"Are the other players coming with us?" Tom was apprehensive about what was going on. But he knew he had a poker face and made every attempt not to let any emotions show. This might be the only way for him to finish the round.

The wooden bench was under a large oak tree, providing relief from the sun. Tom noted a sign showing the bench had been sponsored by a local café, but the sign he focused on was the one that showed the distance from tee to green and the yardage to the stream crossing the fairway. Something hit him on the head and Tom heard some noise above him. He looked up and saw two playful squirrels on the lower limbs. He grinned.

"Would you like a soda, sir?" Ralph reached into his vest pocket and pulled out two twenty-ounce plastic bottles of diet colas.

"Thanks." Tom took the chilled bottle from Ralph, opened it, and took a big swig.

Tom saw Liz coming towards him. He introduced Liz to Ralph and told her what little he knew about what was going on. Liz asked if she could continue on with them. Tom thought it would be okay, but Ralph told them that entrance to the course they were heading to was by invitation only and Liz was not on today's list, nor were the other players.

Liz frowned. Tom knew she was disappointed, but she wouldn't say anything that might jeopardize his opportunity to continue playing. In an attempt to clarify what was going on for both Liz and himself, he again asked, "Why the change in venue?"

Ralph once again stated that he did not know any specific details and that there had been some mix-up in the schedule.

The loud roar of an engine above them halted further conversation. The air whirled as a helicopter landed just in front of the bench.

Ralph pointed at the helicopter. "Our transportation is here. I will get your golf bag and clubs and load them onto the helicopter. Go ahead and get in."

Tom was shocked. "We need a helicopter? Where are we going?"

"I will explain as we travel. We are already behind schedule." Although Tom was not especially fond of helicopters, at this point he saw no alternative if he wanted to finish the round. He looked at Liz. She was looking directly at him, a pleading look in her eyes. He couldn't hear her above the noise of the helicopter, but he read her lips. "Take me with you."

Tom boarded the helicopter, looked out the window at Liz, waved to her and mouthed, "I love you."

The helicopter lifted skyward, pulling Tom and Liz further and further apart.

Chapter 2

THE HELICOPTER RIDE

A FTER TOM GOT settled, Ralph offered him a pillow and blanket. "Sir, it may take a few moments before we arrive at our destination. Close your eyes and relax. I will wake you in plenty of time to be alert when we arrive."

"Where are we going?" Tom asked again. He looked around the helicopter and noted there were only two seats, one on each side of the helicopter and a large open area between the seats. He had not seen any markings on the outside of the helicopter, but guessed it might be owned by the company sponsoring the tournament. *Not very lavish for a corporate aircraft. I was hoping they might have some sodas and snacks. I could sure use an apple and some water now. Guess I'll settle for a nap.* Tom wrapped the blanket around his shoulders.

Ralph shrugged. "I am not sure yet. I need to confirm the flight plans with The Controller."

"Do you have a headset so I can listen to the air traffic communications?"

"That would be a negative."

Despite having a pilot's license and a passion for flying small aircraft, Tom didn't like helicopters, but never could explain why. He hesitated to look out the windows. Right now the helicopter was level with the trees, so they weren't too terribly high. Out of the corner of his eye, he thought he saw movement. *Probably just the wind.* But it was more than the wind. He saw monkeys in the trees. *How strange. I must've gotten dehydrated on the first hole. Now I'm seeing things. I need to force myself to drink gallons of water before I tee off on the second hole.*

Before Tom had an opportunity to ask about the monkeys, the warmth of the sun, the hum of the blades, and the motion of the helicopter lulled him into a peaceful state. As amusing memories of his life drifted through his mind, he felt himself smiling.

Tom didn't notice the medics on the helicopter working on his heart and inserting a breathing tube into his lungs, but Ralph did. Ralph also noted that the medics looked grim when they sent their evaluation of Tom's condition to The Controller. Moments later, the pilot received confirmation of their destination and notified Ralph. Ralph signaled the medics to pack their equipment and conceal it and themselves in a compartment at the rear of the helicopter.

After what seemed like only a few seconds, Tom heard, "Sir."

When Tom didn't flinch, Ralph called in a louder voice, "Sir, we are arriving and you really do need to be alert for our arrival."

Tom moved, but still didn't open his eyes "That was the most refreshing sleep I've had in weeks. I can't get up. I'm stapled to the bed."

When Tom finally opened his eyes, his attention was immediately drawn to the green panorama. The varying shades of green and the outline of the landscape suggested it was a golf course. *Always could sniff out a golf course.*

"Is that the course I'll be playing?" he asked Ralph.

"Possibly. We need to check-in and see what course the starter has you on."

As the helicopter approached, Tom studied the course: the yardage, the slope of the fairways, the doglegs, the size of the greens, and the flag positions. From what he could see from this distance, the golf course had seven sets of tees, immaculately manicured fairways and greens, and a daunting number of strategically positioned hazards. With well-planned and executed shots, trouble could be avoided.

Tom mentally planned his shots, but soon his analytical side kicked in. The area below the golf course was white, like a cloud cover. *How could I be seeing a golf course above the clouds?*

"Ralph, are you sure that's a golf course. Looks more like a mirage."

"You will find out soon enough."

The helicopter landed. Ralph opened the door and signaled for Tom to exit. Tom stepped down onto a soft white surface unlike anything he'd experienced before. His body fairly leapt as he moved away from the helicopter.

I feel like I could be walking on the moon. I'm bouncing around like a kid, gravity barely holding me down.

If I'm asleep and dreaming about a golf course, I think this dream just took an unexpected turn. For some strange reason, I get the feeling I'm not on Earth anymore.

Chapter 3

CHECK-IN

"WHAT'S GOING ON?" Tom demanded. "One minute I'm playing golf, then I'm up in the trees seeing monkeys, and now I'm looking at a golf course sitting on clouds. How on Earth is that possible?"

"Sir, that is your answer. On Earth it is not possible, but in Heaven it is. This is where you are now. You are in Heaven."

Tom stared at the man who claimed to be his caddy. As a rule, Tom loved practical jokes. He recalled a situation he'd read about years ago when some college students prepared a setting that looked like a village where an uprising was taking place. It appeared so authentic, a reporter had picked it up and the fake story was aired on network news. *But nobody I know would have the means to pull that sort of stunt off.* He thought about the jokes he had played through his life. Liz was the only one who could detect them and sometimes she'd join in, which was even better because no one thought she'd play along with him. He looked around at the immaculate greens. *Hmm. Maybe I'm in an amusement park that shows movie settings and special effects.*

Finally, he shook his head. "You're messing with me. If this is someone's idea of a joke, it's not funny."

"Whether you want to believe it or not, this is Heaven."

Generally, Tom was quite good at reading people to determine if they were bluffing. By the look on Ralph's face, the man was serious.

"We need to talk. Do you want to sit over there?" The structure Ralph pointed to looked like a bus stop or a shelter provided at an airport for passengers waiting for a shuttle. The top and three sides were constructed of glass for protection from wind, snow, and rain.

Signs were taped to the sides of the structure. Advertisements, Tom guessed, but he didn't recognize any of the photos or the language. *That doesn't tell me much, but I'm definitely not in the U.S., possibly not on Earth. Maybe I've been captured by aliens. That would sure freak Tony out.*

Tony was a good friend who read and watched everything about space travel and UFO sightings.

But if that's the case, how do I get back to tell him?

Tom followed Ralph toward the structure. As they drew closer, he realized it wasn't like any bus stop or airport shelter he had experienced before. There was no sewer odor, no graffiti, no trash on the ground. The station felt welcoming.

There was a table in the corner. It was covered with a red-and-white checkered tablecloth. In the center of the table was a small vase of wild flowers. Around the table were trays of appetizers: deli meats, cheeses, crackers, cookies, chips and dips, and bite-sized pieces of fruits and veggies. Ralph invited Tom to help himself to the goodies. Tom popped a piece of cheese in his mouth, and realizing he was hungry, he made a small sandwich of ham and cheese on a wheat cracker.

Church bells echoed somewhere close by, sounding like so many he had heard when he'd visited Europe with Liz. He looked around, but as far as he could see there were no other structures.

Tom had always been a good detective, picking up on what might occur in corporate shifts and in relationships between his friends. Something was amiss here, but he couldn't put his finger on it. He sat on the bench in the shelter and Ralph sat next to him.

"Would you like a soda while we talk?" Ralph offered.

"I'll have a diet cola."

Instead of reaching into his vest pocket, Ralph whistled the jingle from a soda commercial. Tom was startled to see two sodas in plastic bottles gliding toward them from above. Trying not to show how shaken he was, Tom casually opened his bottle and downed a big gulp. It was ice cold, the way he liked it, dripping moisture from the sides, but no frosty effects inside. He preferred bottles to cans. With bottles he could recap them to finish later, without any waste. When drinking a beverage from cans, he usually detected a 'metally' taste, something he could do without.

As he took another sip, Tom decided he was not as much alarmed by the floating sodas as he was fascinated. *Pretty cool.* There were several people he'd like to amaze with that trick. One of his pastimes was mastering amateur magic tricks. He'd purchased a handful of special cards to use for tricks and had mastered a couple of tricks. There was always some slight-of-hand or distraction used on the audience. It seemed so easy once he knew the secret. He'd once been invited to a professional magic show and had a front row seat. The show was top-notch, featuring complicated tricks: large animals disappearing and reappearing, cutting women in half. Tom had watched the show intently. There were lots of smoke and mirrors, but at that show, Tom hadn't unlocked any of the secrets he'd wanted to figure out.

The soda bottles were an interesting challenge. *Looks simple. Maybe I can figure it out—if I see it a few more times—or I can ask*

Ralph to teach me if I have to be around here much longer. Hopefully, this is one big magic show and I'll have a chance to talk to him before I leave.

Now he had much larger concerns to face. He needed to listen to Ralph and get to the truth.

Chapter 4

THE WISH

RALPH PRESSED HIS lips together. In a few moments he began to speak. "See the letters GA on my cap? They stand for Guardian Angel. I have been with you ever since you decided to experience a life on Earth. We met before your conception. I was with you when you planned your Earth life. As you got older, I had your back; I was ready to step in if you needed help. But you selected decent people to be with and found good solid Earth angels. There was no need for me to get involved much. That is probably why you did not remember me when I took your bag."

Tom frowned. "So that's what GA stands for. Right now, I think Gigantic Annoyance is a more accurate description."

"I can understand your frustration, sir. But I need to show you something."

Ralph waved his hand downward and a screen came from above. It looked like a screen from Tom's grade school classrooms, the kind that was attached to the ceiling. For some reason, the teachers always had trouble pulling those screens down and generally asked one of the taller lads to help them.

By this time, Tom was no longer curious or amused by the seemingly magic things that were surrounding him. He wanted to find the reality in all of this.

"Sir, do you remember this?" Ralph asked. Tom peered at the screen. The film clip was fuzzy, the pictures faded, like the films of the 80s when those clips were most likely taken.

Tom saw himself driving along a country road on a summer evening as the sun set. Bugs splatted on the windshield. Liz sat in the passenger seat. The Tom in the image turned to her and said, "If I ever have to die, that's how I want to go, quick, like a bug being squished by a windshield."

Tom sighed. He had said that very same thing more than once, but he'd never suspected it would amount to anything.

"There is more." Ralph nodded at the screen.

Tom watched another scene from his life. This time he was with some of his buddies, having a drink after work. They were talking about a friend who had passed away over the weekend. Their friend had suffered a heart attack while playing golf and had died on the course. Tom watched himself on the screen saying, "If I have to go, I want to go fast." Then, in sync with his on-screen image, he joined in, "And it would be even better to die on a golf course."

Having had a career in life and health insurance, Tom knew all too well the realities of dying and the best estimates of life expectancies. The reality of the situation was slowly settling in. *This isn't supposed to be happening to me. Or at least not now, not yet. There were so many things Liz and I wanted to do.*

Tom had never been afraid to let a few tears well up in his eyes at very emotional moments and he didn't hold back the emotion now. He covered his eyes with his hands and choked back an intense sob. He could feel his body quivering. Other than feeling sick to his stomach, he felt empty inside. He needed a hug from Liz, but she wasn't there.

There's got to be a way out of this.

"This has to be a mistake and must be corrected," he said after a moment. He glared at Ralph, then stood and started pacing, stopping occasionally to take small practice golf swings. Even without a club in his hands, the motion of the swing usually helped calm him and get him thinking clearly.

The pacing stopped and Tom looked Ralph squarely in the eye. "Here's the deal. On Earth wishes come in threes. You're right—I did say if I had to die, I wanted to die quickly. I'll admit I said it'd be nice to die on a golf course, too. But technically, I wasn't on the golf course. I was in a freakin' helicopter on the way to the hospital. Here's the kicker—I didn't specify the third part of this wish. I never said *when*."

"That's right, you never said when. The door was wide was open. You could be called back to Heaven any time after you achieved the major objective set in your Earth Life Plan. You did that today."

Earth Life Plan. What's this kook talking about?

"So," Tom said, "it's back to that old adage: 'Watch what you wish for. You just might get it.'" He had one last hope. "Where are the pearly white gates? Where is St. Peter?"

"During life on Earth, each person has a different path," Ralph explained. "In Heaven, every spirit entering will have unique expectations and perspectives. In this moment, the pearly white gates and St. Peter are not on your agenda."

Tom could think of no other possibilities. He heaved a sigh. So he *had* died, but fortunately he'd gone to Heaven. He felt as devastated as he had when he was a boy and had wanted a train set for Christmas. He was sure the present under the tree was the train, but it turned out to be a medical book way beyond his young reading level. He'd had no interest in the book and had hid the book under his bed, never even opening the cover.

Decades earlier, Tom had been short-fused and showed his temper by punching things. He wanted to do that one more time before entering the heavenly realm. He slammed his fist against the glass of the bus station, expecting it to shatter. But his entire arm went through the glass without so much as a crack.

Tom stared at his arm and then at the glass. *Should've guessed something like that would happen. Not the result I wanted, but at least it didn't hurt.*

"Sir, we need to move on. I believe St. Andrew is expecting us."

Chapter 5

St. Andrew's Gate
Heaven's Entrance for Golf Fanatics

Tom followed Ralph, but suddenly came to a stop when he realized he could barely see his hand in front of his face, let alone any details of the golf course that had looked so perfect from the helicopter. They'd evidently walked right into a fog bank. He called for Ralph. "Wait, I can't see in this fog. Where are you?"

"I'm right next to you, sir. In a fog, you say. Take my arm and I will guide you."

Ralph took Tom's arm, but Tom jerked it away. "I don't want you holding on to me. Just tell me how many paces to walk straight and if I need to turn. Call my name every once in a while, so I know I didn't lose you. You can see? Seriously, you're not in a fog?"

"Not at all, sir. My visibility is perfectly clear. I suspect you are experiencing a reaction to your new surroundings and it will clear on its own shortly."

As they walked, Tom heard a chorus of birds chirping. He didn't recognize many of them, but the variety created a beautiful symphony. Frogs croaked somewhere to his left. *Must mean there's water on the course somewhere.*

Tom felt something wet on his right hand and instinctively jerked his hand away, wiping his right hand with his left. "Yuck. What was that?"

"That, sir, was Tully. Tully is the course's collie, very friendly. I am sure you are familiar with the folklore of golf and its origins as a game played by shepherds to pass the time while they watched their flocks. In keeping with that, St. Andrew requested a herd of sheep be kept near the course. Although there is no need for their protection, Tully is here to be a companion to both the sheep and the players on the course."

Tom heard a golf ball falling into a hole. *Kerplink. Always loved that sound.* The *kerplink* was followed by someone whistling a happy little tune. "Are we near the golf course? Is someone playing?"

"No, sir. But we are at the putting green and St. Andrew is here. He is the saint in charge of entry into Heaven for lovers of the game of golf. I shall introduce you."

The fog apparently was not a problem for St. Andrew either. Tom heard an unfamiliar voice say, "Good to see you, Ralph, old buddy. Who do we have here?"

Although Tom still couldn't see anything, he extended his hand in the direction of the voice and felt a firm handshake. "I'm Tom. From what I saw from the helicopter, it looks like you have a nice course."

Always find something nice to say.

"I believe Tom has a tee time for today." Ralph said.

Ralph told St. Andrew about Tom's fog and suggested St. Andrew walk next to Tom to guide him. That way the two could ask each other any questions they might have.

"I have access to the golf records for all eternity in the pro shop. Here we are. Let me get the door for you." St. Andrew opened a door Tom could barely see and guided him to a fog-shrouded counter. "Tom, I know you can't see this, but feel the size of the stack of your records. I pulled them earlier." St. Andrew took Tom's right hand and raised it as far as Tom could reach. "And it goes up even higher. Looks like you played a fair amount of golf. I don't usually see a file this thick unless I'm reviewing the records of a pro. When was the last round you played?"

"I started a round earlier today. Only got to play one hole before Ralph informed me that there'd been a change of venue."

"Do you remember when you played for the first time?" St. Andrew asked.

"Sometime in the summer of '64."

That's one round I'd like to forget.

His first round had been less than spectacular. Tom had been invited to play with a friend and his friend's dad. They'd laughed at every shot Tom hit. Their ridicule, however, was what encouraged Tom to practice the game until his hands bled. The practice paid off. By fall Tom was shooting well enough to make his high school golf team.

"The score cards I have here are for every round you played," St. Andrew explained. "This will to take a while to sort through. While I review these, why don't you hit some balls at the range? Ask Kyle, one of the cart attendants, to set you up. I'll have Ralph come and get you when I have all the paper work finalized."

How am I supposed to hit golf balls in this fog? Sure I can practice my swing, but that won't do any good without seeing how my shots are going.

"Won't it be a little difficult to see the ball in this fog?" Tom asked.

Both Ralph and St. Andrew assured Tom his fog should soon be lifting.

Tom shrugged. "Whatever you say. Ralph, will you direct me? I still can't see a thing."

Ralph escorted Tom to the cart barn and introduced him to Kyle. Tom had no way of telling just where this Kyle fellow was, but extended his hand anyway. "Hi. I'm sorry I can't see you. I'm in some sort of a fog that doesn't seem to be bothering anyone else. But it's nice to meet you." Tom felt a firm handshake and heard a new voice.

"Nice to meet you, too."

Judging from the confidence he heard in Kyle's voice and felt in the handshake, Tom guessed Kyle was a young man and had possibly played college golf.

Tom couldn't see the cart barn either. He heard water running and made an assumption. "Are you hosing down the carts? I didn't think things would get dirty in Heaven."

"They really don't," Kyle said. "Here in Heaven, as on Earth, players respect their surroundings and the equipment, but it's always nice to keep everything in perfect condition."

Ralph interrupted. "Sir, I'll return for you after St. Andrew has the paperwork complete. In the meantime, Kyle, will you find some clubs for Tom to practice with?"

"No problem, Ralph."

After Ralph left, Kyle asked, "Tom, how's your fog? I thought we might check at the helicopter pad first to see if your clubs might be there. It's all the way back in front of the pro shop. I saw the helicopter land and take off, but didn't see if anything was left behind. With all that fog you're experiencing, would you prefer to wait here?"

"I can barely see my hand in front of my face." Tom held his hand in front of him. "Though it's starting to get a little clearer. Is this really Heaven, or is someone pulling an elaborate prank on me?"

"This absolutely is Heaven. Not quite what you imagined, huh?"

Tom shrugged. "Kyle, I don't get something. You mentioned you hadn't seen the helicopter leave any golf clubs behind. On

Earth everyone says, 'You can't take with it you.' Can you bring golf clubs to Heaven?"

"Let me tell you a few things you typically won't hear. On occasion, some items get through our so-called security system, generally when people leave Earth quickly. This is rare, but a few people who die suddenly cling to what they are holding when they cross over."

Tom mulled this over. *Kyle could be a gold mine. Sounds like he has lots of useful information and advice. It'd be good to start up a friendship with him.*

"I won't be much help in looking for clubs, but, if you don't mind directing me, I'd like to come along and chat."

"Okay, then. Follow my voice."

Tom was thirsty. "Tell me if you see anything coming from above. I want to try something." Tom whistled a soda commercial jingle and Kyle let him know a can of diet soda was heading their way.

"I'll get it for you," Kyle said.

Tom reached out and Kyle handed the can to him.

Tom smiled. "Nothing to it. You want one?" He was relieved when Kyle declined. *Not sure I could pull that off again.*

"Did Ralph tell you the secret to that maneuver?" Kyle asked. "He usually doesn't give his techniques away."

"No," Tom admitted. "I watched him do it once and figured I'd give it a try. That was my first attempt."

"I suggest you don't tell Ralph you solved the mystery of whistling up sodas just yet. The guardian angels like to keep new arrivals intrigued for a while. But you do catch on quickly."

"Mind if I ask you a few questions, Kyle?"

"Fire away."

"Tell me about this security system you mentioned."

"Arrivals first pass a check point to verify they're here on the correct date and haven't arrived too soon. Just the other day some guy arrived early. He'd suffered a heat stroke and passed out on the golf course. A helicopter was transporting him to a hospital where he was revived. He was so thrilled he was only having a near-death experience and could return to Earth, he forgot to take the golf clubs that had been in the helicopter with him. In fact, you might want to use those clubs. They're the latest equipment and all."

"Maybe. I'll take a look at them later—if we don't find my clubs and if I ever get completely out of this fog. I don't remember going through a security checkpoint."

"That's not unusual," Kyle explained. "Many people are in a haze when they arrive, residual effects of having traveled through the tunnel toward the white light many experience on their way to Heaven. That may be the case with you. Your crossover may have been so quick that a fog resulted and you're still dazed."

Tom took another sip of his soda. "Next question. The person you talked about, the one who had heat stroke and returned to Earth, could that be happening to me?"

How would he react if he were in that situation? Tom wondered. If he had the opportunity, would he return to life on Earth? He'd never had deep discussions about Heaven and Earth with his friends, but they'd all joked that they'd never get to Heaven anyway and would all end up in the other place.

It's like that old game show. Do I keep what I have now or risk it for another prize? I guess it doesn't get better than this. Even if I had a choice, I think I'd keep this prize package. If I went back to Earth, I might blow the chance of a return by doing something terrible or I might offend the decision-maker and not be invited back. What would really be great is if I could have the best of both worlds.

"I doubt it," Kyle said, startling Tom out of his musing. "It seems Ralph and St. Andrew are taking a long time to review your records. Near-death experiences are usually detected very quickly."

"Oh, great. That's not what I wanted to hear." Tom sighed in exasperation. "I really don't want to be here yet. Yeah, I complained that getting older wasn't any fun, but the aches and pains really aren't that bad. I can get out of bed in the morning. I'm not taking any meds. I have a great relationship with my wife. I actually don't mind going to work, although I grumble about it. But I'm still having fun. There are golf courses to play and vacations to take. There's still a life to live. I feel ripped off. I feel like I'm trapped behind a brick wall."

Chapter 6

KYLE'S SECRET

W HEN TOM HEARD himself say those words about feeling trapped behind a brick wall, the reality of his situation hit him again, but thankfully, no tears came. He needed to divert his focus. Finding some clubs and working on his swing might help. It always had on Earth.

All of a sudden, he realized he could see again. "We can pick up the pace now," he told Kyle. "The fog has lifted and I can see where I'm going. I just want to go back to the driving range, find some clubs, and practice my swing."

This was Tom's first opportunity to see Kyle, a young man who looked to be in his early twenties. He had dark, wavy hair neatly styled, vibrant eyes, and a dazzling smile. He had an athletic physique, with a strong, well-balanced core, perfect for golf. If facial expressions could communicate, Kyle's seemed to say, "I love where I am and what I'm doing at this very moment."

"Oh boy." This was also Tom's first chance to see the golf course and surroundings up close. What had looked so inviting from his view in the helicopter now looked to be more of a dog track with numerous bare spots, unrepaired divots, footprints left unraked in the sand hazards, dying or dead trees. "I may just give up the game if this is how all Heaven's golf courses look. I've got to find a way out. I've got to."

"What are you mumbling about?" Kyle asked.

"Just looking for a way out. Hopefully, hitting some balls will take away some of the frustration."

At the cart barn, Tom didn't notice anything different from the cart barns he'd seen on Earth, except for the upkeep. The barn was a brownish, long building trimmed in green with an opening similar to a garage door through which carts moved in and out. The exterior walls could have stood a fresh coat of paint and the floor could have used a good sweeping. Tom guessed around ninety carts would fit inside There were a few sets of clubs stored along the walls. He spotted a set in the corner. "Are those the clubs you talked about, the ones left by the lucky stiff who got to go back to Earth?"

Kyle nodded. "Yes and I understand they're practically new, used once."

"Mind if I try them?"

"No, go right ahead."

Tom pulled out the seven iron and took a few, easy half swings. He nodded in approval of the feel. "Feels solid. Grip feels good. Shaft stiffness feels right. Do you have a range where I can hit a few shots?"

"Sure."

"Would you mind watching my shots?

"Be glad to"

Golf was Tom's stress reliever; working on his swing usually helped him relax.

They walked to the driving range without a lot of chit chat. *How ironic,* Tom thought. *My heaven is on Earth. My favorite things were being with Liz, traveling, and playing golf. A perfect day was doing all three. Minutes ago all those things were happening. I was out of town, playing in a golf tournament, and Liz was with me.*

When they reached the driving range, Tom set up and hit a few balls. His tempo was off which only added to his frustration. He set the club down and backed away from the hitting area. As he tried to take a few deep breaths, he realized nothing was happening.

"Kyle, take a look at my face. Is it turning blue?"

"No. Why?"

"I just tried to take a couple of deep breaths to relax and didn't get any air, but I don't feel dizzy. One of the last things I remember before I got on the helicopter was that I needed oxygen and couldn't get any. I got dizzy and fell to the ground. What will happen if I don't get any air?"

"No worries. You don't have lungs. Here in Heaven we call what you think of as your body a shell. You don't have any internal organs. Try that movement again—like you're breathing. Tell me if you feel any different."

Tom took another stab at breathing, trying to feel the movement of air against the back of his throat and the pressure filling his lungs. "I feel the motion of my chest moving, but no air coming in. I can smell better. I smell pine trees. I can smell the grass. I had allergies to those scents, but now there's no sneezing or coughing or itchy, watery eyes." *This is nice. Without allergies, maybe being a shell won't be all bad.*

"Can I help you out?" Kyle asked.

"That'd be great. Feel like my swing plane is off. Can you watch me hit a few?"

"Actually, I thought I could help in a different way."

"What do you have in mind?"

"By the looks of you, I'd say you might actually be here before your time. You're younger than most new arrivals and look to be in good health. With the time it's taking to review your records, my guess is there's been a major screw-up—uhh, better restate that—a slight miscalculation . . . in you being here."

Kyle looked around. "I want to be sure Ralph's not within earshot. I'll let you in on a little secret. Don't ever let anyone know you heard this from me."

"Okay." Tom was more than a bit curious. He moved closer to Kyle and Kyle's voice became a mere whisper.

"Let me know if you see Ralph and St. Andrew. Here's the deal—there's a rare opportunity for spirits who come to Heaven too soon to be given a chance to earn a pass that frees them to travel easily through The Veil, the border between Heaven and Earth. There are several regulations regarding the pass, which is sometimes referred to as the SWEEP. All I know for certain is the SWEEP pass has to be offered to you by your guardian angel along with the church and state authorities for your gate of entry. In your case, you are entering the gate for golfers so your representatives would be St. Andrew and Mary, Queen of Scots. There is some sort of hearing to allow you the SWEEP opportunity. Then, if approved, you have to prove yourself worthy by meeting several challenges. You might want to stress to Ralph how strongly you desire to be back on Earth. Again, it's called the SWEEP pass. If he mentions it, don't just brush it off. It may be perfect for you. But don't ever say you heard anything about it from me."

Chapter 7

THE COVER-UP

WITH THIS NEW information from Kyle, Tom was eager to see Ralph. "Let's go to the pro shop and see what's going on."

"Okay, the pro shop is at the end of this path." Kyle pointed down a dirt path to a small building a few yards away.

Tom was quiet along the way. What he saw amazed him and not in a good way. The pro shop was not what he expected. He'd anticipated a heavenly pro shop would be a showcase of classic elegance, but this pro shop was anything but elegant. He'd played courses on Earth where the men's facilities had been larger and more sturdily constructed.

As they neared the pro shop, Tom saw a third person, a woman, with St. Andrew and Ralph. The woman was large, or maybe her dress made her hips look big. She wore a red-and-gold dress of brocade material. A lace collar, the kind that stood up and looked itchy, adorned the neckline. She was wearing a necklace—a large red jewel dangling from a thick gold chain.

Wonder how many carats that puppy is.

A sheer ivory veil edged in pearls draped from the top of her head to below her waist. Above the waist the dress was a tightly fitted bodice; below the waist, yards of fabric made a huge skirt.

She could probably hide a classroom of kids below that skirt. It's so big.

Before Tom could ask, Kyle confirmed his suspicion. "That's Mary, Queen of Scots. She's already played. I have a hunch her presence has something to do with you. Let's hide behind the back wall and listen."

"I like your style." Tom gave him a thumbs-up.

As they squatted down behind the wall in back of the pro shop, Tom could hear St. Andrew briefing the Queen. "I checked the scorecards for Tom. Not only should he have finished the round today, it looks like he was supposed to have about thirty more years to play."

Tom felt an intense anger building inside. He started to stand, but Kyle stopped him. "If you say something now, it might hurt your chances for the SWEEP I think they'll offer you. Let's listen some more."

"Smart move." Tom nodded and they continued to eavesdrop.

"We are piecing the events together," Ralph said. "Our best guess so far is that the evaluation of Tom's condition, which the medics gave to The Controller, was inaccurate. If The Controller had been given the correct information, He might have made a different choice."

"Preliminary reports also suggest the helicopter was delayed in reaching Tom," St. Andrew added. "Had the flight arrived within the acceptable timeframe, the helicopter should have gotten Tom to the hospital in time for him to make a recovery and we'd be looking at a totally different outcome. We know very well from the last meeting that The Controller is not at all happy with the timeliness and accuracy of the medical transportation system."

The queen spoke up. "The Controller was determined to get the transportation system up to speed. He said if the errors and delays continued, there'd be wings and halos flying."

"Ralph," St. Andrew said, "you've known Tom since day one. What's your take?"

"Tom is a reasonable man. Needless to say, he is quite upset about his presence here and has strongly voiced his desire to return to Earth. At this point, he does not have that option. If we offer him a SWEEP, perhaps he will not file a formal complaint with The Controller if and when he discovers the truth. Tom is sharp and chances are he would uncover a mistake like this."

"Offer Tom a SWEEP," the queen said. "We'll never have to reveal the slip-up to The Controller."

"I'm shocked! Where's your integrity? You know we can't do that! We have to let The Controller know what happened," St. Andrew admonished.

"You're right," Mary, Queen of Scots, admitted.

"Are we are in agreement, then?" Ralph said. "We will offer Tom the pass."

St. Andrew and the queen voiced their affirmation.

Tom beamed and silently high-fived Kyle.

"I will talk to him," Ralph said. "I would like to speak to him alone."

❧ ❧ ❧

Tom beckoned to Kyle as he stood from their spying position and walked around the back side of the pro shop to a dirt pathway. They followed the pathway along the side of the pro shop to the front where Ralph, St. Andrew, and the queen stood.

Place needs a few repairs. A board was loose on the side and one of the windows was cracked. Over all the shop needed a fresh coat of paint.

"I was on my way to get you, sir." Ralph stepped away from St. Andrew and Mary, Queen of Scots, to greet Tom.

"Thought you had forgotten me," Tom said.

"Of course not. Mary, Queen of Scots, stopped by and we had some issues to discuss. Come on. Let me introduce you to her. The queen is the civil magistrate for golfers."

Introductions were made and some chitchat followed. Tom was anxious to hear about the SWEEP, but he played it cool, not letting on he'd been eavesdropping.

As their small talk continued, a petite female joined the group and stood next to Ralph. Tom did a double take. She looked remarkably like Liz with short, naturally curly hair and green eyes.

The newcomer apologized. "Sorry to interrupt. Ralph, I need to talk with you. May I pull you away for a few moments?" Ralph and the new arrival took a few steps away from the group.

Tom felt a familiar twinge, the same kind of twinge he'd always felt when Liz was distressed. He and his wife were extremely close. Over the years an unexplainable telepathic link had developed between them. This twinge was the strongest he'd ever experienced. So strong, in fact, it nearly knocked him off his feet.

Oh no. I forgot about Liz. I've been so concerned about my own feelings, I didn't think about how she'd feel. I'm not sure she even knows I've died.

He could delay the discussion about the SWEEP. He needed to find out what was happening with Liz. Tom's instinct told him this woman had information about Liz. Without hesitation, he went to talk to her.

Ralph nodded as Tom walked up. "Tom, I would like to introduce you to Faith, Liz's guardian angel. Faith tells me Liz is beside herself. She won't stop calling for you."

Tom nodded. "I just got a good shock from her myself. Where is she? Is anyone with her?" He glared at Faith. "If you're her guardian angel, shouldn't you be with her?"

"Liz is still in the emergency room at the hospital," Faith said in a calm voice. "Needless to say, she is shattered. I felt, in this moment, she needed her soulmate more than her guardian angel. I left her in the hands of some very competent Earth angels while I slipped away to ask if you could be with her again, if only for a few moments."

"Of course. I want to be with her forever. She's my best friend. I'd do anything for her."

Ralph held up a hand. "As your guardian angel, I have to look out for your best interest. What you might witness in the emergency room could greatly distress you. You will see your physical form and odds are you will have a strong temptation to reenter it. Do not even think about it! Your purpose on this journey is to focus on Liz's needs. Are you up to the challenge?"

A slight grin came over Tom's face. "Liz always was a challenge. That's what I love about her. How can I get to her?"

Ralph glanced at Faith. "Have arrangements been made for our passage?"

Faith held up three prisms. "Anticipating you and Tom would agree to come with me, I stopped by The Controller's office and picked up three round trip tickets for the hot air balloon. The balloon will make the trip to and from the hospital quick."

St. Andrew offered the use of a flying golf cart to get them more quickly to The Veil.

Faith graciously accepted the courtesy, and the three of them—Tom, Ralph, and Faith—jumped into the winged cart and took off.

It seemed they'd just taken off when Faith landed the cart and the three of them stepped from the cart into a balloon's basket. Faith nodded at the pilot and they lifted off. Tom didn't really notice the royal blue-and-gold balloon sailing smoothly through The Veil; his every thought was focused on Liz. Faith had already given their destination to the pilot and he landed the balloon outside the hospital at its emergency entrance.

In his eagerness to see Liz, Tom jumped out of the four-foot basket. Having no idea how the hospital was laid out, he waited at the door for Faith and Ralph. "Faith, please show us the way."

From the hospital emergency entrance, Tom and Ralph followed Faith through the empty hall. There were no carts, no gurneys, no cleaning personnel, or medical staff to get in the way.

Moving along at a quick pace, Tom glanced into a room on his right. The sign outside the room read Family Room #1. He was relieved not to see Liz in that room. Over the past few years, he and Liz had spent more time than they'd wanted in hospitals with the various illnesses, procedures, surgeries, and eventual deaths of their parents. During those long hours, he and Liz had defined the difference between waiting rooms and family rooms. Waiting in a *Waiting Room* was a good indicator the outcome would be good. When they were invited to wait in a *Family Room,* the outcomes were typically not good and a Family Room provided privacy for the family to let out their emotions.

Tom hated hospitals in general and their smell of disinfectant. This one was no different; it made him nauseous. He felt an emptiness in his stomach. *Where is Liz?* "Hurry please. I want to see Liz." Tears burned in his eyes.

He thought about his relationship with Liz. Their closeness had always been the envy of all their friends.

We almost always knew what the other was thinking. Will we still be able to communicate without words? Who knows how this will go?

Hopefully, we can work through this just like other difficulties we've faced in the past. We'd cry, we'd talk, we'd cry some more. And even if we didn't get the issue resolved, we'd find some twist in the situation to laugh about. Laughter pulled us through. Doesn't seem there's anything to laugh at here, but we'll have to find something. That's why Liz loves me; she always told me she loves me because I make her laugh.

Chapter 8

THE HOSPITAL EMERGENCY ROOM

I T WAS GRUESOME, seeing his motionless body on a gurney in the emergency room. It wasn't the outward appearance of the still body that looked like him that made him feel dizzy—that body was clean and unharmed. It was the reaction coming from inside his shell that freaked him out. He felt like his brain had turned into worms creeping around inside him. His empty stomach gnawed at him. He felt like someone had reached inside his chest and torn out his heart, then ripped it into pieces and thrown it on the floor. He wanted to poke out his eyes so he wouldn't have to look at the scene any longer. Before he could actually do any damage to his eyes, though, he saw Liz lying next to his body.

He rubbed his hands across his eyes to get a clear—and probably last—look at Liz. To him she was the most beautiful person in the world and he wanted to remember every detail. At the moment, she wasn't crying, but there was evidence of recent tears on her face. He hated to see anyone sad, especially Liz. He wanted to run from the scene, but couldn't. He and Liz were facing the most difficult situation of their relationship.

Such an odd feeling, watching Liz hold his hand, talking out loud as if she totally expected him to hear her.

"How could this happen to us?" he heard Liz ask. "We're supposed to be together now, talking about your round of golf.

It's not supposed to be me here by myself, figuring out what to do and how to answer the crazy questions people are asking.

"Look at you. Even now you have a smile on your face. You always were smiling, but this isn't funny. Didn't it hurt when the medics put the breathing tube in or used the heart paddles and who knows what else in the helicopter? I fought to ride in the helicopter with you, but they—whoever they were—wouldn't let me. I was so busy fighting with them to let me go with you, I didn't even get a chance to say 'I love you' one last time. But I do love you and I hope you know that wherever you are.

"You may have seen me from above arguing with the nurse to keep trying to revive you, that you were still breathing, but she told me you hadn't been breathing on your own for several minutes; that it was a breathing tube that made it look that way. I begged you to stay, but . . ." Liz's voice trailed off, her eyes filled with tears, and she rested her head on his chest.

Probably a good thing his stomach was empty, Tom realized as reality hit him again—right in the pit of stomach. *So, I'm really dead. Liz kids sometimes, but she wouldn't joke, not about something like this. Wow. We sometimes talked, with no answers, about not knowing what we'd do if something happened to the other. What am I going to do without Liz? Never thought about that side of the dilemma.*

Tom's thoughts were interrupted by Liz's voice. "I guess you're really not coming back. Some people believe when a loved one passes—wow, that sounds so weird when it's my loved one we're talking about—anyway, when someone passes over, if you ask for a sign that they're okay, sometimes they'll give you one. Well, I want a sign. Let's see, what would be good?"

Tom waited.

"You know our CD player is jammed shut. Can you get it opened?" She paused. "No, you tried and couldn't get it. What about the contest I entered? Maybe I could be a finalist. That's not good either. The winner and finalists won't be announced for two or three months. I don't want to wait that long.

"What about a rose, a peach-colored one? You always were good about getting me flowers, but only if I wasn't expecting them. The rose has to come as a surprise. It won't count if someone sends a sympathy arrangement with a peach rose in it. No matter. If you're okay, I'm sure you'll think of something. Love you."

Liz closed her eyes.

"Can I give her a kiss and a hug?" Tom asked around the lump in his throat.

Ralph and Faith nodded.

Tom gently touched Liz's left shoulder and kissed it. He whispered, "I love you." Liz moved her right hand to the spot he had touched and whispered, "I love you, too."

"Time to depart," Ralph said quietly. They turned to leave and Tom took a last glance back. Liz had a small smile on her face and Tom felt himself smiling, too.

Outside the emergency room, Tom stumbled and bumped into the wall. Ralph reached out. "Are you okay, sir?"

Tom brushed Ralph's hand away. "A little overwhelmed right now. I'll be fine." He thought about the last time he'd collapsed—on the golf course. He didn't like that outcome and, although he knew he couldn't die again, he needed to stay alert and in control.

"Ready?" Faith headed for the exit. "The pilot is waiting." The three of them walked out of the hospital and got settled in the hot air balloon waiting for them outside.

෴   ෴   ෴

Chapter 9

RETURN TO HEAVEN

THE RIDE BACK to Heaven was quiet. Tom reflected on his current situation and laid out some tentative plans for his future. On Earth he had developed a multitude of relationships: people who were his friends, people he could trust, and people with various interests who would share their expertise in areas Tom wasn't familiar with.

The important thing was not having all the answers, but knowing where to get the answers.

"Sir, we are approaching The Veil. I will be with you, so the passage will be smooth. Are you ready?"

Tom didn't respond. The balloon was headed there regardless of what he said. Tom sighed as he realized The Veil was one of the things he couldn't avoid and needed to understand. He turned to look where Ralph had pointed.

Definitely looks like a Brick Wall from this side. Maybe I'm missing something. At least now I have something in mind to deal with it. He remembered a tour guide in Germany explaining the position of the statues on the roof of the nation's capital facing the direction of the country's biggest enemy. It was something about needing to keep an eye on your allies, but keep an even closer eye on your foes. To Tom, The Veil—or the Brick Wall, as

Tom referred to it—was his major foe, keeping him from Earth. He felt the best way to overcome it was to understand it.

The reentry was smooth as Ralph promised. Tom didn't feel a thing. *Maybe there is more to this Veil thing than a Brick Wall.*

Ralph directed the pilot to land the balloon at St. Andrew's Gate.

After they were out of the balloon, Faith expressed her need to get back to Liz. "Tom, I came back with you because I wanted to see if you plan to get a sign to Liz to let her know you're okay. If you are, I'll help in any way I can."

Tom nodded. "I don't know how, but she's getting that peach rose. That is possible, isn't it?"

Ralph and Faith exchanged glances and nodded.

Tom thought he might be stretching his limits with his next request. "Can I return to Earth to give it to her? I always love to see her reaction when I give . . . er . . . gave her flowers. She acted like I had given her all the gold in the world, especially when they were a surprise."

"Let me know when you have some ideas," Faith said. "Being at Liz's side, I'll know her tentative plans and will pass that info along to Ralph. You and he can work things out to get you back to Earth so you can see her reaction when she discovers that rose."

"Can you and I be in direct contact?" Tom asked.

Faith shook her head. "Believe me, contact will be quicker between Ralph and myself. Angels have faster communication options than spirits like you. Ralph can explain the difference. Gotta run." She wrapped both her hands around his. "Good luck with Ralph. He's a stickler for rules and I stretched it a bit by agreeing to another visit to Earth for you. But he's a good guy. I know him; he'll help you." She let loose of Tom's hands, stretched up to give him a quick kiss on his cheek, and dashed away.

Tom watched from a distance to see how she handled The Veil. She went through the sheer rainbow fabric like it wasn't there at all. *So, it does look different from this side. That's what I need to do: turn this Brick Wall to nothing. I can work on that. Right now I need to get in good with Ralph—get him loosened up so he'll help with the rose for Liz—and then on to the SWEEP.*

❧❧ ❧❧ ❧❧

SECTION TWO

THE PEACH ROSE

❧❧ ❧❧ ❧❧

Chapter 10

Plans for a Rose

Afteri Faith left, Tom and Ralph remained at St. Andrew's Gate. Tom had several questions and asked Ralph if he had time to talk. Ralph agreed. Conversations over sodas were common for Tom, so he asked Ralph if he would whistle up some sodas. This also gave him a chance to test his idea that the soda jingle whistle was the way to make sodas appear.

Ralph whistled the jingle and sure enough, two sodas floated toward them. They each grabbed one of the twenty-ounce bottles. Tom pointed to one of the benches near the pro shop and suggested they sit.

"First," Tom started, "thanks for getting me to see Liz. She's the most important thing to me."

"I know that, sir. I have seen the two of you together."

"Since this heaven thing is all new to me, I'm counting on your help with the rose." Tom studied Ralph's face. *Some buttering up never hurts.* "I don't think buying flowers from a street vendor or calling a florist would work from here. But before we get to that, I want to ask about something Faith said."

He took a long drink of his bubbling soda. "She said you and she were angels and I'm considered a spirit and we use different communication equipment. What's that all about?"

Ralph nodded. "Yes, she and I are angels. We have been around since the beginning of time. We have spent most of our time on Earth as guardians and guides for mortals, but have not actually lived a mortal life. We have never had the physical inner parts as you had on Earth and have not actually felt the physical pains that mortals feel. However, we have experienced some wonderful human emotions—love and joy—and, unfortunately, some bad emotions—sorrow, sometimes rage, and even hatred.

"Angels operate at higher vibration levels and have faster communication tools and other devices than those available to spirits such as yourself. Spirits have lived a life on Earth. Not all spirits can have—or even want—communication devices. They are relieved to be in Heaven and have no desire to deal with anything on Earth. Other spirits have experienced several lives on Earth, but I can explain that later."

Tom tapped his fingers on his thigh. "Yeah, let's have that conversation another time. I need to take a break to clear my thoughts and stretch my legs. Is that weird?"

"Not really. Spirits have become conditioned to the physical things they experienced on Earth: eating, drinking, exercising. Those activities translate into desires here in Heaven. Yes, a break does sound good, sir. Shall we meet back here in a few minutes?"

"Sounds like a plan." Tom stood up, stretched his shoulders, took a couple of practice swings and strolled around. He became lost in his thoughts, mentally preparing his strategy for his continued discussions with Ralph like he would for a business meeting. He wanted to get to a discussion about the mysterious SWEEP, but would wait. He would absolutely never forgive himself if he didn't get a sign to Liz.

Don't know how talkative this guy normally is or how much time he'll give me today, so I'd better get some priority to my questions now. First the rose details, and then maybe the SWEEP if he'll continue to talk.

The sound of a croaking frog caught Tom's attention and he returned to the bench.

He was about to ask Ralph how angel communications worked when he heard a loud vibration that sounded suspiciously like a cell phone. Ralph reached for the blue bag Tom had noticed he always had with him, opened it, and took out an object about the size of a playing card. He held it up to his face just like the thing *was* a cell phone, though the object was thinner than any cell phone Tom had ever seen.

"Ralph here."

Tom could barely hear Faith's voice, but Ralph motioned Tom closer and held the device slightly away from his face so Tom could listen in on the conversation.

"Things are quiet now," Faith reported. "Liz's sisters have flown in and she had dinner with them. Liz is finally resting. I doubt I'll have anything new until tomorrow, after they have gone to the mortuary to complete the required paperwork and make other necessary arrangements."

"We shall wait to hear from you tomorrow," Ralph said. He returned the card-sized device to the blue bag.

Tom was curious. "Was that a cell phone? And what else do you have in that blue bag?"

"This, sir," Ralph put hand on the blue bag, "is my utility bag. All angels carry one. For fun, we refer to them as our goodie bag. It is filled with an assortment of tools, references, and devices we use on a regular basis. The one I used in communicating with Faith is my Angel Communication Tool, ACT for short. If things go well, you may someday qualify to have a spirit communicator." He winked and pulled the bag closed with its gold drawstring.

Tom felt a little more confident. *That wink, maybe having my own communicator—I'm thinking SWEEP.*

❧ ❧ ❧

THE NEXT MORNING Ralph's ACT vibrated. "Ralph here." He motioned for Tom to listen.

"Liz is on her way to a mortuary," Faith said. "She is upset with Tom, to say the least, because he never discussed his preference for final arrangements. Now she has to make that decision without his input."

Oops.

"She has every right to be ticked," Tom admitted. "She brought up the topic a few months ago and I didn't want to think about it. I knew I'd die at some point, but thought dying was a long way off. Getting sick and dying are things that are supposed to happen to other people, not me. If I have any regrets, it's not discussing my final arrangements. I really didn't—and still don't—care, but I'm sorry I left Liz with this extra burden. I suppose it wouldn't have killed me to have taken a few minutes back then and talked about it. Whatever Liz decides is fine by me."

"Tom, we're at the mortuary. Gotta run. And don't forget about that peach rose."

Ralph put the ACT away as Tom considered what Faith had just said.

"Boy, I really screwed things up." Tom rubbed a hand over his face and looked up. "Liz, I'm so, so sorry. Can you ever forgive me? I promise, I'll get a peach rose to you."

Time to stop being sorry and act. "Ralph, this idea isn't up to my standards, but the best I could come up with is for her to find lots of peach roses at a supermarket or grocery store. It's

49

not uncommon to see them at a store, but maybe we could look the floral departments over and put peach roses in a special location or make them really peach, something that Liz would definitely notice and know were there specially for her. Next time we talk with Faith, can we let her know that's the only idea I have and see if she can help us in that regard? Or maybe she'll have a better idea."

Ralph assured Tom that would be no problem.

A FEW HOURS later, Faith contacted Ralph and Tom to tell them that Liz had left the mortuary and the service rep there had assured Liz everything would be in order by early the next afternoon. The service rep offered to bring the paperwork and other items to the hotel and save Liz a trip to the mortuary. After she had all that was needed from the mortuary, Liz and her sisters planned on, in Liz's words, "Hitting the road, never to return to this awful place again."

Faith paused for a moment. "Tom, no pressure, but Liz told her sisters about her request for a sign from you that you're okay. Have any ideas?"

"Not very original. Best I could think of is to have peach roses at a grocery store or supermarket. Most of them have small floral areas. And I'm sure, at some point, Liz will need to pick up a few things. Can we arrange to have peach roses at a store when she goes?"

To his surprise, Faith said that Tom's plan might work. "In fact, Liz and her sisters have already talked about picking up a few items at the supermarket near her sister's home on their way back. I'll contact some of my friends in the area to help get that store well stocked along with some of the other stores in the area. My guess is that I won't have anything new to tell you until the girls are ready to leave the hotel. Ralph, are you guys going to work on Tom's transportation so he can be on Earth to see Liz's reaction? Sometimes the view through the ELV can get fuzzy."

"That would make good use of our time," Ralph replied. "Thank you for the suggestion. Tom and I will start immediately." Ralph ended the call and returned the ACT to his bag.

Tom had a question. "What was Faith talking about? A view through an ELV? What's that all about?"

Ralph reached into his utility bag again and brought out a handheld object about the size of a remote control for TVs. It had numbered and lettered keys on the bottom portion and a screen on the top. He held out the device so Tom could get a good look. "This is an Earth Location Viewer, also known as an ELV. With it you can locate and view a person on Earth. You can also hear their conversations."

He handed the device to Tom, but Tom didn't take it. He didn't want to get distracted by a new toy. He wanted to focus on getting a peach rose to Liz.

Tom felt light-hearted and apprehensive all at once. He couldn't wait for the chance to see Liz tomorrow. *That seems like an eternity away. What does Eternity feel like? Guess I'm about to find out.*

Chapter 11

A Failed Attempt

W HILE THEY WAITED for their next contact from Faith, Tom and Ralph discussed transportation to Earth. Regardless of the option they would finally decide to use, Tom would need to go through The Veil.

"Sir, given your feelings about your separation from Earth by The Veil, leaving should be easy for you. It will be the return trip you will find difficult since you have indicated you see the outside of The Veil as a Brick Wall."

Tom mentally did a double take and made full use of his poker face. He did not recall ever mentioning to Ralph that The Veil felt more like a Brick Wall to him. "How did you know about the Brick Wall feeling?"

"Sir, remember I have been with you every moment of your Earth life and have developed a sense of your thoughts and feelings, much as you had with Liz, but at a different level. Not only have I picked up on some of your thoughts, I have some reliable sources who, out of concern for you, have shared that information with me. I trust you will not be angry with them."

Ralph winked. "Be assured that when I am with you, I will make the return as smooth as possible. Should you ever find occasion to travel on your own, the return through The Veil may seem more challenging. We should discuss some ways for you to travel."

Tom was a bit confused. *Traveling alone? On the SWEEP pass?*

The first alternative Ralph presented was sliding down a pole like the poles found in fire stations. The drawback was that the poles were rigid and their landing locations could not be changed, which meant Tom and Ralph could end up miles from their intended destination.

"What about using a plane or another hot air balloon?" Tom asked.

"No. Those conveyances are limited in number. The hot air balloons are restricted to emergency uses, as when Liz needed to see you. Planes are difficult to arrange without knowing the proper people."

Sounds like Earth. You need to know the right people.

Tom tried again. "What about elevators?"

"Some elevators are available, but those are slow in comparison to the rope ladders," Ralph said. "I have a rope ladder, and whenever I need it, it is available for my use. I simply attach it to a cloud, go through The Veil, and climb down. The rope ladder has flexibility and lines up directly to where I want to go. It is easily accessible, reliable, and fast. I recommend you give it a try."

Ralph opened his utility bag, pulled out a ladder made from rope, and gave it to Tom to examine. It was lightweight and flexible. Tom wasn't extremely fond of ladders, but this seemed likely to be the best suggestion he was going to get from Ralph.

"Okay," Tom said. "Let's go with the rope ladder."

Suddenly, he felt like a kid waiting for Christmas. He could hardly wait for the next day, anticipating the smile on Liz's face when she got her rose from him.

❧ ❧ ❧

Late the next morning, Faith contacted Ralph and Tom listened in.

"The representative from the mortuary is on his way to the hotel and should arrive in about forty-five minutes. Liz's sisters are loading the car now while Liz is checking out of the hotel. Liz plans a quick departure once she receives what she needs from the mortuary. I contacted several of my angel friends. We have every grocery store and supermarket in the vicinity of your sister-in-law's home stocked with peach roses. Liz has got to notice at least one. I'll let you know when we get close to where the girls plan to shop. They haven't decided yet."

Ralph returned his ACT to his goodie bag. "Now we wait."

Tom sighed. He considered bringing up the topic of the SWEEP, but dropped the thought. He wanted his mind very focused when that discussion came up and now he was distracted by the encounter with Liz. He also remembered—from dealings on Earth, such as salary negotiations—he who throws out the first offer, tends to have the most to lose.

Waiting to see Liz, he actually felt more nervous with each passing moment than he had the moment before, a feeling that intensified as the time for their encounter neared. It was like he was counting down the time for their first date.

Later in the afternoon Ralph's ACT vibrated again.

"Liz decided she wants to stop at the superstore a few exits from her sister's," Faith said. "Do you know where that is?"

Tom nodded. "Yep."

"Tom can get us there," Ralph said. "We will leave immediately. If we arrive before you, we will see if we can arrange something special."

After the conversation ended, Ralph asked, "Are you ready, sir?"

"Lead the way."

Ralph pulled his ELV from his goodie bag. "I will set it to view Liz's current location."

Ralph punched a few buttons and then continued. "The ELV serves two purposes. First, you can keep an eye on your destination as you proceed. Second, it will signal to your rope where you want to go." He handed the device to Tom, but Tom didn't take it.

"Why don't you hold on to the ELV? I want to use both hands to get down the ladder."

Tom started toward The Veil, but Ralph stopped him before he actually reached it. "Sir, perhaps I should explain in more detail how the rope ladder works. We need to attach the ladder to a cloud before exiting through The Veil. Here is the cloud shuttle."

Tom had pictured a shuttle like a commuter train, with several cars for passengers to board. But what he saw was more like a taxi stand except the taxis were clouds. There were numerous clouds lined up waiting for the next passenger.

"The clouds run continually. You will see when we board ours that there are slots off to the bottom left of the cloud. These are the slots you will use to attach the ladder."

Tom was puzzled. *Guess I'll watch Ralph and see what he does.*

Tom and Ralph boarded the next cloud. Tom asked Ralph to demonstrate how to hook the ladder to the cloud. Ralph showed Tom the slots in the cloud and positioned the hooks for the ladder through the slots.

"I get it now," Tom said. "It's like when Liz had a wreath she wanted to hang on a door. Often she used a hanger that went over the top of a door; the hook was short on the back side and was longer in front where the wreath could be displayed."

Tom started to sit, but Ralph informed him the ride would be very short. "In fact, we are already at The Veil."

"Shall I drop the ladder now?" Tom asked.

Ralph shook his head. "No. First we go through the Veil; then we will drop it from the other side. And to reiterate, sir, passage to and from The Veil will be easy when I am with you. All you need to do is make sure the hooks are secure."

Tom and Ralph went through The Veil, without a hitch. Tom was relieved. *That wasn't so bad.* Ralph handed the rope to Tom. "Sir, because there are two of us sharing the rope, one of us will need to hold on to it while the other descends, then anchor the rope for the second person to follow. I suggest, given this is your first excursion, I go down first and wait for you at the bottom."

"No problem with that." Tom mustered up all the courage he could.

"Please drop the ladder and be sure to hold on to it so you will be able to use it after me. Down I go, sir."

Tom dropped the rope. Ralph descended the ladder and waited at the bottom for Tom.

Tom went down the ladder one step at a time, watching every step. When he was five or six, one of his older cousins had put Tom at the top of a slide. Tom didn't know what was worse, sliding at an uncontrollable speed down the slide or trying to back down the slide's ladder. Other cousins stood around, laughing and ridiculing him. It wasn't until sunset and his mom and dad decided to drive off without him that Tom backed down the ladder. Still, as an adult, he tried to avoid stairs and ladders. When ceiling light bulbs needed to be changed at home and a ladder was needed, Liz would volunteer to go up a few steps to change the light bulb so Tom wouldn't have to.

For the chance of seeing Liz, he would take his chances with the ladder, but he was glad Ralph was there in case he needed help.

WHEN TOM GOT to the bottom of the ladder, Ralph helped him to the ground. Ralph showed Tom a button on the bottom of the ladder and asked Tom to push it. When Tom did, the ladder released and retracted. Tom handed the ladder to Ralph who returned it to its proper place in his utility bag.

They reached the entrance of the store just as Liz and her sisters were walking into the entrance.

It's odd being this close to Liz and not able to talk to her or hold the door for her.

Faith greeted them. "So, let's go in and make something happen."

The floral department was located at the store's entrance. Various shades of roses were displayed in buckets on the bottom shelf. The peach roses were last.

Tom saw Liz's sisters point them out. "There's your sign," said one.

"You think that counts?" Liz said with a small laugh. "Tom never gives . . . um . . . never gave me flowers when I expected them and I'd expect to see them here. Plus some were a little more pink, some were yellowish. I want a perfect peach rose. I'll wait a few days. If nothing else pops up, these will do. But I'm pretty sure there'll be a bigger sign."

Chapter 12

REQUEST FOR A MULLIGAN

TOM WAS DISAPPOINTED over Liz's reaction, but he understood.

"Liz is right; that wasn't up to my standards," he confessed to Ralph. "Can I take a mulligan?"

"A mulligan? What is a mulligan, sir?"

Tom raised his eyebrows and put his fingers to his lips. "That's right—you don't play much golf. A mulligan, a do-over. In a friendly game of golf, when someone hits a shot poorly and everyone knows the player can do better, it's not uncommon to give that person another chance, without penalty, to hit again and get a better shot. We didn't have a chance to take a look at the layout of the store beforehand. That's like not planning your shot or not taking a practice swing. Will you and Faith let me have a mulligan?"

Ralph gave his okay, but suggested they check with Faith first. Tom and Ralph found Liz and Faith at the store's exit. Tom asked Faith if they could give it another try on a later day after they had a chance to do more planning.

"Of course," Faith said without hesitation. "Liz is my main concern. I know it would be a tremendous relief to her to know you are safe and still love her. Things should settle down over the next few days. When she's had some time to herself and a chance to do some planning, I'll let you know."

"Sir, we do need to return now."

"How're we getting back?"

"With the rope ladder, the same way we came down," Ralph said. "There is a caveat to getting back with the rope ladder. I saw a coffee shop just around the corner. I suggest we go there to discuss this."

After they turned the corner, Tom saw a familiar coffee shop and detected the rich aroma of a deep roast brewing. He had liked the smell of coffee long before he had acquired a taste for it. He began drinking coffee when he started working since that was what most of his co-workers drank in the morning to jump-start their work day. Initially he'd added cream and sweetener to his coffee and continued to do so throughout his life, although years later he switched to decaf. Most of his coffee drinking had been at work or when eating out. He considered having coffee in a coffee specialty shop a treat and loved to order a specialty drink, usually a latte.

As soon as they entered the door of the small crowded shop, Tom remembered why he usually ordered his drinks to go. The shop was crowded. The few tables were occupied, close together, and difficult to maneuver through. The overall volume of the store—between the conversation of customers, the orders being passed along, names being called when orders were ready, and the screeching of the chairs being moved across the tile floor—was more than Tom wanted to deal with. The coffee was great, the ambience not so much.

"Are we having coffee? Shall I get us a table?" Tom asked as he hurriedly tried to keep pace with Ralph racing through the shop. He bumped into several customers, but no one seemed to notice.

"No need to, sir. We need to go to the men's room."

Tom squinted. "Huh?"

Once inside the men's room, Ralph explained. "When you are ready to return to Heaven—and you must always return—you will need to find the men's room in a coffee shop such as this one, one that has locations worldwide. At the bottom left corner of the back wall in all the men's rooms there will be a crack in one of the tiles. Slip through the crack. From there you can discreetly use the rope."

"Are you insane? Look at my size. I can't fit through a crack. Plus, I'm claustrophobic. This isn't going to work for me." Tom stared at Ralph.

"Sir, remember you are a spirit. You, and anything you might have with you, will have no problem with the crack. Simply tap the crack with the rope and voilà, you and the ladder will ease through the crack where you can discretely use the ladder. It is rather like a genie slipping back into its jar."

Tom squinted and shook his head. "I don't get it."

"Sir, if I remember correctly, magic has always intrigued you. You always loved the 'magic' of some card tricks you mastered on Earth and unceasingly tried to find the secrets at magic shows. You seem to love the sodas that come with a soda jingle. I cannot not explain it all, but on Earth and in Heaven, belief and trust will make seemingly impossible things happen."

Ralph took the ladder from his utility bag and pointed to another small button on the bottom of the ladder. "Once inside the crack, push this small button. The ladder will open like an umbrella, shoot to heaven and attach to a cloud. From there, you can go up the ladder and return to Heaven."

The two of them went into the crack. Tom wasted no time in launching the rope and leading the way. Before he knew it, he was again facing The Veil. The earth side of The Veil still looked like a Brick Wall to him. Ralph caught up to Tom and suggested they pass through The Veil together.

"As I promised, when I am with you, your passage through The Veil will be smooth."

Tom went through The Veil, thankful Ralph was with him and he didn't have to take on the Brick Wall. *Yet.*

Chapter 13

HINKLEY'S

TWO DAYS PASSED before Faith contacted Ralph. Liz's errands for the day included a stop at Hinkley's, a locally-owned grocery store. Tom knew Liz particularly liked Hinkley's floral department for their service and selection, plus he was familiar with Hinkley's location and layout.

Faith gave them an approximate timeline and agreed to contact Ralph and Tom when Liz was on her way to the store.

Tom and Ralph left early. After they landed just outside the entrance to Hinkley's, they went inside and Tom scouted for peach roses. Several dozen were tucked away in water buckets on the floor of the floral department. He knew Liz would only glance at the assortment of flowers—if she went by the area at all.

He tapped a finger to his lips as he studied the assortment. He knew they had to be perfect, given the expression for detail she voiced after the prior attempt. Finally, he found what he was looking for. *Eureka.* When Tom found the perfect roses he felt like he had discovered gold.

"It would be great if we could get a few roses displayed at the checkout area," he told Ralph. "Liz would more likely see them there than in the floral department. It'd be nice to have a few roses placed at the end of the checkout area, near the bagging area. A lot of stores display bouquets at the beginning of the line and it would be more surprising for Liz to see flowers at the end of the checkout line."

"How do you propose we get these flowers moved?"

"Isn't there something called telekinesis?"

"Yes, sir. However, its use in such a public place would raise too many eyebrows. I think we need to find a medium to help us."

Ralph reached into his utility bag and pulled out a device that reminded Tom of a laser pointer used for presentations. Ralph explained it was a medium finder and handed it to Tom.

"Won't people see *this* and wonder what it's doing here?" he asked, turning the device over in his hands.

"Sir, anything we bring from Heaven goes unnoticed by people. There is a special dust, a *visibility* dust, that we use if we want something from Heaven to be seen by those still living."

Ralph turned and appeared to be studying the people around them. "Mediums have the ability to receive messages from spirits and convey them to people. Sometimes you can spot a medium because they have an unmistakable aura around them. Others are less obvious. When you point the medium finder at them, you get a reading that tells you the openness of their heart and how likely it is that they will be able to receive and deliver your message."

Ralph's ACT vibrated, interrupting his explanation. Ralph waved Tom closer.

"Sorry, I didn't have a chance to call sooner," Faith said in her soft voice. "We're at the entrance of the store. Do you want to meet us?"

Ralph agreed and a moment later, they were standing next to Faith. "Liz has started shopping. She has a long list. I feel I can comfortably leave her for a few minutes. Ralph, I see you're showing off one of your toys. You guys and your gadgets."

Faith took the medium finder. "You might not always have a medium finder with you, Tom. Detecting a medium is similar to judging distance on a golf course. The medium finder laser is like using a GPS system on a golf course to figure distance. Eyeing yardage can be difficult at first; a new player may become reliant on tools like a GPS to measure distance. Someone like you, who has played for a while, can estimate the yardage by feel. It's the same thing with finding a medium who will work with you—sometimes it's just instinctive. Look for someone with a radiance around him or her, no matter how subtle."

Ralph took the medium finder back and put it in the bag.

"Oh, keep it out," Faith urged. "We may need it. I just wanted Tom to have a choice if he needs it later. So tell me—you guys got a plan?"

Quickly, Tom told her his idea about getting peach roses positioned in the checkout area.

"Let's make it happen." Faith took a deep breath. "Show me the floral department."

Tom led the way, explaining how Liz would probably only take a quick glance and not see the roses.

Faith looked around. "See the lady over there, the one in the green jacket." She nodded at a rather chubby lady arranging a bouquet. Her name tag said Grace.

"Looks like she may be a medium," Faith said.

"No way. She's definitely an extra-large," Tom retorted.

Ralph rolled his eyes. "Sir, could you please be serious? We are trying to help you and Liz."

"Sorry."

Faith smiled. "I know Liz loved you because you made her laugh. I'm sure she would have loved that. Go ahead and approach Grace. See if she shows any response to your presence."

When Tom was a few feet from Grace, the woman shrugged her shoulders and looked around as though she had heard or felt something. Tom was surprised at her reaction.

Now, if I can get her to move some roses to the checkout area.

"We have so many roses here today," Grace mumbled. "I think I'll put some in the checkout lines."

Tom turned back to Faith and Ralph. "It's like she read my mind. That was awesome." He gave high-fives to the guardian angels.

"Is that how it works? It seems too easy."

Faith patted his shoulder. "One of you," she said, looking at Grace and then back at Tom, "has tremendous powers. I would bet it's you. When you were at the hospital with Liz she responded instantly. Good job. What's next?"

"I need to find a checker who'll point out the roses to Liz and make sure Grace puts roses in that checkout line."

Faith agreed. "Sounds like a plan. Go for it."

Tom moved to the front of the store and looked at the checkout clerks. He detected an aura around a checker named Joy and told Ralph and Faith about his find. He asked if he could try the medium finder to be sure.

Faith agreed it would be fun. Ralph gave a quick demonstration on how to hold and position the medium finder for the best reading. "If the indicator light turns green, you have a medium."

Tom pointed the medium finder at Joy. It turned green.

"Good selection." Faith smiled. "You really didn't even need the gadget."

Tom tossed the medium finder back to Ralph. "We have a medium. What now?"

"If Joy's the checker you want to help you," Faith said, "I'll make sure Liz goes to her line. If you've got a message for Joy to relay, send it to her telepathically. She should be able to receive a message from you and translate it to Liz. I'll go check on Liz."

Tom sent a message to Joy and hoped she received it. This was all so new to him. He waited impatiently for Liz to show up at the front of the store. After what seemed like forever, Liz stepped into Joy's line. While the groceries were being scanned, Liz kept her head down, looking at her list and nothing else.

"Come on, come on," Tom muttered.

"May I interest you in the manager's featured item of the day?" Joy asked. "The floral department has roses on special." She pointed to the bucket at the end of the checkout counter, a bucket holding a dozen peach roses. "Peach-colored roses for someone special, like you."

Tom watched Liz hold back the tears. Finally, she cleared her throat. "The roses are beautiful, but I'll pass on them today. Thank you, though. Thanks for pointing them out."

She knows. She knows they were for her.

He also knew what Liz really meant. *Good job. I wouldn't expect to see flowers at the end of a check stand. Nice touch to have the clerk point them out to me; otherwise, I probably wouldn't have noticed. Thank you. Thank you. That's all I needed. I didn't need to buy them. I just needed to know you're okay. Love you.*

SECTION THREE

THE SWEEP

Chapter 14

THE SWEEP OFFER ON THE TABLE

TOM WAS ECSTATIC that Liz had gotten his message. He barely noticed his journey up the rope ladder. Reality set in when he reached The Veil. Passage was smooth with Ralph at his side, but Tom was sure, if he had been alone, it would have felt like a brick wall. He was determined with every fiber of his soul to make the Brick Wall an easy passageway. If the Berlin Wall could be torn down, he could turn his "Brick Wall" into The Veil as everyone around him seemed to have done.

Life's challenges and rewards had always been a source of happiness for Tom. He had enjoyed life on Earth and had an intense desire to return. Wanting to play it cool, he waited for Ralph or St. Andrew to raise the issue of the SWEEP.

AFTER GETTING THE rose to Liz, things settled into a routine. Tom saw Ralph on a daily basis. Usually they met at the pro shop so Tom could play golf. He always included Ralph, intending to get his guardian angel interested in playing on more than a social basis. After a week, however, there had been no mention of the SWEEP and his patience was waning. One morning

Tom suggested they have breakfast and coffee before they teed off. They ordered breakfast at the grill in the pro shop, poured their own coffees, and sat at the small counter. Tom took a deep breath. "I'd really like to be back on Earth. Anything we can do?"

"There may be something." Ralph rubbed his chin and paused for a few moments. "There is a process called the SWEEP we may be able to offer you."

Tom sipped at his coffee to cover his relief. *Finally, we're getting somewhere.* "The SWEEP. You mean I'd be sweeping floors?" He grinned.

Ralph frowned. "Sir, are you interested or not?"

Let's not mess this up. "Sorry, couldn't resist. I am definitely interested. The floor is all yours."

As soon as he said the words, Tom regretted them. *Oops, I hope he didn't think that was an attempt at another joke. If the info Kyle gave me is correct, I don't want to blow this opportunity. Ralph doesn't seem to appreciate my humor. Better watch what I say.*

"The Seven Wonders Expedition Express Process pass or SWEEP, as it is called, is designed for spirits who miss Earth, but are not seeking a reentry life immediately," Ralph explained. "Special permission has to be granted by the spirit's advocates—in your case, that would be St. Andrew and Mary, Queen of Scots—and The Controller before you can apply for a SWEEP. Testimonies are needed from twelve spirits who knew the SWEEP applicant during his or her most recent life. Relatives are not allowed to give testimony."

Tom raised his eyebrows. *Not sure I know twelve people who are not relatives who might be here.*

"Those who bear witness must reach a unanimous agreement to grant the SWEEP process to the applicant. Once the agreement has been reached, the applicant has to earn the pass.

"Typically, a general pass is available when a spirit has reached the seventh level of vibrations. This pass allows a spirit to easily move between Heaven and Earth. But before getting to the seventh level, a lengthy waiting period is required at each of the lower levels. With a SWEEP pass, the waiting periods between levels are waived."

Tom listened intently as he unwrapped the napkin from the utensils and set the napkin on his lap.

"Earning a SWEEP pass requires interactions with people on Earth. These encounters may come directly to you in the form of a request from someone."

"Like Liz's request for a rose?"

"Exactly. Or The Controller may assign a task when He thinks your specific knowledge or skills would be helpful in a particular situation. Before you earn the actual pass at least seven interactions with people on Earth must be completed, seven encounters which make people wonder."

"Wonder? What would they wonder about?"

"As I understand your society, people do not like to talk or think about death. They fear death and some take extreme measures to stay alive. Life is a remarkable gift they have been given and it is fantastic they value it. Through the contacts you make with people on Earth, he or she may start considering or wondering about an existence after death. If people think there is good stuff to come, death might not be so scary for them."

Sarah, their waitress, came with their breakfasts—French toast and sausage for Ralph, a western omelet and whole wheat toast for Tom. Tom took a bite of the omelet, but barely noticed the taste. He was focused on hearing about the SWEEP.

"Why doesn't everyone apply for a SWEEP?" he asked.

Ralph shrugged. "Most people arrive in Heaven after seventy-five plus years on Earth. They enjoy reunions with family and friends already here or want to wait for loved ones who will soon join them. Some have endured long illnesses or have been involved in fatal accidents. These new arrivals revel in the lack of aches and pains and take delight in the amenities offered such as weather conditions designed for them and instantaneous vacations wherever they want. They have access to phenomena beyond their wildest imagination. The majority of spirits are content to be here and remain at level one." Ralph paused so long Tom wondered if he'd finished, but before Tom could ask more questions, Ralph continued. "There is a downside of applying for a SWEEP."

Tom stared down at his food, suddenly not hungry. *Here we go—if it sounds too good to be true, it probably is.* "Which is?"

"If the hearing results in a denial, the applicant remains at level one with no opportunity to advance to higher levels or to return to Earth via access through The Veil."

Tom wanted the SWEEP more than anything, but he needed to understand it completely before he threw away any chance for advancement through the higher levels. "I'd like to go over a few points. You said I need testimony from twelve spirits, beside relatives, who knew me. I'm not sure I know twelve spirits here. Where would I find witnesses?"

St. Andrew came into the dining area of the pro shop. Tom stood to shake his hand and invited St. Andrew to join them.

"It's been a busy morning out there and I could use a break." St. Andrew took a seat at the counter. He took off his golf cap and wiped the sweat from his brow. Before Tom could ask St. Andrew what he'd like, Sarah had a cup of coffee poured and sitting in front of St. Andrew.

"It's like she reads my mind," St. Andrew said. "So what's going on with you two? Looks like you were having a pretty heavy discussion."

Ralph nodded. "I was telling Tom about the possibility of a SWEEP for him—if you and the queen and The Controller consent."

St. Andrew patted Tom on the back. "The SWEEP pass, you say. Excellent. Consider me on board. There are so many darn details to that thing. I don't understand them all myself, but Ralph is an expert. Would I understand what you were talking about now?"

"I was explaining that Tom would not be responsible for recruiting the witnesses. Those who testify will step forward when they see the notice of the hearing." Ralph turned back to Tom. "If The Controller approves the application, notices will be posted throughout Heaven announcing you are a SWEEP candidate. The posters will give the time and place of your hearing and request testimony from twelve spirits who knew you on Earth."

Tom nodded. "Let's go for it. I like my odds of getting approval for the SWEEP and earning the pass. What do I do to apply? Go to SWEEP.com?"

St. Andrew chuckled.

Ralph frowned. "No, nothing like that. Let me remind you, sir, this is only a possibility. St. Andrew has already agreed, but we also need to talk to Mary, Queen of Scots. If she agrees, I will obtain an application and bring it to you for completion. All applications must be reviewed and approved by The Controller. Usually there are no delays once the paper work reaches His desk for signature."

"How long will it take to get the approval?" Tom asked. "A rough estimate?"

Ralph opened his utility bag and pulled out his spirit communication device. "St. Andrew, do you have time later today to meet with the queen if she is available?"

St. Andrew nodded. Ralph contacted the queen and set up an appointment, then turned back to Tom. "Sir, there is part of your answer. If the queen approves, I can get the application to you later today.

"Back to your question about the time required for approval of the SWEEP process. If your application goes through smoothly, I expect your hearing to begin at the time of the summer solstice, depending on the availability of the Hall of Testimony and if the request for spirits to testify is filled. Once the hearing begins, its duration depends on the length of the testimonies."

Patience, Tom. You've had to play the waiting game before, you can do it again.

Ralph and St. Andrew stood. St. Andrew suggested Tom find Kyle and get him to play a quick eighteen while he and Ralph met with the queen. "Tell him I said he deserves an afternoon off. He's been working too hard."

Ralph and St. Andrew agreed to come back and let Tom know the outcome. Hopefully, if the queen agreed, she would be with them.

St. Andrew held up his hand, crossing his fingers. "With a little luck, we'll have an application for you to complete." He gave Tom a smile, a nod, and a wink.

Tom felt some relief. *Looks like he knows something. I doubt he realizes I already heard them all agree when I was behind the cart barn, but I should be seeing an application soon.*

Ralph and St. Andrew left to meet the queen. Tom found Kyle at the cart barn and the two of them headed out for an afternoon of golf.

RALPH, ST. ANDREW, and Mary, Queen of Scots, returned to the course as Tom tapped in his last putt on the eighteenth hole. There had been very few players on the course and he and Kyle sped around in record time. Both he and Kyle enjoyed playing quickly.

They all greeted each other, then Kyle politely excused himself. "Enjoyed it, Tom. I'd best be getting back to the cart barn. I'll have a few carts to be shined up."

Ralph, St. Andrew, and the queen walked with him back toward the pro shop. The queen had a piece of paper in her hand. Tom tried not to stare. *Hopefully, that's my application. That didn't take long.*

The queen spoke up first. "Tom, I agreed to offer the SWEEP to you, but it's not entirely up to us. The Controller needs to sign your application, which I have here for you to complete. We're all here to give our support and review the rules, which I'm sure Ralph has already done."

Tom felt the desire for a cold beverage kicking in. If Ralph was going to review rules, this could be a long discussion. "Why don't we go inside and get something to drink?" He held the pro shop door for Ralph, St. Andrew, and Mary, Queen of Scots. As the queen entered, he was struck by the contrast between her dark auburn hair, very pale complexion, and barely noticeable eye lashes.

There was only one table in the small dining area. They chose to sit at the table rather than the counter where Tom and Ralph had eaten breakfast earlier. Tom held a chair out for the queen to sit in, took off his golf hat, and set it on the table. He asked what everyone would like to drink and went to the counter to order.

When he returned to the table, St. Andrew started. "Tom, as I told you earlier, I'm not much for knowing all the details of rules and procedures, just the overview. I'll give you what I think are some of the highlights. The queen can review the administrative procedures and Ralph can fill in the details. Sound okay?"

Tom nodded.

Sarah came to the table and served the drinks they had ordered: a beer for Ralph, actually it was root beer; white wine for St. Andrew; hot tea for the queen; a diet cola for Tom.

St. Andrew sipped his wine. "Not as good as the stuff I had at the last supper, but it will do. Tom, as in golf, there are rules for the SWEEP. First, and probably most important, is that twelve spirits need to testify and agree that your life on Earth merits the rewards of the SWEEP. Their testimony could be negative as well as positive. These spirits are simply bearing witness to your life and their statements cannot be rebutted. You have no opportunity to turn anyone away. Those who step forward will speak on a first-come, first to testify basis."

The queen added a cube of sugar to her tea and stirred it. "There will be signs throughout Heaven with pictures of you at various stages of your most recent life. The posters will request testimony from those spirits who knew you on Earth. My office will be responsible for creating the announcement and banners, flyers, and posters, securing a date for the hearing, and taking names of the witnesses. Ralph, do you have anything to add?"

Ralph stood up. "Of course, like in golf, there are penalties. It will take a unanimous decision to be approved for the SWEEP. If the witnesses do not all agree, you will remain at Level One."

Tom stood up, thinking everything had been covered, but Ralph continued. "Should you be approved for the SWEEP, I will be available to assist in your endeavors on Earth to either help someone on Earth or leave them wondering about their existence after a life on Earth; in other words, leave them pondering the question: is there really a Heaven? You may seek advice from me or anyone else about accomplishing your goal—prior to leaving Heaven. But a request for help once you have left Heaven will result in the SWEEP being revoked and you will remain at whatever level you have reached."

"What?" Tom, St. Andrew, and Mary, Queen of Scots, said in unison.

"Yes, explain that please." St. Andrew leaned towards Tom. "I told you I don't know all the details, but I've never heard of that one."

Tom rubbed his hands through his hair and pushed back his chair. He wanted to hear the explanation. This made no sense.

Ralph seemed tongue-tied for a moment. "It is in the rule book." He fumbled through his utility bag. "I have the rules with me, but cannot seem to find them now. I can show it to you later."

The queen sighed and shook her head. "Seems sometimes things get into the rule book just to appease someone. Like who decided three strikes and you're out and how did a strike get defined anyway? Somebody made it up. I like the one I hear many Earth mothers use: Because I'm the mom and I say so. Personally, it sounds to me like the guardian angels stuck that one in to give them more control during a SWEEP process."

Ralph blushed and looked down.

Tom didn't want to rock the boat by questioning the rule, as silly as it seemed. Having worked with insurance rules and regulations for years, he knew crazy rules could be added for no apparent reason. He would just play by the rules and detail every possible scenario where he might need help and then seek that help before he left. Yes, the rule made no sense, but he'd leave it to a future SWEEP applicant to challenge.

Tom completed the application, feeling a lot like he'd felt when he'd applied for his first job—nervously double-checking to make sure his writing was legible. Unlike job applications, however, the SWEEP application didn't ask for his qualifications or why he should be accepted. All that was probably left to the witnesses.

He wrote in all the information regarding date of birth, schools, home addresses, and jobs. Then he got to a line requesting DOD.

"What's this?" he asked Ralph.

Ralph explained it was for the date of his death on Earth. Tom didn't know. The queen offered to look it up and fill it in for him. Then she offered to take the completed application to The Controller's office that evening since it was on the way to her office. She assured Tom she would follow-up in the morning with The Controller's office to get an idea when the application might be signed.

"Do you want to meet here tomorrow morning?" she asked.

"That would be excellent. Sir, is that acceptable to you?" Ralph asked.

Tom nodded. He was hoping to hear sooner, but didn't want to risk losing support by pushing for an answer sooner than his advocates were available. "Tomorrow morning is fine."

Chapter 15

WAITING FOR APPROVAL

MEETING UP WITH Ralph at St. Andrew's gate had become a morning routine for Tom. He had shown up early the day after filling out the application, anxious for the call from the queen. He sat on a bench, twiddling this thumbs, but couldn't sit still, so got up and took a few golf swings with no club in his hand. He fumbled in his pockets to check for tees and ball markers; he had plenty in case he and Ralph played today.

When Ralph showed up, Tom asked if he had heard from the queen.

"Not yet," Ralph said. "Do you want to play a round of golf while we wait, sir?"

"Maybe later. How 'bout we get some coffee and chit chat a bit."

They went into the dining area of the pro shop and sat at the table. Sarah brought them two cups of coffee.

"What do you want to talk about, sir?"

Tom rubbed his hands on his pants, surprised to find his palms felt sweaty. "When we first viewed Liz, you had a device that located her and allowed us to see her. Is that something only angels can use?"

"Are you referring to this?" Ralph pulled out his Earth Location Viewer and showed it to Tom.

Tom nodded. "Is that something that would be available for me?"

"When we reviewed the rules of the SWEEP, we outlined the major benefits, but neglected to tell you about the minor benefits which come with it. If you are approved, you will be given a utility bag filled with devices and tools to use in the pursuit of the pass."

Ralph's spirit communication device vibrated. He glanced at it before answering. "This call is from the queen. Do you want to listen?"

Tom nodded and tried to listen, but the queen's voice was barely audible. He prepared for the worst and was relieved to hear Ralph say, "We will see you later. Thanks for the good news."

Ralph looked up as he slid the communication device back into his utility bag. "Not only was The Controller in today, He took your application and immediately signed it. The queen is on the way to her office to have her staff work on your posters. Things look good. Any other questions?"

"None come to mind right now. Feel like I'm in a new job and there's always something to learn. I thought Heaven would be all golf, all the time."

"It could be," Ralph admitted, "but you are too much a restless soul for that."

Chapter 16

THE SETTING

WITH THE SWEEP weighing on his mind, Tom didn't feel like playing, but suggested they work on Ralph's putting. He and Ralph gathered their putters and a few balls to use for practice. Tom heard a plane, but didn't glance up. It wasn't unusual for a plane to fly over the course. It wasn't until St. Andrew came out of the pro shop and pointed up that Tom realized it was more than just a plane.

"Looks like the queen has things moving along," St. Andrew said. "Flyers are already posted."

Seeing the plane with the banner flying reminded Tom of planes he'd seen on Earth at outdoor sporting events. Some banners advertised products or events while others were personal, announcing marriage proposals and birthday or anniversary greetings. He'd never expected a banner with his name on it for any reason. Number one, it took a chunk of change to hire a plane to carry the banner, and number two, both he and Liz were private people and would rather celebrate a special occasion by taking a vacation. The banner on the plane didn't give much information, only that the SWEEP hearing had been announced. Tom's name and five photos, each depicting a decade of his life, were on the banner.

Ralph's communication device buzzed again. "It is the queen."

When the conversation with the queen ended, Ralph told Tom and St. Andrew that twelve spirits had already signed up to give testimony and hundreds more had to be turned away. "The hall will accommodate observers," he added. "My best guess is this will be standing room only."

St. Andrew gave Tom a slap on the back. "Congratulations. Looks like the hearing will begin on the day we requested and you'll know your outcome in no time."

Tom was stunned, then realized he felt a little resentful. Sounds like this is a spectator event. Standing room only. This isn't entertainment, folks. This is my future on the line.

"With all the preparations completed, I suggest we give up the putting lesson and take a look at the Hall of Testimony." Ralph started to put away his equipment. "If you have any apprehension about the hearing, seeing the location before the testimonies begin may provide a degree of reassurance."

Tom agreed. As the two of them walked long, he glanced at his surroundings. This was the first time he'd gone much beyond St. Andrew's Gate. What he saw would be difficult for him to put into words, even to Liz, who understood everything he said. Within a few Earth blocks he saw a countryside that reminded him of New England towns, with tall, single steeples rising from a few buildings. Nearby some of the lawns brought back memories of Southern plantation gardens he and Liz had strolled through during early spring. A few blocks further, the white picket fences around the homes reminded him of many small towns he and Liz had driven through on road trips. He wondered how there could be so much diversity so close together, but then remembered he was in Heaven now and he was learning that seemingly impossible things were possible.

Tears blurred his vision. He didn't want to look any more. Everything he saw reminded him of Liz and it was painful. He pulled his sunglasses from his shirt pocket and put them on, not wanting Ralph to see the tears he was holding back.

Liz, I hope you know I'm doing this out of love for you. I want to be near you; things don't feel right without you.

They continued walking, finally stopping outside a small mom and pop general store where a young boy was hanging a flyer about the SWEEP on the large front window. Tom looked inside and saw three or four aisles, mostly filled with quick snacks: candy, cookies, ready-to-go sandwiches, beverages.

"Son, do you realize all the testimony spots have been filled?" Ralph asked the boy.

"Yes, sir. Indeed I do, sir, but the owner told me to hang a few anyway. Other folks may be interested."

Tom asked the boy if he had extra copies and if he might have one. He quickly read the copy the boy had handed to him.

The Hot Seat in the Hot Spot

Hearing of Testimonies Speaking Earth's Absolute Truth

in the

Hall of Testimony Seeking Proclamations of Truth

Hearing date: The Summer Solstice

His name and the details of his most recent life—including the names, locations, and dates of the schools Tom had attended; jobs he had held; and places he had lived—were all listed in smaller print with his picture at the very bottom.

He sensed many spirits looking at him as he and Ralph strolled along and he became self-conscious. He felt like a missing child with his picture on a milk carton. Or maybe an outlaw townsfolk wanted to hang. Either way, he wanted to return to St. Andrew's Gate, where he could be alone and just think about the close scrutiny he would soon be under from so many spirits. He told Ralph he wanted to go back to St. Andrew's Gate, but Ralph asked him to walk two blocks further.

Ralph stopped in front of a building situated on a corner and asked Tom what he saw. While Tom studied the building, he heard playful sounds coming from the park across the street. A slight breeze carried the delicate scent of late spring blossoms and Tom was able to enjoy it without allergies. A wrought iron fence about five feet tall surrounded the small lawn outside the building.

Tom sighed before he answered. "A white church trimmed in black. A steeple rising from it. Very plain, except for the gold words over the entry: Thou shalt not bear false witness against thy neighbor."

"Does it suggest anything to you?"

Tom shrugged. *What is this? Some sort of inkblot test?* "Truth is black and white?"

Ralph went inside without answering. Tom followed.

THE INTERIOR WAS decorated with plaques inscribed with quotes invoking honesty and images of people recognized through-out history for their integrity. The windows were transparent, no stained glass. The thirty or so wooden benches on either side of the center aisle could seat about fifteen spirits each and faced a large window. Through the window he could see a tall mountain.

He hadn't seen the mountain from outside the building. It seemed the window made a perfect frame for the scene, forcing one to focus on the mountain. There was a clear lake at the bottom of the mountain. Tall, sturdy trees circled the lake. He was too far away to see details of the trees, only that they were pine trees. Even if he had been close, he wouldn't have been able to identify them. What he knew about trees basically came down to two things: trees were beautiful to look at and there were two types—those with needles and those with leaves. He had allergies to the trees with needles.

Anticipating Ralph would again put him to the test, Tom offered his impression. "I guess the clear windows suggest the truth is clear, as does the clarity of the lake. The height of the mountain and sturdiness of the trees represent truth is strong and rises above all."

Ralph didn't even crack a smile. "I did not plan on asking what you saw, sir, or what it signifies, but it is good to know."

Tom resisted the temptation to roll his eyes. "Can I get some extra credit for my answers? I may need some."

"Extra credit will do no good for the SWEEP, sir. I will keep the request for extra credit in mind, however, for future consideration. Actually, this is not a church, but the hall where the testimonies will be given. I wanted you to see it before Opening Day."

They left the hall and strolled around the building. An uneasiness filled Tom's soul as he sensed the seriousness of his surroundings. The building and its view reminded him of a chapel he and Liz had visited in Alaska. At that time, they had talked about the chapel being a perfect place to repeat their wedding vows on their fortieth anniversary. Not that they would have a ceremony and invite guests, but a place the two of them could come and privately renew their promises to each other.

The uneasiness grew and suddenly he found himself wondering if he'd made the right decision. *What if Liz was right? She always told me I could go to hell for lying. I never really lied, but I exaggerated and made up stuff to set up pranks or to make stories more interesting. Are some of those tales going to come back to haunt me? What have I done? By requesting the SWEEP, have I jeopardized my place in Heaven?*

Tom felt the air flowing around him. He looked around and saw nothing, but the sensation felt like a reassuring hug from Liz. Whether or not that's what it was, he felt renewed by the strength of their love.

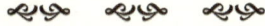

Chapter 17

OPENING DAY

ON THE DAY of the summer solstice, before the hearing began, Tom and Ralph met at St. Andrew's gate. Tom had on a collared white shirt, tie, and sports coat, which he had borrowed from Ralph. He wanted to present a respectable image to the witnesses. If it looked like the testifiers and observers wanted to hang him, he could always do it himself with the tie.

On the way to the Hall of Testimony, Ralph reviewed some of the procedural points with Tom. "Remember, sir, you are present as an observer. This is not a trial. It is a hearing of truthful testimony about your life on Earth. I have watched many TV courtroom shows with you. This hearing is completely for testimony. There are no rebuttals, no redirecting, or re-questioning. Your presence is solely a means for those who are testifying to verify that you are the spirit they knew on Earth."

The gold streets of Heaven were crowded, but festive and very orderly. Several posters detailing the day and time of the testimony were still hanging in shop windows and from lampposts. Tom had the feeling he was being watched. Several spirits looked his way. Most smiled and many young spirits shyly waved. He was relieved he didn't detect any jeers, but felt uneasy about what the reaction would be in the testimony room.

Tom put on his sunglasses and his golf hat. He wanted to cover his face as much as he could to avoid recognition. On Earth he hadn't minded being recognized on the street by his friends; in fact, he loved it. But here in Heaven, he felt uneasy about so much visibility around spirits he didn't know. At least for now, he wanted to hide his identity as best he could.

"Is there a special celebration for the summer solstice?" Tom asked, hoping the solstice was the primary reason for the crowds on the streets, and not that the townspeople on the streets were hoping for a hanging like ones he had seen in old western movies. His hanging.

"Heaven celebrates every day, sir, much as multitudes of people celebrate every day of life they are given. But the solstice is one of the days for special celebrations, such as the Fourth of July in your country. Solstice celebrations on Earth crossed many centuries and civilizations. It was selected as an official day of organized activities for people who have come here from Earth. There are organized games, music and dance performances, and assorted regional foods.

"I suspect, sir, the primary reason for the multitudes on the streets today is to see the opening of your SWEEP hearing. A request for a SWEEP pass is a rarity."

Tom's neck felt tight and he loosened his tie. *What have I gotten myself into?* "Why are there red, white, and blue banners and American flags everywhere?"

"During a SWEEP hearing, it is customary for spirits who lived in the same country as the SWEEP candidate to turn out and support their fellow citizen. I think you will recognize the greeters at the entrance."

Tom heard someone say the hall was filled to capacity. "Why are so many people interested in this hearing?"

"As I mentioned, sir, the day your poster went up, dozens of spirits wanted to testify and some had to be turned away. Apparently, there are many who knew you and care what happens to you. I believe we are entitled to take a shortcut. Come with me." Ralph led Tom to a circle on the street more golden than the rest. The circle was decorated with variations of gold spirals. Tom couldn't say why, but something about the circle reminded him of the points where the cable cars were turned around in San Francisco.

"Step into this circle, sir."

Tom followed Ralph into the circle and the circle began to spin beneath their feet. He was still trying to figure out how the circle could spin while they remained facing the same direction when they were lifted above the crowd. Tom forgot about the upcoming testimonies momentarily as he enjoyed the view from what he imagined as a magic carpet. A magic carpet. *I've been listening to too many of the princess stories Liz reads to her nieces.* What seemed like a heartbeat later, they landed at the entrance of the Hall of Testimony.

Two gentlemen with perfect posture stood outside the entrance door. They weren't mingling with the crowds. One wore a top hat; the other a three-cornered hat, a tricorne if he remembered his history correctly. Tom recognized Abraham Lincoln and George Washington. *Looks like they're guarding the doors. Probably waiting for the arrival of the queen.*

"Sir, I believe these gentlemen are familiar to you."

"They are." Tom shook the men's hands. "Why are you here? I didn't know you, not personally, anyway."

"Maybe not in your most recent life, perhaps earlier," President Lincoln said.

President Washington grinned. "We like to keep an eye on our citizens. We saw so many sacrifices made for life, liberty, and the pursuit of happiness, we want to watch what goes on hundreds of years later."

Tom just had to ask. "*Did* you chop down the cherry tree?"

George Washington winked. "Ralph, I think you should get Tom inside. Word has it that Mary, Queen of Scots, will arrive soon."

George Washington had a device in his ear similar to ones worn by Secret Service agents on Earth. Resisting the urge to scratch his head, Tom nodded at the two men and followed Ralph inside. *Why would there be protection agents in Heaven? Probably just ceremonial.*

As Ralph escorted Tom down the center aisle to their seats, Tom removed his hat and sunglasses. He was nervous and had to keep talking to relax. "Ralph you gave me some reasons why not many spirits request the SWEEP, like waiting for loved ones. Are there other reasons I should know about?"

"Many feel they got here, in Earth vernacular, 'by the skin of their teeth.' They fear if the testimonies are not favorable, they will forfeit their acceptance into Heaven."

Tom heard the door to the testimony room close. *What have I done?* he thought again. *Have I put myself in the lion's den?*

SECTION FOUR
TESTIMONIES

Chapter 18

JOHNNY

S T. ANDREW STOOD in the front of the room and asked for attention. The hall was pretty much as Tom remembered it from his preview with Ralph, except that the wooden benches had been replaced with chairs. The main focal point was behind the queen's bench—the window and its view. Chairs squeaked and groaned as people settled down. There were chairs in rows behind where he and Ralph were sitting. The annoying sound of chairs being dragged across a floor came from somewhere overhead and he realized there was an upper balcony. Twelve men and women spirits sat off to his right.

Mary, Queen of Scots, entered and took her seat at the judge's bench. She reviewed the purpose of the hearing—to determine if the applicant qualified for the SWEEP—and underscored the importance of honesty in all testimony given.

When St. Andrew called for the first witness, a neatly dressed male spirit with an athletic physique stood in the area reserved for the testifiers and approached the queen. Tom did not recognize him.

"State your name for the record, please," the queen said.

The man straightened. "Johnny Johnson."

"Mr. Johnson, do you recognize the SWEEP applicant, Tom Malone?" she asked.

"Yes, ma'am," the witness responded.

"I have no idea who this is," Tom whispered to Ralph.

Ralph put a finger to his lips.

"Can you tell me when you met Mr. Malone?" the queen asked.

"I don't know exactly, probably twenty-five years ago."

"What were the circumstances of your meeting?"

"Tom was transferred to the office where I worked because the office was growing. Tom was in a management training program and the home office sent him to manage the service area."

Tom slumped in his chair, then sat up again. He tapped Ralph on the shoulder and whispered in his ear. "I'm a dead man."

"Of course you are. Otherwise you would not be here."

"Now's not the time to get funny," Tom whispered back.

The Queen of Scots looked at Ralph. "Please keep your charge quiet."

"I will, Your Majesty. However, may we take a few moments for me to listen to what he wants to say?"

The queen consented and Ralph turned to Tom. "Sir, what is your concern?"

"I'm sure this guy wants to screw me over," Tom said, keeping his voice low. "Johnny had a problem with drugs and alcohol. It affected his work. We warned him about his work performance and absences. The company offered to pay for counseling programs, but he refused. After all avenues to retain him were exhausted, we had no choice but to terminate him. Since he was on my team, I was the one who had to deliver the news to him."

"Ralph," the queen asked, "are you ready to resume?"

Ralph nodded. "Yes, Your Majesty. I believe now I understand my charge's association with the witness."

Ralph whispered to Tom, "Sir, please try to keep quiet."

The queen asked Johnny to continue.

"The support staff hated Tom. He enforced corporate guidelines that required us to work harder. Heck man, that's not why we were there. The only reason we showed up was to get a paycheck."

"Mr. Johnson, did your acquaintance with Mr. Malone change your life in any way?"

Here we go. Tom felt his stomach tie up in knots, the same way his stomach would have tied up if he had still been alive. He was thankful for the ability to keep a poker face—he didn't want to let on that he was concerned. He looked around the sides of the room and up at the balcony where more observers were seated. He thought he recognized a classmate from high school, someone who was killed in Viet Nam. He saw a couple of guys he had worked with—both had suffered with long bouts of cancer—then noticed a couple of his dad's brothers, a cousin...

Wonder where my dad is? he suddenly thought. *Probably in a workshop somewhere.* He saw his father-in-law, Rayme, and smiled at him. Seeing his father-in-law eased some of the tension Tom was feeling, however, and the knot in his stomach relaxed.

"Yes, ma'am. He accused me of coming to work drunk and fired me. I was angry. After that I blamed him for all the bad things that happened. I drank all day. Eventually money ran out for my booze. I couldn't pay my rent and got kicked out of my apartment."

Tom slumped in his chair, sure he was going to get creamed. He'd be looking at denial of the SWEEP after the first testimony. How many times had he been told the decision had to be unanimous? He looked over at the other witnesses; a couple of the faces looked vaguely familiar, but he wasn't sure. *Wish I'd been better at remembering names and faces. What does it matter anyway? With Johnny's testimony, I'm sure I'm out.*

"Would you say your relationship with Mr. Malone had a negative impact on your life?"

Tom really didn't want to hear this answer, fearing the worst. He wished he could close his ears. But his attention was distracted. A star-shaped piece of paper floated down from seemingly out of nowhere and landed on the table in front of Tom. There was writing on the paper and Tom tried to be discreet while he read the note.

> Hi, whatcha doing? Wish I knew what you're up to today. Anyway, just wanted to say "Hi," and that I love you. Your Best Friend.

Liz. Tom was blown away. He hadn't expected to be able to communicate with Liz, but apparently she could get a message to him. He'd ask Ralph about it later, but for now, the note gave Tom the strength to listen to what Johnny had to say.

"No, ma'am. I thought about the way Mr. Malone had treated me. I realized, except for the day I got fired, he actually never came across as a boss. He was supportive. He had offered extra training to help me do my job. He had encouraged me to get into the clean-up programs sponsored by the company. Even on the day he fired me, he supported me as a person. He told me to get some help. I just wasn't ready to hear it."

"So what happened?"

"I thought about the suggestions he made. He believed in me when I hadn't believed in myself. I decided to clean up my act and found a local men's shelter, a place to sleep and eat for a few days. The shelter helped me find a rehab program and a few short-term minimum wage jobs.

"I saved some of my wages and eventually took some classes. It was in one of those classes I met a beautiful lady. Cynthia was the type of lady I never would have met while I was making a mess of my life. Instead of liquor and a one-night stand, we went for coffee and talked. We dated for several months, fell madly in love, and eventually got married. She encouraged me to continue taking classes. After I got a full-time job as a youth counselor, we started a family. We managed to buy a house, but it was in a tough neighborhood. I was killed by a gang member who was angry because I helped his brother get off the streets and find a job."

Tom was stunned by Johnny's attitude. A few weeks after he fired Johnny, Tom had been promoted to another location. It was common for the old office to have farewell dinner parties when someone left the office, usually at one of the office's favorite restaurants that served Greek food. One of the team managers Tom had kept in touch with let him know there was indeed a dinner celebrating Tom's transfer after he left. Johnny was at the dinner, venting his hatred for Tom. *I can't believe he's crediting me with his turnaround.*

The queen asked about Johnny's current situation.

"I've decided to stay in Heaven. It's the best place for me to watch my wife and daughter and keep them safe. They live in a nicer neighborhood now, but it's a crazy world with all the drugs, alcohol, and violence. It will be some time before my wife and daughter cross over. While I wait, I'm working with young spirits who were challenged during their time on Earth with a number of problems: broken homes, drugs, alcohol, gang violence. I help those young spirits who want a chance to live a clean life on Earth develop the skills they'll need to achieve their dreams."

The Queen of Scots asked for a summation.

"I credit Mr. Malone with turning my life around. Although I hated him when he fired me, he didn't judge me or look down on me. He told me how to get help. He apologized for firing me, but explained he had to."

Tom sat straight in his chair, overwhelmingly relieved by what he was hearing.

Johnny looked at Tom.

"Mr. Malone, being fired was my wake-up call. Eventually I worked through my anger towards you and found the respect for myself that you had for me as an individual even with all my problems. I'm grateful for your concern and your inspiration, Mr. Malone. If you have a chance, come by the teen center and meet some of spirits there."

Tom's head swam as the queen asked Johnny for any further comments. He had none. "Mr. Johnson, you are excused. Thank you for your testimony. We'll take a short break before we hear from the next witness."

❧ ❧ ❧

RALPH ESCORTED TOM out of the courtroom into a waiting area, which was actually just a hallway outside the hearing room. The hallway was long and narrow with large windows at both ends of the hall. Opposite the door of the hearing room was an elevator, a door leading to the staircase, and the doors for the restrooms. A bench across the hall from the restrooms had copies of the day's newspaper on it. Tom sat on the hard wooden bench and picked up the paper, but set it on his lap without opening it.

"I dodged a bullet there," Tom said in relief. "I thought he'd want to rip me apart for firing him. I saw him a few weeks after he'd been let go. He was in the stairwell, waiting for some of the girls who worked in the office to return from lunch. I tried to say hello, but he turned away. It was payday and I later heard that he'd been trying to get loans from some of the girls. The talk in the breakroom was how much the staff hated me for what I had done to Johnny.

"I would have never guessed that, by firing him, he'd credit me for impacting his life in a positive way. I was doing what I had to do as his boss. And no matter what, I try to respect everyone, whether I agree with their lifestyles or not. Don't understand how he relates the changes in his life to me, but I'll take credit for it, if it helps me with the pass."

"One of the lessons people need to learn is forgiveness," Ralph said. "If they feel an action was unfair, whether it was or not, people need to forgive. Johnny not only forgave you for doing what you had to do, he used his anger to push himself forward. I speculate he may have used your respect for him as a motivating factor."

Tom took a deep breath. He glanced toward the men's room door and saw his father-in-law go in. He wanted to sneak up on his father-in-law, Rayme, when he came out and surprise him. He kept an eye on the door while he listened to Ralph.

"The first testimony is tough," Ralph continued. "You do not know what to expect. Often the first witness has the most damaging testimony. This one turned out quite well. What you get is typically what you gave. Based on Johnny's testimony, I would say you each received something positive from the other."

Tom spotted beverage and snack machines at the end of the hallway and realized he was thirsty. "Want a soda?"

"No, thank you."

"I'm gonna get one." Tom walked to the machines and selected a soda. When he walked back to Ralph, he saw a grin on Ralph's face. Tom turned around to see if there was something funny behind him; he didn't see anything. He wondered what brought the smile to Ralph's face. The guardian angel hadn't seemed to have much of a sense of humor, though Tom would love to find the guy's funny bone.

"What are you smiling about?" Tom asked as he sat back down. "Did I do something against the rules? Are the machines off limits?"

"No. We need to work on your telekinetic skills and have the soda come to you. Maybe next time. Right now we only have a few moments."

Tom took a long drink, smothering his grin.

Glad I didn't use the jingle trick. Ralph doesn't know I figured it out. Sounds like he'll be willing to share it with me. I need to ask him soon, so I don't accidentally use it before he teaches me and is disappointed I learned it on my own.

The door of the men's restroom door opened and Tom saw his father-in-law come out. He hurried down the hall and touched Rayme's shoulder from behind. "Boo."

He was disappointed Rayme showed no indication he was startled, which was what Tom wanted to do in a playful way. Rayme turned around.

"They treating you right here?" Tom asked.

His father-in-law could usually find something to complain about and this time he was concerned with not being able to find a hot cup of coffee and a decent breakfast. "How long have you been here?"

Tom said he really didn't know. He had been busy keeping an eye on Liz and preparing for the SWEEP. He knew Rayme would appreciate the fact he was watching out for Liz; his father-in-law had threated Tom on their wedding day, vowing to punch his lights out if he ever did anything that upset Liz.

"Good to see you," Tom said. "One of these days after I finish this SWEEP deal, we'll get together and find a hot cup of coffee for you."

Tom thought of other relatives and people he knew from school and work who might be in Heaven, people he should try to find. He just hadn't thought about it because he'd been focused on the SWEEP. The outcome of the process was beyond his control, but he was hoping for the best and preparing for the worst.

Ralph walked up and Tom made introductions. Then he told Tom the queen was ready to resume. The three walked back into the hearing room. Rayme returned to the balcony; Tom and Ralph took their seats. St. Andrew asked the spirits to rise for the queen. Mary returned from her chamber off to the left of the hearing room, sat in her chair, called the hall to order, and asked St. Andrew to call the next witness.

Chapter 19

LEONA

THE NEXT WITNESS was Leona Baxter. Tom thought the elderly lady might be in her early eighties. Her ash-gray hair was pulled back and neatly secured in a bun; she wore wire-rimmed glasses. He didn't recognize the lady or her name. He passed a note to Ralph.

If these people know me, why don't I know them?

Ralph wrote back.

You never know when you make an impression on someone. It sounds as if you were a person who unknowingly made major impacts.

Leona introduced herself as the roommate of Tom's Aunt Fran when she and Fran had been in St. Joseph's nursing home.

"I was a very bitter old lady. I had been an only child. I was madly in love with my husband, but had been a widow for forty years. We never did have any children," Leona stated. "Tom visited Fran two or three times a year. When he came by to see her, he'd always smile and say 'hi' to me. Boy, Fran could get so huffy when he talked to me. She'd find some reason to interrupt us, like needing a pillow or something. She made it very clear she didn't want him to pay attention to anyone except her."

Tom smiled as he remembered a particular incident at the nursing home. Leona couldn't find the remote for her TV. Tom went to her side of the room to help find it. His aunt immediately started screaming for water. The glass of water in front of her that she could reach wasn't cold enough. She needed a fresh pitcher of water, with ice. And she needed it now! Tom shook his head. Something like that had always been always going on; dealing with Aunt Fran had certainly helped him learn to be patient.

"One morning near Christmas," Leona continued, "Tom stopped to see Fran. She kicked him out because she wanted to take a nap. After her nap, it was lunchtime. Fran and I went to the dining room where we had the typical cold soup and stale sandwiches. When I returned to our room several packages were arranged on my bed tray. There were chocolates, a tin of cookies, a perfume and body lotion set, a small artificial Christmas tree decorated with red bows, a poinsettia, and a Christmas pin, which I have on today." She pointed to the pin on her sweater. "There was a card among all the gifts. The card read: *Dear Leona, Didn't know what was on your list, so here are some surprises. Merry Christmas.*

"Tom returned to visit his aunt late that afternoon. I waited until Fran went to the bathroom before I tried to thank him for the gifts, which I was sure came from him. I didn't want Fran to get all bent out of shape when I talked to her nephew. He denied any responsibility for the gifts. However, the twinkle in his eye conveyed a different message.

"It had been years since I had received Christmas presents that were picked out just for me. Oh, there were the usual gift exchanges at work and with various organizations I belonged to. And when I got to be a senior citizen, I'd get food and maybe a hat and scarf because some social worker decided that I qualified for a charitable handout.

"During the Christmases at the nursing home somebody from a local charity would ask us what we wanted from Santa. The requests were hung on angel trees around the city. Well-meaning people filled the wishes and gifts were delivered anonymously to the nursing home. It's very kind that people want to give something, but old folks in nursing homes are lonely. Most of us would prefer to see a face than receive a gift. Tom's face was always a welcome sight. He always looked at me with a smile when he came in. If Fran was in a decent mood, he'd say 'hi' to me and include me in the conversations with Fran and himself. If Fran was grumpy, he'd just wink at me. During those times, I'd eavesdrop on them. Tom always had such funny stories and jokes to tell.

"The gifts on the tray seemed very personal, even though I had allergies to the chocolate and the perfume. I had felt old and abandoned in the nursing home, but the unexpected gesture of someone taking time to do something specifically for me gave me an emotional lift. I felt I still had value as a person. Much of my bitterness and self-pity went away.

"Later in the week, the activity director arranged for Christmas music to be played in the lobby. I asked one of the assistants to help me downstairs to listen to it. She was shocked because I seldom left my room except for meals. While listening to the familiar melodies, my mind danced away to the happy years with my dear husband, Howard. Memories of the vacations we took, the laughs we shared and the intense love we felt floated into my mind like a gentle snowfall. I cried for the first time in years. That night I dreamt about Howard and saw his face. I heard him whisper, 'You'll be home for Christmas.'

"It was still dark outside when I woke early Christmas morning, but the room was filled with a radiance I could never have imagined. I saw Howard. He was accompanied by two strangers. 'We're here to take you home,' he said and lightly took my hand. I was home for Christmas."

Chapter 20

GREG

I T WAS A hot and windy night," began the young man who had taken the witness seat after another brief break.

"Sounds like you'll be telling us a story," Mary, Queen of Scots, said with a frown.

"Oh no. I'm here to tell the truth, the whole truth, and nothing but the truth."

"We're not quite that formal here. We do want some information about your acquaintance with Tom. Let's start with your name."

"My name is Greg Parker."

Greg looked to be around twenty years old. His light brown hair was wavy and fell between his ears and shoulders. He wore navy pants, a white golf shirt with a collar, and a red golf cap. The cap and the pocket on the shirt were embossed with the design of a putter done in black. His shoes needed a polish and his shirttail hung out of his pants.

Tom nodded and grinned slightly. Now that he had a name, he recalled palling around with Greg decades ago. *Wow! Is that right? It's been more than thirty years since I've seen him.*

"You're here to testify regarding the SWEEP applicant, Tom Malone. Is that correct?"

"Yes, Your Honor."

"Please tell us when you met Mr. Malone and the role he played in your life."

"We met the summer of '69 at the local university." The young man rubbed his hands on his legs. "Actually, we met at a burger joint in our neighborhood, ordering burgers to go. Tom picked up his order and headed to the door. When he saw me, he stopped. He said he recognized me, but had no idea from where. After a few questions back and forth, we realized we were both enduring the misery of a quantitative analysis class.

"Tom was quite a chitchatter and we decided to eat together at one of the tables outside. We found out we both still lived with our parents and that our houses were only a few blocks from each other. Neither of us had a girlfriend or many friends at all, actually. Tom's family had recently moved back to town after living in another state during Tom's high school years. Most of the friends he had before then were in the military or away at college.

"That summer, after our morning classes, we hung out. Some afternoons we went bowling or played pinball. Tom worked most nights and weekends. I didn't go back to school in the fall. My parents were pressuring me to move out. By then, I had a girlfriend. She also was pressuring me to get an apartment for the two of us. I was working two jobs to scrape together funds for the deposits required to move into an apartment—"

The queen interrupted. "Since you didn't return to college, did you continue to hang out with Tom?"

Greg stretched his shoulders before he continued and Tom's thoughts drifted for a few seconds. His mom had mentioned she had read in the newspaper that Greg had died, but that was years ago, after Tom and Greg had lost contact. Tom never followed up to see if there was any truth to the article or if it was the even same person.

Greg continued his testimony and Tom refocused his attention.

"Didn't see Tom much throughout the fall and winter. We just passed each other on the way to and from work. We bumped into each other in early spring at the burger joint and had a chance to catch up. I mentioned how hard it was to find a job with decent pay. Tom told me about an opportunity he might have. He had met a man, Mr. Sheppard, who owned several family entertainment centers in the area. The centers featured miniature golf courses, water slides, and pinball machines. Sheppard had offered Tom the manager's job at one location, provided Tom attend a training class.

"Tom said if I was interested, he'd talk to the owner about me managing the other location. Tom boasted that these weren't typical hourly paying jobs, they were management positions. The hours were long—most nights, some hours during the day for maintenance work, and weekend nights were a must since that was the busiest time for the centers. The weekly pay was low. I thought Tom had lost his marbles. Who would want to work a lot of hours for little pay?

"He explained that the appeal of the job was the potential for a large bonus at the end of the season if we stayed until the centers closed. Sheppard had shown Tom financial results from the past year for locations in markets similar to ours. Tom was great at numbers and thought this was an opportunity for beaucoup bucks.

"Tom cautioned me that Sheppard carefully watched expenses. By keeping overall costs down, the potential amount of our bonuses increased. No free play or discounts were allowed. I liked the idea of a bonus at the end of the season. It made the job sound important. Tom talked me into taking the second manager position."

Here it comes. Tom leaned over and whispered to Ralph, "He's gonna cream me 'cuz we really put in some long hours. I didn't think finding him a job would come back to haunt me."

Mary, Queen of Scots, frowned at Tom; she didn't need to say anything. He sat back in his seat with an apologetic smile.

"The night Tom really impacted my life was a warm July night. The center was busy. We usually closed at one a.m., but if customers showed up at closing time, we had to let them play. This particular night it was around two a.m. when the last person left. As soon as the last customers were gone, I dumped the money from the register onto the counter. The night had been busy and the receipts were not sorted.

"Putting the cash on the counter wasn't such a good idea. I hadn't noticed a storm coming. The winds blew some of the bills off the counter and out to the parking lot. I put my arms on the counter in an attempt to hold down the rest of the money."

"Was the money outside?" the queen asked.

"Yes, Your Honor. The structure where customers paid and got tickets and snacks was outdoors and open on three sides. There was a counter at the front and that's where I had dumped the money.

"I was focusing on sorting and counting the receipts when I heard an unexpected voice tell me 'This is a stick up; hand me all your money.' My heart stopped, but started again when I turned around and saw it was Tom.

"Tom asked why the lights were still on. As I looked around, I realized I had forgotten to turn off the lights. The marquee light was still on and so were the lights all around the center."

Tom snickered, remembering Greg's reaction to his voice and the threat of a stickup. Greg had jumped, looking like he'd seen a ghost. At the time, Tom thought it had been hysterical.

"After Tom stated the obvious about having one freakin' mess on my hands and pointing out that I could have been robbed, he took control. He sorted the money on the counter and suggested I gather the money blowing in the parking lot and around the water slides and golf course. He asked if I had any idea how much money was supposed to be there.

"I didn't, but knew it was a lot. The night had been the busiest of the season.

"When I returned with the all money I could find Tom asked, 'Have you been drinking? You smell like alcohol.'

"I admitted there were a few beers stashed in the soda machine. I had put an out-of-order sign on a selection no one ever bought. A couple beers were left and I asked Tom if he wanted one. I went to get one for myself. Tom flatly declined and stopped me. He asked what I was thinking."

"Yes. What were you thinking?" the queen asked. "You could have been fired for drinking on the job. You were probably underage, too, and could have been arrested. Lucky you got into Heaven."

Greg hung his head and sighed. "I know. My excuse was that I was angry. My girlfriend, Terri, and I had been talking before I went to work. She threatened to break up without more of a commitment. She wanted a promise ring and for us to move in together."

Greg stood up, tucked in his shirt, and cleared his throat. When the queen asked what he was doing, Greg explained he was going to try repeat what Tom had said that night and he wanted to get more into the Tom role. "Tom had always had his shirt tucked in."

The queen shook her head and raised her eyebrows. "Go ahead with your performance, sir. I'm sure it will be of Shakespearean quality."

Greg straightened his back, deepened his voice and continued in a decent imitation. "'We can talk about your romance problems after we get this mess straightened out. Then we'll go to the diner for onion rings and a shake. For now, let's see how close you are to what the register tape shows. If there's a shortage, you know you need to take responsibility and cover what's missing. If you can't, you'll have to fess up to Sheppard and will probably get fired.'" Greg took a bow, the spirits in the testimony room applauded, and Greg sat back down in the chair next to the queen.

"Fortunately the shortage was small. I had the funds to cover it, with the help of a ten-dollar loan from Tom. He asked that I pay him back the next payday, which I did.

"Since I'd had a bit too much to drink, Tom prepared the daily receipt report and completed the bank deposit slip. He insisted on driving to the bank to deposit the funds at the overnight depository, leaving my car in the parking lot. After we finished at the bank, we went to the diner to grab something to eat.

"As I sobered up, I asked Tom what made him swing by the course. He told me he'd sensed something was wrong. He made it sound like a mysterious ESP thing and freaked me out. When I was sober enough to drive home, he took me back to my car.

"The rest of the summer, Tom called every night I worked. His excuse was to meet for a burger and shake after we closed, but I'm sure the real reason was to make sure I was sober. We went to the diner most Friday and Saturday nights. The big topic was girls. Tom had started dating someone. Rhoda—our regular waitress—and I had to give him a bad time. He tried to act macho about it, but it was obvious he was quite smitten.

"I felt comfortable talking man-to-man to Tom about my relationship with Terri. I liked her and had fun when I was with her, but wasn't up to the commitment she wanted. Tom didn't claim to be a relationship expert, but freely threw out his ideas. He said he wanted to marry someone he thought would be his best friend forever.

"Tom's encouragement kept me on the job 'til the end of season. We got our bonuses. As Tom had predicted, there were significant dollars involved."

"Did your friendship with Tom continue after the end of the season?" the queen asked.

"We were still friends, but rarely saw each other." Greg said. "Tom went back to school. I looked for another job. I was still under pressure to get my own place, but was in no hurry to do so. Terri and I continued to date. When she hit me with the news she thought she was pregnant, I caved in and gave her a promise ring. I told her I'd find a place for us to live and did.

"It was a cold, early winter Sunday afternoon. Snow was falling and the roads were icy. I had loaded my car with the few things I owned and was headed to our new apartment. One of the last things I had packed was my bowling ball.

"I started the car and backed out of my parents' driveway for what would be the last time. On the way to the apartment, the driver of the car in front of me stopped quickly to avoid hitting a dog. When I slammed on my brakes, my bowling bag flew from the back seat and struck me in the head. I died at the scene."

Chapter 21

MEG AND CLARE

THE NEXT WITNESSES to approach the queen were a woman and a young girl. The woman appeared to be in her early thirties. Her long, dark brown hair was pulled back and secured into a ponytail. She sported a pink baseball cap through which her ponytail hung, swaying in rhythm with her confident walk. The young blonde girl accompanying the woman had her hair woven into a single braid decorated with red, white, and blue ribbons at the end. The girl wore a white t-shirt embellished with red and blue stars.

Before the queen could say anything, the young girl spoke. "Good morning, Mary, Queen of Scots, or should I address you as Your Honor?"

"Queen Mary is fine."

"My name is Clare. I'm six years old. This is my mom, Meg. She's old. She's thir—"

Meg stepped behind Clare and placed one hand on Clare's shoulders, playfully covering Clare's mouth with the other. "I'll talk now. I don't think the queen needs to know every detail of our lives, just how we know Mr. Malone."

"Please take a seat." The queen pointed at a chair to her left. Meg sat down and Clare sat on her lap. "How do you know Mr. Malone?"

"We met Mr. Malone around a Fourth of July weekend. Our family had recently moved to Elk City because my husband, Brad, got a job promotion. Clare was sad to leave our home, as were Brad and I, but as parents, we felt a small town was a much better place to raise a family. The move gave us a huge increase in income. I could be a stay-at-home mom and get involved in Clare's activities. My parents—"

"That's Granny and Gramps," Clare explained.

"Yes, that's right," Meg said with a tolerant smile. "Granny and Gramps still lived in the hometown where Brad and I grew up and where Clare was born. We missed them and planned a visit for the July Fourth holiday.

"We had already made our travel arrangements when Brad's company scheduled a meeting back in our hometown. The meeting was scheduled the week before our planned vacation. After discussing alternatives, Brad and I decided he'd fly in for the conference and Clare and I would stick with our original travel reservations and fly in a week later. Brad would pick up a rental car so, as soon as our flight arrived and we had our luggage, we could hop in the car and head to Granny and Gramps.

"Clare was very excited when we got to the airport the morning of our flight. Not only would she see her daddy and Granny and Gramps, this was her first flight."

Clare blurted out, "I wanted to get wings from the pilot. Betsy, my best friend, got wings the first time she rode on a plane. I was 'cited too because we were going to a park with lots of rides. I forget the name of it. But since I was six, I'd be tall enough for the big roller coaster. Not the really, really huge one—that one's for teenagers—but the big one for first graders, not the baby one for little kids."

The queen smiled. "Clare, thank you for sharing your story. I'd love to hear more of it later. For now, please let your mom tell me about your meeting with Mr. Malone."

"When we got to the gate," Meg continued, "the attendant told me the flight was overbooked. She said with the number of people already checked in, only one seat was left and she couldn't get both of us on the flight. I explained the situation to Clare and she immediately burst into tears."

Clare made a sad face and tugged on her braid. "I didn't think I'd ever get to see Granny and Gramps or go the 'musement park."

Meg continued. "I felt like crying, too, but had to hold up for Clare's sake. The gate attendant made a heartwarming plea. She explained the situation and asked for a volunteer to give up their seat. Clare and I went off to the side. I knelt next to Clare and hugged her tightly. Her little body was quivering, trying to suppress her tears.

"Out of the corner of my eye, I saw Tom walk to the counter and talk to the airline representative. I overheard them making arrangements for another flight. The attendant called me back up and told me that Tom had generously given up his seat which meant there would be room for both Clare and me on the flight.

"While I waited for the paperwork and boarding passes, Tom went to Clare. He asked what her tears were for and he bet her he could put a smile on her face. He pretended to pull his thumb off and make it disappear. When his thumb came back, he reached behind Clare's ear and pulled out a coin. That made her smile. He handed the coin to Clare and told her to buy cotton candy with it at the 'musement park."

Tom thought about the countless times he had done that trick for his nephews, nieces, and neighbor kids. He always gave the coin to the child, saying, "Look what I found behind your ear. Don't you ever clean behind your ears?" The smile he'd gotten from Clare that day had pleased Tom then and hearing that Clare still remembered it, warmed his heart now. He always liked to make people smile.

Clare smiled at Tom and waved.

Meg continued. "Clare talked about how funny Tom was as we hurried to board the plane. I agreed and commented he had a very big heart."

"Mama," Clare interrupted again. She studied Tom, focusing on his chest. "I still don't know how you can say that. I can't see his heart. How can you?"

"I'll explain it later."

The queen asked how this incident with Mr. Malone related to Meg and her daughter now being in Heaven.

"It doesn't. We remembered what a nice thing he had done for us. When we heard he needed some references, we wanted to do something for him.

"We had a great vacation. Clare got her wings from the pilot. Brad, Clare, and I had a nice week with Granny and Gramps. We went to the amusement park where Clare got to ride the first grade roller coaster. We flew back home without any problem. It was a few weeks later, right before Clare was ready to start first grade, when we unexpectedly got our tickets to Heaven.

"Clare's school had an ice cream social the week before classes began, giving the kids a chance to meet their new teachers and classmates. Parents got to mingle with other families, to exchange phone numbers and email addresses for possible carpool arrangements and play dates.

"It was an amazing late summer evening and we decided to walk to school to enjoy the weather. We could also see how well

Clare knew the way to school. On the way home, Brad stopped to talk to a neighbor about the upcoming football season. As Clare and I continued walking, I heard a car approaching from behind us at a high speed, much too fast for a residential area. I heard Brad scream something. Before I could hear what Brad was saying and see who was driving that fast, I felt a horrific blow from behind. I fell and hit the street.

"I heard sirens and voices I didn't recognize. I tried to open my eyes to see Clare, but my eyes wouldn't open. I heard Brad whisper, 'Clare, Meg, I love you. Stay with me.' I heard Brad's sobs. I heard nothing."

Meg took a deep breath.

Tom sighed. His eyes burned; he felt like he could cry. *Guess it's not just me. Being separated from your loved ones hurts for everyone.*

Meg cleared her throat. "The speeding driver was under-age and intoxicated. She lost control of the car and hit us. Both Clare and I died at the scene. Brad now donates most of his salary and time after work to raise awareness of the tragedy caused by driving while intoxicated. To honor the memory of our precious daughter, Brad designed a poster featuring a photo of Clare. Above her picture is a caption—*Think before you drink!* At the bottom of the poster are the dates of her birth and death. The posters are all over town. The town loved Clare. Although we were new to the community, Clare's exuberance had captured the hearts of everyone.

"The young lady who hit us pled guilty to driving under the influence, vehicular homicide, and whatever other charges were thrown at her. We watched her on the day she admitted to her huge mistake. She made a video with pictures from the party where she had been drinking, the scenes of the accident, family photos of Clare, and finally photos of the memorial service. She narrated the video to tell people, especially high school students, the tragedies that can happen when driving under the influence."

Meg wiped away a tear. In a barely audible voice she continued, "Just as one kind act like Mr. Malone's made a lifelong memory, one thoughtless moment created a lifetime of hurt for Brad."

The queen waited a moment, then quietly asked if there were any further comments. Clare asked to talk to Tom and the queen agreed.

Clare ran over to Tom and gave him a big hug. She pulled away, holding something tight in her right hand. She handed him a coin. "Look what I found. Don't you ever clean behind your ears?"

Tom laughed and acted surprised. He rubbed his hand behind his ear to see if there was anything else hidden away.

She winked and said, "Thanks. Thanks for the nice thing you did for me and my mom. Have a coconut ice cream cone at Gramps' Ice Cream store. Tell him Clare sent you."

As Clare skipped back to her mom, Tom turned to Ralph. "Nice kid. The world needs more kids like her. Seems a waste she's already here."

Chapter 22

SHARON

Tom's interest was immediately grabbed by the next witness. He looked around to see if anyone besides him was checking out this beautiful lady. Indeed, they were. He recognized several observers. Many were high school classmates. He hadn't kept in contact with any of them since he had moved out of state immediately after graduation. But his mom had remained in touch with several of his classmates' parents and told him every once in a while about someone who'd been killed in Vietnam or who'd died from a drug overdose. Tom didn't know why, but he had a sense those same classmates were highly interested in the upcoming witness and her testimony.

The witness appeared to be in her forties and, as if mesmerized by a beautiful sunrise on Earth, all eyes followed her as she confidently walked to the chair next to the queen and took a seat. A young male clerk carrying files for the queen did not take his eyes off the witness. He tripped and dropped the papers.

The queen waited as the clerk got reorganized.

"You know this babe?" Ralph asked.

Tom's mouth dropped and he leaned back in his chair. "Ralph, I can't believe you just said that."

Ralph hung his head and his face turned red. Tom patted him on the shoulder. "That's okay, but you being an angel and all, I didn't think you'd notice."

"Even guardian angels need to recognize The Controller's most beautiful creations and she certainly is one."

Tom nodded. "Apparently I must know her if she's here to testify. There is something familiar about her, but I can't place her. Who'd forget a face like that? Those green eyes look right through you and her blonde hair looks so soft, makes you want to stroke it."

Tom had been a sucker for girls with blonde hair and green eyes before he met his wife. He gazed at the woman in white. She wore white linen pants with a matching tunic. Although her clothes fit loosely, Tom could see she was amply endowed. *Who is she?*

The queen's voice brought Tom's attention back to the matter at hand.

"State your name."

"Sharon Dees."

"Do you know Mr. Malone?"

"Yes, we dated one summer."

Several men in the room gave Tom a thumbs-up. His reaction was not as favorable.

She's a liar. I'd certainly remember dating someone that beautiful. When does she think we dated? Tom was greatly concerned. *If she has no problem lying about the two of us dating, what's next? Will she accuse me of taking advantage of her? That would certainly kill any hope of the SWEEP.*

"When did you date?" asked the queen.

"It was the summer between our junior and senior years of high school."

Tom pieced the clues together. He remembered a girl in his class named Sharon Larkin and her boyfriend, Bill. Before Bill had left for summer vacation he asked Tom to date Sharon during his absence. He told Tom that Tom was the only guy Bill trusted with Sharon. At the time Bill was arranging this deal, he had reminded Tom word around the school was that Tom was a nice guy. Many girls wanted to date him because he was so nice; it took several dates before Tom would even do as much as hold a girl's hand. But Tom's last girlfriend had broken up with him because he was too slow. He grimaced, remembering how much he had hated that nice guy reputation.

He also remembered that Sharon's trademark in high school was the tight, low-cut sweaters she'd worn. The sweaters emphasized her well-developed breasts, which Bill freely boasted was the only reason he dated her. Bill confided to Tom that he was certain all the other guys wanted to score with her and Tom's responsibility would be to keep everyone else away from her.

"Was it a serious relationship between you and Tom?" the queen asked.

"My steady boyfriend, Bill, arranged it. Bill, Tom, and I met before Bill left with his family for summer vacation. Bill told us how things were going to be. Tom was the only guy I could date while Bill was gone. If Tom saw me with another guy, he was to beat up the other guy. Tom and I could date, but Bill insisted physical contact was limited to letting Tom feel my breasts with my sweater and bra on."

"Your boyfriend told you who to date and what you could do?" The queen raised an eyebrow. "Sounds unconventional to me. Tell me more."

Sharon shrugged. "On our first date Tom picked me up on time. He came to the front door and walked me to his car. The exterior was sparkling clean. He opened the car door and waited for me to get situated before he closed the door and went to the driver's side. Not at all like Bill. Bill always honked for me to come out of the house and practically raced off before I had time to get into the car.

"Tom asked if it was okay to go to a movie. I couldn't believe he actually asked what I wanted to do. Bill never did. Tom asked what movie I wanted to see. I had no idea. Bill and I went to movies all the time, but I rarely got to see much of the movie. Bill started to make out before the previews began.

"On the way to the theater Tom told me humorous stories about his day at work. After he parked the car, I reached for the handle to open the door. He told me to wait; he'd get the door. We walked to the ticket window and looked over the selection of movies. He asked if I had a preference, which I didn't. Someone said the movie in theater four was good, so he bought two tickets for theater four. Bill usually told me to stand in line for the tickets while he hung out smoking with his friends. He rarely gave me money to pay for the tickets.

"Once inside, Tom went to the refreshment counter and asked what I'd like. I was shocked. Bill always hurried into the theater so we could start kissing and stuff. I told Tom popcorn and a soda would be nice. Tom ordered two large bags of popcorn, two sodas, and a chocolate bar. Before I could open my purse, he paid for everything. He tried carrying it all, but it was a little too much for him. He apologetically asked if I'd mind taking some of it. At the door to theater four he nearly spilled the soda while he tried to open the door for me.

"We agreed to sit in the back row; I was happy with this choice. It would give us some privacy. I hoped he might try something. In the forty-five minutes or so since he'd picked me up, I dreamt about going all the way with Tom, despite Bill's limited touching rules. After the movie, Tom took me home, opened the car door, walked me to my front door, and waited until I was safely inside before he returned to his car. No attempt to hold hands or kiss, just a polite 'Had a nice time. I'll call in a few days.'"

Tom remembered the evening. On his way home, he didn't think about whether or not he'd ask her out again. That was a given, since Bill had made it clear Tom would date her all summer. When Tom got home and was getting ready for bed, he was horrified. His pants were unzipped. *When did that happen?* He thought and tried to remember last time he went to the bathroom; that had to be before he picked up Sharon. His pants were unzipped all night! *How embarrassing.* If Sharon noticed, she never mentioned it. Thankfully, Bill had already left for vacation. If Bill had heard about the unzipped pants, Tom would've been a dead man a long time ago, no questions asked.

"The second time we went out we played miniature golf. We laughed and joked. It was fun, but again no physical contact. On our third date we doubled with another couple. We were going to an amusement park where there was a free concert. I suggested Tom's friend drive. I thought if Tom and I were in the back seat, I might get some action. Nothing. No fake yawning or stretching. None of the stuff guys sometimes do to get their arm behind a girl, then reach down to cop a feel. I wondered what was wrong with this boy. I almost missed Bill and his pushiness.

"By our next date, I had made up my mind that Tom was going to see and touch my breasts. When we hit the main street, I took off my sweater and threw it out the window. 'Hey, Tom, look at these,' I shouted."

"Tell me, sir, were they beautiful?" Ralph asked in a barely audible whisper.

Tom rolled his eyes. "How would I know? I didn't look. Besides, if you were always with me, as you claim you were, you had as good a chance as I did to check them out."

The queen directed her "be quiet" look at Ralph and asked Sharon to continue.

"Tom calmly pulled the car to the curb and parked it. I thought he was going to throw me out. But he took a deep breath, got out of the car, and walked back to pick up my sweater. When he returned, he looked away and handed me my sweater through the rolled-down window. 'Put this back on,' he told me. 'I won't look.'

"After I was dressed, he got back in the car. He wanted to know why I'd thrown my sweater out. I began crying and asked, 'Don't you like me?' Tom assured me that he liked me and suggested we go to a diner to talk.

"When I cried around Bill, he'd get mad, throw me out of the car, and drive off. Sometimes he'd come back, depending on how horny he was. There were times I ended up walking home. But with Tom, he shyly reached over and put his hand on my shoulder. Tom had manners. He pulled a handkerchief from his pants pocket and gave it to me so I could wipe my eyes. I thought again how I would let Tom go all the way with me, but he was too much of a gentleman to try.

"We went to a diner. Tom reached across the table and took my hand. He looked me straight in the eye and told me, 'You have more to offer than sex. I've seen the way Bill treats you. He bosses you around and walks over you like a doormat. You deserve better.' Tom told me I was a nice girl and should respect myself and expect respect from others.

"I didn't hear from Tom for a few days and thought my behavior may have ended our relationship. When he called, he apologized for not phoning earlier, but his work schedule had changed. He asked if I'd like to go out the next night and I agreed. He told me to think about what to do. I didn't give it much thought—Tom always had fun, adventurous ideas. I was sure he'd have a plan.

"The next night Tom insisted that I decide what to do. I wasted half the night trying to decide. I wanted to choose something fun, but something that wouldn't cost a lot of money. Tom had paid for everything all summer. I finally suggested a walk. He agreed and drove to a nearby park. We strolled along the grounds and came across a small duck pond. Several people were feeding the ducks. He told me to stay where I was and ran off, only to return in a few minutes, smiling like he always did. He handed me a loaf of bread. 'This is for the ducks,' he said. Then he sheepishly handed me a white rose. I asked what it was for. He told me it was because he was proud of me for making a decision.

"I had that rose until the day I died. My husband was jealous that I had kept a rose from a prior relationship. When I explained it was my freedom rose, the rose that gave me the courage to stand up and speak for myself, he was glad I had it and never said another word against it."

Tom didn't remember buying the rose, but if she said he did, he must have. He had given Liz many little trinkets; she kept them and could remember when and why he had given them to her. *Must be a girl thing.*

"The summer had been lots of fun. I thought about the good times and also about the serious discussions we had had. I made another a decision and wanted to talk to Tom about it. Although it was unheard of in those days for a girl to call a boy, I broke those rules and called him.

"I told Tom I needed to talk to him and asked if he'd have some time off soon. He said it sounded serious and I told him it was. He tried to get me to talk about it over the phone, but with my new self-confidence I told him I'd prefer to talk face-to-face. He had Thursday off. I told him that would be perfect. He suggested we get dressed up and do something special. I thought that would be fun. We agreed he'd pick me up at seven.

"That night Tom took me to a fancy restaurant, the kind you go to for homecoming or prom. Bill had taken me to homecomings, but never to dinner. He couldn't see wasting time at dinner when he could spend time doing what Bill liked to do best.

"I reminded Tom that Bill was returning in a week. Tom listened as I told him I'd decided to break up with Bill. He nodded in agreement. I asked if he'd tell Bill for me. His response was something along the lines of not wanting to get killed. I suggested it would be easier if he was with me when I talked to Bill, but he assured me I could handle it on my own. He offered to help me with some practice conversations.

"I broke up with Bill when he returned. He responded in his macho manner and said he had decided he was bored with me. He ordered me out of the car. My feet barely hit the street before he took off. I thought if he was that ready to move on, so was I—to more respectful relationships."

"I'm curious," the queen interrupted. "Did you and Tom continue dating?"

"No, we both agreed Bill's jealous nature could be harmful to either one or possibly both of us. Tom did kiss me once, after my breakup with Bill. It was a very sweet gentle kiss and I knew what we had was a respectful friendship, not a passionate romance. I dated a few boys during senior year. Some were nice, but not as much fun as Tom. Others were like Bill, looking only for the physical thing."

Tom reflected on the new, confident Sharon. He had seen many women walked all over and treated like doormats. If he had helped even one, like Sharon, gain confidence and think and speak up for herself, he was glad for his nice guy reputation.

"After high school I found a good job," Sharon continued. "It was at work that I met my wonderful husband, George. He was funny and adventurous, like Tom in many respects. He treated me like a princess, but still gave me the strength to make my own decisions.

"We had a daughter, Jennifer, and absolutely adored her. I worried about her during her high school years. Jennifer tended to go after men who took advantage of her beauty. Many boys she dated reminded me of Bill. She and I were close and I tried to make sure she got the message not to be someone's doormat. Some of her relationships were borderline abusive, maybe the path I would have been on if I hadn't dated Tom and then later met George. I was relieved when Jennifer met a man who respected her and married him."

The queen held up her hand, interrupting once again. "Mrs. Dees, I assume this is not how you looked in high school. Why did you choose this age?"

"As I understood the reasoning behind the 'shell,' the reason most spirits take one on is to be recognized by other spirits. I was forty-eight when I died. Since I was still considered young by Earth standards when I arrived here, I figured there wouldn't be many spirits here who would know me anyway. Although today I see several spirits I know from high school." She looked at the observation seating area where Tom thought he'd seen guys he knew. Tom turned to see them. Sharon waved to their classmates.

"So when I took on my shell," Sharon continued, "I chose the happiest time of my life. That was shortly after my daughter's wedding, a few months before I died."

"What are your plans now?" the queen asked.

"Jennifer and her husband are finally planning a family after six years of marriage. I've applied for reentry to be Jennifer's child so I can watch Jennifer and help keep her away from any harmful relationships she might be drawn to down the road, although she is happily married now. I overcame an abusive relationship. It wasn't physical abuse I put up with from Bill; it was mental abuse in not being respected."

"Fair enough," the queen said with a brisk nod. "Do you have any further comments?"

"None come to mind, except that I am grateful Tom came into my life and set me on the path to self-respect and confidence."

Chapter 23

WILLIE

A GENTLEMAN APPEARING to be in his mid-eighties gave the next testimony. Thin, gray hair peeped from under his plaid golf cap, the kind of cap that looked like it belonged on a newspaper boy from the twenties. He sported a white shirt, a light brown vest, plaid knickers, argyle stockings, highly polished golf shoes, and a gold bow tie.

Tom knew this guy had to be a golfer; no one except a golfer would wear knickers and argyle socks. Tom had played so many rounds of golf and had met so many people playing the game, he guessed this was someone he had been paired up with at some point, so he relaxed a bit. He had never cheated on the course, or anyplace else for that matter, and—except for one time when his ball accidently hit the back of a shoe of a player in front of him—had never harmed anyone on a golf course. He always had found golfers to be friendly people and hoped for a favorable testimony from this witness.

"State your name for the record, please." Mary, Queen of Scotts, started with the usual request.

"William Edward Jones. Just call me Willie."

"Do you know Mr. Malone?"

"Yes."

"When did you meet?"

A twinkle lit Willie's pale blue eyes as a charming smile shed twenty years from his face. "Can't say exactly, but it was the last day I spent on Earth."

"Did Mr. Malone have anything to do with your demise?"

"Indirectly."

A gasp echoed through the room, followed by a stillness similar to a soft snowfall hushing the earth on a calm winter's night.

The queen's voice revived the shocked courtroom. "Tell me about that day."

"I went to the golf course to play with my usual golf buddies," Willie began. "Ed, Joey, and Dean weren't there yet, so I practiced. After about thirty minutes, the guys still hadn't arrived, so I went back to the pro shop to see if any of them had checked in or called to say they weren't coming. Once you get to our age—we're all in our eighties and I was the baby in the group at eighty-one—it wasn't unusual for someone to forget that their wife had scheduled a doctor's appointment on golf day or maybe they just weren't feeling up to par."

Tom chuckled at Willie's pun and winked at him. "Don't know who he is or where we met, but he's got a sense of humor and he plays golf so he's gotta be a good guy," he whispered to Ralph.

The queen's glance curtailed further remarks.

"Continue, please," the queen directed.

"I asked Nathan, the kid in the pro shop, if any of the guys were there yet. He said no and checked the schedule. He told me our tee time was for the next day. Then I remembered we had changed our regular play day that week because Joey had to take his wife to a doctor's appointment.

"I decided to practice some more. I could putt better than the other guys and usually won a few bucks from them through our various bets on putting. The old geezers I played with still tried to muscle the ball and had the yips when it came to the short game. Not me. I hit it short and straight, but beat them on the greens every time. Drive for show, putt for dough."

Tom smiled and nodded in agreement. He knows the fundamentals of the game. Don't know where he's headed with his testimony; hopefully, it will be favorable.

"As I left to practice, Tom and another guy came into the pro shop. I heard their laughter when they came out, watched as they stopped at the snack counter for chips and sodas, and then went back to the parking lot to change shoes and get their clubs.

"The first tee was wide open. Most younger guys would jump right on the course, especially if they saw an old guy like me on the practice green. No way would they want to get stuck playing behind a pokey old man like me. Tom and his friend stopped to hit a few putts. Before they went to tee off, Tom politely asked if I was playing, as they didn't want to cut in front of me. I told them, 'You boys, go ahead. I'd just hold you up.' Tom smiled and said I was welcome to play with them. They hadn't played the course before and I could show them around.

"I thought it would be fun to play with a couple young fellas who could hit the ball a ways, a couple of nice guys, just out to enjoy the day and the game. I decided to play. On the way to the first tee, Tom introduced himself and his friend, Larry.

"Off the first tee, I watched Tom hit a long drive with a little draw. I never could hit a draw. I wanted to play from the back tees with them but knew from there I wouldn't even get the ball past the forward tees. So, regrettably, I hit from the senior markers. My shot went less than a hundred yards. I was happy—at least it was in the fairway."

The queen nodded. "Being in the fairway is good."

"I had a great time. We told jokes, gave each other high fives on good shots, and razzed one another when a shot went astray. It was all in good fun. Being around these guys made me feel twenty years younger and I hit the ball better than I had in years.

"The seventh hole was a par three and required a shot over water. Tom and his friend hit. Both their shots reached the green. I went to tee off from the other side of the water. Tom asked what I was doing. I explained that I had lost so many freakin' balls in that darn water, I'd given up trying and just hit from the other side.

"Tom says to me, 'I've seen the shots you hit. You can carry the water with any one of the tee shots you hit today. Come on, give it a try.'

"His friend also told me to go for it. I finally agreed to give it a shot with a water ball. But Tom pulled a ball from his bag and reminded me a new ball would fly better than an old hacked-up one. He teed it up.

"After a couple practice swings and making some minor adjustments suggested by Tom, I addressed the ball. Feeling confident, I took the nicest, easiest swing I could imagine. I felt the club make solid contact with the ball. That *is* the best feeling in the world. I watched the ball in flight, amazed I was the one who'd hit the shot. Not only did the ball fly over the water, it landed inches from the hole and rolled right into the center of the cup. A hole-in-one!"

Willie paused and stared out the window into the distance.

"A hole-in-one! Congratulations," the queen said. "That's quite an accomplishment. Is that when you died, from the excitement?"

Willie looked at the queen. "No. I was excited; I felt young again. I couldn't wait to tell Ethel, my wife, about the hole-in-one. When I got home, I gave her a big hug and kiss, even tried to pick her up, but this tired body wasn't quite up to that. I told her to put on her best dress and do whatever gals do to get gussied up. We were going to paint the town.

"We had steak and wine for dinner. On the way home I stopped and picked up some flowers and chocolates for Ethel. We got home and went to bed. I was feeling frisky; Ethel was amused. She didn't do her usual 'not tonight, I have a headache' routine when I reached over to kiss her. I performed without any of those drugs that cause four-hour erections. I had a great climax. And I don't mind boasting—Ethel was quite satisfied, too. I died in my sleep."

Willie was quiet.

"You knew Tom for only a few hours—is that correct?" the queen asked.

"Yes, ma'am."

"He must have had some impact on your life for you to be here today. What was it?"

"On the way home from the golf course, I knew it would be a day I'd always remember. Although the hole-in-one was a thrill, I also knew I would not forget the impression Tom made on me. He gave me confidence. He helped create one of the greatest moments of my life. Maybe I would have died anyway, but without him I wouldn't have played golf that day. I'd been pissed at forgetting we'd changed the day we were playing that week and would've gone home, kicked the dog, yelled at my wife, and sulked."

"One last question, more for my own curiosity. What are you doing now?" the queen asked.

"Waiting for my sweetheart, Ethel. She should be here soon. I can't wait. I want her to golf with me when she gets here. I need someone to teach her the game."

Willie turned to Tom. "Tom, you helped me so much in one unforgettable afternoon. Would you teach her how to play?"

Tom stood up, smiled, nodded, and took a nice easy practice swing. Willie did likewise.

Chapter 24

MATTHEW, MARK, LUKE, AND JOHN

GROUP OF four rather shabby-looking gentlemen strolled around the courtroom for the next session of testimonies. Despite their scruffy beards, torn clothing, mismatched socks and shoes—or being shoeless—the happy tune they whistled as they sauntered around the testimony room gave the impression they had no cares in Heaven or on Earth.

The four carried folding lounge chairs and a variety of small musical instruments: a flute, a harmonica, a tambourine, and cymbals. As the quartet made their way to the witness stand, Ralph asked, "Close friends of yours, sir?"

Tom shrugged. "Looks like some of the street people who hung around my office. I've been surprised by some of the previous witnesses. Nothing would surprise me now."

When the queen asked their names, they harmonized, "We're Spare Change." They sang their names individually.

"Matthew."

"Mark."

"Luke."

"John."

Their rich voices sang a message, "Now appearing nightly at The Top of Heaven Lounge."

The queen told them to be seated. Luke asked permission to set up their own chairs. "We find them very comfortable and take them wherever we go. These were hard to find in Heaven."

The queen waved her hand. "Go right ahead."

As the four got themselves situated, she assured them she'd be sure to catch their show. Once again, the typical questions were asked: "Do you know Tom? How do you know him?"

"Wouldn't say we really knew the bloke," Matthew said.

Mark looked at his friend as if he had two heads. "What do you mean, we didn't know him?"

"Does anyone really know another person?" Luke asked, absently fingering his flute.

"Tom was the president of our fan club," John said, slapping his knee with one hand.

Matthew looked bewildered. "I didn't know we had a fan club."

Luke appeared even more confused. "I didn't know we had any fans."

The queen raised a hand. "Let's keep focused here. Are you here to testify for Tom?"

The quartet nodded.

"May I request you speak one at a time and stay on the subject?"

The group looked at one another and again nodded in unison.

The queen asked, "Do you know the gentleman in question?"

Matthew spoke for the group. "Your Honor, we didn't know his name, but we recognized his face on the posters we saw regarding his request for the SWEEP."

"Why are you here if you don't even know his name?"

Mark fielded this question. "He was one of those people who created magic moments. You know, one of those 'random acts of kindness' things."

"Can you be more specific?"

"We hung out on the streets in the area where Tom worked and saw him frequently," Luke said. "Our typical location was under a bridge between his office and the lot where he parked his car. We'd play music and sing during lunch and again during the evening rush hour."

Tom smiled, remembering. He had walked past many street people in the business district where he had worked. These four had caught his attention because they had seemed happy living as they did and always said amusing things as people passed by.

"That's when most people hit the streets," John said, "and we had the best chance of getting spare change from the business people passing by."

Matthew continued. "The majority of people ignored us and hurried past. Tom was a different sort of guy. More often than not, he'd put some change into our cup."

"After a few times of tossing some coins our way and continuing on, he stopped to listen," Mark added, his face thoughtful. "He made comments like 'Wanted to see if you knew all the words to the song' or 'You sounded a little off key.'"

"He treated us like real people, not street people," Luke said. "Can't tell you how many times people would cross to the other side of the street to avoid us."

"So many people reacted as if we had some dreaded disease," John said.

"Or looked like we were going to attack them," Matthew added.

One by one, the members of Spare Change listed their memories of the stranger who had passed through their lives.

They had not known his name when they'd met on Earth, but he'd made a lasting impression on them.

"Tom was different," Matthew remarked. "Always had a smile on his face. Sometimes he'd have a bouquet of flowers. Those times he'd apologize, 'Sorry, guys, for not having any spare change.' He'd spent it all on flowers for his wife."

Luke added, "We'd kid him about his wife being mad at him and the flowers were to get back in her good graces. He always denied he was in trouble. He told us he hoped the flowers would surprise her and help him get lucky."

"The time I remember most is an evening in December," John said. "He had a super huge bouquet. We commented on its size and the fact that the bouquet probably meant no spare change for us for a while. Tom told us it was a few days before some obscure anniversary his wife always made a fuss over, something like their first date or the night he gave her an engagement ring. He said his wife might anticipate that he'd give her flowers on special days, but he liked to throw her off and bring her a bouquet a few days ahead of time."

"That's the night we learned 'The No L' song," Mark said.

The queen interrupted. "Most children learn that Christmas carol in elementary school or in Sunday school. You mean you didn't learn it until you were adults?"

John responded. "Oh no, ma'am. 'The No L' song, not the 'Noel' Christmas carol. Tom offered us twenty dollars if we'd sing 'The No L' song. So we started singing the Christmas carol, just like you thought. Tom stopped us and sang the song, the alphabet song—A B C D E F G H I J K . . . M N O P. Get it, there's no L in the song?"

Mark shrugged. "It's pretty lame. And the man sure couldn't carry a tune. But we sang it and Tom gave us a bit more than twenty bucks."

"It was enough we each got a decent sandwich and a cup of coffee, once we found a deli that would let us sit down," Luke said. "Many places wouldn't let us in because of the way we looked. We asked people in the deli if they wanted to hear 'The No L' song. Most folks ignored us. A few listened, chuckled, and gave us some coins."

"Previous witnesses have testified to big changes in their lives after their encounters with Tom," the queen said. "Are you going to tell me you recorded 'The NO L' song, it was a best seller, and you became rich and famous?"

"No," Mark piped up. "Nothing like that, but we met a memorable, nameless friend. We happened to be singing outside St. Andrew's Gate the day Tom arrived and recognized him."

John summed it up. "Tom was a special guy. The time he took to talk to us made us feel like royalty. It's remarkable how one person, even if you don't know their name, can bring a moment of happiness that leaves a lasting memory."

When Mary, Queen of Scots, asked if they had anything further to say, the members of Spare Change exchanged glances and shook their heads. Individually they each sang out, "No." Then in harmony sang, "No L."

The Spare Change group gathered their chairs and instruments, then paraded around the room before heading back to their seats. They were singing "The NO L" song. As they passed Tom, Matthew tipped his hat. Mark put out his hand for some spare change. Tom grinned and held his empty hands out. "Sorry, nothing today." He applauded when they finished their song.

Luke reached up the sleeve of his worn jacket and pulled out a bouquet of flowers, peach-colored roses. "For your wife next time you see her."

John winked and pointed to the flowers. "Hope you get lucky."

Tom nodded and smiled as he stood and watched the four parade around the room. He was stunned that something as simple as talking to a stranger could make a memory for someone. For him it had just seemed like a natural thing to do. And for them to remember his wife's favorite flower, the peach roses. Incredible!

Chapter 25

KATHY

THE QUEEN CALLED for the next witness and advised the spirits in the hearing room the next witness would be entering through the back door. The door in the back of the room opened. A young female spirit, probably around seven years old, entered. She was chubby with curly red hair and was wearing thick glasses. Her face was covered with freckles. She was riding a bike, swerving from side to side down the aisle towards Queen Mary. Her bike had a basket on the handlebars; the basket was filled with hard-cover textbooks and soft-cover workbooks. About halfway down the aisle, she lost her balance and fell off her bike. Her bike fell on top of her and her books scattered in the aisle.

Tom was seated with Ralph in the front row at a table facing the queen. He had turned around to watch the spirit come down the aisle. When she fell, some observers in the room laughed.

Tom jumped to his feet, retrieved the girl's books, and picked up her bike. He asked if she was okay and extended his hand to help her to her feet. She smiled at Tom, reassured him she was fine, and thanked him. The girl carefully returned the books to the basket as if they were her most precious possessions. She walked her bike to the chair next to the queen and dropped her bike on the floor in the space between the queen's desk and the witness chair. The books fell from the basket again.

"Stupid thing," she muttered. Then she very carefully arranged her books and slid them under the chair. She brushed off the plaid uniform-type skirt she wore. She turned to the queen first, then looked around at the other spirits who had testified and the observers in the room. "And that's pretty much a reenactment of what happened some forty or forty-five years ago."

She looked at the queen and asked for permission to sit down. The queen nodded.

Another spirit person Tom didn't recognize.

Poor kid, she has three strikes against her: the hair, the glasses, and being chubby, a prime target for being teased as a kid. Hope I didn't say anything mean that she overheard.

The girl shyly introduced herself. "Hi, I'm Kathy. I was in second grade when I first met Tom. I was riding my bike home from school, with all my books, just like I showed you. Even the books I didn't have homework in, 'cuz I wanted to study for tests at the end of the week. I heard some older girls, fourth graders, behind me. They were saying mean things and making fun of me. They called me Four Eyes. They laughed at the color of my hair and said I was a fat freak. I tried to ignore them and ride faster so I couldn't hear 'em. I had tears in my eyes and didn't see the tree root making a crack in the sidewalk. I lost control of the bike when it hit the crack and I fell off. The girls pointed at me and snickered as they walked by.

"Tom and his friends were across the street, riding their bikes. Tom stopped to see if I was okay. He took a hankie from his pants pocket and cleaned my scraped knee. He said that I must be pretty smart, carrying all the books I had. I told him I kinda was. Then Tom picked up my books and helped me up from the sidewalk. He handed me my books and gave me a piece of bubblegum from his pocket. He told me the gum would put a smile on my face; he was right. He got back on his bike and rode off the other way. Tom was my knight on the shiny red bike."

Tom had never thought of himself as a knight. He chuckled softly as he imagined what he would look like in shining armor.

Kathy asked if she could get some water. The queen graciously asked one of her aides to get water for Kathy and for herself.

The testimony continued. "I saw Tom again one day during summer vacation. I went to Shorty's to get a frozen drink. Shorty's was a neighborhood store where kids went for ice cream and candy. When I opened the door, I saw the mean girls inside. I turned around to leave, hoping they hadn't seen me. But before I got out of the store, the girls were making fun of me. I stood in front of the store with the door partially open and debated whether to go in and face the mean girls. Tom rode up on his bike. He got off his bike, held the door for me, and followed me inside.

"The girls were in the back of the store where there was a small area with magazines about movie stars and teen idols. They pretended to read those, but I could hear them whispering and giggling. I knew they were making fun of me. One of the girls saw Tom with me and her mouth dropped open. I didn't look at the girls directly but watched them out of the corner of my eye.

"Tom asked what I was getting. I told him a frozen lemonade. He said that sounded good and decided to get one. He told Shorty he wanted two frozen lemonades and asked him for a couple pieces of bubblegum. He put his money on the counter and I put mine there, too. Tom gave my money back to me. He said he'd buy my drink. After Shorty handed Tom the drinks, the gum, and his change, Tom gave me my drink and a piece of gum. When he walked out the door with me, I felt like a princess.

"My sister was in the same grade as the mean girls, but in a different class. My sister's friend, Diane, knew those girls. Diane told my sister one of the girls who made fun of me had a crush on Tom. That girl was really mad when she saw Tom buy me a lemonade. Me and my sister thought it was funny."

The assistant returned with two glasses of water and handed one to Kathy. She paused to take a drink before continuing.

"Later that year, I got cancer. I spent a lot of time in the hospital before I died. When I had treatments and was really hurting, I thought about Tom as my Prince Charming coming to rescue me. It made me feel better.

"I really did feel like a freak when I was sick. All my hair fell out and I had to wear funny-looking scarves and hats to cover my head. When you're sick and people think you're gonna die soon they do all sorts of nice things because they feel sorry for you. I think sometimes people do nice things for sick kids so they can feel good about themselves. I think Tom did something nice for me because he wanted me to feel good about me."

Tom relaxed, but not completely. He felt the testimonies had gone well, but the final decision about the SWEEP was still out of his hands. He let his mind drift back to the fifties when he was a kid and life was simpler. His generation all seemed to agree they'd grown up just fine. They hadn't needed organized activities to keep busy. They played baseball in the streets or rode their bikes all over the neighborhood. They only had three TV channels and he and the boys in his class had faithfully watched Saturday afternoon baseball. They didn't get killed without seatbelts or bike helmets. Back in those days, the street lights coming on and parents' voices and whistles told kids when it was time to come inside. Families were lucky to have a phone with a private line.

His generation had survived the political upheaval and riots of the sixties and the inflation of the seventies, and they worked hard, raising families and taking on responsibilities. As they aged, he and his friends admitted the aches and pains were setting in. Most of his friends planned on working until it wasn't fun anymore and most agreed they wouldn't want to be part of the current generation. Life had been good. Tom only wished he'd had a chance to live more of it.

Chapter 26

THE VERDICT

FTER KATHY FINISHED her testimony, the queen invited the observers to remain in the testimony room if they desired, but asked them to remain quite while she explained the criteria for granting the SWEEP to Tom and what achieving the SWEEP pass meant. The queen turned to her right to face the area where the twelve spirits who had given testimony were seated together. She reminded them that their decision must be unanimous. If granted the right to earn the SWEEP, Tom would be permitted to travel to Earth on a restricted basis to answer requests for help from people on Earth. Actually earning the pass would be up to Tom. She charged the twelve witnesses with the final decision: should Tom be given the right to earn the pass?

The twelve witnesses looked at each other, simultaneously nodded approval, and signaled with a thumbs-up.

"As spokesperson for this group, I am pleased to announce that it is our unanimous decision the SWEEP be given to Mr. Malone," Clare said.

Every spirit in the room applauded and went crazy trying to reach Tom and offer their congratulations.

The queen smiled as she watched the exuberance of the crowd. The excitement continued for a few more moments and finally the queen tapped her gavel on her desk. When the crowd quieted, the queen spoke. "You definitely are all in agreement, but we need to follow protocol and have the official decision made behind closed doors." She asked one of the guard angels to escort the witnesses to a meeting room.

Then the queen suggested that Tom and Ralph wait in one of the chamber rooms or outside if they wanted some fresh air. She recommended they stay close.

As he and Ralph walked out of the testimony room, Tom reflected on the current situation. He felt like he had when waiting for all the other players in a golf tournament to finish. There had been tournaments when he'd finished playing sooner than the players and guessed he might be one of the top finishers. But he'd had to wait for the remaining players to post their scores. In those tournaments, as in all tournaments, he had done as well as he could and the final outcome was out of his hands.

He felt the same way now. He had lived life as best he could and now the decision for the SWEEP was completely out of his hands.

Before going to one of the chamber rooms, Ralph asked, "Would you like a soda, sir?"

Tom never had been one to turn down a soda. "Sounds good. Make mine a diet."

Ralph offered to tell Tom how to pull sodas from the air. Tom didn't have the heart to tell Ralph he had mastered the soda trick on his own. "That would be great."

Ralph shared the secret. Tom whistled, got one soda, and started to work on the second. He stopped mid-whistle when he saw the witnesses returning.

He and Ralph followed the witnesses back into the testimony room where everyone returned to their original seats—the witnesses across from the queen and Tom and Ralph in their seats facing her. The queen asked if a decision had been made. Clare stood and admitted their original decision had been made way too quickly and without much thought.

She paused long enough Tom's stomach started to do flip flops. *They're gonna take it away.*

"We want to add an addendum to our original decision. Mr. Malone, if we didn't get a chance to tell you on Earth, we'd like to tell you now—Thank you for the difference you made in our lives."

The twelve witnesses jumped to their feet and crowded around Tom, showering him with hugs, slaps on the back, and high fives. Mary, Queen of Scots, held up her hand. "I'm sure you all are anxious to express your gratitude and congratulations to Mr. Malone, but before you do, we have a piece of business to take care of. St. Andrew, Ralph, please step forward and present Mr. Malone with his utility bag."

She nodded at Tom. "As you know, based on the decision of these twelve spirits, you have been granted the opportunity to earn the pass. In order to earn the pass, you need to create seven 'wonder moments' with people on Earth, moments that will get people to think about an existence that begins after the physical body dies. To assist you in making those moments happen, you will need some tools."

Ralph held up a bag similar to the one he wore. "Sir, this is your utility bag," Ralph said. "You are already familiar with some of its items, such as the ELV—also known as the Earth Location Viewer—the medium finder, and the rope ladder. Also in the bag are two pockets filled with dust: one to make items you take from Heaven visible to people on Earth, the other to make items from Earth invisible to people. You now also have your own spirit-to-spirit communication device. A new convenience item has been included in your bag. You will be the first to have it. It is a spray to give you mobility options. If you should need a way to maneuver around more easily when seeking out mediums, it will give you options, such as gliding, floating, hovering. It might even come in handy when traveling over tough terrain. Simply spray it on your shell and you are good to go, in more ways than one."

St. Andrew handed Tom the utility bag. It was a royal blue drawstring pouch fashioned from velvet fabric. "These are the major tools you will use. Other tools may be given to you along the way. Good luck."

Tom thanked the queen, St. Andrew, and Ralph for his utility bag. Then he turned back to the witnesses and the observers who had gathered close.

Ralph tapped Tom on the shoulder. "Sir, I am sorry to disturb you, but I think we need to leave soon. A message star is headed your way." Ralph pointed to an approaching star.

SECTION FIVE

WONDERS AND DISCOVERIES

Chapter 27

SANDRA

STAR MESSAGES

THE GREEN STAR stopped in front of Tom. It was a five-pointed star, about five inches across. It reminded Tom of the star-shaped cookie cutter Liz's family used when they got together and baked Christmas cookies.

"I can get messages?" Tom asked, wondering if he should try to touch the glimmering object.

"Yes, sir, you can receive messages—star messages. And in fact, you have already received one. Do you recall the note you received from Liz during the testimonies?"

Tom remembered. "I thought that was just a thought from Liz, since on Earth we could often sense what the other was thinking. But back to my question, can I get messages from people on Earth other than Liz?"

"When someone on Earth thinks about you in any way," Ralph said, "their thoughts come to you by way of message stars. The stars come in various colors and sizes reflecting the intent of the sender. Typically, a green star, such as this one, is from someone who wishes you were still on Earth because they would like your help on something. Red stars tell you the sender loves you; blue stars let you know the sender misses you. Yellow-and-gold stars, the sunshine cards, may not have a message inside, but are to let you know the sender has a happy memory of you or something you did to make them smile or laugh. A white star is like a friendship card, a 'thinking of you' message. The stars I am sure you will not want to see are purple stars with flaming orange edges. A star like that would come from a person who is angry."

"What do I with it?"

"I suggest you take the star and read it."

Tom gingerly took hold of the star. "I thought it might be hot, but it's not even warm." He turned the star over in his hands to examine it.

"The star opens like a greeting card," Ralph said. "The outside will typically show the name of the person who sent the message. Generally, their message is inside."

The name *Sandra* was on the outside of the card.

Tom frowned. "Sandra. Sandra is ... uh ... *was* my assistant."

He looked inside. "I can't read this. It looks like gobbledygook." He handed the star to Ralph. "What does it say?"

While Tom waited for Ralph to decipher the strange message, he thought about Sandra and how much she had changed over the twenty-plus years they had worked together.

"Do you remember Sandra?" he asked Ralph.

"Though I saw all of the people you encountered, some were more memorable than others. If she is someone you knew, I most likely saw her. However, I do not recall her specifically."

"I remember the day we met," Tom said. "She came into my office to apply for a typist position. She was timid and had never worked full time. She had planned to attend college, establish a career, and travel the world before getting married and having a family. But when she fell in love and got pregnant, her plans changed."

"Unexpected things happen."

"Yeah, tell me about it." Tom thought about his current predicament, feeling like a large portion of his life had been taken away without any notice and he was trapped behind a brick wall. *But now that I have an opportunity with the SWEEP, I can earn the pass for free travel. This part is up to me and I can do it!*

"Have you figured out the message yet?" Tom asked.

"Sir, I am unable to translate it precisely. It is written in a higher code than I typically see. I suggest we contact Ms. Perez at the Education Complex. She is an expert at higher encryptions."

"Encryptions? Why would a message be written in a code in the first place and how would a person know what the code was? The message probably says something like 'eat your veggies'."

Tom remembered the secret messages on cereal boxes he'd deciphered as a kid. Every few weeks, new clues had shown up on cereal boxes to get kids hooked on a certain brand. He'd given up on the messages when one he'd decoded told kids to eat their breakfast.

Ralph's voice brought Tom back from Memory Lane. "Often when people are under stress and need help, their thoughts become jumbled and are not clearly communicated. Sometimes a star gets damaged en route from Earth to Heaven. Some young spirits in the mailroom are pranksters and like to alter the messages a bit, which is another possibility. They mean no harm, but their handiwork can be annoying.

"My guess is Sandra is under some time constraint. In order to save time, I need some assistance from Ms. Perez. Ms. Perez has a busy schedule. It is simpler to find her while she is at work in the Education Complex, but she will not be there all day. We best be on our way, sir."

As Tom and Ralph made their way to the Education Complex, Tom continued telling Ralph about Sandra. "After her daughter was born, she and her husband decided it would be good for Sandra to work. The extra income would help the family save for vacations, college education, retirement, and extra needs.

"I knew there was something special about her when I interviewed her. The position required two years of college. If I had followed the company's guidelines, I wouldn't have hired her. But I consider myself a good judge of people. I knew she'd give the job her all. She had great enthusiasm and showed potential, so I gave her a chance."

Tom paused for a second, wiped his hand across his mouth, and chuckled. "One day, I had a meeting out of the office first thing in the morning. When I got in around ten, Sandra came to me in tears and apologized because she didn't get any work done. She couldn't get the typewriter to work.

"From across the office, I could see the typewriter was unplugged. I didn't want to just plug the cord in. I thought if she solved the problem on her own, it would build her confidence."

Tom pictured the scene in his mind as he continued the story. "Sandra sobbed as I walked with her to her desk. 'I didn't want to call a repair service without your approval,' she said. 'When we get it fixed, I'll stay late and get the work done.'

"I looked around the sparsely furnished office. The office had recently opened and I had my first shot at being an actual manager, not an assistant. Sandra was my first hire and I really hoped she would work out. I was hoping she would be the office manager as the office grew.

"'I don't think you'll need to stay late,' I told Sandra. 'We'll get this resolved and you'll get through it. Here.' I handed her a tissue from her desk, then suggested we check the power switch, the ribbon, the keys. 'What's on the floor?' I asked. She picked up the cord. 'Look. It's not plugged in.' She put the plug into the outlet and the typewriter hummed. I gave her a high five to congratulate her. In the afternoon, Sandra came into my office to report the work was caught up. 'That includes what was in today's mail.'

"I knew she would be embarrassed if I praised her too much, so I kidded and asked, 'Great, but do you have tomorrow's work done?' The stunned look on her face told me she was not sure how to take my teasing. I added 'good job' hoping she would realize my remark about tomorrow's work was intended as a compliment."

Through the years, Tom had watched Sandra's career blossom. Her decision-making abilities and initiative grew. He promoted her to office manager and kept an eye on her as she trained and motivated others. Together they cultivated a top-notch team. Their office consistently earned company recognition for on-time service, customer satisfaction, and accuracy.

Although there were no corporate awards for fun, Sandra had once told him that team members repeatedly remarked how much they enjoyed working for him. They appreciated the morning snacks he frequently brought in and the casual dress-down Fridays he allowed. The team considered the greatest show of his appreciation was permitting the staff, if they were caught up, to leave early while he stayed and covered the phones.

When Tom had been promoted and transferred to another city, Sandra accepted the service manager position. Various company mergers, acquisitions, and relocations led to Tom and Sandra working together again, but for a different company.

"She really is good," he told Ralph. "She is great at details and has presentations ready days before meetings. She sometimes runs . . . er . . . ran things by me if she had a question or sugges-tion. Her ideas were always right on the mark. I can't imagine she'd need my help now. It must be serious. Can I check on her?"

"The ELV in your utility bag should help you. We can dis-cuss this later, sir. We have arrived at the Education Complex."

Chapter 28

MS. PEREZ

To Tom, the Education Complex did not seem much different than the college campuses he had seen on Earth. As he and Ralph walked through the campus, Tom was intrigued by the spirit students and their activities. There were students riding bikes back and forth between classes, couples on benches pretending to study. If they were like couples of his generation, they most likely were studying each other. Some students were walking, some were jogging, a few were seated in groups on the grass.

Some of the study tools captured Tom's attention. Most had textbooks like the ones he had used, or should have used; some were peering closely at long, handwritten scrolls. He was fascinated by a student using an abacus, but was more intrigued by group of students sitting with their eyes closed, making motions with their hands as if writing or making calculations.

There's gotta be some spirits here from advanced civilizations. Wonder if that is their way to study?

The buildings varied in architectural styles: stately columned buildings, red brick structures covered with ivy, modern reflective geometric designs. Historical studies were in a pyramid-shaped building and natural sciences were in a large tree house. Tom thought the language department building had a classical Roman influence. *Seems appropriate if I remember my sixth grade world history. Romans spoke Latin and Latin is the basis for many modern languages. Now how'd did I remember that?*

He followed Ralph into the language building and down a hallway, approximately one hundred paces long. Along both sides of the deserted hall were offices with glassed-in windows and doors. Many offices were empty; a few had workers seated at the desks in the offices. At the far end of the hall was an office with two glass doors. Emblazoned on the doors were two lines:

Language Department
Ms. Isabella Perez, Director

I know that name. I know I know it, but I don't remember where I heard it. Perez is such a common name. I didn't think much of it before. But Isabella—that's unusual. I wish I had been better with names.

A woman inside the office took a seat behind a counter that faced the doors. She wore a purple suit. Her coffee-brown hair was pulled back from her face and arranged in a bun. When she glanced toward the entrance and Tom saw her face, he put the name and face together and came to an abrupt stop.

That can't be. She looks like my Spanish teacher from high school. I sure hope not.

Ralph's pace quickened.

Tom continued to hold back. "I'm not feeling well. Where's the men's room?"

Ralph turned and frowned. "Sir, remember what I told you—you are a spirit now. There are no physical internal parts; there is no need to use a restroom. Ms. Perez sees us coming. If you want to get your message from Sandra read, we need to see her. Are you ready?"

Tom nodded.

Before they entered the office, Ralph smoothed his pants and tucked in his shirt. The smile on Ms. Perez's face when she saw Ralph made Tom suspect there was more between Ralph and Ms. Perez than merely being colleagues.

"Good morning, Ms. Perez." Although Ralph's greeting was formal, Tom detected a sweetness in his voice that hadn't been there before.

"Buenos dias."

The two shook hands and made eye contact. Tom noticed the firm handshake softened into holding hands while the eye contact continued.

Looks like we have a couple of lovebirds here.

If he'd seen a couple of friends holding hands and making goo-goo eyes during his time on Earth, he would have kidded them and suggested they get a room, but he was sure Ralph would not be amused, so he held that remark and quietly cleared his throat.

Ms. Perez turned to Tom. "And who is your companion, Ralph?"

"Excuse my manners, Ms. Perez. This is Tom."

"Malone," she said as she extended her hand. Tom quickly resolved not to let his previous experience with Ms. Perez taint her willingness to help him now. He confidently shook her hand.

"Nice to see you again." Tom paused for a moment and cautiously looked around. He had heard a person could go to Hell for lying. Since he had already died and made it into Heaven, he wanted to make sure he did not change directions. Fortunately, his surroundings stayed the same.

"Tom was one of my Spanish students at Lincoln High School," Ms. Perez told Ralph. "One of the students a teacher never forgets."

Tom remembered an incident in her class, one he hoped she *had* forgotten. "Ralph, I'm sure Ms. Perez is busy and we don't want to waste her time. Why don't you tell Ms. Perez why we're here so we can get out of her hair and she can get back to what she was doing?" He handed the star to Ralph.

"Oh, yes." Ralph held the star out so Ms. Perez could see it. "Tom recently arrived here and has been granted a SWEEP. He has already received a message requesting his assistance. I was hoping you would help translate the message for him."

Ms. Perez took the star and gave it a quick glance. "Shouldn't be too difficult."

She placed the star on the counter. "Let me tell you a story about Señor Malone. It won't take long."

I'm a dead man, in more ways than one. When Ralph hears the story I think she's going to tell, he'll have no interest in helping me. I really wish Sandra was here. She could come in and politely interrupt me for whatever reason and I could excuse myself from this conversation. Ugh! I really don't want to be here right now.

"Tom was in a first year Spanish class, one of a handful of students not already fluent in the language. I called on him to translate 'See the dog' into Spanish. He stood and hesitated, but couldn't answer. Several boys around Tom whispered to him, pretending they were trying to help. Tom finally repeated the words they fed to him. The class broke into laughter. What he said translated to an obscene phrase.

"I wanted to laugh, too, but had to maintain control. I hustled Tom to Mr. Gordon's office. Gordon was the vice principal for young men."

Tom remembered it all too well—one of the worst days of his life. He remembered the laughter, the embarrassment. But most of all he remembered the paddle.

The paddle. How different things are today.

In the world he'd just left, a teacher or coach would be fired and probably charged with abuse for even having a paddle in his or her office. But he'd often compared notes with his buddies about their childhoods. It was not uncommon for parents to exercise physical discipline: a hand, a belt, a stick, a rolling pin. And no questions were asked when physical discipline occurred in the schools. Even in younger grades, a swat on the hands with a wooden ruler was not uncommon. Parents and teachers wanted the kids to learn respect for adults. And his friends—now in their fifties and sixties—all agreed they came out okay.

The more he thought about the incident, the more vivid the memory became . . .

Normally, the walk down the hall of the newly built high school seemed very long. Not on that day. When Ms. Perez took him into the office, she requested an immediate meeting with Mr. Gordon. When the secretary informed her the vice principal was not available, Ms. Perez asked for paper and a pen and jotted a note. "Please see Mr. Gordon gets this as soon as he returns."

She told Tom to wait in the office until the vice principal returned or the period ended, whichever came first.

He'd waited and watched the clock. He thought it was broken. Every time he glanced at it, the hands had barely moved. Although he tried to avoid it, his attention was drawn to the paddle outside Mr. Gordon's door. Mr. Gordon was also the wrestling coach. Rumor had it the paddle, along with his powerful physique, could yield ferocious welts that lasted for weeks.

Thankfully, the bell signaling the end of the period rang before Mr. Gordon returned . . .

Laughter from Ralph and Ms. Perez pulled Tom's focus back to the present.

"So, Señor Malone was a troublemaker in his youth," Ralph said.

Ralph's comment angered Tom, but he stayed calm. As his guardian angel, Ralph was with him all the time. He should know Tom was not a troublemaker, a prankster maybe, but not one to get into serious trouble.

Ms. Perez gave Ralph an admonishing slap on the shoulder. "That's not true. Tom was a highly regarded student. When I shared the incident in the faculty lounge the next morning, everyone, including Mr. Gordon, got a good laugh. We all agreed Tom was a great young man. He might not have had the highest GPA, but he was always a gentleman and had an incredible knack for bringing a smile to everyone's face."

Ms. Perez reached for the star laying on the counter.

Tom squinted his eyes and tilted his head. "Hold on a minute. I need to understand this. Mr. Gordon laughed? So what would have happened if he had come into the office? Would I have been on the receiving end of his paddle?"

Ms. Perez smiled. "I knew he was off campus at a conference and nothing would happen to you. I had to get you out of class to maintain control and I didn't want you to face all the heckling I knew you'd get after class. Plus, I wanted you to think about the consequences of taking bad advice. You were so trusting of everyone. I wanted you to learn that not everyone has your best interest at heart. I felt that understanding trustworthiness would be more valuable to you than all the Spanish in the world."

Hearing Ms. Perez's side of his embarrassing incident changed Tom's perception of his high school experience *and* of Ms. Perez. "Thank you. I never realized where I learned to look for friends and associates I could trust, but now I have an idea where it began." He wasn't sure if he should shake her hand or give her a hug. He went with the hug and she didn't object. *Seems weird hugging a teacher.*

Chapter 29

SANDRA'S MESSAGE TRANSLATED

Ms. PEREZ HELD the star in her left hand and brushed her right hand over it, sending gritty dust everywhere. It reminded Tom of dust from sand storms he had experienced when traveling through deserts.

"Looks like this could have been launched through a dust devil," she said.

"Good one." Ralph laughed. "A dust devil bringing something to Heaven."

Tom raised an eyebrow. *Ralph doesn't generally find anything I say funny; maybe there is a sense of humor in him after all.*

"I guess it was rather funny," Ms. Perez said. "I was thinking of a dust devil like the ones in the desert. I didn't intend for it to be a pun. Let me clean this." She grabbed a tissue from a box on the counter and removed several layers of dust. "The message seems pretty simple."

To Tom's surprise Ralph's face actually turned red.

"The letters look entirely different without all the dust," Ms. Perez explained.

Was that an attempt to spare Ralph's ego? Tom bit his lip. If Ms. Perez was sensitive enough to protect me from class ridicule nearly forty years ago and she's caring enough now to see the embarrassed look on Ralph's face and spare his ego, she's okay.

"Ralph," Ms. Perez said, "now that we've gotten the message cleaned up, do you want to take a stab at interpreting it?" She handed the star to Ralph and he read the message out loud.

Tom,

I never realized how much I'd miss you. Things are so quiet and dull without you. I could really use your help for about thirty seconds. I'm working on a presentation that's due Friday. I'm using the program we updated last month, but I'm stuck. I know what function to use, but don't remember where it is. If you could just walk me through that one section, I know I could handle the rest.

Where are you when I really need you? I wish you were on a golf course with a client so I could call and bug you—like you'd really have your cell phone on. I know how phones on the golf course annoyed you. Well, wherever you are, I hope there's a golf course.

Miss you,

Sandra

Tom momentarily forgot about the separation that existed between Sandra and himself. The note seemed so natural.

That's right; it's only a note. I can't just walk across the hall to help her. What can I do?

"Good job." Ms. Perez beamed at Ralph. He flushed again.

"I feel foolish," Ralph said. "Let me apologize for taking your time with a message I should have been able to handle myself."

"No problem. In your eagerness to help Tom, you simply didn't consider that dust could make such a huge difference. You recognized your need for help and came to me."

More and more intriguing, Tom thought as he watched the exchange with interest. He held back a big grin and stretched out his hand. "Muchas gracias. It was nice to see you again." This time he meant it.

Ms. Perez gave a graceful nod as she shook his hand. "My pleasure."

Ralph extended his hand, too. "May I take you for a glass of wine to thank you for your help?"

Tom again sensed that special connection between Ralph and Ms. Perez and excused himself, saying he wanted to check out a golf course he had seen from the window.

"I thought you'd be anxious to check in with Sandra," Ms. Perez said.

"I am, but I'll only be a moment."

"Ralph, I'd enjoy going for wine. Send me a star."

Before Tom had a chance to go over to the window and give Ms. Perez and Ralph some time alone, Ms. Perez escorted Ralph and Tom to the door and opened it. "We all have things to do. Now, the two of you, scoot."

Chapter 30

SANDRA'S PROBLEM

A**FTER LEAVING THE** Education Complex, Ralph nodded at Tom's new utility bag. "Why don't you pull out the Earth Location Viewer?"

Tom did, staring at the device with a frown. The ELV was roughly the size of the TV remote control he had used on Earth. At the top of the hand-held instrument was a screen to view the location on Earth he wanted to see. Below the screen was a keypad similar to one on the mobile phone he'd had on Earth. This was used to key in either the name of the person he wanted to see or the location he wanted to look at. At the bottom of the ELV was a dial to rotate the view up or down or left or right.

"Here." Ralph showed him how to set the viewer finder and soon Tom was watching Sandra in her office. Her office was small, with barely enough space for her desk, a chair, and a small bookcase for reference manuals. The bookcase also served as a stand for a printer. There were no windows in her office. Sandra was a private person, no photos of family and friends. The only photo on her desk was one of Tom and Sandra and their team of co-workers holding a reward for their sales achievements.

The rest of the staff had gone home. It was after hours and not unusual for Sandra to work late. She sat in front of her computer monitor. Her arms were crossed on her desk and her head rested on her arms.

Her body trembled and she raised her head, looking around.

"She appears to be highly sensitive to your vibrations," Ralph said. "Did you notice how she shuddered when you set the ELV on her?"

Tom sighed. "I always thought she was a bit touchy."

Sandra looked at the screen and moved the computer mouse around. Black lines of mascara streaked both of her cheeks.

"Drat, where is it?" she asked the empty office.

"She always did talk to herself." Tom chuckled. "I loved it when I'd cruise by her office and catch her saying something. She'd get so flustered when I answered, not knowing I was nearby."

She lifted her head and rolled it side to side, back and forth. She lifted her arms over her head and grasped her palms together in a long stretch. She put her arms down and got out of her chair.

"A break might help," she said. She walked out of the office and down the hall to the restroom.

Tom adjusted the ELV to continue watching Sandra. He was curious about seeing a ladies' room. He had wondered why women often asked other ladies to go with them. Was there a secret ritual that went on in their restrooms or were the women afraid of the dark if the lights weren't on when they entered?

He didn't find the answers to those questions. What he saw was that the ladies' room was much tidier than the typical men's rooms, no tissues on the floor or newspapers left behind for reading material.

"What a mess I am," she said to her image in the mirror as she splashed water on her face.

The door of the restroom opened and Celeste, someone who worked for another company in the building, walked in. Celeste was one of Sandra's numerous friends. Sandra had a knack of keeping in contact with all of her friends on a regular basis, either through a lunch date or drinks after work. He'd gone with Sandra and Celeste to a wine-and-cheese bar once after work. He wasn't fond of wine, but went along to be social. He'd been uncomfortable around Celeste, which was unusual for Tom. He clicked with most people. Her preferred topic of conversation was explicit books and movies. Although he didn't state that as the reason, he politely had turned down subsequent invitations that included Celeste.

"Looks like you're having a tough day." Celeste said. "Either you've been crying or you need a different brand of mascara. What's got you down?"

"I'm working on a project the client wants done by the end of the week," Sandra explained. "It should be straight forward, but last month Tom and I reworked parts of the program. I don't have all the new functions down yet. I know what to do, but I can't find it in the revised program."

"Ask Tom for help."

"Didn't you hear? He passed away."

"I know, but ask anyway. You might be surprised by how much he can still help," Celeste said.

Celeste walked Sandra back to her office. Tom followed them by adjusting the ELV. Celeste waved at the framed photo sitting on Sandra's desk. "You worked well together from what I heard," Celeste said.

Sandra nodded. "We had a great team. We all helped each other, especially Tom. He was good at everything and brought everyone together. He was one of a kind; no one can ever take his place."

"I don't know anything about what you do, so I can't help you solve your problem," Celeste said. She picked up the photo and handed it to Sandra. "Seriously, why don't you tell him about it. I'm sure he'd help."

Sandra shrugged and gently set the photo back on her desk. "Actually, I thought about doing just that a few minutes ago, but thought it was a bit out there. If Tom knew I'd tried to talk to people who died, he'd poke fun of me and make spooky sounds. I wanted to get this project done before I went home, but it'll have to wait. The team can help me in the morning. Thanks for listening."

Tom turned to Ralph. "So her just thinking about asking me for help generated the message on the star?"

Ralph shrugged. "That sounds like a strong possibility. The message presented a general idea of her problem, but no specific details. From my observation, sir, starting with Liz and the people who helped you show her a peach rose, and now with Sandra, you have shown an exceptionally high vibration level. You not only have a high sensitivity to picking up on the needs of others, but others respond quickly to the vibrations sent from you."

Tom nodded ever so slightly, taking in all this new information. He returned his attention to the ELV.

"Talk to Tom, then go home." Celeste hugged Sandra and left. Tom watched a few minutes longer, realizing he could feel a vibration connecting him and Sandra.

Sandra spoke to the empty office. "Guess it wouldn't hurt anything if I asked Tom for help. I've already thought about it; maybe I should give him more detail." She looked at the picture of Tom. "This feels weird. I already feel like you are watching me, but here goes." Sandra listed the specifics of the problem she was facing, even going so far as to move the cursor around and showing Tom the problem as if he was standing at her desk.

Then she shut down her computer. As she neared the door to leave her office, she turned and looked at the team picture.

She made a fist and shook it at the photo. Tom was reminded of the old days when she would, in a kidding way, pretend to get irritated by one of his smart remarks and fling a file at him. He loved pulling her strings.

"Tom, you brat, I wish you were here. This sure isn't any fun without you." She turned out the light and walked away.

Tom knew the answer to Sandra's problem. "If I can point the cursor to the correct option," he explained to Ralph, "I'm confident Sandra will find the solution she needs."

Although Tom was anxious to get the job done, he wanted to see Sandra's expression close up when she found the answer right in front of her. He decided to wait until morning to go to her office and be there when she arrived.

He turned off his ELV. He was confident about solving Sandra's problem. But this would be his first time using the rope ladder and getting to Earth and back without Ralph. Tom had some concerns about the procedure, which he reviewed with Ralph.

❧ ❧ ❧

EARLY THE NEXT morning, Tom went to The Veil and paid close attention to it before attempting to pass through. It did look like a sheer, lightweight fabric with a rainbow of colors, one that could easily blow with a slight breeze. Then Tom remembered that Ralph had told him leaving would be easy, since that is what Tom wanted to do. It would be on his return from Earth, which Tom did not want to do, when the separation between the two realms would be difficult and he would be facing his Brick Wall.

He hooked his rope ladder to the next cloud on the shuttle and took a quick leap through The Veil like he was getting on an elevator with its door closing. He sighed with relief when he passed through. He used the location finder on his ELV to set his destination to Sandra's office, threw down the rope ladder, and cautiously descended.

Sandra's routine had always been to turn on her computer, then go get coffee in the break room while the system warmed up. This morning was no different. When Tom arrived, Sandra had her coffee mug in hand on her way for coffee.

He quickly went to her computer and positioned the cursor to the function she needed, then stepped back to watch her reaction. When she returned, Sandra looked at her computer screen, then at the team picture, and gave the photo a thumbs-up. "That's it. That's what I need." She clicked the mouse. Her face relaxed as the proper report appeared on the screen.

Sandra thoughtfully picked up the team photo and stared at it. "How cool. It's like you heard about my problem and fixed it."

She picked up the receiver of the phone on her desk and made a quick call to Celeste. "You won't believe this." Sandra filled her friend in on the request for help last night and what had happened with her computer this morning. "I feel Tom is watching me now. Makes me wonder what's going on."

Tom mentally gave himself a pat on the back for fixing the problem. Despite his strong desire to stay on Earth, he knew he had to return. He wandered down to the breakroom to see if anyone was there and if anyone had brought in donuts. No donuts today, but a couple of guys were hanging around, telling jokes. He wished he could show off his new whistling-for-sodas trick, but that wasn't possible. He had to go back to Heaven and continue earning his SWEEP pass.

Quickly, Tom found the nearest coffee shop, checked the indicator to make sure the rope had attached securely to a cloud, and started back up the rope ladder. When he reached the top and saw the Brick Wall, he shuddered as he passed through, but the Brick Wall felt different this time.

Hmm. That felt more like going through drywall, like I'd know how that would feel.

Chapter 31

WRAP UP

RALPH MET TOM on Heaven's side of The Veil, helped him haul up his rope ladder, and suggested they walk to St. Andrew's clubhouse for coffee or soft drinks so they could discuss Tom's experience with Sandra's problem.

"It seems your plan worked flawlessly," Ralph said, as they walked to the clubhouse. "Do you have any comments?"

"That was it? That was a challenge? It seemed so natural."

Tom felt jubilant; he felt like it was only January and he had just closed his first substantial piece of business for the year. To put what was happening in terms he was more familiar with—he still had a long way to go to earn the year-end bonuses and incentives that came with reaching his sales goal, but he had momentum and confidence on his side.

"Ralph, are there any time constraints for completing the SWEEP? Do I have to wait a year? Or do I only have a year before the offer expires?"

"Sir, unlike grade levels in school or winning games in sports tournaments, proceeding to the next level is not predetermined nor is the time set. You do not necessarily finish one level and immediately go on to the next. Some of the situations that create 'I wonder' moments will come from direct requests, such as the one you just received from Sandra. You can also generate your own opportunities for 'I wonder' moments by careful interpretation of the messages the stars bring and the vibrations you still feel from your friends and family on Earth."

Tom rubbed his chin, a habit he had when he was absorbing new information. "What's next?"

Ralph shrugged. "Much like life itself, you never know what the next challenge will be or when it will start or end. You may not even realize you faced a challenge until long after the event has passed."

"Well, I'm fired up."

"Glad to hear that, sir. Given your enthusiasm and desire and the high vibration level you show, I believe you will quickly achieve your dream."

Tom knew that it was all up to him, but he'd be the fastest SWEEP achiever Heaven had ever seen.

Chapter 32

WILLIE AND A DAY OF GOLF

WHEN THEY ARRIVED at the course near St. Andrew's, Tom wondered if they were at the right place. The fairways seemed lusher, the sand hazards were all raked and looked easier to hit from. Even the flags on the green looked brighter.

"Are you sure this is right? The pro shop looks different. Last time I was here I thought it looked like a shack. Now it looks like the typical setup one would see at a muni course on Earth."

"Things are looking better, are they, sir? Might I say your perspective of Heaven is changing?"

I really don't want to answer that question. Tom saw St. Andrew and waved. His first impression of St. Andrew had been just that—an impression—formed when he was still in the fog upon his arrival to Heaven. All he really remembered was the firm handshake. Now he knew St. Andrew had a very muscular build. Somewhere along the line, Tom had learned St. Andrew had been a fisherman on Earth; that might be reason for the strength Tom was now seeing.

St. Andrew approached them and said, "Heard you've been working on your first 'I wonder' moment. How'd it go?"

"It went well. Anything going on here?" Tom was anxious to think about something besides Ralph's statement. Heaven was looking better, but it reminded Tom of falling in love—it was really too early in the process to express changes in feelings.

"There's another star for you," St. Andrew said. "I'll get it." He snatched at the air, then handed Tom a yellow star.

This star's message was very legible. It was a note from Willie asking Tom if he'd like to play golf. Tom excused himself and gave Willie a call on his Spirits Only Communication Apparatus (SOCA). During their conversation, Willie agreed to meet at St. Andrew's Gate and give Tom a tour of the different courses before Tom decided where he'd like to play their first round together.

Ralph chatted with St. Andrew while Tom waited for Willie. Tom tried to follow the conversation, but all he could think about was Sandra's expression when she'd realized what had happened. He was startled when Willie landed his flying golf cart in front of them outside the pro shop. The flying golf cart looked like a golf cart one would see on Earth, except it had two white feathered wings, one on each side, behind the opening for the passengers to enter. On top of the cart was a golden halo.

"I thought we'd cover more territory with a flying cart since there are so many courses to check out," Willie said.

"Ralph, do you want to go along?" Tom asked. "Should we get another cart?"

Ralph shook his head. "Thanks for asking, but no. I'll stay here and practice, maybe talk to St. Andrew. Willie, you're familiar with golf in Heaven as well as on Earth. You are in a good position to help Tom select a suitable course."

Before Tom and Willie left, the queen arrived at the golf course with two other people. She introduced her companions as Mr. Tom Morris and Ms. Babe Didrikson Zaharias, champion golfers during their time on Earth.

Tom shook hands. "It is an honor to meet you. I've read about your contributions to the game." He'd been interested in all aspects of golf. Not only had he read about its history, he'd constantly watched TV specials about the game's development. He knew Mr. Morris was considered by some to be the father of the game and Babe was not only a golfer, but she had participated in the Olympics.

He wouldn't have recognized them if they had just walked onto the golf course. Tom wasn't one to care about how people looked or dressed. To him people were people, or to make the analogy more relevant to his current situation—in Heaven, spirits were spirits. He tried to use hair as a memory trigger. He did note Mr. Morris had a long beard, and Babe had wavy, dark-brown hair.

Tom's eyes widened as an idea occurred to him. "Hey, Willie, Ralph, wouldn't it be fun to find a fourth player and challenge St. Andrew, Queen Mary, and her playing partners to a little tournament? Maybe in a week or so?"

The queen liked the idea and proposed a little wager.

"Ah, a betting woman." Tom rubbed his chin and nodded in approval. "I like that. Loser buys lunch?"

The queen agreed. "If my team wins," she said, "you'll arrange a lunch of bangers and mash, shepherds' pie, and pints. If your team wins," the queen looked down her nose, "I'll provide a lunch of hamburgers, hot dogs, chips, beer, and soda."

With the wager set and a tentative tee time scheduled for the following week, Queen Mary and her two playing partners prepared to play. The queen asked St. Andrew if he could still play with them.

St. Andrew pressed his lips together. "Oh, I don't know. I might just hang around here and practice with Ralph. My game could stand some work, especially if we have a competition coming up."

Tom caught what was going on here, or so he guessed. St. Andrew was planning on playing with the queen and already had a foursome set up. When Tom had earlier invited Ralph to come with him and Willie, Ralph had declined by saying he'd hang out with St. Andrew. Now that Tom knew St. Andrew had arrangements to play, Tom didn't want Ralph to be left out. He again extended the offer to Ralph to come with him and Willie.

Ralph waved him off. "Go. Go. I have some trick shots up my sleeve that I have been working on with Kyle. Perhaps he can help me now."

St. Andrew scratched his head and grinned. "I shouldn't say anything to help my competitors, but might I suggest you invite Kyle as your fourth—he's quite a player."

Ralph and Willie agreed. Tom said he would talk to Kyle. He winked at St. Andrew. "Now don't tell him he can't have that day off."

St. Andrew smiled.

Chapter 33

HEAVEN'S GOLF COURSES

SINCE THEY WERE already there, Willie gave Tom a tour of the course at St. Andrew's Gate, Paradise Greens at Angels' Ridge. Willie said, "Tommy, I'm sure you've played this course already, but I want to show you their extensive equipment selection. The pro shop has clubs that have been used throughout the centuries. Every design of clubs and balls are available for players to use."

"That brings up a question—where can I get a set of clubs?" Tom asked.

"The majority of us don't bother to get our own clubs. The courses make so many club choices available and players like to borrow whatever equipment they feel suited for that day. A very popular choice is to play a long yardage course with feather balls and the wooden-shafted clubs from centuries ago. It makes for a very challenging round."

"I bet. I want to try that sometime."

After leaving St. Andrew's Gate, Willie flew them to a nearby course, Enchanted Hollows, only about a mile away in Earth distance. Tom studied the course from the cart. He squinted at the greens. "Can't seem to get a focus on the course. Can we pick up a scorecard and review the layout?" On Earth Tom had found the scorecard a good way for him to evaluate a course.

Willie laughed. "Won't do you any good here. Players take turns at designing a hole. They prepare a mental image and the hole is laid out accordingly. The players determine the layout and length along with the placement and condition of the hazards. It's important to know your opponents' strengths and weaknesses to strategically place obstacles. That's probably the reason you can't focus on the course; someone is probably changing it now. That's why there are no score cards mapping the layout. The designer of the hole will tell you the design he's laid out and what the intended par for the hole is. It's easy to find a piece of paper to write down the score. This is probably not the best course to play until after you have an idea how your partners control their shots and know if they get freaked out by particular conditions or hazards."

Tom took off his sunglasses to clean them. After removing the smudges, he put the glasses back on. "Still can't get a clear vision of the hole. You're right; someone must be changing the hole now." He loved the concept. "Interesting. But you're right—not a good course to play until you know how your partner likes to play. When some of my friends get here, though, I can really trip them up."

Willie chuckled. "Can't wait for those old geezers I played with on Earth to get here and have them play this course. Already have a few designs in mind." He grinned, then continued. "Wait until you see Parting Waters. It's a gimmicky course, with lots of water hazards. Each hazard has a *spot*. If your ball lands there, the waters part and you're hitting from a dry area without a penalty stroke. If you don't hit the *spot* and the waters don't part, you score your shots like you do on Earth."

"Sounds like you need to feel lucky when you play that course," Tom said. "Does the location for the landing area to part the waters stay the same? That would make it easier to figure out."

"No. The tricky part is that it changes daily, like changing the flag position on the greens."

Next Willie and Tom flew over a course called Lightning Greens.

"I think the name speaks for itself," Willie said. "The greens are extremely large and fast with subtle undulations and breaks."

Off in the distance, Tom spotted another course that appeared to be mostly sand. "Tell me about that one."

"It's called Drifting Sands, Shifting Sands. Lots of bunkers, but the sand is good to hit from. The bunkers can be very steep. The groundskeepers move the bunkers on a regular basis and a player never knows from one round to the next where the bunkers will be."

Next they visited Shepherds' Fields, so named because Earth lore credited the origins of golf to shepherds. Shepherds would hit stones with sticks to pass the time while tending their flocks. They eventually made a game based on this activity and found ways to improve their sporting equipment.

The golf cart began to descend. "Let's land here," Willie said. "Unlike many of the courses we looked over that change layout on a regular basis, this one stays pretty consistent, except for changes you would see on Earth, such as changing flag positions. Plus, this course has some background that I think you may find interesting."

Upon landing, they approached a pro shop constructed of gray stone blocks. The landscaping varied from hole to hole as far as Tom could tell. Willie and Tom walked into the pro shop and were greeted by the female pro. She was dressed in a plaid kilt and a crisp, neatly pressed white blouse. Willie asked Nickie, the pro, to tell Tom about the course.

Nickie picked up a club and took a few practice swings as she gave a description. "Each of the eighteen holes is a replica of a hole from the most renowned courses on Earth. Some holes date back to the origins of the game, but won't be found on Earth any longer as they have been redesigned or no longer exist."

Tom nodded. He had played a few courses on Earth that were based on a similar idea: modifications of famous holes.

Willie and Tom thanked Nickie for the information and returned to the flying golf cart. Before they climbed in, Tom straightened his shoulders. "You know, I had a pilot's license on Earth. Think I could fly this puppy around?"

Willie waved his hand at the pilot's seat. "Give it a whirl. Ask if you need help, but I think you'll find the controls similar to single engine planes on Earth."

Tom took off without a hitch. The ride was smooth. The flying conditions were comfortable; he enjoyed the slight breeze that flowed through the cart's openings. It was exhilarating. "All we need now is some in-flight beverage service."

After looking at a few more courses, Tom asked Willie if he would like to play at Paradise Greens at Angels' Ridge.

"It's a nice little course, a few doglegs and not too many hazards."

Willie agreed. They returned to St. Andrew's Gate to set up a tee-time. Kyle was behind the desk and got them on the course immediately. Before Tom went to choose some clubs, he invited Kyle to be the fourth in his group for the match against Mary, Queen of Scots, and her team. Kyle accepted with a grin.

Tom selected some equipment and headed for the first tee. He saw Ralph on the practice area and invited him to come along. Ralph did.

When they finished, Tom described the round as a "heavenly experience."

Chapter 34

THE MATCH AGAINST MARY, QUEEN OF SCOTS

THE PLAYERS ALL agreed the match between Tom's team and the queen's team should be played at Shepherds' Fields because of its historical significance.

Tom's team lost. He shanked shots and missed easy putts all day. On one hole he took six putts. But walking down the eighteenth fairway, he felt like he had just won a major championship.

As a teenager, Tom had imagined what it would feel like to walk down that eighteenth fairway leading a tournament. He had watched some very emotional finishes on televised events. Fathers' Day events were often tear-jerkers because the winning player's dad had taught the game to his son. Tom had sat on his sofa and cried tears of happiness along with the players who had just won their first tournament as a pro and cried tears of sadness along with players who had struggled for victory while they had loved ones at home fighting illnesses or dying or were playing a tournament in honor of a loved one who had recently passed away.

To Tom, the golf course was the best place to learn what a person was really like. And he'd never met a golfer he didn't like.

And the course he'd played today! The most immaculately groomed course he had ever seen. No divots anywhere, very strategic hazard placements for all levels of player, no weeds—come to think of it, there were no ball marks on any of the greens. He was anxious to show this course to his friends: Larry, Bob, Glenn, Doug, Mike, and countless others.

How would my friends react to the course requirements? If they knew in order to play this course, they actually have to die.

That last thought jolted Tom. How do I feel about being here? I guess it's still too early to tell; it's like you go someplace on vacation and think you might want to live there. But I can't return to Earth and life as I knew it. Best I can do is work on the pass.

He sighed and made sure he had his happy face on. Liz had told him time and time again his smile was the most beautiful feature he had. Tom graciously congratulated the other team and apologized to his teammates for his poor play.

"Sir," Ralph said before Tom could get any further. "I may have neglected to inform you—there has been a change in the dinner arrangements. Because of the uniqueness of the match, St. Andrew invited The Controller to the festivities after the round. The Controller declined the invitation, since He rarely makes public appearances, but offered to use His connections to have the catering done by The Last Supper Bread and Wine." He assured Tom the menu would meet the preferences for all the players.

St. Andrew had arranged for limos to drive the players to The Last Supper facilities, although it was just around the corner from the golf course. The Last Supper had a catering business operating on the lower level of a two-story building and several private party rooms on the second floor. St. Andrew directed the players to their room and suggested seating arrangements.

The setting reminded Tom of paintings he had seen of the Last Supper, except for the seating arrangements. Of course the players weren't going to be having their images painted and didn't need to be all facing the same way. It made it easier for conversation to have four players on each side of the table, rather than seated along one long table of eight, and that was exactly how the table was arranged. The wooden floor must have been centuries old and was uneven, probably due to persistent foot traffic. The wooden chairs were a bit wobbly and the wooden table was uncovered. The table was already set for eight with white china serving pieces, utensils wrapped in linen, goblets for wine, glasses filled with water.

The players had barely gotten seated when the wait staff bought out baskets of fresh bread. Tom saw the steam coming from the just-out-of-the-oven bread and rolls. He loved the smell and taste of fresh bread. He missed the rainy stay-at-home Sunday afternoons when Liz would make homemade bread. With butter melting into the warm bread, it was quite a treat. The players quickly emptied the baskets and requested refills.

A monk named Vince was the wine master. Tom guessed Vince to be in his late twenties. Tom was sure, if that was his age, Vince would not like Tom thinking of him as a choir boy— he had rosy cheeks and an innocent smile. But his balding pattern added some years to his youthful appearance—he had a thin bit of light brown hair in the shape of a circle still on his head. Almost looked like his hair could have been drawn on with one of those eye pencil thingies women used.

Vince had wire-rimmed glasses and wore a very loose-fitting, brown hooded floor-length robe. Around his waist was a braided belt made from ropes. A cross was tied to one end of the belt.

He poured a sample of the wine intended to be served during the evening and offered it to Tom for tasting. Tom looked at the label. It identified the wine as a selection from the Garden of Eden Vineyards, Perfection in Every Bottle. Tom sniffed the cork, because he had seen people do that when he was on wine-tasting tours in the Napa Valley. He motioned Vince closer and whispered in his ear, "What is this supposed to smell like?"

Vince whispered to Tom, "It has a fruity fragrance," and Tom repeated that description to the guests. He twirled the glass of wine around, holding the stem of the goblet with his hand, and watched the ripples run down the inside of the glass. He took a small sip of wine and swished it around in his mouth for taste and swallowed. Then, because he couldn't resist, he announced to Vince and the people at his table, "Very dry. Has a distinct taste. I detect a hint of cobweb in this vintage."

Ralph's face turned red. "Sir, I think you owe St. Andrew an apology."

St. Andrew had covered his mouth with hands, Queen Mary held her napkin in front of her mouth. Babe bit her lip and Mr. Morris sat back in his chair. Kyle rubbed his eyes and Vince stood there with the bottle of wine waiting to be poured.

Looked like he'd gone a bit too far. Tom hadn't considered the reaction of the spirits around him. "I'm so sorry. I wasn't thinking. That was something I would have said to my friends on Earth. I guess I feel surrounded by new friends here. I just blurted it out. I apologize to everyone. No offense was intended. I'm just not a wine connoisseur."

St. Andrew uncovered his mouth and let out a long, hearty laugh. Mary, Mr. Morris, Babe, and Kyle all joined in the laughter. Even Ralph smiled. Vince quietly held the bottle of wine.

St. Andrew moved behind Tom and squeezed his shoulders. "Well, I guess we all know now, you are definitely not a wine connoisseur." St. Andrew nodded to Vince. "Go ahead and pour the wine for the rest of us. I think they'll find it acceptable." St. Andrew took a taste of the wine Vince had poured for him. "Quite good, in my opinion. Tom, what is *your* beverage of choice?"

"Diet soda. Let me treat you to one." Tom whistled the tune from the soda commercial and a bottle of soda floated down from above. He never had bothered to ask Ralph how far the sodas traveled; he really didn't care. He just thought it was a pretty cool trick. He grabbed the bottle and started to hand it to St. Andrew, then hesitated. "Actually the variety in ice cold glass bottles from the old days is better. Let me see if I can whip you up one of those. I'll also need a bottle opener. How did the earlier jingle go?" He thought a moment and whistled an older version of the ditty from the commercial. He grinned as another bottle floated down. "Knew all the trivia stuck in my head would come in handy at some point."

He opened the bottle and handed it to St. Andrew.

St. Andrew tasted it. "Not bad, but I think I'll stick with the wine."

"To each his own. Just means more soda for me. Mind if I finish yours?"

"Help yourself."

Tom took a drink from the bottle. "Haven't had one of these for a long time. Soda sure was better in the sixties when it was served in glass bottles. You could get it ice cold from a vending machine for a nickel and didn't have to worry about the sugar-free, caffeine-free varieties. Now this is Heaven—an ice cold soda after a great round of golf."

After Vince served wine to everyone at the table, he returned to Tom. "Always wanted to try one of those sodas. Would you mind getting one for me?"

"No problem." Tom whistled the tune and Vince caught the soda coming his way. He tried it and liked it.

Queen Mary and Babe excused themselves and left for the ladies' room. Once they were out of earshot, Tom asked the guys if female spirits were like those on Earth, always asking another female to accompany them to the restroom. The guys all nodded and showed various expressions of puzzlement. Willie piped up. "Being the most recent to come to Heaven, with the exception of Tom, of course, I'd have to say when it comes to figuring the great mysteries of life, like life and death and Heaven, that's the easy one. The real mystery is trying to figure out women."

The guys all laughed, but stopped when the women returned to the table. Mary and Babe were talking like they had been best friends forever. They were chatting about changing their wardrobes and getting more comfortable clothing than the skirts they both had on.

Mr. Morris loosened his tie and unbuttoned his vest. St. Andrew took off his sunglasses and placed them on the table. Kyle removed his hat and ran his fingers through his hair. Ralph removed his tie and Tom ribbed him for wearing one. Tom excused himself and went to the men's room. He removed his hat, ran a comb through his hair, and neatly tucked his shirt tail into his golf shorts before going back to the table.

Vince soon returned to the room. "Apparently one of our waiters left early tonight, so I will be taking your orders." He looked at Tom. "Except for you, Tom. I won't be taking any wine orders from you."

Tom smiled.

Mary asked if Scottie was in the kitchen. After Vince told her he was, Mary said, "Then I'd like the shepherd's pie. He makes the best shepherd's pie ever."

"I have to be true to one of my professions on Earth. I'll have the catch of the day," St. Andrew said.

Babe ordered angel hair pasta. Mr. Morris had a taste for prime rib.

Then it was Willie's turn to order. "What's the dish we're supposed to be eating if we lost? Bangers and mash, or something like that?"

Vince nodded.

"Well then, by gosh, that's what I'll have. A golfer's got to be a man of his word." He gulped. "But what I could really sink my teeth into is a thick, juicy T-bone."

St. Andrew suggested that Vince bring both dishes to Willie.

Kyle ordered nachos and wings as appetizers and a double cheeseburger, onion rings, and a vanilla shake for his main course.

What would Ralph be having for dinner? Tom wondered. He thought it would be funny to see someone as proper as Ralph eat with his fingers. Tom had never seen anyone, even the most sophisticated, refined people, who was able to eat barbequed ribs, fried chicken, or corn-on-the cob without having to pick it up at some point, and end up with sauce and butter all over their hands and face. He smirked at that thought and asked Ralph if he could order for him. Ralph gave him the go ahead and Tom placed the order. "And bring lots of extra napkins," he added.

Tom was relieved the menu had been expanded; the bangers and mash was something he had suggested for the purpose of the wager. He'd tried it once when he had visited Scotland, but hadn't acquired a taste for it. Tonight, Tom ordered a filet, just a little pink in the center; a loaded baked potato with butter, chives, sour cream, onions, bacon bits, everything but the kitchen sink; and a side salad with ranch dressing.

About midway through dinner, Tom glanced over at Ralph. He wanted to burst out laughing, but considering how much he had embarrassed Ralph earlier with his reaction to the wine, he held in his laughter. Ralph had barbeque sauce all over his face, and was looking at his hands, which were dripping with butter from the corn on the cob. Tom just smiled.

"You should see yourself." Tom picked up a few of the napkins Vince had brought to the table. "Let me clean up your face." Tom dipped a napkin into his untouched glass of water and cleaned Ralph's face the way his mother used to clean Tom when he had a messy face. "Here." Tom handed Ralph another napkin. "Use this to wipe off your hands."

"How's your food?" Tom asked Ralph.

"Delightful, sir."

Tom was glad Ralph was enjoying it. He felt badly that he'd ordered messy food in an attempt to make Ralph look foolish.

After everyone completed their meals and the plates were cleared away, Vince brought in a tray displaying dessert options. Tom swore to himself he wasn't going to go for dessert, but when he spotted pink champagne cake tucked away among the tarts, cookies, pies, and other cakes, he couldn't pass it up. "Vince, could I also get a cup of coffee with cream and sugar?"

Vince smiled. "Of course. And I take it you won't be having any after-dinner wine."

Tom returned the smile.

Vince served the desserts and after-dinner drinks.

Ralph stirred his coffee "Sir, back to your comment about a great round of golf, I would hardly say you had a stellar round. You shot 120," Ralph reminded him. "Your score has got to be right up there with your first round of golf. How can you call it great?"

"My game is always off when I'm excited about playing an exceptional course and this definitely fits that description. I'll play it again. The day was fantastic: playing with fun spirits, a great layout, perfectly manicured fairways and greens. On Earth we used to say, 'The worst day of golf is a heck of a lot better than the best day of work.' To me, golf's not always about the score. I admit it's more fun when I play well, but golf is about the game and the people you meet."

After Tom thanked everyone for an enjoyable day, he stepped outside with Ralph and Willie. The evening climate they had chosen was ideal. It was warm, with a touch of humidity and a refreshing breeze. He enjoyed the slight scent of the petunias hanging from the baskets outside the restaurant. The good news was that there was no sneezing; on Earth he had been highly allergic to night air. He watched in delight as the lighting bugs danced. As a kid, he had spent hours catching them in glass jars and releasing them at the end of the evening.

As far as bugs went, this really was Heaven—no mosquitoes. Thank goodness for that; those were pesky little buggers.

Willie reached into his pocket and handed Tom a gold golf ball. "I think you'll appreciate this. It's a feather golf ball I got ahold of. I figure as much as you love the game, you'd take good care of it. It's been good luck for me. Hold on to it. It could be helpful in some way during your pursuit of the SWEEP."

Tom was overcome with the thoughtful gift. He patted Willie on the back. "Thanks. Is it good for making a hole-in-one?"

"Well, I don't know about that."

Tom jabbed a finger in Willie's stomach. "Willie, you're sure looking good, been working out? Looks like your hair is darker and thicker. Spiffing up a bit, are we?"

"As a matter of fact, I am. I've been going to Leona's. She has a boutique where I can decide if I want to make changes to my shell. I received an alert that my wife, Ethel, will arrive soon and I want to look as good as possible when she comes."

He looked Tom over. "You might want to visit Leona yourself and see what she has to offer."

"I'll do that."

As their conversation wound down, a glowing purple star with flaming orange edges raced towards Tom. He dodged to get out of its path. The star screeched to a halt, just inches from his face. "What the heck? That thing almost hit me!"

"Looks like you're in big trouble. That's an angry star," Willie warned. "If you were on Earth, I'd say you musta' forgot an anniversary, a birthday, or some important date. Ralph, have you explained the purple-and-orange stars to Tom?"

"Yes, I have, but I never expected Tom would receive any."

Willie eyed the star and excused himself. "I'll catch you fellas later."

"You may remember purple-and-orange stars are from someone who is angry with you," Ralph said. "Grab the star. We can go inside after you read it and talk about it if you want."

Chapter 35

Jeremiah and the
Golf Tournament Tickets

Tom angrily snatched the card hovering around him. He was still shaken by the stupid thing almost knocking him over.

"It's from Jeremiah. He's my brother." Tom opened the star, but there was no message. "Great, do people think I can read minds now?"

"Sir, would you like to go inside, get something to drink, and talk about this?"

"No thanks. I know it's from my brother. He's mad at me. And something Willie said gave me an idea what this might be about. But it's not something I want to talk about. I want to get this taken care of. For now, I'd like to do some checking around with my ELV and think about this. I'll let you know if I have any questions. Thanks. See ya tomorrow."

Tom walked about six Earth blocks until he found a bench that looked like a good place to rest. He sat there to think things through about the star message.

He'd spent a lot of time tinkering with new innovations back on Earth, but new expensive versions came out every few months, making it costly to keep up. Now he had a new toy, his ELV. Whenever he had some time alone, he played around with it.

The first thing he had discovered was that he could check on Liz even without a star message from her. He had expanded his exploration to other people, such as his brother, Jeremiah. He had checked on his brother a few weeks ago. But the comment Willie had made, what he had said about forgotten birthdays, sparked a clue in Tom's mind.

Jeremiah's birthday is tomorrow.

Tom had put Jeremiah's birthday out of his mind, knowing he had a special surprise for his little brother's birthday. Several weeks ago, he had made arrangements for it. During one of his ELV checks on Liz, he found her at a bookstore. The two of them had often gone to bookstores together. She'd look for whatever she was interested in and Tom usually looked around in the magazine section.

During that particular viewing, he had adjusted his ELV to take a glance at the magazines. One of the magazines had an article about the Queensberry Open—what Tom had considered the most prestigious golf tournament on tour—as its feature story. Unless you were a member of the club where the tournament was held, tickets were only available for purchase if your name was selected in a drawing. For years, both he and Jeremiah had submitted applications for the drawing. In fact, he'd submitted an application just before he passed into Heaven and he knew Jeremiah had mailed his.

The date for the drawing was two weeks before Jeremiah's birthday and announcements were mailed soon after the selection drawing. Tom and Jeremiah had always kidded, but they were serious at the same time, about what a great birthday present it would be if either one of them received an announcement around Jeremiah's birthday that they had won tickets.

A couple of weeks ago, Tom had tinkered around with his ELV and his medium finder. He didn't know if it would work, but he had always figured crazy ideas were worth a shot. The worst that could happen was that they wouldn't work. He'd set his ELV to the location for the ticket selection drawing. He looked through the selection committee—just a handful of people really: one to spin the barrel the names were in, one to draw the names from the barrel, one to read the names, one to record the names and keep track of how many names were left to be drawn, and finally a person to hand-address the envelope for the selected name.

He had fumbled around, trying to run his medium finder over his ELV. He wasn't sure how accurate any readings would be, but what the heck. His medium finder lit up when he scanned it over the image of the person drawing the names. Then, with an even more bizarre idea, Tom sent a telepathic message to the gentleman drawing the names, *Draw Jeremiah Malone's name.*

Tom was sure he had gone off his rocker when he heard through the ELV that the first name drawn was Jeremiah. He continued watching until the envelope was addressed.

He looked at the purple-and-orange star again, picked it up and turned it over and over in his hands. *Looking at this isn't going to do any good, I need to look in on Jeremiah.*

Tom picked up his ELV and focused on his brother's home. Jeremiah and Lynn, his wife, were sitting at their kitchen table, relaxing for the evening. Many an hour had been spent at that table when the four of them, Tom and Liz and Jeremiah and Lynn, had played card games, especially hearts. He'd always felt triumphant when he could dump the queen of spades on Lynn. He remembered her glare, pretending to get so mad at him, but she got in her share of revenge moves.

Tonight their home was quiet. Jeremiah was working a sudoku puzzle. Lynn had some paper on the table and a pencil in her hand, a ruler nearby. Tom guessed she was creating a new design. She was always working on something: quilts, stained glass designs, wood-working projects.

"What time are you playing golf tomorrow?" Lynn asked.

"What makes you think I am?" Jeremiah snapped back. Tom heard the tone in his voice; that explained the anger in the star.

It made Tom think of something else. He missed Liz and his family and friends, but he never thought they might miss him too. That could explain some of the anger. *Maybe I should check on more people once I get this Jeremiah thing straightened out.*

"It's your birthday; you always play."

"That's when Tom was around. We'd play golf, have a gourmet lunch of hot dogs and chips, and if we had time, play another quick nine."

Those were fun days. Tom thought about the time Jeremiah's drive was hit way off to the right, directly towards an apartment where the occupants were on their deck, barbequing. The ball hit the lid of the grill and closed it. The occupant picked the ball up and threw it back into the fairway. Then there was the time they both got too close to a skunk and returned home with a new "cologne."

During the night Tom worked on a plan to get the ticket selection announcement in Jeremiah's hands. He also worked on a well-worded explanation for Ralph. He hadn't left Heaven when putting his planned surprise together; he had just used his ELV and medium finder. As he saw it, he hadn't done anything wrong, but it seemed Ralph always had a zillion questions about what Tom was up to.

There wasn't anything down on Earth he could do tonight, but Tom wanted to leave first thing in the morning. One thing he could do, however, was contact Ralph and let him know he'd be leaving in the morning in response to the star and as part of his SWEEP pursuit.

He used his spirit communication system to contact Ralph. After Ralph answered, Tom explained the reason for the call. "I need to check on this star. I'm sure it has to do with Jeremiah's birthday tomorrow and me not being there to play golf with him. I arranged a little birthday surprise for Jeremiah. It should arrive at his home tomorrow. I'm leaving in the morning to check on it."

"Do you think that is really necessary, sir?"

"Yeah. I wanna get Jeremiah out of that nasty mood, plus this might be an opportunity to make one of those wonder moments for my SWEEP."

Ralph didn't ask for details about the surprise. "Okay, sir. Do you want me to meet you at the exit in the morning?"

Tom was anxious to end the communication before Ralph asked for more details. "No thanks. I'll be fine. See ya when I return."

ক্ষ   ক্ষ   ক্ষ

THE NEXT MORNING Tom dug around in his pockets and found the gold golf ball Willie had given him. *This might come in handy.* He placed the golf ball in his utility bag and made sure he had visibility dust—the dust that made things brought from Heaven visible on Earth if he wanted them to be seen—in his bag. Then he headed to The Veil.

Tom hung his rope ladder over a cloud and made his way to Earth.

Going through his Brick Wall and The Veil was easy this time. That's right, leaving is always easy. Remember that, Tom. It's the return trip, coming back into Heaven, that feels like a Brick Wall to me.

ক্ষ   ক্ষ   ক্ষ

TOM WASN'T SURE where to start, but figured Jeremiah's home was as good as anyplace. His alignment was perfect. When Tom reached the bottom of the ladder, he was in front of his brother's home, a two-story house in a suburb southwest of town. The lawn looked to be freshly mowed. Tom was thankful he didn't feel that need to sneeze; freshly mowed grass had been one of his biggest allergies on Earth.

It was fairly early in the morning, around seven o'clock. The morning dew was still on the grass, and there were a few clouds, though the sky was mostly sunny. He could feel the humidity rising. Although Tom loved thunderstorms, he hoped he wouldn't see any today. He didn't know how, but if Jeremiah hadn't already changed his mind about playing golf, Tom was determined to get the ticket selection notice into Jeremiah's hand. That should put Jeremiah in a better mood and, hopefully, get him out on a golf course.

The garage door opened and Jeremiah and Lynn came out with their dog, Pooch. It looked like they were ready for one of Pooch's favorite activities, her walk. Both Jeremiah and Lynn were wearing shorts. Lynn had a tan tank top on and Jeremiah was wearing a royal-blue golf shirt. Pooch, a whippet, was proudly modeling a colorful scarf around her neck. Jeremiah had been holding the leash, but handed it to Lynn while he put sunglass lenses over his prescription glasses. He took the leash back and that was Pooch's signal to go. She did and at a fast pace.

Tom followed them, still not sure how to complete his intention for getting the ticket announcement to Jeremiah. About three-quarters of mile later, Tom saw a postal worker returning to her delivery truck. He thought about trying to use her as a medium.

Why not?

Arlene, as the name embroidered on her shirt indicated, looked weather-beaten. Her face was deeply wrinkled, her gray, shoulder-length hair wiry, probably from the daily long exposure to the elements, but there was an aura around her. Right now, it seemed to be his only hope. When he got near her, he attempted to reach into her bag. He wasn't going to tamper with the mail, just test to see Arlene's reaction. She took a swat as if she had sensed a bug or something near her bag.

Good. She senses my presence. Next step. I'll try a telepathic message.

"Arlene, can you check to see if you have any mail for 4973 Birch Street?"

Arlene looked through the pieces of mail for the next few blocks. Tom watched over her shoulder and saw nothing. But she returned to her truck and searched through her next bundle for delivery. She saw it and Tom did too—an envelope marked *Urgent* with a return address from the Queensberry Open golf ticket selection committee.

Tom told Arlene she had a special ability. "That family isn't home right now and I don't know if you know them or not. With a little luck and good timing, they may be returning home about the same time you reach their house. It's an important piece of mail. If you could hand-deliver it or ring their door-bell—anything you can do to make sure they see it would be appreciated."

Arlene nodded in understanding. Tom crossed his fingers as he had done when he was a child, hoping his plan would come together.

Then he had another idea. Pooch seemed to be the pace set-ter of the group. Tom had seen a TV show years back about a pet trainer who claimed he could control animals by talking to them. At the time, Tom had thought the guy was nuts, but at this point he couldn't come up with anything else. He had also heard several animal lovers claim dogs possess a higher level of smell and hearing than humans. He would test Pooch to see if she detected his presence.

Tom left Arlene and caught up with Pooch. She started sniffing. He walked a few paces and Pooch followed, pulling Jeremiah along. *Hopefully, she'll stay on my path and follow my pace back to Jeremiah's. And I'll follow Arlene's pace.*

Tom heard Jeremiah say to Lynn. "She seems to be sniffing at something. Wonder what it is."

Arlene's pace was slower than Pooch's as she had mail to deliver along the way. Tom adjusted his speed and direction so as to be just slightly ahead of Arlene so she could hand the envelope to Jeremiah before they entered their house.

The timing was perfect. Arlene stopped at the homes along the way to drop off the mail and occasionally took some extra time at a stop to sort the next batch of mail, making it easy for Tom to keep up with her while still setting a pace for Pooch who led the way for Jeremiah and Lynn. Arlene and her mail truck arrived at Jeremiah's driveway just as Lynn was entering the code for the garage door to open. Arlene walked up to Jeremiah instead of the mailbox, showed him the envelope, and asked if that was his. "It's marked 'Urgent' and I wanted to be sure it got into the proper hands."

Jeremiah thanked her and Tom heaved a big sigh of relief. That was a lot of work. *It better get him in a good mood and out on the golf course.*

Jeremiah's mouth dropped. He turned to Lynn. "You know for years Tom and I have entered a drawing for tickets to Tom's favorite golf tournament, the Queensbury Open. It's a very prestigious tournament and tickets are next to impossible to get unless you are a member. A few tickets are held back for purchase by the names selected in a drawing. Looks like this year my name was drawn! I can't believe it! It's played on a course on the east coast in the spring. Next year you and I will have to go and be part of the gallery watching the tournament."

Jeremiah took a couple of practice swings. "Now I'm jazzed and want to play today. Wanna walk the course with me?"

Lynn smiled. "Let me just get cleaned up a bit."

They went inside to put on fresh shirts; the ones they had worn during their walk were drenched in sweat. Lynn also wanted to curl her hair. While she did that, Jeremiah filled a couple of water bottles to take with them, then he sat on a kitchen chair while he put on his shoes. He called Pooch over and scratched her ears. It looked like he was talking to the dog, but his words were directed at Tom.

"Tom, I usually don't talk to you because I feel weird when I try. I have a sneaky suspicion you had something to do with the tickets. You always did make stuff happen."

He gave Pooch a final pat and went to the garage to load his clubs into the car. Tom followed him to the garage and shook his head a little bit. It was always amazing how neat Jeremiah's garage was. No oil stains on the floor. All the tools and sporting equipment were organized, hanging from racks on the walls. Tom hadn't been one to take the time for such neatness. As long as there was room in his garage for the cars to fit in and space for the golf clubs—that was all that mattered, and Tom's clubs were usually in back of his car.

The exterior of the sedan was spotless and the interior was equally neat: vacuumed floors and seats, drink holders cleaned out and ready for the next soda—Tom and his brother both had a passion for sodas.

Tom slipped into the car to catch a ride to the golf course.

❧ ❧ ❧

The parking lot at the course was practically empty, maybe a half dozen cars.

"Tom woulda loved this," Jeremiah said. "With nobody ahead of us, we coulda sped around, probably got thirty-six in and still been home in time for a birthday dinner."

Tom was happy to see Jeremiah playing with the putter Tom had given him the previous Christmas. He felt honored when he heard Jeremiah tell Lynn he was going to play two balls—one for himself and one for Tom—and keep scores for each of them. After the last hole, Jeremiah and Lynn stopped at the snack counter inside the clubhouse for the traditional birthday lunch of hot dogs, chips, and a soda. They opted to sit at a small table near the window to eat and tally the scores. One score was in the low seventies; the other was eighty-one, Tom's usual score.

The server from the snack counter pointed to a chocolate cake on the table next to them. "Earlier, several groups of ladies played to celebrate one of their birthdays. They brought a cake in for dessert after lunch. They had some left over and asked that I offer it to other players. Would you like some?"

"Looks good. Thank you." Lynn got up to get plates and forks and cut one large piece of cake to share with Jeremiah.

❧ ❧ ❧

When they got home, Jeremiah and Lynn freshened up for dinner, both needing showers and fresh clothes after the sweat they'd worked up on the golf course. While waiting for Lynn, Jeremiah sat down to play with Pooch and talk to Tom.

"Guess you were my playing partner today. Thanks for the unforgettable birthday."

Lynn came out dressed for dinner, wearing black shorts and a loose-fitting maroon-and-black top. She said, "You know I was thinking—"

"You were thinking?" Jeremiah said. "I didn't know you could do that."

Lynn affectionately slapped him on his arm. "Doesn't it seem strange you received the notice about the tournament tickets today? The tickets, shooting Tom's score of eighty-one, having birthday cake in the clubhouse—it all makes you wonder."

Jeremiah agreed. "Yepper. Makes you wonder."

With those words Tom made sure he had his utility bag and left to find a coffee shop.

That was a tough day. Never thought such a simple surprise could get so complicated.

Chapter 36

LEONA'S BOUTIQUE

I T HAD BEEN a long day and Tom was thankful he didn't run into Ralph on his return to Heaven. He headed straight to his favorite bench for some rest. It wasn't physical rest he needed, but he wanted to do some mental unwinding. He had enjoyed being on the golf course and hanging out with Jeremiah and Lynn was fun. He hadn't realized how much he missed them until he had spent the day with them. And the task of actually getting his birthday surprise in Jeremiah's hands was much more difficult than he had anticipated.

The plan had been a challenge from the beginning—getting Jeremiah's name selected in the drawing—but the really complicated piece had come at the end. Tom always expected to be in control of making things happen. He wasn't happy needing to find mediums to help him, but he appreciated the service the postal worker had provided.

THE NEXT MORNING, Tom meandered his way to the clubhouse for coffee. He hadn't contacted Ralph upon his return the previous evening. Ralph was probably already at the clubhouse or would arrive soon. Ralph wasn't one for changing his schedule.

Ralph was already seated at the counter when Tom arrived. He had a cup in front of him. Tom sat next to Ralph and Sarah poured a cup of coffee and served it to Tom.

"How was your Brick Wall upon your return?" Ralph asked.

"It was easier, I guess. Felt more like poster board this time. Anything new here?"

"No. Things have been quiet."

"When we played golf, Willie mentioned that Leona has a place for enhancing the look of your shell. I might check into that today. How would I get there?"

"I am sure she would be delighted to help you. Do you mind if I come along? I am anxious to see the new you."

"Sure. Come along. How do we get there again?" Tom repeated his request for directions.

Ralph smiled. "Sir, I suggest we take the rail system. It is about a twenty-minute ride and will give you an opportunity to see more of Heaven than you have seen so far. Actually, there is a rail station a few blocks from here. You may not have noticed it, but that station would be the easiest access."

Tom thought about asking Ralph if it was okay to go dressed as he was, but realized he didn't have anything else to wear.

How long have I been wearing the same shorts and shirt? A few weeks now? Good thing shells don't perspire; I'd really be a stinky boy.

As they neared the station, Tom saw a rail system above them. It reminded him of the elevated rail systems in several large metropolitan areas on Earth. A train was approaching and Ralph and Tom jumped on.

Never expected Heaven to be so much like Earth . . . then again, I never gave Heaven much thought. I think Liz will love this place; I know she plans on getting here someday. This place could be very tolerable once more of my family and friends get here. I could be their guide.

On the ride to Leona's, Ralph talked incessantly, pointing out parks, residential areas, churches, schools, shopping areas, fresh food markets, cafes. Tom didn't give Ralph his undivided attention since he was busy taking in all the sights. With his good sense of direction, he could return on his own to the places that interested him most.

Ralph indicated the stop for Leona's. They exited in an area that again reminded Tom of downtown areas of Earth's large cities: high rise buildings, traffic lights, busy streets. He'd investigate later.

Leona's boutique, Stellar Impressions, was about a block from the main street. The front doors were glass, with large windows on either side, allowing spirits passing by to look in before deciding if they wanted to visit the store. The shop was very inviting. Inside near each window were seating areas where Leona consulted with her clients or where spouses and friends could wait for their shopping companions to come out of the dressing rooms to show off new selections.

Tom and Ralph entered the store. It was about thirty-one thousand square feet. The walls were painted a soft blue-gray. At the back of the store were two draped openings. Tom assumed those were fitting rooms.

Leona greeted them. After exchanging a few pleasantries, Ralph brought the conversation to the business at hand. "Tom is considering some adjustments to his shell. Perhaps you could explain the options."

"I'd be glad to. Do you have time today?"

Tom nodded.

Leona pointed to the consulting table and chairs on her left and invited Tom and Ralph to sit down and help themselves to the beverages and snacks on the table. Tom poured himself a cup of coffee with cream and sugar and selected two cookies—one, a chocolate chip, the other, oatmeal raisin.

Leona reviewed her services. "I do the repair work after a life on Earth. Based on the lives people have lived, spirits select an approximate age they want displayed through their shell. Some make their selection on a weight they were or the amount of hair they had or its natural color."

"Do people—or spirits, I should say—always take on their perfect look?" Tom asked.

Ralph interrupted. "Sir, before we answer your question, I have a question for you. How would you describe the perfect look?"

Here we go again. Better watch how I answer this one. Seems when Ralph starts asking questions, he likes to trip me up somehow. I think he tries to make me flustered, but so far, I've been able to hold my own.

He considered a few moments before he replied.

"Some people do look better than others," Tom finally said. "Even some of the most attractive people could be improved upon: better muscle tone, a few inches taller or shorter, a straighter nose, whiter teeth. Come to think of it, I can't say I know anyone with a truly perfect look . . ." He paused. Then he remembered Catherine.

"Wait a minute. There was a girl who worked in the same office building as I did during the seventies. Back then people rated attractiveness on a scale from one to ten. Hardly anyone was considered a ten. But every guy agreed Catherine was a ten, even most women gave her a ten. On the elevator, at the water fountains, walking to different departments to deliver files, everyone stopped. They couldn't take their eyes off her. But no one talked to her. Most of the guys had her on a pedestal and worried she would laugh at them if they ever asked her for a date. Several years later, I met the man she married. I joked about how an average Joe like him got such a prize for a wife. He told me he just asked her out and she accepted. She had never been asked out before and thought everyone hated her. Her husband told me she was shy, but others took her quietness for being a snob. So, I guess, what was beauty for everyone else was really a curse for her." He paused again, thinking. "Is that the point you want to make by asking me about perfection? What's perfect for some maybe a curse to others? In that the case, Leona, don't make me too perfect." Tom winked.

"Don't worry, I won't." Leona smiled and winked back. "People tend to focus on the outside of others, in other words— their looks. If another person doesn't have what someone considers the *right* look, they might avoid that person. People often neglect to recognize the character within."

Tom summed it up. "You're talking about the old saying— something about 'It's not what's on the outside, but what's inside that matters?'" He considered that adage and thought about how he had lived his life. He admitted he was terrible with names and faces, but when he saw people he had met, he could remember the places they had traveled, how they swung a golf club, how many kids they had, the music they enjoyed. But their looks—he really hadn't paid much attention to. He hoped he had focused on the right stuff.

"Now that we've solved the perfection concept, Tom, are you ready to talk about your shell?" Leona asked.

"Let's do it." Tom was a man of action—once he knew what he wanted, he was ready to get it done, but done correctly.

"I hope you won't feel that I'm staring at you, but I'd like to start by studying your current shell for a few moments, if you don't mind. Just relax. While I'm looking it over and making a few notes, you might want to consider any changes that are of interest to you." Leona's voice was soothing. Tom did relax, to the point that he was nearly in what he considered a hypnotic state. Leona was quiet. The shop was quiet, except for very soft background music coming from a harp. Tom detected a hint of a candle burning, giving off the scent of a sea breeze. He felt like he could stay in that peaceful state forever. He was too much a restless spirit for that, but in his present state of calmness he had a good opportunity to clear his mind and think about what changes he wanted made to his shell.

He thought of questions he wished he would have asked Leona before she started studying him, but for now, he'd remain quiet. The worst that could happen was that his request would be turned down. He had lived with his body for fifty-plus years and now that there were no aches and pains from the inner parts, it would still serve him well.

Let's start at the top of my head. I'd like a fuller head of hair, not so much of a receding hairline. I know there's a thinning spot in the back; maybe that can be filled in, perhaps a little more pepper and a little less salt.

Tom thought about his face. He had looked at it every day for years and was happy with it. He had deep wrinkles in his forehead. The wrinkles really didn't bother him, but he knew most people, if they could afford it, would pay megabucks to have their wrinkles filled in. He figured why not go for it. The sags over all could stand a lift: his chin, abs, buttocks. But what he wanted most was the unsightly varicose veins to disappear. His varicose veins had developed at an early age, but Tom never thought of having them treated. That would require surgery and Tom had watched his dad go through a painful surgery and a long recovery; he didn't want that. Another reason he didn't want the surgery was the recovery would keep him off the golf course. He never tried to hide the varicose veins; he had worn shorts at every opportunity. But it sure would be nice to get rid of them.

"Tom," Leona's gentle, soft voice roused him from his peaceful state. "Are you ready to discuss your shell? I've made some notes and assume you have some thoughts."

Tom shook his head a few times as if wakening from a deep sleep.

She asked if he had an age in mind for his shell.

"I'd like to show forty-seven."

"Sir, I am surprised. I thought you might want to be twenty-five. Is that not considered the prime of life?" Ralph asked.

"It might be the prime of life for some people, but it wasn't for me. At twenty-five I was gaining weight. Back then, hairstyles were longer with side burns. Lots of men had facial hair, which I could never get to grow. I really didn't like the seventies look. The fashions were rather sloppy in my opinion, compared to twenty-some years later. Overall, I felt more confident at forty-seven than I did at twenty-five. I think the self-assuredness and a little maturity was a plus for appearance, despite the wrinkles and gray hair that had shown up. I had lost several pounds and was at a good weight, but on the downside I had also lost some hair and my varicose veins got worse. Any chance those could be repaired?"

Leona made a notation on the pad of paper she had in her hand. "No problem.

"But Tom, I should warn you that if your shell takes on a younger age than the age you actually died, you might lose some of the significant lessons you learned during that time. Are you sure you want to take that risk?"

"What the heck? I probably lost a lot of brain cells anyway during that time. Senior moments and things like that."

Leona asked if there was anything else.

Tom thought a moment. He listed off the other thoughts he had had while she was studying his shell: his hair, the wrinkles, the sags.

Leona added those items to her list. "Seems easy enough to do. What about your glasses?"

"I guess I don't need them since there are no physical parts. But I like wearing them. I think they make me look distinguished."

Leona suggested he wear them as an accessory. "Not all physical reminders are abandoned. Some spirits like the feel of a good sweat after a workout, and some, mostly females, like to show tears with their emotions, whether the tears be happy or sad."

Ralph suggested Tom try a pair of ZAG glasses. "ZAG is short for Zoom Ability Glasses. Since you are in the midst of the SWEEP, you most likely would enjoy the ability to zoom in for a more detailed view if you need it."

Tom started his own list. "Perfect. That will be the first item on my shopping list. Leona, when can you whip up this new shell for me?" Now that he knew what adjustments were going to be made, he was as excited about revising his shell as when he ordered custom-made drivers.

"Let me check my appointments." Leona looked at her calendar. "The rest of the day is free for me. I can start now. Your requests are routine; I may even be able to finish today."

Tom thought that would be perfect.

Leona told him the next thing was to get his spirit out of the shell. "If you'd like some privacy, you may use one of the fitting rooms at the back of the shop—behind the curtains. Would you like some help?"

Tom nodded and Leona led him to the fitting room.

He had no idea what to expect. "What now?"

"I need to push your navel. That will release your spirit from your shell, like a genie being released from a bottle."

Tom wasn't comfortable with that idea. It sounded like it would tickle and he didn't like being tickled. "Can I do it myself?"

Before Leona could respond, Tom pushed his navel. He felt a light air rushing from the top of his head, swirling around him. Then he saw the air glowing with the pastel colors of a rainbow.

Ralph spoke through the fitting room curtain. "Sir, you should see your spirit; it is filling the entire shop. Actually, it is quite beautiful, sir."

Tom was not one to blush, but considering the words had come from Ralph, he was a bit humbled. His spirit enjoyed the feeling of expansion. He wondered if his feeling might compare to a Jack-in-the-Box being released.

He looked down at the shell now laying on the floor like a balloon that had lost its air. Leona picked up the shell and told Tom she was going to do the initial work at the front of the shop where the lighting was better. She invited him to browse the shop if he felt comfortable wandering around without his shell or he could remain in the fitting room if he wanted privacy.

"I need some shirts and shorts and probably some other things. Shoes, I definitely could use some shoes and socks. What else?" Tom elected to shop while Leona altered his shell. He was excited about his custom shell and about getting new clothes to go along with it.

He started with shirts. They were the most fun to shop for with their variety of colors and designs. He mostly stuck with solid colors since they were easiest to coordinate with shorts. He might try some patterned ones; they could be fun. He saw a shirt with a gold paisley design on a black background. It reminded him of a shirt that Bob, one of his friends, wore. It was not something Tom would typically select as he thought it was a little on the wild side. But he picked up the shirt and started filling a shopping bag.

Why not? I'm trying so many different things. Maybe I'll like the less conservative shirts, or maybe not.

He picked up a dozen shirts, then wondered if any were on sale. It didn't matter if they were or not; he needed them.

Next Tom looked at golf shorts. He had always worn what he considered traditional golf attire: collared pullover shirts, either in solid colors or stripes, and solid-color pants or shorts.

He picked up an assortment of shorts, various shades of black, tans, navy blues. Then he saw a must-have—a pair of hound's-tooth shorts. On Earth he had had a jacket of similar fabric. Liz had always liked the jacket and it had been one of his favorites as well. He picked up the shorts. It was crazy, he knew. But sometimes it was fun to do something out of the ordinary. He wished Liz was there with him right now. He could try on the paisley shirt with the hound's-tooth shorts. He was sure she'd get a good laugh and that would be the end of it. But he had to get them and somehow show them to Liz.

Tom held his new outfit in front of him and asked Leona and Ralph what they thought. "I should show up in a dream with this outfit. Anyone who sees this would never forget it. Rather unusual, isn't it?"

"It is definitely not something one would forget, sir. Have you appeared in the dreams of other people?" Ralph asked.

"Not that I know of. Liz used to tell me when she'd dream about me, but now I have no way of knowing."

Leona asked Ralph if he had told Tom about dream potions.

"No, actually. We have had so many other matters to discuss, I had not thought about it. I know you have some available in the shop. Do you want to tell Tom about it?"

Leona pointed to a counter. "Tom, there's some on the counter. Why don't you pick up a bottle? If you put some into a beverage that a person drinks before falling asleep, the potion promotes dreams and allows you to appear in their dreams as long as the dreams won't be frightening. Using the potion does require a quick trip to Earth to get the potion into a beverage. Once a person has taken the potion, you have the ability to direct their dreams, either as a way to say hi, give cheer and inspiration, or to help solve a problem. Since you had the idea of appearing in a dream, I recommend you take some dream-inducing potion with you."

Tom picked up a bottle and dropped it into his shopping bag, then continued shopping. Leona turned her attention back to the alterations and Ralph became engrossed in watching Heavenly Hues, a video with tips on selecting clothing to enhance shell tone and coloring. Tom watched the show for a few moments. The host and guests on the show were discussing how the colors a spirit wore worked best with the tone of their shell. They also talked about how the colors a shell wore reflected some personality traits of the spirit inside.

The show's topic reminded Tom of a business breakfast meeting he had attended years before. The association's program director, who selected speakers for the meeting, wanted to do something fun for the holiday meeting. At that time, fashion consultants earned substantial incomes by advising business professionals what wearing certain colors could say about one's personality, especially when it came to accessories such as ties and shirts for men and scarves and blouses for women. Red was a power color. There were colors associated with humor, warmth, trustworthiness. That was back in the days when people met face to face for meetings, agreements were signed in person, and job candidates went to offices for interviews.

Leona stood up, shell in hand. "Tom, I'm almost done. I need to make the final adjustments on my machines in the back. I'll call you back when it's complete."

Tom went to the fragrance counter. He was afraid he'd sneeze but he didn't even detect any twitching reaction where his nose would have been. He ran across a cologne he had used when he started dating Liz. They'd both loved it, but when he needed to replace it, it was off the market. He hadn't used up the final drops. He saved them to run under Liz's nose every once in a while. It drove her crazy and he reaped the benefit of those results. They saved the fragrance until it got stale.

He added the cologne to his shopping bag along with other items: belts, sunglasses, handkerchiefs—he no longer needed them for sneezing and watery eyes, but he could use them for cleaning his sunglasses and his new ZAG glasses. He checked his shopping bag and didn't see the ZAG glasses in the bag so he chose a pair and added them to his selection.

His bag was full. He was getting tired of shopping, but still had to get some of what he considered necessities. He filled a second bag with socks, underwear, shoes for golf, and sneakers to wear when he wasn't golfing. He considered dress slacks, shirts, and possibly a tie, then decided those could wait for another day.

He was ready to rest. He was about to sit down with Ralph, watch the video, and enjoy a soda when Leona called out from the fitting room. "Tom, I have your shell finished. Do you want to come and try it on?"

Tom raced to the fitting room, anxious to see the results.

"Sir, may—"

Tom was sure Ralph wanted to see the shell. He motioned

for Ralph to follow. "Sure. Come on back and take a look."

Leona showed Tom an opening in the top of the shell. "Once we get your spirit back in the shell, you can press your navel and the opening will close."

Tom's spirit was large and Leona couldn't get it all to fit into the new shell. She asked Ralph to help.

The three of them worked on getting his spirit into his altered shell. Finally, the rainbow light from his free spirit was gone from the shop and was now contained in his shell.

Ralph nodded. "Sir, I am not one to give compliments easily, but you have a tremendous spirit." He walked out of the room and Tom was relieved. He felt like he could get teary-eyed and he didn't want that to happen.

Leona took a quick look at her craftsmanship and gave a satisfied nod. "Do you need help buttoning up or can you handle it yourself?"

Tom wanted to be alone. He told Leona he could handle it and asked if she had a mirror. She pointed to one in the corner of the fitting room before she departed.

Tom pushed his navel; he didn't want any of his spirit escaping through the opening in his head. He loved every bit of his spirit. The push of the belly button did tickle. He let out a giggle and hoped no one heard him.

He caught his image in the mirror. The results were extremely pleasing. *Not too bad, if I do say so myself. Even better with the varicose veins gone and the wrinkles removed. And I have hair.* He ran his fingers through his hair. It was still soft, but now fuller, more gray than white. He was pleased with the short style; the receding hair line had been brought forward. It was neatly trimmed, with none of the natural curl from his younger years remaining.

He wanted to be dressed when he modeled for Ralph and

Leona, but his shopping bags were still out in the store. He poked his head out of the curtain and asked Ralph to bring the bags to him. Ralph picked up the bags and handed them to Tom through the fitting room curtain.

"I'll be out soon if you still want to hang around in the shop," Tom said.

"I am quite anxious to see your new look, sir. I will be waiting." Ralph left to watch more of the video. Tom dressed in one of his new shirts and a pair of new shorts. He put on a belt, his socks and sneakers and stuck a handkerchief in his back pocket. He reached for a wallet to put in his other back pocket and remembered he didn't have one. Perhaps there would be no need for one. If that turned out to be the case, he might go ahead and get one later, just because it was part of his dressing routine.

He looked in the mirror once again and gave the image he saw a thumbs up. He was ready to introduce his new shell to the world or at least to Heaven.

He strutted out into the main part of the store. He had his ZAG glasses in his hand and put them on as he strolled past Ralph.

"These really do make me look distinguished, don't you think?"

"Most certainly, sir. But then again. I always thought you looked tremendous inside and out."

He gave Ralph a long look. Wonder what's with Ralph today. Throwing compliments around. He's a good guy, but I don't want him getting sentimental on me. I need to get him back to his old self. I've kinda gotten used to his properness.

Leona stood back and looked over her work. "Have to admit I did a pretty darn good job, but I had good material to start with."

Tom loved all the compliments. He thanked Leona for her

great job and asked what he owed her for her services and the articles he had in his shopping bag. Leona asked if Tom was on the no-pay list and Ralph confirmed.

"Sir, there is a banking system in Heaven. Most spirits do not need to pay for goods and services, but some elect to do so for a variety of reasons. Perhaps we will go to the bank some-day next week."

"Sounds like a plan," Tom said. "Are you ready to leave?"

"I would like to see the end of the video," Ralph said. "I am going to stay. Perhaps I will select some new shirts to keep up with your wardrobe. Do you know your way back?"

"I'm sure I can find it. I'd like to do some exploring around this area. Catch ya later."

Once again, Tom thanked Leona. On his way out, he saw the cookies again and politely asked if he could have a couple more. Leona nodded. He took two more and briskly exited the store, feeling confident and ready to take in some self-guided exploration of Heaven.

Chapter 37

Banking in Heaven

TOM WALKED OUT of Leona's shop feeling confident and ready for an afternoon of exploration. He retraced the few blocks he and Ralph had walked until he reached the point where they had exited the rail system. He assumed this was the main street—maybe not of Heaven in its entirety— but at least in this area of Heaven. The surroundings reminded him of business districts and shopping areas in large metropolitan areas where he had worked on Earth. The street was more golden than other streets he had seen while riding the rail. He looked up at the street sign.

How appropriate. Heaven Street. The intersecting street is Seventh. Here I am, on the corner of Seventh and Heaven. Wonder if this is a landmark, like the Golden Gate Bridge or the Statue of Liberty, where spirits take photos to show their spirit friends they've been here.

Tom wasn't surprised by the color of the streets. He hadn't thought much about Heaven when he'd been on Earth. However, a few weeks prior to his passing he had been playing around on his home computer, listening for music selections to add to his collection. One of the songs was about Heaven. Its lyrics had described Heaven and its streets of gold. He'd liked the song, paid for it, and downloaded it to his computer.

The streets were busier now than when he and Ralph had arrived earlier to visit Leona. Tom guessed it must be around lunchtime.

He stopped at the intersection along with other pedestrian spirits waiting for a walk sign. Tom wondered why there was a need for a traffic light. Around the golf courses and other places he had been, he hadn't noticed transportation other than golf carts and the train they'd ridden today. But as he looked around now, he saw a variety of ways spirits were moving on the streets: riding on dinosaurs, camels, elephants; unicycles, bicycles, bicycles built for two, motorcycles; horses, horse and buggies, covered wagons; cars of every model since, he guessed, the invention of the automobile. Some vehicles he didn't recognize: possibly from planets other than Earth or, he speculated, designs from the future?

Suddenly, he felt a slap on his back. Tom gulped at the unexpected contact. Would somebody try to rob me? Of what? My utility bag? My new stuff from Leona's?

He turned to see who it was and was relieved to see a familiar face. It was Greg, the friend who had testified at Tom's SWEEP hearing.

"Great to see you, man." Greg gave Tom a pat on the shoulder. "You're looking really good."

Tom was still feeling good about his new shell. "Just came from Leona's shop. She did a great job with my shell, don't you think?" He looked Greg over. "You're looking—the same."

"Yeah, I guess. Really didn't feel like making a change. Still don't. Hey, listen. I'm headed out for a quick bite. I was gonna grab something and take it back to the office, but do you want to come along? We can sit while we eat and catch up on what's going on. I can tell you a little about the bank where I work. Then, if you're interested, I'll give you a quick tour of the bank."

Tom was intrigued by the ideas—both of the work concept in Heaven and the need for a bank. *Pennies from Heaven.* "Are you sure you don't mind?" he asked. "Don't want to hold you back. I was a working man for too many years; I remember those nasty time constraints on breaks and lunch hours. But I'd love to join you."

Greg waved him on. "Follow me. There's a greasy spoon about three blocks down; it's on the right hand side of the street."

They walked briskly through the throngs of spirits. Tom was glad he had the experience of maneuvering through the busy streets on Earth. Greg was leading the way, a few paces ahead, and Tom kept an eye on him. As he followed, Tom heard musicians playing various instruments: drums, guitars, clarinets, saxophones. Out of the corner of his eye, he saw spirit vendors selling foods from their carts. He detected aromas of pizza, hot dogs and sausages, pretzels, waffle cones.

It reminded Tom of working in "the big city." *Sure don't miss those days.*

Greg had gotten ahead of Tom and was waiting for him at the door of the diner. Most spirits were taking their lunches to go, but Tom and Greg slid into the only empty booth. Dirty dishes were on the table. The benches had not been wiped down, but Tom and Greg moved the dirty dishes aside and brushed off the table and benches as best they could.

Both ordered cheeseburgers, onion rings, and soft drinks. While they waited for their order, Tom pointed to one of the paper bags being carried out. The brown bag was dripping with grease. "A real greasy spoon, huh?"

Greg grabbed a handful of napkins. "Not the best tasting burgers, but quick service."

After they got their food, Tom bit into his burger and felt grease dripping down his chin. Soon he was surrounded by flies. *Flies. Not surprising. What would a greasy spoon be without flies?*

Greg swatted the flies away. "Tom, what were you thinking? Not about flies, I hope."

Tom answered. "As a matter of fact, I was. I was thinking about the greasy spoon places Liz and I sought out on holiday weekends. The more flies, the better the food; the dives with the most flies were given a five-fly rating. Kinda dumb."

"Quit thinking about flies. Sometimes you'll find that here in Heaven just thinking about something will make it happen."

"Sorry." Tom cleared the thoughts of flies from his mind and the flies disappeared.

"So tell me about the work thing and about the bank. Should I be getting a job?" Tom asked.

"In Heaven no spirit has to work," Greg said. "If I remember correctly from Earth, not working is one of the things people dream about. But surprisingly, many spirits eventually want to find a way to keep active; they have found work as a way to identify themselves. At the bank, I hear from many spirit customers who retired on Earth that they enjoyed being active after retirement. After retiring, they did something they enjoyed and still do so in Heaven. But again, it isn't required. If you want to do something, that's up to you."

Tom asked about the bank and about paying for things.

"As I understand it," Greg said, "there are many spirits who had trouble handling money and dealing with financial concerns while they lived on Earth. Those spirits have chips to alert the shop owners here in Heaven that they need to pay. There are also spirits who have been plagued in previous lifetimes by overspending, gambling addictions, or embezzlement issues. Some of these spirits are employed by the bank in order to put them in tempting positions as they strive to overcome old habits. They are audited frequently to measure their suitability to move on to another Earth life and face its challenges."

Greg took a bite of his burger before continuing. "As for paying, most spirits don't have to pay."

That's right. Ralph did say at Leona's that I was on the no-pay list.

Greg wiped his chin with a napkin. "One of the programs at Johnny's youth center trains young spirits who want to re-enter Earth and develop financial responsibility. They learn about holding a job, buying cars, paying rent, and supporting families. They maintain accounts at the bank and are required to pay for goods and services."

Tom and Greg noted the diner was getting crowded and spirits were waiting for booths or tables. Since they had finished eating, they agreed to give up their seats and head to the bank. As they cleared their booth, Greg continued. "The spirits of service personnel like to have funds to slip into pockets, purses, and piggy banks to help their families through hard times. Other spirits drop coins to loved ones on Earth to let them know they're watching them or are with them on special days."

As they walked along Heaven Street past Seventh Street and on to the bank, Tom asked Greg how he'd felt when he arrived in Heaven.

"I was actually very glad," Greg said. "My parents were happy to have me moving out of their house—not that they hated me or anything like that—and that didn't make me feel too good. Shortly after I arrived here, I found an Earth-viewing device available for all spirits to use, so I checked on my supposed girlfriend to see how her pregnancy was coming along. Turns out that was a false alarm; there was no baby. Just an attempt to get a promise ring out of me and a live-in boyfriend so she could brag to her friends, not because she was in love with me. You were the only friend I really had, and we rarely saw each other after the summer we worked together, so I didn't really leave behind much." He jabbed Tom's arm.

Tom understood. *Now that's one of the things I really miss; guys being able to joke around and kid each other.*

At Heaven and First Street, Greg stopped. "Here we are."

The bank was built in a style reflecting the late 1890s. A dozen or so stairs led from the sidewalk to the entrance. The railings on either side of the stairs were being polished. At the top of the stairs a greeter, wearing a gray three-piece suit, white shirt, red bow tie, and top hat trimmed in red, opened the door and welcomed them.

The lobby accommodated about ten teller windows on the left side of the lobby facing the entrance. The windows had iron bars between the tellers and the customers. Small openings under the bars allowed for sliding deposits, withdrawal requests, and currency from one side to the other. Dark wood paneling went from below the teller windows to the floor.

The floor was covered in black-and-white tiles. On the right side of the lobby were six offices. Greg pointed down the row. "My office is the last one."

Between the teller windows and offices were two round tables with large bouquets in the center of each table. The flowers featured in the arrangements were oriental lilies, sending their scent throughout the bank. In addition to peach roses, oriental lilies were one of Liz's favorites. On Earth he'd been highly sensitive to the lilies. When he sent them to Liz, he'd sent them to her office. No matter where Liz would place the lilies at home, his eyes would water and the sneezing was nonstop. But now, without his allergies, Tom could enjoy their fragrance.

Between the tables was an oblong table, a place for completing withdrawal slips and deposit forms. All three tables were cherry wood, matching the paneling under the tellers' windows.

Greg stopped and talked to a white-haired lady; she had a scent of cinnamon around her. She was pleasantly plump, wearing a red sweater over her house dress and carrying a red purse with a snapping clasp. She reminded Tom of his grandma, who'd always been in her kitchen cooking something.

"How's your day, Mrs. Blake?" Greg asked. "Don't you have some grandchildren with birthdays soon?"

Mrs. Blake smiled. "Thank you for asking. Yes, I do. I'm dropping coins for great-grandchildren now, three of them next month. I have two more greats on the way; that'll bring me to eighteen. Can't believe the grandkids are grown up and having kids of their own. The younger ones and the new ones won't know me, but I hope their parents will tell them about me."

A wistful look crossed her face. "I need to go home and bake some cookies. No one to bake them for really. I'll bring some by the bank tomorrow for your customers."

"Customers? I doubt that," Greg said. "I'll have them eaten myself before any customers have a chance to get to them."

She smiled at Greg and Tom and headed to the exit.

Tom thought of his grandmother. She'd had similar hair color, done up in a bun with a few wisps that couldn't be controlled. "Reminds me of my granny."

"Mine too. Mrs. Blake loved that role in her life. She told me that's why she kept that look for her shell. The favorite time of her life was her granny years."

Greg waved at a young spirit standing at a teller's window. "Jason, what's going on with you?"

Jason appeared to be in his early twenties, very athletic-looking, wearing a sleeveless shirt, and displaying a strong shell.

Wonder if he was an athlete of some sort?

"My older brother's getting married soon," Jason said. "Thought I should have a mint-condition nickel ready for his big celebration. What's your opinion—do you think it's appropriate to give him a nickel with the year of his fiancé's birth?"

Greg clapped Jason on the shoulder. "Sounds good to me. Have fun finding a good place for it."

A small group of young military service spirits were standing in line—some shells were missing limbs, other shells reflected the wounds they had suffered. All were proudly wearing the uniform of the branch they had served.

Greg stopped and thanked them for protecting the rights of all people on Earth. Tom did likewise. He had great respect for those who volunteered to protect his country and his freedoms. On Earth, if he'd seen someone in uniform, he always thanked them for their service. If they were in a restaurant, he would pick up their tab.

Greg invited the military personnel to follow him to the head teller, Tim. They did and Tom followed as well. Greg asked Tim to give a generous amount to the service spirits.

"They ask for so little and have given so much," he explained to Tom. "Their loved ones struggle to pay bills and put food on the table. I figure with a few extra dollars, maybe their families can afford some special surprises for the holidays or add to an education fund."

Tim, the teller, was dressed in a white golf shirt with the emblem of the bank embroidered on the sleeve: the outline of an angel's face with a gold halo over its head and wings where arms might be on a person. Tim had light black, wavy hair and wore glasses with black frames. He reminded Tom of the tellers at his bank on Earth, probably a college student working to earn credits for a degree in finance.

Continuing to his office, Greg stopped to talk to another young spirit in another line. They shook hands and Greg gave him a friendly slap on the back. "Curtis, don't tell me you're in here for another loan?"

"No way. I got a job delivering pizza. I'm here to deposit my first paycheck. See?" Curtis beamed as he showed Greg his check. Curtis showed it to Tom, too.

Tom congratulated him and wished him luck with his new job. He silently applauded Curtis. *Lose that ponytail and tuck in your shirt. You'll get raises and promotions quicker that way.*

He was excited for the young spirit. On Earth, he'd always respected young people eager to earn a few dollars, whether it be working for fast food restaurants, working part-time at retail stores, or standing on street corners waving advertisement signs.

"Do you know all your customers?" Tom asked Greg when they reached his office.

Greg moved a stack of papers off one of the chairs facing his desk and offered Tom a place to sit. The office was cluttered and reminded Tom of the night Greg had ended up with money blowing all over the amusement center where they'd worked. Before he sat down in his chair, Greg cleared off a space on his desk. He sat in his chair and put his feet up in the space he had just cleared.

"Really don't have too many customers, but I try to remember them. Some spirits, like Mrs. Blake, drop shiny coins to Earth for her great-grandchildren's birthdays and special occasions. She gets coins with the year of their birth on them. She'll drop the coins in plain view, easy for a child to find. Most of her grandkids know an unexpected coin is a gift from Grannie."

Tom shrugged. "So where does this money come from?"

Greg snickered. "Heaven learned a trick from governments on Earth—if you need more money, just print it. It's used to pay the spirits who work in the work-for-pay programs and use the money to pay their bills and make purchases."

Greg got up from his chair and walked over to what looked to be a small vending machine. He opened its door; it was actually a small refrigerator.

"Diet cola for you, Tom?"

"Have any beer in there?" Tom asked.

"Root beer. Didn't think you drank." Greg looked surprised.

"I don't, but the vending machine reminded me of the night you had some beers stashed away for yourself." They both shook their heads and laughed.

Tom hadn't had a root beer in ages and requested one. Greg pulled out two cans of root beer and tossed one to Tom.

"Thanks." Tom opened his soda while Greg sat back down and propped his feet on his desk. He listened while Greg continued with his explanation.

"The money that service spirits send to their families and the coins that spirits such as Mrs. Blake and Jason like to drop, go to Earth and need to be spendable there. Ever wonder what happens to coins tossed into a wishing well or a fountain or to money dropped on the ground?"

Tom shrugged and shook his head.

"Heaven has vacuuming hose lines that are discreetly dropped to Earth during the night. Money is suctioned by the hoses to Heaven. The vacuum is programmed to search and pick up loose money from fountains and wishing wells as well as loose change found on the streets.

"After the money is gathered, it is sorted. The coins that were tossed into a fountain or wishing well are set aside with the name of the person who made the wish and what they wished for. Specific wishes, if they are not harmful to anyone, are earmarked to make those wishes come true—if possible. The other money, tossed on lark or dropped on the ground somewhere, goes in another pile and is used by spirits who want to get extra money to send to the families they left behind and for the spirits who want to drop a few coins every now and then as a way to say 'Hi'.

"Jason, the young man you just met, was an excellent swimmer, but drowned in an attempt to save a friend. As he mentioned, he's getting a coin for his older brother's wedding. He likes to leave nickels with special dates on them as a 'Hello, I'm here' to his family.

"Last year, his younger brother, Kevin, was to give the class president's speech at his high school graduation. The students were told to be at the school early to make sure they were in their caps and gowns and lined up correctly in plenty of time before the ceremony began. Jason's dad dropped the family off so Kevin could get with his class and his mom could make sure their seats were reserved. After his dad parked the car, Kevin met him at the door. 'Dad, don't panic, but I think I left the notes for my speech at home. It should be on my desk. I probably could get by without them, but I think there's time for you to dash home and get them to be on the safe side.'

"Jason was watching this through a public ELV, one any spirit can use for a limited time. He felt this occasion called for one of the special nickels he routinely left for his family on important days as a way for him to say 'Hi.' He found a nickel with the graduation year on it and let it fall. When his dad found the speech notes, the nickel was on top of them. His dad sped back to the school and found Kevin in line just as the graduate procession was beginning. He put the notes in one of Kevin's hands and squeezed the nickel into the other hand. The two of them hugged, smiled, and nodded as Jason watched. After the ceremony, Kevin was more anxious to show off his special nickel than his diploma. The family did their traditional group hug, then all looked upward and waved."

"Wow." Tom stood and stretched his shoulders and took a short practice swing. "I've taken up a lot of your time. You probably work bankers' hours and it's past time for you to leave."

Greg stood up and stretched his shoulders. "Yeah, I'm ready to blow this popsicle stand. Do you have any questions?"

"I've always wanted to ask a banker if they give out samples." Tom laughed, anticipating he would be told no.

"As a matter of fact, we do. In fact, I thought you might want a sample or two. In your quest for the SWEEP, you may need a few bills and coins in your pocket. They're good attention getters. I'll be right back."

Greg left and returned a few moments later with a handful of paper money and coins.

Tom felt the crisp bills in his hand. He held them to his nose. "I smell ink. Were these freshly printed?"

"No, this money can be spent on Earth. Most of this is in dollars, but I've thrown in some foreign currency. You never know where a journey may take you."

Tom raised his eyebrows. *Interesting thought.*

"Thanks, Greg. It's been a fun afternoon. It was good to see you and not just because you gave me free money. I should bring my father-in-law here. He always said a bank should give out samples."

"Bring him in. We can load his pockets."

Chapter 38

THE SHOWER CURTAIN

BEFORE TOM REACHED the front door of the bank, he received another star. He was relieved to see it was not purple-and-orange. There were tiny markings on the outside of the star that he couldn't really make out. He adjusted the glasses Leona had given him and zoomed in on the marks. The name Doug was printed in tiny, barely legible letters on front of the star. Doug was his nine-year-old nephew, the oldest child of Liz's sister, Suzanne. Liz had two sisters. They'd been only four and nine when Tom and Liz began dating and he felt like her sisters were his sisters, too.

As far as Tom could tell, no message was inside. He used his ELV and saw Doug was at the desk in his bedroom, doing homework.

Through his ELV, Tom looked around Doug's bedroom. Doug was a collector: dinosaur models, books, unique pens and pencils. Despite all the items in his room, the room was neatly organized, not a bit of clutter. There were bunk beds in the room; Doug slept on the bottom bunk.

Doug was looking at a paper with some homework instructions on it. With the zooming glasses Tom was able to see the assignment sheet. The paper's instructions were to prepare an outline for an essay about a person you admire. Doug's printing was so small Tom had to refocus the glasses and zoom in for a closer look.

On the line for Title, Doug had written *Tom*.

The next section of the outline was Characteristics. The first thing Doug had written was *Had fun together*. Under the subsection for Examples, Doug listed: *Showed me magic tricks*. Another example was *Played card games with me*.

I could really mess with his mind if I left a coin on his desk while he's asleep, Tom thought. He contacted Ralph using his spirit communications system. He told Ralph about the star from Doug and about his encounter with Greg. "Even though Doug didn't ask for my help, I think it'd be fun to slip down to Earth while he's asleep and leave a coin on his paper. I'd want to stay overnight to see his reaction in the morning. So I'll see you when I return."

Ralph thanked Tom for advising him of his plans and agreed to meet Tom upon his return.

Tom looked through the samples Greg had just given him, searching for a coin with Doug's year of birth on it, preferably a dime. Doug was thrifty and had a whole list of things to do with a dime. Tom found the appropriate coin and put it into the visibility dust compartment of his utility bag. He took his rope ladder from his utility bag, closed the bag, and headed to The Veil.

On the way Tom thought about Doug. His nephew had quite an imagination. Together they had made up stories about how the Grand Canyon was formed. Tom had shown Doug magic tricks and Doug had always figured them out.

Doug had a game he loved to play, a game that required strategic thinking and used characters with various powers. The characters were depicted on sets of cards one could purchase. Doug told Tom the card sets to buy, but Tom didn't get around to buying any. Doug gladly shared his cards, even some with good, strong powers so Tom could have a chance to win.

TOM WENT TO the cloud shuttle, attached his rope ladder, boarded the shuttle, and went through The Veil. He set his destination to Doug's room.

This time Tom missed his mark, landing behind the shower curtain in the main bathroom, the one that Doug shared with his two sisters. He got tangled in the curtain and accidentally knocked it down, rod and all.

He was embarrassed and hoped he hadn't wakened anyone. He'd done a similar thing on his last visit to the family when he was still on Earth. Only that time the rod had been broken and needed to be replaced. Tom had gone to a local hardware store and bought a new one. Suzanne approved of the replacement, saying it had better tension than the old one and should stay put.

Wonder why I missed my mark.

Tom considered possible reasons: maybe he'd been thinking too hard about Doug and not keeping an eye on his ELV. Maybe the skylight in the bathroom had been easier to get through. He'd ask Ralph when he got back.

Before Tom could pick up the shower curtain and rod to rehang it, Suzanne came into the room. Her eyes were half shut and she was tiptoeing. Tom figured she probably had made the trip to the kids' bathroom so many times during the night when the kids had been sick or had woken up from bad dreams that she didn't need to turn on the light switch. A small plug-in nightlight gave some light. She picked up the rod and shower curtain, adjusted the tension in the rod, and set it in its proper position between the walls.

"That hasn't happened since Tom was here," she mumbled.

Tom watched as Suzanne checked each of the kids' bedrooms before returning to bed herself.

The bathroom smelled of bubblegum, probably from the kids' toothpaste or mouthwash. Though the nightlight was dim, Tom could tell the bathroom was painted yellow with matching towels, tooth brush holders, and soap dishes.

After Suzanne left, Tom went to Doug's room. He looked at the essay on Doug's desk and when he read it, the memory of playing games with his nephew triggered another idea. The game he and Doug had played featured characters with special strengths. Tom searched Doug's room and found the game. He chose the card of the character with all the powers and placed it on Doug's paper along with the coin.

Tom went downstairs to wait until morning. He didn't want to stay in the house and possibly disturb the family, so he slipped out the patio door and waited in the shed in the backyard. While he waited he thought of the nights when he and Liz had visited. Suzanne's husband would get a bunch of guys together to play cards. Nothing serious, mainly a chance for some pizza and beers—or sodas, in Tom's case—and a lot of laughs. He had so many wonderful memories; his mind darted quickly from one to another.

Knowing Suzanne was an earlier riser, Tom went back into the house just before dawn. He looked at the family pictures clipped on the fridge along with notes and reminders. One paper came loose and fell to the floor. Tom picked it up and tried to recall where it might have fallen from. He saw it was her to-do list and put it on the center of the door, guessing that might be where it had been.

At sunrise, Suzanne came into the kitchen, showing no evidence of being woken up during the night. She reviewed her to-do list for the day while she waited for the kids to come downstairs for breakfast.

Doug's seven-year-old sister, Felicity, came into the kitchen, brushing her long, blond hair, and asked Suzanne if she'd heard the noise during the night and knew what it was.

"The shower curtain came down."

"I couldn't get back to sleep after that. Who was in the shower anyway?"

"Nobody. I didn't see anything unusual; I just put it back up."

"Remember last time Uncle Tom visited? He broke the shower rod and the curtain came down. That was funny." Felicity giggled.

Doug came into the kitchen, a puzzled look on his usually smiling face. "Mom, one of the girls was in my room last night. When I went to bed the only thing on my desk was my paper for English. This morning I found this card and coin on top of the essay."

Felicity denied having anything to do with the card.

"By the way, did anyone hear the commotion in the bathroom last night? Was Dad in the shower?" Doug asked.

"No, the shower curtain just came down," Suzanne and Felicity said at the same time. They looked at each other and started laughing.

Mary, a second-grader, was searching through her backpack as she wandered into the kitchen. She placed her backpack over her chair and sat down at the table. Not one to be left out, she asked what the laughing was about and was told about the shower curtain.

"Mom, for some reason, I'd like waffles this morning. Do we have time?" Mary asked.

Suzanne checked her watch. "If we don't dilly-dally, we do. Do you want to make them?"

"Sure," Mary said.

"I'll help." Doug grabbed milk from the refrigerator while Felicity set the table.

Mary kept an eye on the waffles. "I don't think we've had waffles since the last time Uncle Tom was here. He knocked the shower curtain down, too, didn't he?"

Doug showed Mary the card and coin he'd found on his desk. "Do you know anything about this?"

"Why should I?" Mary glanced at the card and tried to grab it. "Let me see."

Doug held on to the card. "When I went to bed last night, the only thing on my desk was my English assignment. This morning, I found this card and coin on top of my paper. I want to know which one of you two came into my room." He looked at Felicity, then back to Mary.

Mary shook her head. "I know better than even go in your room. Where do you think it came from?"

"I don't know. I don't think I've played this game since the last time Uncle Tom was here. Maybe he was the one who left the card on my desk."

"While you figure out how the card got on Doug's desk, I'm going to check the weather and traffic before I take you to school and head for work." Suzanne turned the radio on.

The radio was playing a familiar tune. Tom knew this song by heart. He didn't remember how he came to love it so much. On Earth, when he heard this song and Liz was with him, he'd sing the song to her and pat her knee in rhythm with the song. It was unofficially their song.

"Wasn't that Uncle Tom's favorite song?" Mary asked.

Suzanne nodded.

"Maybe Uncle Tom knocked the shower curtain down and put the card on Doug's desk," Felicity said, her eyes wide. "Maybe Uncle Tom turned into a ghost." Felicity shuddered. "That would be spooky. Doug, can I sleep in your room tonight? I'll keep my flashlight under the covers."

"I bet if it was Uncle Tom," Mary said, "he'd be a friendly ghost and play funny tricks. Doug, can I bring in my sleeping bag and sleep in your room, too? Maybe we can catch Uncle Tom doing something sneaky."

Doug asked his mom to help him decide what to do about the girls. Suzanne said, "It's Friday night; there's no school tomorrow. You guys figure it out."

While eating breakfast, the kids talked about all sleeping in Doug's room and staying awake to see if Ghost Tom would return. There was a loft upstairs outside their bedrooms and they decided that would be a better place for a stakeout. Suzanne gave her okay.

After they cleaned their plates and put them in the dishwasher, the girls raced off to the bathroom for one last check of their hair and clothes.

"All clues point to Uncle Tom playing a trick on us: the shower curtain, the waffles, the song on the radio," Doug said as he helped Suzanne finish cleaning up. "After school, I'm going to check some things on the Internet. I'll get this figured out."

Suzanne nodded. "I'm sure you will."

Before Suzanne gathered her cell phone, her keys, and her tote bag, she looked at a picture of Tom that hung with other family photos in a collage in the hallway. "Tom, you always could get the kids going. Tonight could get pretty crazy."

Too bad he couldn't hang around. Tom gathered his utility bag and his rope ladder.

Suzanne gave the signal. "Okay, guys, we're leaving." The kids raced to the car and took their places. Tom followed them out and watched from the driveway until Suzanne backed out.

Tonight should be interesting. They all have such vivid imaginations. Who knows what they'll come up with?

He sought out the nearest coffee shop for his return.

I can't stay here, much as I'd like to. I'll play out the SWEEP and see what happens. Then maybe I can come back and spend some time.

Going through The Veil and his Brick Wall felt more like breaking through a piece of plastic wrap this time, and before he knew it, Tom was back in Heaven.

Ralph was right, going through is getting easier each time.

❧❧ ❧❧ ❧❧

SECTION SIX

A DAY OF CELEBRATION

❧❧ ❧❧ ❧❧

Chapter 39

CELEBRATION OF LIFE

T OM SENSED SOMETHING unusual was about to happen. *Feels like the day I died. I need some time alone. Think I'll find a secluded spot to sit and watch the earth go by.*

As Tom wandered around, he came across a flat green area. It was about three city blocks long and two city blocks wide. Tom thought it might be a park, however there were no picnic tables, no benches, no walking paths, no playground equipment; nothing he would expect to see in a park on Earth. The only thing in this green area was a tree in the far right corner. The tree had a long trunk and a large overhanging of leaves which looked good for shade. The area was quiet and Tom decided it was the perfect place to be alone while he figured out what his funk was all about and how to get out of it.

Tom walked over to the tree and sat down under it, his back up against the trunk. He took his ELV from his utility bag. He didn't use the ELV, but watched the movement of the clouds for a few moments.

His mind wandered and he found himself thinking about the day he and Liz had strolled along a beach in northern California. The blue ocean had been to their left and rocky cliffs to their right. They had climbed some rocks to the top of one of the cliffs and sat to watch the waves coming and going. They enjoyed the view and relaxed to the point they didn't notice the tide getting closer and closer. They got soaked by spray from one of the waves and decided it was time to move on.

He didn't know why he felt so lethargic today. If he had been on Earth, and it had been a work day, he probably would've declared a "mental health day" and called in sick. If it had happened on a weekend, what he would have done to get out of the funk depended on Liz's plans. If she had errands to do out of the house, he probably would've stayed home and played around on his computer. If she was staying home to do chores, he most likely would've gone someplace to play nickel slots, both activities that, for him, didn't require too much thinking.

Although he had his ELV out, he didn't want to set his sights on anyone or anyplace in particular. He closed his eyes and let his thoughts wander back to his days on Earth.

Imagining and remembering sure aren't as good as being there. I miss those crazy people. What I'd give for one more day. But, then I'd just want another. Guess I could use my ELV and get a view of what's going on.

"There you are, sir." Tom heard Ralph calling him from a distance. He didn't want to be disturbed and hoped if he continued to keep his eyes closed, Ralph would just go away. But Ralph persisted. When Ralph was right next to him, Tom opened his eyes and rubbed them as though he had been in a deep sleep.

"Ralph, what are you doing way out here? I hoped no one else knew about this place. I was looking for a quiet, secluded spot and this seemed remote enough." *Ralph, you really are being a pain. Please go away. I just want to be left alone until I get out of this funk. I need time to myself!*

"Have you not seen all the star messages around you? There must be dozens."

Actually, Tom had not seen them. His eyes had been closed. Now everywhere he looked there were stars, so many stars he was reminded of the junk emails he used to get.

"I'll look at them later."

"I do have an important message from The Controller. He asked me to personally deliver it to you on His behalf. Why don't you look at some of these other messages first? They may give you a hint at what The Controller wants you to know."

Ralph grabbed a few messages and read them to Tom.

"'Thinking of you and Liz today. Sorry I can't be there. I'm on vacation with my family. I sure miss working with you. Especially miss the golf meetings. JRT.'

"This one says, 'Happy Birthday, Uncle Tom. Miss you. Can we blow out the candles on your birthday cake and make a wish? We wish you were here. Love you.'"

This message jolted Tom. *My birthday? Maybe that's why I'm in such a funk.*

The next message Ralph selected read, "'Tom, We're all in shock. You were a great guy. I hope I can find something appropriate to say to Liz. The two of you were an amazing couple. Love, Laura.'"

Ralph grabbed a smaller star. "This one says 'Happy Birthday, Big Guy!' Did most of your friends call you Big Guy?"

"Just one very special little buddy of mine."

"I see," Ralph said quietly.

Tom was confused. *Where did JRT want to be?* Maybe reading more of the messages would help make sense of this whole thing.

Tom sighed. "I guess I should take a look at the messages. You said you had one from The Controller. Guess I should read it first."

Tom opened the large gold envelope from The Controller. He put on his glasses and read:

Greetings Tom,

Today is a special day for you. It marks the anniversary of the start of your most recent life on Earth. It is also the day your family and friends have chosen to gather and celebrate the time you shared with them.

I have been bombarded with messages from Earth concerning you. Some are thankful for the opportunity to have known you. Others are mad because you are no longer on Earth with them and think I took you from them too soon. Most are asking that I bless you.

In keeping with our policy for Celebrations of Life, enclosed are two passes for you and your guardian angel to attend this event and any pre- or post-event gatherings. The pass is valid for one Earth day and is restricted to a fifty-mile radius of the site of the Celebration.

I've made arrangements for your transportation to the golf course where your Celebration will be held. You'll be riding the wind. The wind quickens your arrival to the Celebration. Give the passes to Ralph; he will know how to call the wind.

Yes! There will be birthday cake! Bring me back a piece—if it's angel food.

Be sure to return within one day. I know how you tend to lose track of time when you're with friends. Ralph, I'm sure, will keep you punctual.

Enjoy the day and recognize you are considered "A friend to all."

Bless you,

The Controller

❧ ❧ ❧

Chapter 40

RIDING THE WIND

TOM PUT DOWN the letter and the sentiments of the messages came together. It was his birthday. A celebration of his life was planned for today. That must be what JRT was referring to.

He handed the passes to Ralph. Ralph pressed a small button on each of them and a loud whistle sounded. The wind was in front of them within an instant. Ralph hopped onto the wind; Tom followed. The wind was flat and Tom imagined he was going on a magic carpet ride. As soon as they were on board, the wind headed for Earth. No Veil to go through, no ropes to set. He felt like he had his own personal jet.

Tom jabbered nonstop on the way to his Celebration. He was so excited about his destination and its purpose that he didn't even glance around to see what might be below or above him, as he usually liked to do when he was flying. Leave it to Liz to hold his memorial services on his birthday. He couldn't have asked for a better gift—except to attend the celebration and The Controller had taken care of that.

"I doubt anyone will be there except for Liz and our families. But I hope some of my friends show up. I'd like you to meet a few of them. Liz told me once memorial services were not for the deceased, but for the living as way to share their grief. I hope tons of people are there for her."

Tom couldn't contain his eagerness to get to the golf course. "I'm curious about this one being held at a golf course. I know people have weddings and receptions at golf courses. But can't say I ever heard of a Celebration of Life at one. A bit out of the ordinary, but Liz and I tried never to do anything the conventional way."

Tom hadn't been this excited in weeks. As they approached the golf course he saw there were actually some people milling around.

He got out his trusty ELV. He didn't know whether he'd need it or not, but he had it with him just in case. It worked and he saw many people he recognized.

He nudged Ralph with his elbow. "The Devil is here. He's one person I really want you to meet."

Ralph raised an eyebrow. "Excuse me?"

"Oh, not the real devil. *The Devil* was the code name my friend Ken and I had for each other. On nice afternoons, one of us would tempt the other to sneak out of work early to play a little golf. It didn't take much arm twisting to get us headed to the golf course under the pretext of an emergency meeting."

"Sir, please refrain from referring to him as *the Devil*. Something about your code name seems so wrong, especially today, considering The Controller Himself took time to recognize you."

"Ken's so funny." Tom chuckled. "He's always losing something besides lots of golf balls. I bet he loses two pairs of sunglasses every month."

The vicinity where the course was located was typically windy, especially late in the afternoon. The gust of wind Tom and Ralph rode seemed normal and blended in nicely with the hot summer winds coming off the hills. The wind made a smooth landing at the course. It stopped near the pro shop and Tom and Ralph stepped off.

The day was extremely hot, well over one hundred degrees. That was one thing Tom did not miss about Earth—the extreme heat, or the extreme cold, for that matter. The sky was a brilliant blue, there were no clouds to give shade.

The course looked lush and well maintained as always. Although it seemed forever, Tom guessed it had been less than two months since he had last played this course.

The veranda, or tent, as Tom preferred to call it, was set up for a special event.

Tom held his hand to his chest. He couldn't believe how many people were milling about. He recognized every one of them as a friend, someone there because of *him*, not to play golf. A few feet in front of him, he saw his friend, Ken, aka The Devil.

He nudged Ralph. "Look there's Ken. He's the one with the glass of wine. Let's get closer and hear what he has to say." Ken was surrounded by about eight or so people.

Tom listened in on their conversation as he looked around at other friends in the group. He was shocked when he saw his friend and co-worker, Phil. Phil hadn't come into the office for several weeks before Tom's passing because of the terrible back pain he'd been experiencing. Tom had talked to him on a regular basis, but hadn't actually seen him. He still seemed to be in a lot of pain, limping so much he could hardly walk.

What a friend. Don't know that I could have gotten here in that kind of pain.

And there was Rick. Rick had come from halfway across the country to be there. Tom wished he could talk to the guy; Rick was now completely bald at an unusually young age. Tom would have loved to razz him about the new hairstyle, or lack thereof.

On the other hand, Tom was glad he couldn't be heard when he saw Bill and Marsha. They looked like they had aged about ten years since he had last seen them. Actually, it had been over five years ago. He was sure he would have blurted out something he would have regretted. Also he was glad he could not be seen. Although he had a poker face most of the time, he didn't think he would have been able to hide his initial shock at their current appearance.

Ken was talking about where he'd been when he heard the shocking news of Tom's passing. He was on the twelfth hole of the golf course when he got a call telling him Tom had passed away. He had no desire to finish the round, so he got into his cart and sped toward the clubhouse. On the way, his sunglasses, which had been in the cart, fell out. He heard them hit the cart path, but didn't take time to stop for them. He wanted to be with his friends gathering at Froggy's as soon as possible.

Ken joked. "Don't know what was worse, losing Tom or losing those darn sunglasses. The glasses had all the latest technology: scratchproof, smudge-proof, automatic brightness control. Wish I could find them, but they probably got run over by another cart."

Tom grinned and nodded. *There he goes again; another pair of sunglasses lost. And comparing losing sunglasses to me dying—that deserves me getting back at him if I can.*

The group broke up to mingle with other guests. Ken and several others headed to the veranda where appetizers and drinks were available. Tom followed to see who else was there. The veranda was a large tent set on a grassy area outside the banquet room of the golf club facilities. Today, inside the veranda, over one hundred and fifty folding chairs were arranged in rows. A podium had been set up in the front center of the room. An audio-video presentation was playing on a screen in the left front corner. In the right front corner, pictures of and tributes to Tom brought by friends and family were displayed.

The right side of the tent was open so guests who could not find seating inside could sit at outside tables and see in.

In the back left corner was a bar where Ken was getting another glass of wine. A buffet table was off to the left featuring cheese and crackers, fruit, veggies, dip, carved turkey, and shrimp.

The Controller had been right. On another table to the right of the appetizers there was a birthday cake with candles. Seeing the cake and candles hit Tom hard. He realized even more how much he missed Earth and its celebrations with family and friends. He felt a sadness stirring inside him. He bit his lip hard and turned away from the cake table.

Today would have been my fifty-fifth birthday. It's not fair! This wasn't supposed to happen to me.

A few friends were viewing the audio-visual slide presentation. Tom heard a few of his favorite songs and viewed a few of the photos. But hearing the music and seeing photos of vacations, holidays, and golf tournaments that had been such a happy part of his life made him depressed again. He missed those things.

He'd lived a good life and he was the first to admit it and be thankful for it. He had worked hard for his achievements, but recognized good supporters and opportunities had helped him along the way. He and Liz had a comfortable home, careers that were satisfying, and had been able to pursue activities they both enjoyed. They'd loved playing golf, traveling, exploring new places, and taking in an occasional concert or play.

The most important thing to Tom was his relationship with Liz. It surpassed love; they were best friends and soulmates. Their love was usually silly and joking, carefree with the two of them smiling and walking hand in hand. They were blessed and they knew it.

Sometimes their serious sides had kicked in and they would ask, "What would I do without you?" thinking of what would happen to the one still on Earth after the other passed. Now Tom was facing the same question, only from the other side.

How could his spirit survive without Liz?

Tom turned his attention to something else. He looked to see who was watching the video. Mostly they were friends of Liz. He recognized a few as ladies she often had lunch with. A few others he didn't recognize. But after listening to some of their conversation, he guessed they were friends from one of her volunteer activities.

He needed a distraction to put his sadness aside if he could. He looked around for Ralph and spotted him eating some shrimp. Ralph even had a glass of wine in his hand. Tom walked over to Ralph. "I want to mess with Ken. If I can find his lost sunglasses and place them somewhere he can discover them today, he'll freak out. I'm going to check around and look in the cart barn."

Tom went into the cart barn where the golf carts were maintained and lost items were stored. This cart barn held approximately one hundred carts and was a metal structure. It was where carts were cleaned after use and prepared for the next group. Many items were forgotten in the carts: jackets, phones, club covers, sunglasses, wallets, keys. When such items were left behind, they were held in Lost and Found.

He not only checked the lost and found items that were stored in a box, he checked all of the carts currently in the barn in case the sunglasses had been overlooked, but came up empty-handed.

Ralph was waiting outside and Tom let him know he was going to check the clubhouse. Tom went inside and combed every inch. He checked the pro shop, including behind the check-in desk. He checked around the merchandise displays. He checked the restaurant and bar areas. He checked both the men's and women's locker rooms. In the men's locker room, he picked up a piece of cinnamon gum. The club provided items for its members' use to freshen up after a round of golf: combs, toothpaste, deodorant. Included were pieces of cinnamon gum, another way to freshen breath. Tom always chewed a piece after golf. He wondered about taking a piece, but he figured Liz had kept up with their dues and it would okay. He popped a stick of gum into his mouth and enjoyed the burst of flavor.

He did not find a pair of sunglasses. He wasn't surprised. Ken's probably right. Most likely the glasses were run over. Ken would be so freaked out if he found his sunglasses today.

Tom headed to the exit. As he did, he saw Liz coming into the clubhouse; she was talking to the catering manager. She didn't even flinch when their paths crossed. He slumped and walked over to where Ralph was waiting.

~~ ~~ ~~

"WHERE'S THAT GUST of wind we rode in on?" Ralph asked. "You'll never get around to all these guests unless you pick up your speed."

Tom attempted to make a joke and cover his disappointment at Liz not sensing his presence. "Yeah, I guess some of the wind has been taken from my sails. I didn't find the sunglasses, but I did see Liz. I just wanted to grab her and hug her tight and never let her go."

"Didn't you expect to see her today?"

"I guess I knew I'd see her. I really hadn't thought about how I'd feel when I did. I don't think she had any idea I was so close to her."

"She might have been distracted since she was talking to someone. I'm sure her mind is on you. After all, today is all about you."

Tom appreciated that Ralph was trying to cheer him up a bit. He tried to smile, but couldn't.

Ralph took charge. "Enough of this pity party. I think I know what will put a smile on your face. You need sunglasses for your friend."

"How do you suggest we pull that off? The glasses Ken had were a one-time special TV offer."

"Sir, I am highly trained in vibration and energy levels," Ralph said. "You have quite the imagination. We can . . . no, we *will* pull it off!"

Tom had never seen that level of excitement from Ralph and was encouraged.

Ralph covered his eyes with his hands. When he uncovered his eyes, a pair of oversized, bright yellow plastic sunglasses adorned his face.

Tom winced. "Those look like part of a kid's Halloween costume. Good attempt, though. Can I try?"

"Go ahead, sir. Just cover your eyes. Visualize the style of the sunglasses you want and focus all your energy on that image."

Tom's first attempt produced a pair of plastic glasses with a fake nose and mustache. "Always wanted a pair of these. Can I keep them? They might come in handy for a joke."

"Whatever you want, sir. Now think. Do you know exactly what Ken's glasses looked like?"

"I should. When he bought 'em he showed me every detail. He bragged about the glasses having the latest technology. Ken's a salesperson's dream; he falls for any gimmick. What he needs is a pair of sunglasses that can't be lost, but that feature hasn't been developed yet."

Tom made several attempts to recreate Ken's sunglasses. He produced piles of sunglasses, but none duplicated Ken's.

"I remember the initials, KS, were on the temples. Ken told me the glasses were personalized for him, Ken Starr. The KS on the glasses were actually the initials for the name of the design company."

He scratched his head. "Wish I could remember. Wait. I know! When I was watching the video earlier, I saw a photo from a recent golf tournament Ken and I played in. Ken was wearing those sunglasses. I need to look at that picture again."

Tom and Ralph went into the reception area. The coordinator of the Celebration of Life event had just invited everyone to watch the Eighteen-Shot Salute, which would take place on the driving range. It was a steep walk to the range, so carts were available. The guests stood and headed for the exit.

When the area cleared, Tom moved close to the screen and waited for the slide presentation to show the photo of Ken with the sunglasses. While they waited for the correct photo, Ralph helped Tom capture the residual positive vibrations from the presence of friends and family. When the correct photo showed up, using every ounce of his own energy along with the energy in the room, Tom focused on the image of Ken's sunglasses. He held the visual in his mind and closed his eyes. He felt a pair of glasses being slipped onto his face. He opened his eyes, took off the glasses, and examined them closely.

They were an exact replica of Ken's sunglasses.

"Voila! Nothing to this." He showed the sunglasses to Ralph. "Now we can go to the driving range for this eighteen-shot thing and I can put the glasses in Ken's cart." Tom felt as if he'd won the lottery.

❧ ❧ ❧

Chapter 41

THE EIGHTEEN-SHOT SALUTE

TOM LED RALPH to the cart barn where several carts had been cleaned and lined up outside, ready for players' use. Tom slid into the driver's side of the first cart. "This one is good to go. Hop in."

A crazy idea struck him. Ralph will think I've lost my marbles. But what the heck; the worst he can do is say no.

"Think we could fly this puppy?" Tom asked. "Since flying around with Willie in his golf cart, I've wanted to try flying a golf cart on Earth. Now will probably be my only chance."

He'd always viewed Ralph as a stickler for rules and not as an adventurous angel. He was sure Ralph would put the kibosh on the idea.

"Sir, since this is a day to celebrate you, I will make that happen. I need to retrieve some items from my utility bag."

Tom watched in surprise as Ralph pulled out two packets of dust and sprinkled them on the golf cart. "Sir, since this is an Earth object, something that people would normally be able to see, we need to use the invisibility dust. Also, since the cart can be heard on Earth, we need to use this silencer dust."

Ralph reached into his utility bag again and fumbled around for something. His hands came out empty and he looked flustered. He reached into his bag once again and pulled out his spirit communication device. "Excuse me, sir. I need to have a private conversation."

Ralph walked toward the end of the cart barn. Tom watched his guardian angel pace back and forth while communicating with a spirit on the other end of the line. *Very un-Ralph-like. Wonder what's going on. Hope our passes didn't get called back.*

After a few minutes, Ralph returned to the cart. "Sir, I need to apologize. I had known about the Celebration planned for you today and was waiting for The Controller's note before looking for you. Knowing how much you love to fly, I had planned to put wings in my utility bag. I thought I could surprise you with a special flight at some point during the day. But in the excitement, after I received notice that The Controller's note was ready to present to you, it seems I picked up my utility bag, but forgot the wings. I am deeply sorry, sir."

Tom opened his mouth to let Ralph know it was no problem, but Ralph continued without allowing him to say a word.

"Sir, I have called the heaven help line and requested that they bring us a set of wings; however, none are available to lend out for the day. The spirit assisting me suggested an alternative, something about using a ball marker if I have one."

Ralph removed a clip from the brim of his golf hat and pointed to the small round piece attached to it. "Is this what she was referring to, sir?"

Tom had to grin at Ralph's lack of knowledge about golf, especially since the guardian angel had been with Tom his entire life and Tom had played quite a bit of golf. "Imagine so."

"She said to attach it to the cart somehow. She suggested the spot near the ignition key might work or we could try attaching the clip and the ball marker to a visor on the cart. Then we simply tell it to fly. Tell it something like, 'Make this golf cart fly'."

With those words the cart inched forward a few feet.

"Really?" Tom frowned and furrowed his eyebrows. "And that will work?"

"Sir, you have spent some time in Heaven and have only witnessed an inkling of what is possible there. Heaven is a place to make things happen—if one believes. This is only a small thing in comparison to the big problems Heaven has to handle. Please give it a try as my gift to you. I am sorry it is not with the wings as I planned, but I hope this will be acceptable."

Tom gave Ralph a slap on the back, the kind of slap guys give their teammates in sports, and thanked him. He couldn't verbalize what he felt, though his heart was filled with gratitude. He totally would not have expected that kind of thoughtfulness from Ralph.

Tom took the clip and ball marker and attached them near the ignition key inside the cart.

Ralph directed his voice at the ball marker, "Make this golf cart fly."

And they were off and flying a few feet above the ground.

Tom guided the flying golf cart along the cart path. There was a fork in the path. To the left, the path led to the first hole of the course. To the right, the path went uphill to the driving range. They took the turn for the driving range and flew to the top of the hill. Below and to his left, Tom saw the groundskeepers watering the area around the first green. The course needed frequent hand-watering throughout the day to keep it so lush.

He desperately wanted to play the golf course, but now he had a job to do. When the flying cart neared the driving range, he verbally gave the cart instructions to land behind and to the left of the driving range to be out of the way of the participants and the observers assembled for the Eighteen-Shot Salute. Tom looked around as the cart settled to the ground.

There must easily be over a hundred people here.

It was nearing sunset, but still very warm. Many people, especially the women, were fanning themselves with programs they had picked up in the pavilion. There were no trees for shade and the angle of the sun was such that there was no shade available anywhere, even sitting in a golf cart.

The driving range was at the top of the hill and was arranged with nine places for nine people to hit.

Tom found the cart Ken was using. He knew it had to be the one Ken was driving when he saw a set of keys on the driver's seat. The key chain had a place for a photo and a picture of Ken's dog, Lucky, was with the keys. Tom placed the sunglasses next to the keys.

Mission accomplished!

Ralph had a puzzled look on his face. "Sir, I am curious about the Eighteen-Shot Salute. How does it work?"

"Your guess is as good as mine. I've never heard of one before. Musta been one of Liz's brainstorms."

He was still amazed at the number of people who'd gathered for the ceremony. Some of them had traveled from as far away as the east coast. He watched as nine of his closest friends and family members lined up at hitting stations and one-by-one hit a shot onto the driving range. After Liz hit the first shot, she stepped back and waited as the others in the first group hit their shots. Included in the first group were Tom's brothers-in-law, a nephew, several guys Tom had worked with on a daily basis, and Ken.

After nine shots had been hit, the first group moved back and another nine friends stepped forward, completing eighteen shots in Tom's honor. This group included guys Tom knew from the club, a few of his clients, and a couple of guys he had worked with years ago. The last to hit was his brother, Jeremiah. This was especially appropriate since Jeremiah was the last person Tom had played a full round of golf with while on Earth. Tom watched their shots and realized he had influenced each one of their golf games.

Looks like Chuck is still playing with the clubs I helped him pick out during a lunch break over twenty years ago.

Tom thought back to one of his winter hobbies, making custom clubs. That was before everything was available online. He had gotten catalogs by snail mail and ordered the equipment to put the clubs together: scales, balancing tools, tapes, epoxy. He and his customer would experiment with different clubs for shaft stiffness, loft, flight pattern of the ball, and Tom would order, again by snail mail, the equipment his customer felt gave him the most favorable results. Tom would put everything together once he got all the parts. His customers, mostly close friends, got their own customized club at very little cost, just the price of the club head, shaft, and grip. Tom did the work for free. *Jack's swinging well with the club I made for him. I had forgotten about that club since I hadn't seen him for ages.*

And Walt, what can I say? He really should get a new driver. The one I gave him after I replaced mine is too stiff for his swing. But he's too cheap to buy something new.

"I never thought this many people would show up for me," Tom admitted.

"Sir, do you remember the comment in the message from The Controller? You were considered 'A Friend to All'."

"Didn't have a clue. I didn't have a clue."

❧ ❧ ❧

AFTER THE EIGHTEENTH shot landed on the driving range, Tom's friends returned to their carts and paraded back to the pavilion in single file.

Ralph offered to fly the cart they were using. "I shall fly low enough for you to get a good view of everyone."

"Thanks," Tom said with a smile. "I'd love to see who is here. Everyone keeps milling around and I'm sure I've haven't noticed several people."

Ralph made a smooth takeoff and flew low, as he had promised. Tom got a good look at all the attendees: several of the staff from prior jobs, clients, vendors. Even some of the employees of the company that invited him to play in the pro-am golf tournament that fateful day were in attendance. He shook his head in amazement at the tribute being paid to him. He really didn't know whether to laugh or cry. He went with laughing; after all, his smile and laughter were what Liz loved best about him. He uttered, "Unbelievable, simply unbelievable" over and over again.

As Ralph prepared to land the golf cart back at the pavilion, Tom conjured up happy memories he had shared with these people. He told himself to smile and send off happy vibes in case anyone sensed his presence.

The guests returned to the pavilion where they had been previously. Tom looked inside. It was arranged now with tables covered with white linen cloths. Eight chairs were set around each table.

Several groups formed inside and outside. Tom wanted to be with all of them, but couldn't. Until his spirit learned how it could be more than one place at a time, he'd have to make a decision.

Liz and her sisters, along with Jeremiah, were moving from group to group and introducing themselves. There were people he had worked with years ago, some of them from different companies; friends connected because of their shared interest in other sporting activities, like college football; acquaintances from

Froggy's, the sports bar and grill where he and his co-workers met for a cold one after work on Friday nights; members of the business association he presided over; and Liz's friends.

He'd never stopped to think about how diverse his circle of friends was. He felt very blessed and honored that they had all come to celebrate the life he'd shared with them.

His golfing buddies and associates grabbed his attention first.

Bob, a long-time business associate, was wearing a shirt similar to the black-and-gold paisley shirt Tom had picked up at Leona's. Bob reminisced about a time he had asked Tom to help his wife with her position on top. Tom had taken the opportunity to make an off-colored remark that had embarrassed them all.

Jon, a former co-worker, was wearing glasses now.

Guess that aging thing hits us all in some way.

Jon explained Tom's rules for client golf. "Tom loved to take clients out for a game of golf. He was up front with everyone on the first tee. He told clients the game would be nice and friendly for the first six holes. We'd discuss business on the next six. After the twelfth hole, if we had reached an agreement, the game would be relaxed again, with lots of mulligans and gimme putts."

A young man wearing a dress shirt and tie spoke up. Tom didn't recognize him. "I'm new to the business and had always heard Tom was a highly respected leader in the industry. I had an opportunity to meet him the week before he passed away. It was only a quick handshake. He was on his way out for a meeting and I had an appointment with someone else in his office. But he promised to meet with me after he returned from his trip. What you just said doesn't make him sound very professional."

Wes, a client Tom had known for many years, took off his sunglasses and cleaned them. "What's your name, son?"

"Adam."

Now Tom recognized the guy.

"Adam, I'm glad to meet you and want to set the record straight. What you heard about Tom is correct and I'm sorry you're not going to be able to experience the upstanding gentleman we all knew. I left myself open for the client golf rules once." Wes put his sunglasses back on. "Here's the real scoop. When we started doing business together, Tom always invited me to play golf. I turned him down time and time again, because my days were heavily scheduled with corporate meetings. In fact, I usually had to ask Tom to arrange our meetings after traditional business hours. He was always accommodating.

"Finally, he had a draft for the proposal, which he anticipated would be the final draft and would have a renewal contract prepared if I approved and initialed the proposal. He asked again if he could take me out for a round of golf and I think I surprised him with a yes. That's when he told me about his rules for client golf." Wes took a sip of wine from the glass he held.

"Adam, like you, I thought those rules sounded harsh and not like Tom at all. But I accepted and invited myself to lunch before golf. Two reasons—I heard the restaurant here had the best Reuben sandwiches in the area and I wanted to try one. And I wanted to see the proposal before we teed off. I didn't want to spend a miserable afternoon talking business and having my arm twisted out on the course. Golf is frustrating enough for most of us. Bottom line is Tom's two-page proposal was right on the mark. I had my initials on it before Tom even had the lunch tab to sign." Wes took an appetizer and napkin from a tray a server was walking around with.

"By the way, if you like Reubens, I'd highly suggest you try the ones here. They are the best."

Tom was unhappy. He never realized anyone took his client golf rules seriously. Most of his clients knew him better.

But the next story lifted his mood. He had a shirt just like the one Paul was wearing today. The shirts had been given to players in a recent tournament. Tom listened as Paul recalled a charity scramble tournament that they, along with two other guys, had played in about a month before Tom died.

"With a few holes left we figured our team was probably in the top three," Paul said, "but we wanted to win. We took a birdie on the seventeenth hole and figured with another birdie on the eighteenth, we'd finish first.

"Tom was the last to hit on the eighteenth hole. The afternoon breezes had come up and Tom wanted to see how the wind impacted our shots. He adjusted accordingly and his ball landed in the middle of the fairway about thirty yards past the others. His next shot reached the fringe of the par five. The ball was puttable. He took a last look at the putt and knocked it in for an eagle. His play on the last hole won the tournament for us."

Tom smiled at remembering the tournament. It was always nice to win, not so much for the trophy and whatever other prizes there might be, but for the bragging rights.

Even though he was enjoying the conversations, Tom was anxious for Ken to return. Knowing Ken, after I did all that work, he probably didn't even notice the glasses and sat on them.

A cart raced in from the driving range. Ken was driving, waving a pair of sunglasses like a flag. He brought the cart to an abrupt halt and jumped out before the cart stopped.

"Look at this." Ken waved the sunglasses for everyone to see. "You're not going to believe this. I found the sunglasses I lost the day Tom died. They were in my cart after the Eighteen-Shot Salute. Weird, huh?"

Ken's wife, Cheryl, approached the group and invited everyone to come inside the pavilion for more appetizers, another drink or two, and a few more stories. The couple held hands as they went inside.

Cheryl's the perfect wife for Ken. Although everyone loves Ken, he has a tendency to get sidetracked. Cheryl seems able to put up with it and keep him moving along. She's one beautiful, classy lady.

Ken asked if she had heard about his sunglasses. She nodded and sighed. "Really amazing. But then again, Tom was an amazing guy. It's almost like he's here. It makes one wonder."

Tom and Ralph followed everyone back to the pavilion. Along the way, Tom thought about Cheryl's remark. *Funny what people will say about someone when they don't know that person is listening. I guess talking behind someone's back doesn't necessarily mean bad things. If I knew how to strut around like a proud peacock, I would.*

It was very close to sunset. The winds had subsided and Bob suggested everyone gather outside on the veranda overlooking the lake to watch the sunset and for a final toast. Everyone raised a glass.

"To Tom, a friend to all."

Chapter 42

REFLECTIONS

A FTER THE TOAST, Tom followed his friends around the clubhouse and out to the parking lot. A majority of the people slowly left.

He wondered how they could leave before they had any of the cake, but realized a couple of things. As adults, many of his friends no longer cared about celebrating birthdays and having cake the way he still did. And today was about him. His friends had come to honor him, and he had had some pretty amazing friends.

Some of the couples walked hand in hand. Some friends who hadn't seen each other for a while lingered to say good-bye, agreeing to do lunch soon. Tom realized as he looked back at life, that most of the time, the 'let's do lunch' thing never happened. Maybe after today, some of his friends would realize the importance of making the important things in life happen: the smiles, the hugs, the laughs, the incredible moments of friendship.

There was a bench outside the front of the clubhouse and Tom sat down. Like earlier in the day, he wanted a few moments alone to think. He was alone now. Ralph was still at the pavilion having another glass of wine. *Wonder if guardian angels can get drunk.* Tom smirked as the idea of taking an inebriated Ralph back to Heaven floated across his mind.

But, unlike this morning, now he wasn't in a funk; he was on an incredible high and needed to take it all in emotionally. A lot of the guys he used to meet with at Froggy's had wondered why Tom didn't drink. They all liked the buzz they got from beer or wine. Tom didn't need that stuff to get a good feeling; he got a natural high on life.

Besides the unexpected turnout, Tom's head was spinning from the number of smiles he had seen and the outbursts of laughter he had heard. To him, that was the most important part of his life—well, after his relationship with Liz—making people smile and laugh. He hoped that he might be remembered again by his friends and that they would smile at the memories.

He sat a few more moments, then slapped his hands on his knees and got up. *There's still more to this day.*

He wanted to see about getting a piece of birthday cake and, hopefully, catch a ride home with Liz.

TOM DIDN'T HAVE long to wait as his younger nieces and nephews reminded Liz about the birthday cake. He would really miss birthday cake. *Maybe there is birthday cake in Heaven. I had cake at the dinner after the golf match with Queen Mary. If there are cakes in Heaven, shouldn't be too difficult to decorate them for special occasions. Maybe I can start a new tradition.*

Tom's cake was a round two-layer cake with white frosting and extra decorative frosting around the bottom edge. The top had a green background like a golf course and had a small plastic golfer standing on top.

As a kid, his mom would only let him have a tiny piece of his birthday cake. As an adult, Tom wondered if his mom had been ahead of the times in her nutritional knowledge or if she had just flat-out hated spending time in the kitchen. When he was growing up, it was normal to have homemade desserts after the evening meal: cakes, cookies, pies. Tom's mom begrudgingly fulfilled this expectation, but kept track of every cookie or piece of cake she doled out. She didn't want to be baking every day. Tom and his dad had often joked she had drawn serial numbers on the cookies and measured the cake on a regular basis. Every time his dad had snuck into the kitchen later in the evening for a cookie or, with the precision of a surgeon, cut the tiniest slice of cake, Mom knew about it. Naturally, Tom was blamed. He was never the culprit—he wasn't brave enough to try—but he didn't rat his dad out. The two of them had an understanding that if Mom dealt out some ridiculous punishment for whatever reason, Dad would overrule the sentence. One of her favorite punishments was no TV for twenty years. Tom laughed to himself. *If it was up to Mom, I still wouldn't be watching TV.*

When he'd met Liz and her family, Tom had experienced a whole new level of birthday celebration. Birthdays in Liz's family were a big deal and cakes were an important part of the day.

Tom and Liz's nieces and nephews were the only kids at the Celebration. In addition to Doug and his two sisters, who Tom had seen recently in their home when he had knocked down the shower curtain, there was another family of three girls all under the under the age of ten, completing the group of cousins, as they called themselves.

Jeremiah's daughter, Beth, was also there. She would be starting college in the fall. Tom still thought of her as the little girl who loved to play hide-and-seek, but now noted that she had turned into a beautiful young woman.

The younger kids were waiting at the cake table for Liz to give the okay for them to start the cake ceremony: lighting the candles, singing the birthday song, and eating the cake. Liz was talking to Ken. Kayla, the oldest of the three sisters, offered to get Liz. She pranced over, but politely waited until Liz finished her conversation with Ken to ask about the cake. Liz returned with Kayla to the cake table.

"We need to find your moms and dads to see if they want to sing and have some cake. They might be putting some things back in my car."

Mary and Felicity raced off to find their parents. One of Mary's flip-flops came off and Felicity kicked it halfway across the pavilion. Mary chased after her. Felicity got to the flip-flop first. She picked it up and handed it back to Mary, then both proceeded to find Mom and Dad.

Before Felicity and Mary returned with their parents, another sister of Liz's, Donna—and her husband, Tony—came over to see what was going on.

Jeremiah and his family joined the group. "Can't have cake without me," Jeremiah said.

Felicity and Mary playfully dragged their mom and dad over.

"Looks like we're all here. Does anyone want cake?" Liz asked.

The response was lots of jumping up and down, waving arms, shouts of, "Yes, yes, yes!"

Liz looked around and crinkled her nose. "I think I'll put on the candles." She had two numbered candles, both fives, that she arranged in the center of the cake.

"Beth, when I say ready, will you light the candles?" Liz asked.

Beth picked up the lighter from the table. Then the kids argued over who was going to blow out the candles.

"After the candles are lit, we'll all sing 'Happy Birthday'," Liz said. "Doug, after the song, please count to three as a signal for everyone to blow out the candles together."

Doug didn't look like a little boy today, with his button-down shirt and long khaki pants. He nodded solemnly at Liz, as if she'd just given him a serious chore. He never had a chance to count to three, however. Before the song was over, the candles went out.

Mary stomped. "It's not fair. Felt like the wind blew them out."

Smiley, who had been given the nickname by her grandpa because she was always smiling, shook her head. "No, it felt like Uncle Tom did it."

Doug held up his hands. "We'll light them again. On the count of three, we'll all blow them out."

"I wish Uncle Tom would come back," Mary whispered.

"You said your wish out loud; now it will never happen," Kayla reminded her.

"My mom says Uncle Tom will always be in our hearts," Felicity said.

Leigh added, "Uncle Tom was my godfather. Liz says Uncle Tom is my special guardian angel."

AFTER BETH LIT the candles, Tom heard the sincerest version of "Happy Birthday" ever. He was facing the kids. There wasn't much light from the two candles, but Tom detected a light in the kids' eyes and the expressions on their faces gave him great expectations they would lead fulfilling lives and bring hope to the future of the world.

"One, two, three!" Doug barely got the count finished and the candles were out, this time the kids had blown them out.

Miley bounced on her toes and clapped. "Now we'll all get our wishes."

Tom hoped so, because he, too, had made a wish for his nieces and nephews. *I hope you all find happiness and a best friend for life. If you find half of the happiness I did, you'll have great lives.*

All the kids wanted the first piece of cake. Liz ended the squabbling by saying they would be served by age, with the youngest getting the first piece.

Two-year-old Leigh smiled at that decision. She took a plate and held it against her chest as she got in line to be first. Her mom stood behind her and readjusted Leigh's two ponytails which had loosened during the course of the day.

Leigh requested extra frosting.

Liz looked at her sisters. "Will you two cut the cake? You know how much you want your kids to have; I don't want to be responsible for any sugar highs you have to deal with tonight."

There was only one table and set of chairs still set up in the pavilion. The kids sat there and Tom watched them smiling and enjoying the cake, licking frosting off with their fingers. The smiles on the kids' faces delighted him.

Even things as simple as a piece of cake brought joy to a child. The girls were swinging their legs and comparing their new flip-flops and the colors on their toenails: bright shades of pink, green, orange, yellow, blue. Tom grimaced when he saw the nail colors, but he knew the girls loved them.

Finally, their families were ready to leave and Liz walked with them to the parking lot. Her purse was still in the pavilion, so Tom and Ralph knew she would be back.

"Sir, I want to try some of this cake. The kids seemed to enjoy it so much. Let me know if Liz is on her way back. I'm going to get the invisibility dust out and put it on a couple pieces for us." Ralph quickly sprinkled the cake and then handed Tom a slice before tasting it himself. "Uhm. Quite tasty, sir. It does seem to be special compared to other cakes. Is there a secret ingredient?"

Tom had to laugh. Ralph had cake all over his face, like a toddler with his or her first birthday cake. "Maybe it's the extra frosting," Tom said, "or maybe it's the excitement and happiness that comes with it."

They had their cake finished before Liz came back for her purse. They followed her to the parking lot.

Tom watched her get into her car. "Okay if I go for a little ride?"

Ralph looked at the sky. "Looks like you have sufficient time before our passes expire. Go for it. I shall follow you on the wind."

Tom got into the car on the passenger side and patted Liz's right knee. Liz reached with her right hand and touched the same spot. She looked his direction and smiled.

She knows. She knows I'm here.

"Need to roll down the window and get things cooled off." Liz rolled down the window and a small white feather blew in and landed on her right knee. She picked it up and tried to let it go back out the opened window. The feather came back and landed again on her knee.

"Okay," she said to the feather. "I guess you can come along for the ride."

Tom made a mental note about the feather. Some spirits like Mrs. Blake, the woman he had met at the bank, dropped coins to let their families know when they were thinking about them. Liz had paid particular attention to the feather. He would try to use feathers as a sign to Liz that he was watching over her. He was sure she would get it. And he was sure that in Heaven he could get his hands on some feathers that might drop from angels' wings.

When Liz came to a stop at the next red light, she looked over at the passenger seat. Tom saw her eyes look directly into his, as if she could really visualize him. "How about you? You want to ride around with me?"

Tom telepathically answered yes.

"Alrighty then. Want some music? I do." She slid a CD into the player. "I hope I made good choices. I wanted some of your favorites to play at your celebration."

Liz turned up the volume. For the moment, music made a connection between the two of them.

She turned into their driveway and waited for the garage door to open. Liz looked over at the passenger seat again. "Makes me wonder," she said. Then with her right hand, she patted Tom's knee and added. "No! I don't wonder. I know!" She smiled, but not the big carefree smile she'd had before they were torn apart.

Tom was glad she'd responded to his presence, but how long would they be able to keep their connection going?

Liz pulled into the garage, opened her car door, and headed into the house. Tom went out the garage door to the driveway. The wind and Ralph were waiting for him.

≈≈ ≈≈ ≈≈

SECTION SEVEN

MORE WONDERS AND DISCOVERIES

≈≈ ≈≈ ≈≈

Chapter 43

BETH AND A MOOSE

TOM WAS AT the golf course with Ralph. It was early and the ground was covered with morning dew. The course had the smell of freshly mowed grass, which Tom could now enjoy without the sneezing and watery eyes that had come with his allergies on Earth.

They were at Paradise Greens at Angels Ridge, the course at St. Andrew's Gate, practicing chip shots. Tom was teaching Ralph how to play golf. In spite of all the years Ralph had been around Tom, Ralph hadn't picked up on the golf swing or playing strategy, even with as much golf as Tom had played.

Tom had started by working with Ralph on the driver and fairway woods, but Ralph got frustrated with that part of the game. A change of pace would probably be good, so Tom planned to work on Ralph's short game. Tom had been the envy of his friends on Earth because of his short game: the pitch shots, the chip shots, shots from the sand. Hopefully, Ralph would enjoy that aspect of the game as much as he did.

Paradise Greens had great practice facilities: an area for chip shots, a practice green surrounded by sand hazards for working on sand shots, and a green for putting. He liked coming to Paradise Greens with Ralph because if St. Andrew and Kyle were there and had time, they would pair up with Tom and Ralph to play a quick round. Both St. Andrew and Kyle gave Tom great tips.

Ralph was catching on quickly to the short game, knocking a few shots close to the hole. St. Andrew came out of the pro shop to say "hi" and see how things were going. Ralph's next shot fell into the hole.

"Impressive." St. Andrew said. "You fellas playing today?"

"No, just sharpening our game," Tom said. "Need to keep up with you next time we play."

"Well, have fun. But your plans may be changing." St. Andrew pointed to a white star approaching Tom.

The star was from Beth, one of his nieces.

Hi Tom,

I'm on vacation with some friends. Today we're hiking in a national forest. It would be so awesome if we saw a moose. There are moose in the park, but the rangers told us we probably wouldn't see any. I guess moose don't hang out near the trail we'll be on.

Maybe, if I wish hard enough and keep my fingers crossed, I'll spot one.

Remember your stuffed animal, W. S. Moose? The stories you told me about him when I was little were 'a-moosing.'

It was funny when my bear, Ms. Bear, married W. S. Moose.

Anyway, hope to get a glimpse of a moose. They remind me of you.

Love ya,

Beth

Tom chuckled after reading the star and handed it Ralph. "Take a look at this. I have a little surprise in mind that could be fun for Beth, but I might need some help with it."

Ralph read the note and gave it back to Tom. "And what is it you are scheming, sir?"

"Before I tell you about it, I want to make sure I'm not jeopardizing the SWEEP. It's okay if I ask for help before I leave, right?"

Ralph nodded.

"It would be so cool to have Beth see a moose today. Are there any mediums, like the people with the special abilities who helped me with the peach roses for Liz, who can talk to animals?"

I'd love to have Beth see a moose. Always wanted to see a bull moose myself, but never got a chance.

"Let me think." Ralph rubbed the back of his neck. "I do know someone who has a close relationship with animals; he may be helpful. We should go see Noah."

"Noah. You mean the flood Noah?" Tom grinned. Before he came to Heaven, he'd never thought about who he might see in Heaven. *This could be exciting.*

"I never heard it put that way, sir, but yes, Noah from the ark and the flood. He is probably at the Ark Park."

"Is that Heaven's zoo?"

"I would not call it a zoo, sir. It is an area where the spirits of Earth animals congregate. All creatures consider Noah a great friend and protector." Ralph looked at the sky. "It is about a forty-five-minute walk to Noah's park. It is a lovely day. Shall we walk?"

Tom grimaced. "Actually, I'm concerned about the time frame. Beth didn't say when they were hiking. She usually likes to get an early start and may already be on her way. Is there a quicker way?"

"There is." St. Andrew offered to take them in a flying golf cart. Before either Tom or Ralph could respond, St. Andrew had a cart ready. Tom and Ralph jumped in. St. Andrew took off, and in a blink of an eye, they arrived at Ark Park. Tom thanked St. Andrew for the lift. He and Ralph hopped out of the cart.

Just inside the entrance stood a spirit surrounded by animals. He wore a sleeveless robe striped in shades of reds, blues, and violets, and had a braided rope hung with keys and whistles around his waist. He had sandals on his feet. His straight, gray hair was long, about midway between his shoulders and waist, and his beard was equally as long. The man's upper body was quite muscular.

This must be Noah.

The animals near Noah were ones Tom would expect to see in a children's petting zoo on Earth: sheep, pigs, horses. The area had the odor of zoos on Earth, which he always had assumed was a combination of the scents from the droppings of the animals and their urine. Noah and the animals near him stood in a large, circular grassy area, which was surrounded by a dirt path leading off in a number of directions.

Noah was busy checking the animals' food and water supplies. He had a pail of oats in his hand, but put the pail down when he saw Ralph and Tom.

He wiped his hands on his robe and held out his hand to shake Ralph's. "Ralph, good to see you. What brings you around here?"

Ralph apologized for coming by unannounced and asked Noah if he had a moment to speak with him and Tom, which Noah did.

"This is Tom," Ralph continued. "I kept an eye on him while he was on Earth. Now he is in pursuit of a SWEEP pass. He has an opportunity to make a wish come true and wants to improve his chances of success."

Ralph turned to Tom. "Sir, this is Noah. If you need to know anything about animals, this is your man."

Tom stuck out his hand. *How cool is this?* He'd always been at ease meeting famous people, not that he was a person who purposely sought them out. On Earth he had met profession-al sports figures, TV personalities, political leaders, CEOs of world-wide businesses. He had never felt shy or awkward meeting anyone, no matter who the person was or what they did for a living. Each new encounter was an opportunity to learn something new.

"Nice to meet you, Noah." Tom shook the spirit's hand, then showed Noah the star from Beth. "It would be fun to have Beth see a moose during her hike today. Possibly when she and her friends stop for lunch."

Tom told Noah about his experience with mediums. "Is there a similar way to convey messages to animals?"

Noah smiled. "I may have an idea or two. Let's see. I have a moose horn around here somewhere." He looked through the assortment around his waist. "It's usually here, but I don't see it. It must be in my office. I'm assuming you plan to go to Earth and see Beth's reaction if we figure out the details?"

Tom nodded.

"If a moose on Earth agrees to help, a signal from you with a moose horn will notify the Earth moose when your niece is nearby. When you get to Earth, you can use the horn to direct the moose to a specific location, provided the area is not harm-ful for the animal."

Tom loved innovative tools and gadgets. The idea of a moose horn intrigued him. "Great, sounds like it'd do the job. Where can I get one?"

"There's no need to get your own. I have an extra one that's out for repair. It's supposed to be ready today. If it is, you can borrow mine."

Noah led the way to his office, which was only about a hun-dred and fifty paces from the round grassy area where they'd been standing. They approached a log cabin and Tom assumed the structure was Noah's office as well as his home. Three stairs led up to a covered porch which extended across the front and around the right side. Noah opened the door and cautioned Tom and Ralph to watch their step as there was another step up from the porch to the door.

The inside was one room, approximately twelve by fourteen feet. On the left, was a cot covered with books and magazines. To the right was a desk covered with papers, newspaper clippings, maps. The cracked walls were a dingy beige as far as Tom could tell. Nearly every inch of the walls was covered with a multitude of cork boards which were covered with photos, diagrams, maps, and letters.

Noah picked up some papers from his desk. "As you may have guessed, I am quite the collector. When I cared for animals on the Ark, it was mostly by instinct. Since the time of the Ark, so many books about animals have been written. I pick up every book I can get my hands on. Don't know why, since I rarely read. I'd rather spend time with the animals. But every once in a while, I need a quick reference." Noah found the horn, picked it up, and handed it to Tom. "Let's go outside to test it."

Tom and Ralph followed Noah back to the grassy area and around to a forest. They didn't enter the forest, but stood at its edge. From their vantage point, the place looked similar to forests Tom had seen on Earth. He and Liz had loved to explore—he would drive while she kept her eye out for wildlife. Looking into Noah's forest, Tom could see multitudes of pine trees, giving shade to the thick growth of ferns and other foliage below. There were several varieties of pines, but he couldn't identify one from the other.

Noah handed Tom the horn. "Go ahead, give it a try."

Tom blew the horn, but heard nothing. Disappointed, he handed it back to Noah. "Doesn't seem to be working."

"Oh, I think it does. Look." A second later, a huge moose came out of the forest, ambling towards Noah. "That's Clarence."

Tom guessed Clarence must've been about six feet tall. His antlers were a little shy of eighty inches across and had a velvety look to them.

After Noah introduced everyone to the moose, he turned back to Tom.

"This might look a bit odd," Noah said, "but here in Heaven, animals speak in sign language, using movements of the head and limbs."

Noah turned back to Clarence and told the moose about the request from Tom's niece. He dipped and swung his head and stamped his feet as he spoke. "Do you have a friend on Earth who could go to the area where his niece is?" Noah asked. "Then Tom could use this horn to lead your buddy to his niece and her friends."

Tom added, "And hang around long enough for them to get a few good shots?"

He wasn't sure how to say that in sign language, but Clarence seemed to get the message. The moose's jaw dropped, his eyes widened, and he backed way.

"What's wrong?" Tom asked. "He looks horrified."

"Wouldn't you be horrified if you thought someone was going to take a shot at one of your friends?" Noah asked.

Tom felt awful and apologized. "Clarence, I'm so sorry. The words in our language can be confusing. I meant a shot with their cameras, a photo, not a shot with any weapons that could harm your friend. No one I know personally would even consider harming a moose."

Noah interpreted Tom's message to Clarence and Clarence replied by tossing his head and stamping his feet.

"Clarence thanks you for your apology. He told me, now that he knows his friends will be safe, that he thinks the idea sounds fun and is sure he can find a friend or two to help. He has one buddy, Wild Bill, who loves to be photographed. The more details you have about Beth's location, the better the chances are he'll be able to direct Wild Bill or one of his cohorts to be close by."

Ralph suggested that Tom take out his ELV. "This is getting exciting, sir. I find some of your schemes quite imaginative."

Tom took out his ELV and set the viewer on Beth. She was with two girls Tom didn't know. He'd never met any of Beth's friends or even heard her mention them. They all had long, light brown hair, great smiles, and dazzling white, straight teeth. One was loaded down with camera equipment; the other carried a backpack and Tom saw several reference guides sticking out of the pockets.

They were standing at a trailhead in a spot just off the main trail. The ground was covered with crushed gravel. A sign at the top of a wooden post indicated they were at the start of a trail, but Tom couldn't make out the name. Beth had a map in her hands and all three girls were studying the map on the trail post. Beth referred to the map in her hands and compared it the one shown on the post. She traced the trail on the post with her finger and pointed to a spot. "Guys, this is where we should be around lunchtime. There's a pond in the area. Do you want to try to take a break there?"

Her friends agreed. Beth asked if they were ready to start and they gathered the equipment they had put on the ground.

Beth asked, "Sarah, do you need any help in carrying some of your camera equipment?"

"Thanks, but no," Beth's friend with all the camera equipment shook her head. "If I hope to become a professional wildlife photographer, I better get used to carrying it on my own. I'm used to hauling all this around. Right now I know exactly where everything is. You lead the way since you have a good sense of direction. Plus you have all the maps."

Beth said she would be glad to. She checked with her other friend. "Amy, you have all the information if we want to know anything about the plants and animals we see?"

Amy patted the side of her forest-green pack. "It's all right here. Every guidebook I could get my hands on with information for this trail."

The girls got started with Beth leading the way.

Noah and Clarence watched the ELV over Tom's shoulder. Tom zoomed in so they could get the name of the trail. It was Cherry Creek Trail. Clarence let out a bellow, which, Noah explained, was Clarence's way to communicate with his friends on Earth.

Tom asked, "If animals in Heaven can be heard by their friends on Earth, why can't spirits in Heaven speak loudly and be heard by their friends on Earth?"

"Sir, you are aware, are you not, that species of Earth animals have various sensory levels?" Ralph said. "I am sure you know that dogs are much better than people with their hearing and smelling senses. In Heaven, spirits gain entirely different levels of vibrations that are not detected by people on Earth. It is all right here in this book."

Ralph held out a book for Tom and Noah to see. Ralph blushed. "Noah, I picked up this from your office. I had every intention of returning it to you before we left and thought I could learn something new. I hope you don't mind."

Noah smiled. "No worries. Perhaps after we finish our business here, you can fill me in on what you learned."

While waiting for Clarence to hear back from his friends, Tom asked Noah to tell him about the Ark Park.

Noah sighed. "There is so much to tell, but I'll start with where we are now. If you look around, you'll see several pathways heading off in different directions. Each path leads to different habitats that support various species. There are rain forests, jungles, deserts, plains, mountains, streams, rivers, and numerous other environments."

Tom listened, and in the background he could hear animal sounds coming at him from all directions: roars and grunts from large animals, a variety of songs from birds, buzzing from insects. He even heard a dog or two barking.

Clarence nudged Noah. Through the movements of his head and legs, Clarence gave Noah a message. Noah gave Tom a rough translation.

"Looks like Clarence got several replies," Noah said, "including one from Wild Bill. According to Clarence, Wild Bill is quite friendly and loves to show off for people. He is familiar with the trail your niece is hiking. Moose are rarely seen in that area of the park, so when he's there, he gets lots of attention. Wild Bill will be the designated contact, but Clarence has plenty of backups."

Tom had to ask. "How did Clarence get his buddy's message?"

Noah patted Clarence. "When his Earth friends want to communicate with Clarence, they let out a bellow, much like the one you heard Clarence make. Their bellow is set at a vibration level that Clarence can receive here in Heaven."

Tom's imagination was blown away by the growing likelihood that his crazy idea might actually happen. He nudged Ralph. "Love it when a plan comes together."

He wanted to know if the pond along the trail would be good for Wild Bill and Noah passed the question onto Clarence.

Clarence sent another call. Within moments, Clarence had an answer that Noah interpreted. "Looks like Wild Bill's already on his way,"

"Sounds simple enough," Tom said, studying the horn in his hand. "I just blow the horn after I get down there and Wild Bill will come?"

"Hopefully, that's all there is to it," Noah said.

Tom gathered his utility bag, confirming that his rope ladder, the moose horn, his ELV, visibility and invisibility dusts, spirit communication device, and all his other paraphernalia were with him. He gave his shell a squirt of the new mobility spray and tucked the spray into the bag with everything else.

Satisfied he had everything he needed, Tom headed to the cloud shuttle and attached the ladder to the next cloud. Then he went through The Veil and set his destination to join Beth and her friends.

❧ ❧ ❧

BETH AND HER friends were already on the trail. Tom enjoyed the great views of the mountains and being able to soar close enough to observe the details of the tiniest flora and fauna.

This is cool. Love that new mobility spray!

Tom spotted the pond and tried out the horn. He detected movement in the trees on the other side of the pond. He glided to the other side of the pond and blew the horn again. Next thing he knew he was face to face, or in this case, spirit to moose, with a moose he presumed to be Wild Bill. He wanted to thank Wild Bill for his cooperation, but had no idea how. Maybe brushing away some of the insects from his back might be appreciated? He shooed the insects away. The moose, if it was Wild Bill, nodded his head as if in approval.

Tom glided back to the other side of the pond, the side the trail was on. He heard Beth and her friends say they were ready for lunch. Beth checked the map. "We're near the pond. It's just a few minutes from here."

She led the way to a picnic area off the main trail. A few fir trees were growing around the area they had chosen for their break. The ground was covered with gravel. It was quiet except for the occasional sounds of birds and the buzzing of unseen insects.

Tom watched Beth prepare a peanut butter and jelly sandwich. She grabbed an apple and some water, then set her lunch on a roundish rock about one hundred yards from the edge of the pond. The rock she chose was currently catching the warmth of the sun and stood about waist high. Beth placed her hands behind her and boosted herself onto the gray rock.

No sooner than she sat down on the rock, she jumped up. "Oh my goodness." She put one hand over her heart and covered her mouth with the other. She uncovered her mouth and pointed to a spot in the pond. "Look, guys! Sarah. Amy. Come here. Quick. There's a moose on the other side of the pond."

Her friends, who were still preparing their lunches, dropped what they were doing, hurried to the edge of the pond, and looked in the direction she indicated. Beth jumped off the rock and joined her friends at the edge of the pond. Wild Bill waded into the pond and stopped in the middle where he munched on lily pads and drank the pond water.

Beth took a few quick photos, then asked Sarah if she would mind sharing the photos she captured. "You can get much better shots with all your fancy equipment than I can."

Amy said, "Me, too. I want copies."

Sarah agreed on the condition Beth would finish making her lunch. Beth went back to make the sandwiches for Amy and

Sarah, grabbed hers from where she had left it on the rock, and returned to the edge of the pond.

Amy pulled a guidebook from the side pocket of her pack and opened it. "What do you want to know about moose? Did you know that moose like to come into ponds for the salty plants they need to supplement their diet and to help them get relief from insects that swarm around them on land?"

Beth shook her head.

"Says here they shed their antlers every winter and the antlers regrow in the spring. Their average size is about six feet tall and their antlers average about eighty inches across."

Beth guessed the moose in the pond was about that size.

Sarah seemed to be the most excited about Wild Bill. "Watch the way he looks our direction and how he turns his head. He seems to be posing so we can capture his best side."

Wild Bill basked in the sun and enjoyed his lunch for nearly thirty minutes. As he made his way back to the far side of the pond, the big moose looked back several times.

"It's like he knows we're here." Sarah took one last shot.

After Wild Bill disappeared into the shade of the trees on the other side, Beth and Amy gathered around Sarah and reviewed a few of her digital shots. Sarah complemented a few of her own shots. "That was awesome. I got some great close-ups. Look at this one; you can see the details of his eyes."

Tom was pleased with their reaction. He had seen many smiles from Beth while she had watched Wild Bill. His niece was not one who showed her emotions easily and her smiles were enough of a reward for Tom. And he was sure from the comments of Sarah she had also enjoyed the experience.

Beth, Amy, and Sarah packed up their lunches and cleaned the area. Before they headed off on the second part of the hike,

Beth glanced around. Her eyes glistened. Her friends gathered around her and gave Beth a hug.

"My uncle would have loved this. I don't think he ever got to see a bull moose in the wild, although he always wanted to. This morning I thought about Uncle Tom and his old stuffed moose and then I see a moose where the ranger said we'd have practically no chance of seeing one. Makes ya wonder." She wiped away a tear.

She's right, Tom thought as he headed to the café he'd set up as his return. *In my entire lifetime, I never even saw a bull moose, never mind got close enough to get a decent photo of one. Today I not only got to see a moose, I talked to one, even though it was through an interpreter and a horn. So what. I communicated with a real moose. Makes me wonder how many seemingly impossible dreams and wishes are possible with a little imagination and a little help from the right sources?*

Chapter 44

Earth Life Planning Center

Need to review Tom's plan

WHEN TOM HAD passed through The Veil and back into Heaven, Ralph was waiting.

"Sir, I know you had a busy day. In your absence, I received notice from the Earth Life Planning Center. They have an opening in their schedule tomorrow. I made an appointment for you to meet with St. Peter. It is routine for all spirits to meet with St. Peter after their arrival in Heaven to review the life plan they mapped out before their birth on Earth. It is customary to have a limo take the spirit and guardian angel to the planning center. I requested a limo meet us at the clubhouse mid-morning. I will see you then, sir?"

Tom nodded and Ralph left.

Despite what Ralph had said about the meeting being routine, Tom was concerned. *Has there been a mistake? Am I supposed to be in the other place? I never thought I'd actually make it into Heaven.*

He felt like he was a kid again and his mom had told him she'd made a doctor's appointment for him the next day and he'd be getting a shot or the same way he'd felt when he walked into a class and the teacher announced there would be a pop quiz.

But—he *had* had an amazing day and wanted to focus on his moose experience. He could worry about tomorrow, tomorrow.

THE NEXT MORNING when Tom arrived at the clubhouse, a white limo was parked in front. Ralph was waiting and had a cup of coffee for Tom. The limo's back doors were already open and Ralph signaled for Tom to get in. Once situated, he handed Tom the coffee. Ralph got in on the other side and both their doors slid closed. The sliding window between the driver and passengers was darkly tinted and Tom never saw the driver.

On their way to the planning center, Ralph explained some of the work done there. "When a spirit decides to take on a life on Earth, the spirit works with guides in Heaven to prepare a life plan. They chart out lessons to learn, personality traits to develop, people to help. Their objectives are mapped in detail. However, once inside a womb, the destination and routes become buried deeper and deeper inside the subconscious, until at birth, the person has no recollection of the purpose for its existence and needs to rediscover the established goals."

"Why waste all the time planning, then?" Tom asked. "Or why not write cheat notes on your hand?"

"Good question, sir. I will present your question to St. Peter. He can give you an explanation."

Tom was concerned about this meeting with St. Peter, especially after his question about the cheat notes which he was certain Ralph would raise. He had been kidding. Ralph just didn't get his sense of humor. He held his warm cup of coffee in both hands. He took a sip. It was perfect, a bold blend still piping hot.

"Sir, the purpose of today's meeting is to see how closely your most recent life on Earth met the goals you established before you were born. Perhaps when you review the achievements of your most recent life compared to your original goals, you will see there were situations you wanted to experience during that lifetime, but did not have the opportunity. There may be something you would like to take on immediately and so decide you would like to prepare a quick reentry life for yourself."

Tom frowned. "When I really think about my options, what it comes down to is this: although I've said I'd like to be on Earth, surprisingly enough, I feel like I want to continue the SWEEP and see how things are when I finish."

The limo stopped and the side rear doors slid open.

"Sir, we have arrived at the planning center." Ralph got out of the limo and Tom did likewise.

Tom thought the Earth Life Planning Center was cleverly designed. It was in the shape of the earth and the exterior displayed the oceans, the continents, and all the details that would normally be shown on a globe.

They located the help desk, which was basically a counter about three and one-half feet tall. On the counter was a communication device and a computer. A few feet behind the counter were rows and rows of shelves perpendicular to the counter and stretching back so far Tom couldn't see the end. The shelves were at least ten feet high and filled with neatly filed sturdy brown office folders.

"Please let St. Peter know Tom and Ralph are here to see him," Ralph said.

Tom looked around. Was Ralph talking through an intercom system, like a security gate or a fast-food order window? He saw a communication device floating above the desk and heard a perfectly normal female voice say, "St. Peter, Ralph and

Tom are here to see you. I'll show them to a meeting room, get Tom's file, and bring it to the meeting room for you."

Tom couldn't figure out what was going on. He gave Ralph a puzzled look. Ralph put his finger to his lips.

Tom again heard the female voice, though he still couldn't tell where it was coming from. "St. Peter is on his way. Come with me. I'll show you to a meeting room."

Tom had no idea who he was supposed to be following, but Ralph seemed to, so Tom stayed close behind Ralph, following him into a small room.

Unsure whether to speak or not, Tom shrugged his shoulders and held out his hands in a questioning manner.

"Sir, I guess this is your first encounter with a spirit who has elected not to take on a shell. When the spirit returns with your file, use your senses and see if you can detect a presence. Is there a scent you detect? Any hints of color?"

"I did hear a female voice." Tom thought that was a good starting point, but was interested to see if he'd pick up other clues when the file was brought into the room.

The room was very plain. There were no windows. The furniture consisted of a desk with an executive-style chair behind it and chairs for visitors in front of the desk. The desk looked like it had been picked up at a secondhand store. Tom and Ralph sat in the visitors' chairs. There were no personal effects on the desk, nothing on the plain walls desperately calling out for a fresh coat of paint.

Tom squirmed in his chair. "Hope this meeting won't be long. This chair is uncomfortable."

"I can assure you, sir, the meeting will be short. This room was not designed to be cozy. St. Peter is an extremely busy spirit. It is his responsibility to meet with every spirit who comes to Heaven and review their most recent life on Earth. He does have helpers. St. Andrew, for example, greets people who had an interest in golf and gives the entering spirit a quick approval or denial.

"St. Peter is responsible for helping spirits evaluate how closely they met the goals they set for their most recent lifetime on Earth. He is busy, so the meetings are just a quick in and out. Do not expect to be offered any coffee or a cold drink."

Chapter 45

Saint Peter

St. Peter arrived wearing a white cotton robe trimmed in gold fringe. He had a gold chain around his neck with a cross hanging from it. He was a tall man with shoulder-length dark brown hair. He wore glasses and had a friendly smile that made Tom feel as if he had known him forever. Ralph introduced Tom and they shook hands.

While they waited for Tom's file, St. Peter asked if Tom had any questions.

Ralph told St. Peter that Tom was curious about the planning process, specifically why go through the trouble to create a plan if you're only going to forget it when you're born? "His main question, I believe, was why not write cheat notes?"

Tom felt his face burn. *Why did Ralph have to go and ask that question? Hope St. Peter doesn't think I was trying to be a smart aleck. I need to watch what I say to Ralph until he understands my sense of humor.*

"It's all part of the adventure," St. Peter said. "Figuring out what you signed up for. Everyone starts without a clue as to what he or she is supposed to do. Their bodies are outfitted with the physical attributes they chose and they are born into or placed with the appropriate family and are surrounded by associates they preselected. But the original plan is buried deep in the spirit soul. The purpose of your life on Earth finds its way to consciousness if the heart and mind listen and feel the vibrations of the soul. That is difficult for many people to do.

"But, let me tell you, a twist of your so-called cheat notes has been suggested before, not as cheat notes, but as markings that show up later in life. People have their permanent teeth come through years after birth and then there's the puberty change. Some spirits are conducting a feasibility study for markings similar to tattoos to develop at some point if the spirit, in planning their Earth life, requests some hints such as your cheat notes. So far there hasn't been much of an interest."

Now Tom didn't feel so stupid. Others had thought of similar ideas.

The help desk spirit returned with Tom's paper file. When Tom saw the thick brown file floating into the room, he paid close attention and detected a tinge of pale blue and a slight whiff of an ocean breeze. He imagined the help desk spirit as a young lady who had spent much of her Earth time near a beach.

St. Peter thumbed through the file, occasionally nodding his head. There were frequent moments when he broke into laughter.

"Looks like the major goal you set for yourself in your most recent life on Earth was to make people smile and let them know someone cared about them. You did that on a daily basis. You were true to your spirit's goal in every aspect of your life."

St. Peter thumbed through a few more pages.

"Looks like you've had many lives on Earth. You've been making trips almost since the beginning of time. That's one reason your file is so thick. Interesting—in most of your previous Earth life plans, your top priority was to make people smile. Ever consider being a comedian?"

Tom laughed. "Don't think I could make a living in that profession."

"You're a restless soul, that much is evident. Are you sure you're not ready to take on another life?"

Tom shook his head. "Not just yet. I want to get the SWEEP pass and see how things are. I hope my best friend and soul-mate will share another lifetime with me when she arrives. In the meantime, I want to scope out options for a new adventure with her if she agrees."

"I saw a couple of side notes in your file about the unusual-ly close relationship you shared with Liz. I'm sure she'd be glad to share another adventure with you," Saint Peter said.

St. Peter set down the file. "I don't have anything else to talk about. I won't take up any more of your time. Any addi-tional questions before I leave?"

Tom shook his head. He stood and shook St. Peter's hand, thanking him for his time.

Before St. Peter left, he patted Tom on the back. "Job well done. Welcome to Heaven."

Tom felt a ton of pressure lifted from his shoulders. His acceptance into Heaven hadn't been a mistake and he was ec-static that his relationship with Liz had been noted in his file. Their relationship was the pride of his life. He felt like he was on cloud nine—whatever that cliché meant—but he was sure his spirit was swirling with happiness.

❧ ❧ ❧

TOM WAS GLAD to get away from the uncomfortable chair. "Hope you know the way out. I was following you and didn't pay attention to how we got here."

"The exit is straight down the hallway to the left, sir."

The hallway was narrow, barely wide enough for three people to walk through at the same time. It reminded Tom of recruiting centers at a university. The walls were covered with flyers seeking spirits interested in potential lives, both for the next generation and for hundreds of years in the future.

Tom saw Sharon, one of the women who'd given testimony for him, in the hallway. He stopped to talk to her after they greeted with a hug.

"I don't know if you remember," Sharon said, "but during my testimony, I mentioned my plans to reenter Earth as my daughter's child. Kathy and I have had several conversations about her innovative treatment for childhood cancers. She and the spirit colleagues she met in Heaven have worked together to develop a treatment that would be less painful, and hopefully more effective, for children on Earth who have cancers. They feel it is ready for testing on Earth and I'm one of the candidates in line to 'discover and test' the concept through my planned career as a medical researcher. There can only be one who makes the discovery, though. The finalist will be announced at an open house at the Cancer Research Center, here in Heaven, sometime next month. I'll ask Kathy to invite you. I'm sure she would love for you to come."

Tom was intrigued by the idea of cancer research being done in Heaven. He'd never thought about that. Then again, he had never thought about a bank being in Heaven, either. It would be fun to see Kathy. He'd barely known her before she testified at his hearing. He wanted to thank her for again for doing that.

"Sounds like a plan," Tom said. "I'll see you there.

Chapter 46

THE THUNDERSTORM

MOST MORNINGS, EVEN if they didn't have a tee time or plans to practice, Tom and Ralph met at the clubhouse at St. Andrew's Gate for a cup of coffee and to peruse the newspapers. Sometimes, Willie or St. Andrew or Kyle joined them. With St. Andrew and Kyle, the visit would be quick as they had work to do around the course and St. Andrew usually had a full schedule of greeting newcomers at his gate.

Willie used to come by to chat, but his wife had recently arrived and he now spent most of his time with her. He had been so excited when she was "born" — a term used to describe a spirit's entry into Heaven. Willie had been beaming when he showed Tom and Ralph her birth announcement in the paper. Tom thought it ironic, birth announcements in Heaven were followed with the same type of interest people on Earth followed obituaries. Spirits were curious to see if any of their acquaintances had snuck into Heaven so they could reunite with old friends.

Ralph was usually at the clubhouse first, but this time he wasn't there when Tom arrived. Tom went to the snack area and ordered a latte and a cherry muffin. Cherry muffins were his favorite and weren't always available, but when they were, he'd treat himself. Maybe a cherry muffin would help cheer him up a little, though he doubted it. He went to a table near the corner window and sat down. Ralph joined him a few moments later.

After finishing their beverages and glancing through the papers, Ralph asked, "Sir, are you up for a little golf?"

"Not feeling like it today. I want some quiet time. Maybe I'll take in a movie."

"Anything you would like to talk about, sir?"

Tom was hesitant to tell Ralph why he was feeling despondent. Today was his and Liz's wedding anniversary, a joyous day for both of them. They had been married for so long, they no longer exchanged gifts as they had everything they wanted. Their celebrations included a nice dinner the evening before their anniversary, an enormous bouquet for Liz which had to be delivered a day or two prior to their anniversary to surprise her, and a long weekend get-away the weekend before or after their anniversary. Sometimes, they'd take in a play or a concert if they found something of interest.

Tom guessed Ralph probably knew how important their anniversary was to them. On Earth, Tom and his buddies used to joke about being in big trouble with their wives if they forgot their anniversary. Tom always remembered—marrying Liz and sharing a great relationship with her was the happiest part of his life.

"No, I'll be okay. If you don't mind, I'd just like some time to be alone."

"Of course, sir, do what you want. Might I suggest a magic carpet ride, perhaps a guided tour to visit sights and places you have not seen. You could rent a carpet and have the carpet customize a tour centered around your interests. Another option would be to simply fly the carpet yourself and go wherever you please."

"A magic carpet ride could be fun. Where can I rent one?"

Before Ralph could answer, a huge gold star accompanied by zillions of smaller blue-and-gold stars surrounded Tom.

Wonder what this is all about. Tom read the message on the largest star first. It was from Liz.

Happy anniversary. Thank you for choosing me as your life partner. I miss you terribly. Love you forever.

Tom sighed. He read the other stars and realized Liz had sent thirty-four stars, not zillions. He had exaggerated, but it could have been zillions for the emotional impact it had on him. This would have been their thirty-fourth anniversary. He doubted Liz knew about his ability to receive star messages. Maybe she had been planning the messages to put in a memory book for an inexpensive, but meaningful anniversary gift, things she had prepared before he passed into Heaven.

Each card represented a different year and highlighted something special they had done during that year of their marriage. Tom sighed; he wished he had done some planning and had arranged to get a huge bouquet or some bedazzling gift to her. She really wouldn't be expecting anything this year. With all the stars caressing him, he told Ralph about their anniversary.

"Wish I could surprise her in some way," he added.

"I understand, sir. I will certainly help any way I can to get something special to Liz that she will know is from you."

Tom pulled out his Earth Location Viewer and, with Ralph watching over his shoulder, brought up a view of Liz. She was at a neighborhood coffee shop with Regina, the lady who lived across the street from Liz. The small cafe had been recently re-opened by new owners according to a banner outside. Liz and Regina had placed their orders, and while they were waiting, Tom used his ELV to look around. The shop had about five or six tables squeezed together and two bookcases full of used books for customers to borrow. After their coffees were ready, Tom watched Regina push the door open with her elbow, pull her baby stroller outside, and select a table shaded from the bright sun. He listened in on their conversation.

"Is this okay for you, Liz?"

"Perfect. Does Bryan have a full day of school today?" Liz pulled out a chair and sat at the round, wrought-iron table.

"He gets out at two. Preschoolers, I have to tell ya. Bryan thinks he's a big boy now. He's not little anymore and is definitely developing a mind of his own. He insisted this morning that we walk to school and he wants me to come back with the stroller to pick him up. He told me he didn't want to ride 'in no car.' I think that was his way of telling me he didn't want me doing any errands after school. It's a good thing the school is only another half mile or so from here. The walks give me the chance to get some exercise in."

Regina situated the stroller with her sleeping toddler, David, next to her chair.

Tom had only met Regina once, at a neighborhood Christmas gathering, the winter before he died. She and her family were new to the neighborhood—mom, dad, and two little boys. They had recently moved into the house across the street from Tom and Liz. Starting the night of the party, their area had been hit with massive snowstorms, keeping the neighbors inside most of the winter.

Tom saw Liz look up at the sky. "Hope the weather holds out so you can walk to school to pick him up. I heard there's a chance for thunder showers this afternoon."

Liz took a sip of coffee, then continued. "Tom was a weather freak. I loved riding around with him on summer afternoons. He'd look at the skies and tell me if he thought there'd be storms later in the day. He'd watch the big thunderheads he called 'anvil heads' build and explain to me how storms develop. He especially loved storms at night when he could see the amazing patterns formed by the lightning."

Tom *had* definitely loved storms—at a safe distance where he could enjoy them. He recalled one night, however, that was pretty darn scary. He and Liz were startled in the middle of the night by bursts of thunder, each clap louder than the previous. They'd gotten got out of bed and from their bedroom window saw lightning everywhere. At times, the lightning came so quickly the skies were nearly as bright as day. They also heard lots of sirens. They turned on their emergency radio and heard non-stop reports of homes and apartment buildings being struck by lightning and catching on fire. A couple of the addresses mentioned were near homes of some friends and they hoped for their friends' safety.

The rains that night came in torrents. Despite the usually good drainage system, the rains flooded over the curbs of the parking lot in their apartment complex. It was hard for Tom and Liz to get back to sleep after the storm subsided, and first thing in the morning they checked with friends. One reported the building next to them had caught on fire. Another lived in a building that was struck, but his apartment was spared from any flames or smoke damage.

"Tom knew when to head for cover, though," Liz said. "If he saw lightning on a golf course, he'd be the first to seek shelter. 'If you get stuck on a golf course in the middle of a lightning storm, take out a one iron. Even God can't hit a one-iron,' he always kidded."

Tom chuckled to himself, remembering the day he and Liz were on vacation and playing golf. They were on the third hole when warning sirens screamed through the air, a signal storms were approaching and to get off the course. He and Liz had their rain jackets and rain pants handy and scrambled to put them on and to get their clubs covered. But the torrential rains began immediately and they were soaked. In the clubhouse, they waited with the other drenched players for the storm to pass over, hoping they could continue play. But the club pro had to deliver the news every golfer hates to hear—even if the storm stopped immediately, the course conditions would not be playable.

That was a nice course. Too bad we didn't get to finish the round.

Tom sighed and shook his head. "It's not fair," he told Ralph. "Liz and I should be playing golf together. She shouldn't just be going for coffee."

"Maybe Earth is due for a small lightning show," Ralph said. "I know where some extra lightning bolts are stored. If we can get our hands on few of those, we can generate a quick storm. I doubt that would upset anyone."

If he'd had a physical body, his eyes would probably have popped out of his head. He was blown away that Ralph, who always seemed to do everything by the book, had come up with such an intriguing idea. The thought of creating a storm was exhilarating. Tom felt like a little boy who'd just gotten an amazing surprise birthday gift and had to hold back from peeing his pants.

Incredible! Making a thunderstorm!

That was beyond his wildest dreams!

Ralph led the way to a wooden structure about the size of a storage unit one would see in a backyard on Earth. The wood was weather beaten; its shingled roof sloped down. Tall wildflowers adorned the front on either side of the door. Behind the shed were bins of lightning bolts marked *Defective*. Ralph pulled a fistful of bolts out of the first bin and handed them to

Tom, then grabbed another fistful and handed those to Tom as well, then took another fistful for himself.

The lightning bolts' shapes were as varied as one would see in the skies during a storm. Some were jagged, some were short, some were long, some were straight. Tom was thankful he didn't feel any energy flowing through the ones Ralph had handed to him. Tom had great respect for the effects lightning could generate. He held on to them gingerly, not wanting to do anything to set them off.

"Should we really be taking these?" Tom had serious doubts about what was going on here. He felt like he and Ralph had traded roles and he was watching over Ralph, trying to keep him out of trouble. He knew how dangerous lightning could be, defective or not. He had loved the idea of making a storm for Liz, but not at the chance of blowing up Heaven and possibly Earth with defective lightning bolts. He decided to wait a little longer and see how Ralph's scheme would progress before he put a halt to it.

They walked back to the front of the shed. Tom was startled when he saw a beautiful green spirit—without any definitive shell—arranging some clouds. He glanced around and realized it was not a storage shed. An overhead sign outside the structure identified the small structure as Mother Nature's Supply Shop.

"Mother Nature, what a surprise to find you here. I thought you spent most of your energy on Earth." Ralph dropped the lightning bolts and held out his arms to greet her with a hug.

Tom was stunned and relieved. He was stunned at meeting Mother Nature. *Mother Nature?* Had holding the lightning bolts made him delusional? Or maybe he had walked into a storybook. He'd never considered Mother Nature to be real. She was just a concept. He couldn't tell for sure, but guessed Ralph's reason for dropping the lightning bolts was that he'd gotten caught red-handed. The lightning bolts weren't meant to be taken. The hug was a cover up. And he was relieved that nothing happened, there was no explosion when Ralph dropped the defective bolts.

"You're right," the spirit said, "I'm on Earth most of the time. However, with the seasons changing, I needed to check our inventory. Right now, I'm choreographing the clouds for the new season. I think I recognize you. Isn't your name Ralph?"

Ralph nodded.

"Are you and your friend looking for something special today?"

"Mother Nature, I must apologize. I neglected to introduce Tom. I watched over him while he was on Earth."

"Nice to meet you. You do some awesome work." Having just met her, Tom didn't feel comfortable hugging Mother Nature as Ralph had done. He extended his hand, but wasn't sure she could shake hands without a shell. She welcomed him with a hug. He felt a softness, like trying to embrace warm air. On closer contact Tom saw her aura was a pale spring green and he thought he detected the delicate scent of lily of the valley.

Ralph told Mother Nature about Tom's love of thunderstorms and that today was his anniversary. "I told him we could create a little thunderstorm for his wife."

Although she had no shell, Mother Nature's next movement reminded Tom of a woman angry with her husband. He pictured her with one hand on her hip and the other hand pointing a finger and shaking it at Ralph. Her voice turned raspy and her green aura deepened. "So you thought you could just come in and take some things. Do you know what it takes to make a storm or were you going to just throw a few lightning bolts around?"

Her voice softened and her aura returned to spring green as she directed her attention back to Tom. "I recognize you from Earth," she said. "You were always looking skyward, checking out clouds, their formations and movement. You had a great respect for my work. If you like, for you, I'll prepare a nice little storm."

She suggested they use decent lightning bolts, then add some thunder and some rain. "And especially for an anniversary, you need to finish off the storm with a rainbow."

She paused thoughtfully. "Tom, I have a hunch you might like to view the storm from Earth, mostly to see your wife's reaction up close. Ralph also may be more helpful there. I'll arrange for a wind to take you down."

Tom jumped on that offer. A wind was a great way to get to Earth and not worry about The Veil and the rope ladder. He could focus on Liz. "I would love that. Thank you."

Mother Nature contacted the wind through her spirit communications system. "The wind will come to the garden and wait there until you and Ralph are ready to depart."

She looked around as if searching for something. "Now, let me see if I can find my daughters, Spring and Rainbow, to assist. They're probably in the flower garden. Spring likes to practice her control over rainfall by watering the garden, and Rainbow likes to work on her gymnastics so she can create amazing formations with rainbows."

The trio took off for the garden. Mother Nature flew overhead, her spirit glowing and blinking, reminding Tom of the lightning bugs he and his friends had chased in their backyards when they were kids. He and Ralph followed on foot until they arrived at two wrought iron gates marking the entrance to the garden. Beyond the gates, the paved pathway branched out in countless directions like a maze. Flowers and shrubs stretched back and out to the sides as far as Tom could see. His eyes were drawn to a tall bank of red-and-pink azaleas.

He and Liz had visited plantation gardens in the southern United States and a similar flower bank had become a focal point for many of their photos. By luck, one of the snapshots had turned out exceptionally well for the rank-amateur photographer he considered himself to be. Liz had had it enlarged and framed and had hung it in their family room. But the photo and the garden on Earth paled in comparison to the majestic work of nature in front of him.

Spring and Rainbow were in the garden as Mother Nature had suspected. Two other spirits—Ben and Franklin, according to Mother Nature—were with them.

The four had shells, but lacked hair and distinguishing facial features. The shells were colorful: yellow, red, rainbow, and one shell whose color continually changed. They were dressed in colors to match their shells. The yellow and rainbow shells wore coordinating skirts and tops; the other two wore loose-fitting knee-length black shorts. The red shell's shorts had a fiery red stripe on the side, the flashing shell's shorts looked like it had been worn in a paint ball battle and was covered in splashes of various colors and sizes.

"Once they hear about the plans brewing for a storm later today," Mother Nature said, "they'll be terribly excited and I probably won't have time to properly introduce them to you, so let me tell you a little about them now.

"The yellow spirit is Spring. She is practicing her telekinetic skills to control rainfall. In the rainbow-colored shell, as you might have guessed, is Rainbow. She works nonstop on creating innovative gymnastic moves for unique rainbow formations."

Mother Nature's aura shuddered. "Those two with them—I hate to think what would happen if I didn't keep an eye on them. Ben is younger than Franklin and has an artsy side to him that he tries to hide. He's great with color and sound and rhythms. I'm trying to develop those talents so he can take on full responsibility for the fall foliage, the sounds of thunder, and the rhythms of the wind, but for now he wants to be macho and focus on physical activities. Franklin has a predisposition for activities requiring strength, such as handling lightning bolts and generating hazardous storms. Ben and Franklin are rambunctious; Earth would be hit constantly with earthquakes, volcanoes, tsunamis, tornadoes, floods if they had their way."

As Tom, Ralph, and Mother Nature neared the young spirits, Tom heard the four of them talking about the upcoming season and how anxious they were to use the skills they'd been practicing. Even as they talked, the four were very active. Spring was holding out her right arm, pointing one of her fingers at a yellow pail filled with water. The pail moved up and down and sideways according to the movement of her hand and finger. Rainbow was turning somersaults and Ben and Franklin were competing in throwing lightning bolts for distance and size.

"I may have just the opportunity you're hoping for," Mother Nature announced. "We have a request for a small storm from these two nice spirits, Ralph and Tom. Maybe you'd like to demonstrate your new skills this afternoon."

"Can we really, Mom?" Spring and Rainbow hugged Mother Nature, then clapped, squealed, and jumped up and down. "Can Ben and Franklin help us with the thunder and lightning?"

Mother Nature consented.

Except for his nieces and nephews, Tom hadn't been around kids much. But he guessed Spring and Rainbow to be about seven or eight. Ben and Franklin might be older, twelve or thirteen.

The storm team prepared a plan. Mother Nature glided to her shop and returned with more than enough clouds for a small storm. She asked Ben to add tinges of storm colors to the clouds.

"Tom, I think you will enjoy this experience," Mother Nature said. "You'll watch these little clouds transform from small formations in the sky to the anvil heads you used to watch develop from Earth."

Tom rubbed his hands in anticipation. "Thanks for doing this. I love storms and I hope my wife will enjoy this one."

Franklin loosened up like an athlete preparing for an event, demonstrating different throwing styles. He invited Tom to join him.

Tom declined. "I'll let you handle the lightning. I'd prefer to sit back and enjoy the show." He didn't want to admit his fear of lightning bolts. He'd only held the bolts earlier because Ralph had thrust them into his hands. Tom had even been afraid to handle lit sparklers at Fourth of July celebrations.

It was decided that Rainbow would travel to Earth on the wind with Tom and Ralph so she would have the opportunity to view her work as seen on Earth as well as handle any special requests for rainbow positions or colors.

Everyone wanted Tom to enjoy the display and Liz's reaction, so it was agreed Ralph would communicate with Mother Nature to relay any special requests or questions that might come up later. Ben would be the spirit behind the timing and volume of the thunder. Franklin was on the lightning. Spring planned a steady, but gentle rainfall that would last about five minutes. Rainbow was eager to handle her specialty.

Tom set his ELV to Liz. He wanted to know her location if she was running errands, so she wouldn't miss the storm being prepared for her. She was in their backyard, pulling weeds. She put a lot of time and effort into their yard. Liz admitted she couldn't get anything to grow, but the landscapers he'd hired the summer before he died did compliment her on her weed control. She would love to have a garden like the one he was currently in.

As he watched, Liz picked up a trash bag and began filling it with the weeds she had pulled and leaves she had apparently raked from under the bushes. Tom recognized her work pattern and knew she planned to go inside soon. He asked for the storm clouds to be sent to grab her attention before she went inside. Once she was inside, if she wasn't near a window, she might not notice the changes in the sky.

Mother Nature, along with Ben, sent the storm-colored clouds to Earth, covering the sunlight and shading the ground. Tom thought the timing was right for the sound of distant thunder.

Before they could jump on the wind, a green star slid to a stop in front of Tom. He paused to read its message.

Dear Tom,

I only met you once at a neighborhood party, but Liz and I have become acquainted and we talk about you. Our family loves her and we wish we could have known you better.

I heard you have a passion for thunderstorms and it looks like one is heading our way. I just picked up my older boy from preschool and we're walking home. The younger boy is with me, too. They're both sleeping in the stroller. I'm pushing as fast as I can. If there's anything you can do to hold off any rain until I get the boys home, I'd appreciate it. Regina

Tom read the last part of the message about delaying the storm aloud to the storm team.

"Let's hold back on the rain."

He set his ELV to find Regina and the boys. She was on the trail that ran behind the houses in their neighborhood. The trail was mostly wetland and was home to several species of butter-flies, birds, and small animals such as rabbits and an occasion squirrel.

He saw Regina start running. She was in great physical shape and pushed the two-seat, front-and-back stroller uphill as effortlessly as if she'd been on a leisurely walk.

"She's almost home," Tom said. "I don't want her and her boys to get wet, but I think it's okay for distant lightning and thunder."

Ben showed a sensitive side. "I'll keep the thunder at a quiet rumble so it shouldn't wake the boys."

Tom thanked him and Ben started his job as Franklin tossed some distant lightning. Spring patiently waited for her chance to begin the rain. Mother Nature offered to use her ELV to keep an eye on Regina's progress. Tom helped Mother Nature locate Regina, then Tom, Ralph, and Rainbow boarded the wind and headed to Regina's driveway.

They landed as Regina opened her garage door. Ralph contacted Mother Nature and told her they were ready for the rains to begin; Regina and her boys were safely home and under cover. As soon as he ended the conversation the light rain began. Regina pulled out her cell phone, and called Liz.

"The boys fell asleep on the way home and I don't want to wake them. Would you mind coming over and keeping an eye on Bryan while I take the little one in? I think if I try to lift the stroller up the stairs to the house, the jostling around would wake them both and I don't think I can manage carrying them both at the same time. If I take them in one at a time, I think they'll stay asleep. They both could use longer naps. Oh . . . It's just started raining. You might enjoy seeing the rain."

Tom saw the garage door of his home open and was elat-ed when Liz came out. She crossed the street and stood with

Regina in her garage. Regina picked up David and took him inside. She returned to the garage and picked up the older boy without waking him and carried him in. She came back to the garage to watch the rain with Liz.

Regina told Liz about the prayer she had sent to Tom, asking if he could do anything to hold off the storm until she got the boys home. "It really makes me wonder what powers are out there."

They watched the rain a little longer. Then Regina went inside.

Liz crossed the street to her home. The rain stopped and Tom signaled for Rainbow to do her job. The young spirit created a perfect arch, one that reached from one horizon to the other.

"Bravo! A true masterpiece!" Tom clapped and asked for another. Without hesitation, Rainbow drew another rainbow across the sky, this one parallel to the first, smaller, but more vibrant.

He hoped Liz was enjoying it. He didn't know if she would realize the storm was meant for her, but he was grateful to Ralph for his suggestion, giving an anniversary gift both Liz and Tom could enjoy.

He felt the wind approaching. Rainbow wanted to try bouncing her way back to Heaven. She promised Ralph she would call her mom if she had trouble getting back. She took one big leap and disappeared from Tom's sight.

"What's that all about?" Tom shook his head in bewilderment.

"Sir, Mother Nature and her helpers are in a special category and have been endowed with unique abilities. They have not lived on Earth, so are not spirits, nor are they classified as angels. The Controller saw a need for some special assistants, such as Mother Nature, and gave them the talents they need to perform their duties. Bouncing around is a skill Rainbow needs to do her job."

Before hopping aboard the wind for their return to Heaven and Mother Nature's garden, Tom gave Ralph a high-five. "I needed that."

"What fun, sir."

The wind got Tom and Ralph back to Heaven before Tom had any time to take in all that he had just witnessed. *That was fast.* But even faster was Rainbow; she was back in Heaven before Tom and Ralph.

Tom never really expected anything from anyone. He was overcome with joy by all that had been done on his behalf today. Even if he could find adequate words to express his gratitude, he doubted he could verbally convey them as he couldn't stop laughing from the great fun that had been created. He went to each team member—Ben, Franklin, Spring, Rainbow, Mother Nature, and Ralph—and gave them a high-five and thanked them for the wonder moment they had created for him.

A brilliant gold star floated in front of Tom. The outside read, "Your best friend." When he opened it, there was an audio message.

"That was nice what you did for Regina," Liz whispered. "And what you did for me. That rainbow was the very best ever. I don't wonder anymore. I know there's good stuff ahead!"

Chapter 47

KATHY'S CANCER TREATMENT

TOM RECEIVED AN invitation from Kathy to an open house at the Medical Research Center. During the event, Kathy was to explain the innovation for treating childhood cancer that she and her colleagues had developed. There also would be an official announcement of the reentry candidate selected to head the research team to test Kathy's concept on Earth. Tom had invited Ralph to go with him, but Ralph declined, explaining he wanted an evening to himself.

When Tom arrived, Kathy was near the entrance. She was kneeling on the floor, surrounded by children, making balloon animals and giving them to the kids. She stood when she saw Tom. She was wearing a pair of fake glasses, black ones with a large nose and a fake mustache. They were like the glasses Tom had conjured up at his Celebration of Life while he was trying to "find" the lost sunglasses for his friend, Ken.

"Wish I would have brought my glasses, but I thought this might be a more formal event." Tom smiled and gave her a wink.

"No worries." Kathy reached into the large pocket of her white lab coat and pulled out another pair. "Now we can be twins. You might want to wear these while I give you a quick tour. Everyone here needs to display some sense of humor."

To the right was a long hallway wide enough for about six spirits with shells to pass through. Several large picture windows were along the exterior wall. Kathy pointed out one of the windows at the large trees and the tree houses built in them. "Looks like fun, doesn't it?"

Tom shrugged. "For some, maybe. I never was a fan of climbing."

Along the interior side of the hallway, Kathy pointed out various rooms for treatment, recovery, and discussions. The rooms had large windows and were decorated in vivid colors: blues, reds, yellows. Some rooms had plastic tables and chairs; others were equipped with toy bins and shelves filled with books and puzzles. The walls in all the rooms were covered with handprints from the spirit kids and pictures and essays they had created. Tom thought the medical center looked more like a toy store than a medical facility. He didn't see any scary equipment.

At the end of the hallway, they turned left, and Kathy explained they were going to the auditorium where her new concept would be presented and the spirits selected to bring her idea to Earth would be announced.

It only took a minute to reach their destination. At the front of the auditorium stood a lectern and a screen for a presentation to be shown. Tom guessed there were about fifty or sixty round tables set up, each table with seating for eight spirits. The tables had pitchers of water and water glasses on them. The walls were decorated in a style similar to what Tom had seen in the rooms along the hall, with handprints, art work, and essays done by the kids.

No one was sitting yet. Spirits milled around socializing, sipping drinks, and sampling appetizers.

"I want to introduce you to my team, the spirits who worked with me to develop my idea and refine it into a potentially effective treatment. There." Kathy pointed to the far corner. "I see them. Follow me." She grabbed Tom's arm and they made their way to her colleagues.

Along the way, many spirits stopped Kathy to congratulate her on her success. She introduced Tom to everyone who stopped her, telling them Tom was one of the kindest people she'd known on Earth.

When Kathy and Tom reached her colleagues, she made the introductions. Tom recognized their names: Hippocrates, Louis Pasteur, Madame Curie, and Clara Barton. They had all made tremendous contributions to medicine during their Earth lives. No wonder Kathy had asked to work with them to turn her childhood idea into a reality.

He vaguely recalled seeing pictures of these people in textbooks, but wouldn't have recognized them. Hippocrates had neon-blue spiked hair. Louis Pasteur was wearing a baseball cap sideways and had a long ponytail. Madame Curie had on a big red clown nose that squeaked when it was pinched, and Clara Barton had an oversized hypodermic needle in her pocket. Tom noticed the kids in the auditorium loved to come up and steal it from her. He wondered why, then saw the reason. She would chase them, threatening to give them a shot. She'd be all ready to give them an injection, but when she did, the needle squirted water back at her. The kids really thought that was funny. Tom did too. He felt like he was at a family carnival, not at a medical research center.

A deep voice in the background introduced Kathy and called her to the lectern. A parade of kids escorted her. Kathy told the audience the spirit children with her were the test patients who participated in her study and were with her tonight to demonstrate the treatment. She introduced Abby, Branden, Hayley, Taylor, Tyler, and Josh.

"On Earth, groups of four to six children requiring the same treatment will gather in a circle and hold hands," Kathy said, gesturing at the children. The kids extended their arms, held hands, swayed back and forth, and softly began humming songs.

"The Earth children will be taught to use the energy and vibrations around them to spread the treatment to the others in the group."

Tom thought he had detected a hint of pale auras from the kids when they initially held hands. Now the auras intensified and he was reminded of laser light shows he had seen on Earth.

Kathy continued, "The number of children in a group depends on the level at which each child is able to transmit energy. Only one child, designated as the leader for the session, actually receives the treatment; the remaining children use their energy to transfer the therapy to one another. The kids take turns being the leader. Tonight Josh is our leader. Josh, are you ready?"

Josh, a lad of about thirteen, had bright light brown eyes and a brilliant smile that could light up a room. He stepped forward, waved to the audience, and returned to his position with the group.

Clara Barton came up with her huge needle and pretended to inject Josh. He fell to the floor, as if he had fainted. The audience gasped, but Josh quickly stood and asked Ms. Barton if she could be serious. She returned the huge needle to her pocket and came out with a much smaller needle.

"This is the size needle actually used in the treatment," Ms. Barton explained to the audience. "Tonight the needle will be filled with a placebo, rather than the treatment, but I will be giving Josh an injection." She gave Josh a shot in the arm. "Be truthful, Josh. Did that hurt?"

"Ms. Clara," Josh rubbed his arm, "you're losing your touch. I did feel a little pinch."

Clara looked like her feelings had been hurt, but Josh hugged her and grinned. "Didn't feel a thing."

The audience burst out with laughter, cheers, and applause. Before the spirit kids returned to their seats, Ms. Clara explained that, since this was for demonstration and no actual treatment had been injected into Josh tonight, the young spirits would not be able to show the transfer of energy that typically would occur. The actual treatment material was needed to ignite the energy to be transferred. The young spirits moved into a line, still holding hands. Ms. Barton joined the line and sang with the kids as they returned to their seats.

Kathy talked about her days as a cancer patient on Earth where the idea had come to her while she endured painful hours of treatment. "When I met other kids in the recovery room, we noticed we felt remarkably better being together, holding hands and singing songs. One day a friend commented it would be nice if we could get cured by just holding hands. I thought about that until the day I died. I tried to imagine ways to turn the positive energy young patients felt when they were connected with each other into a possible treatment.

"When I reached Heaven, I asked to work with experts in the medical field to help me turn a child's idea of an easier and more effective treatment into a reality. I have many distinguished colleagues to thank." She acknowledged Hippocrates, Louis Pasteur, Madame Curie, and Clara Barton. The spirits in the auditorium, young and old alike, cheered. Some young spirits raced around the auditorium on foot; more were on scooters, skateboards, or bicycles.

After thanking and recognizing her research team, Kathy introduced Sharon as the reentry candidate to head the research.

She also introduced a team of reentry volunteers to be part of Sharon's reentry life as classmates, research assistants, and patients.

"Sharon won't be able to do this all on her own. She'll need parents who are already on Earth, anxiously hoping for a baby. It's not a coincidence, but Sharon will be born to her daughter and son-in-law. There are also people currently on Earth who are preparing for careers as teachers and role models who will inspire Sharon to study medicine and specialize in research for childhood cancers. Still in Heaven, but soon to be Earthbound are those who will be Sharon's fellow classmates and research colleagues. In the future, spirits will choose Earth lives to be test patients for this treatment."

When the presentation ended, Tom had an opportunity to quickly congratulate Kathy before she was surrounded by other spirits wanting to add their praises and wish her success.

Tom wanted to chat with Kathy some more. He had learned so much that evening and wished Liz was there to talk about what he had seen, not just the center and Kathy's idea, but the entire process.

While Tom waited for the well-wishers to clear, he had a multitude of thoughts to mull over. *Is this what is meant by the Circle of Life?*

Kathy had been on Earth when she'd gotten the idea. She developed the idea in Heaven and now her new and improved idea was going back to Earth. Kathy's name would not be in history books, though. Sharon would probably be given credit for the discovery.

After the last of the well-wishing spirits left, Tom again praised Kathy for her innovation and wished her great success. "Guess I should be leaving. Thanks for the invitation. I learned a lot."

"You're welcome back anytime. Let me walk with you to the door."

Before he left the medical center, Tom eyed a candy dish on the appetizer table. The dish was filled with bubblegum. "Mind if I have a piece?"

"Take a handful. If you need an attention-getter for a child, a piece of bubblegum is a sure way to get it. It's also a good way to get your words into someone else's mouth—if you ever need to."

"Interesting. How does that work?" Tom was intrigued by that idea. His mind was already racing with how he could put that notion to good use, mainly for fun and pranks, though he would never do anything mean or harmful with it.

"A person just chews a piece of gum you made available. Your words will come to them, along with any ideas you want them to have."

"Very interesting." Tom took a few handfuls and put them in his pants pockets, some in the left, some in the right. And— for good measure—a few pieces in his shirt pocket. Finally, he popped a piece into his mouth. He had smelled bubblegum all night and wondered why. This was probably the reason. But now that he was chewing it, he enjoyed both the smell and the flavor. He tried to blow a bubble, but had never been good at that.

Ralph interrupted Tom and Kathy. "Excuse me, Kathy. I need to talk to Tom."

"Ralph, I didn't think you were coming," Tom said, surprised to see Ralph. Maybe the building would be open long enough to give Ralph a quick tour of the facility. He had been so impressed by what he had seen and he thought Ralph would enjoy it, too.

"I just arrived, sir. I have a request for you from The Controller. We need to discuss it immediately."

Tom quickly thanked Kathy again for inviting him to the open house and for the bubblegum, then turned back to Ralph, trying not to be nervous.

What could be so urgent from The Controller that we need to discuss immediately? Guess I shouldn't question The Controller.

Chapter 48

THE BUSINESS DEAL

T OM AND RALPH stopped outside the doors of the medical center and Ralph again apologized for interrupting Tom's conversation with Kathy. He held a brown envelope addressed *Ralph, Guardian Angel for Tom*, and marked *Confidential*.

"Sir, did you know a person named Steve Brady when you were on Earth?"

Tom immediately recognized the name. "Sure. Steve and I go back a long way. Why do you ask?"

"It appears you are needed for a special project on Earth involving Steve. Are you interested?"

Tom thought about Steve. They'd known each other for close to twenty years and had worked together years ago.

Over the years Tom and Steve had seen many changes in the employee benefits business, taking their careers in different directions. Tom was promoted to another office, which eventually closed due to market shifts. He took a position with another company which called for another relocation. When Steve's office was downsized, Steve accepted a transfer to the home office and apparently had done very well.

"So what's going on?"

"I assume you know he has been promoted several times and is now president of the company where the two of you worked?"

"So I heard. Not surprised he worked his way up the ladder. After all, he learned the business from me." Tom patted himself on the back. "When he started with the company, fresh out of college, his first assignment was as the service rep for my accounts."

"Steve has requested your help. The details are in this package from The Controller."

"Why would a request come from The Controller and not Steve?"

"My guess is that Steve did not know how to contact you. Perhaps he was not aware you had crossed over. His thought about wanting your advice went out as a general request. Messages like these are received and sorted in Heaven's mailroom. The majority are forwarded to The Controller to evaluate and He assigns the request to the spirit He feels most capable to fulfill the need."

Ralph read the note out loud.

Ralph,

Please refer to the attached request. It came to me because Steve apparently didn't know Tom had completed his life's tasks. Steve's situation looks like it might be long term. Please review the general requirements for a long assignment on Earth with Tom, especially the ones regarding strict confidentiality. Contacts with Earth people are not allowed except for Steve and those involved in his negotiations. It could involve full-time work on Earth for several days, possibly weeks.

Bless you,

The Controller

"So what's Steve up to? Trying his luck at the poker tables again?" Tom said. He thought about the time he and Steve had met with a client in Las Vegas. After the business had been completed, Steve had wanted to test his skill at the gaming tables. Steve was a numbers-cruncher and statistically knew what should be dealt. The two of them stayed up all night. Tom had come out a few dollars ahead, while Steve had lost big time. Steve was concerned his wife would kill him, not only for gambling, but for the money he lost. Tom talked Steve into getting money from an ATM, confident they'd be able to recapture Steve's losses by playing the poker machines. Tom, for some reason he couldn't explain, felt he had the ability to sense a machine that was hot and ready to pay off. He found a machine for Steve to try. Steve made a withdrawal from the ATM, played the machine Tom had selected, and recovered his losses.

"Sir, I hardly think The Controller would agree to assist someone at the gaming tables. Steve is dealing with a major challenge. The company is looking at a merger and Steve is in charge of the negotiations. Steve sent out a message, wishing you were around for a fresh perspective on some of the details. I will review the highlights and we can discuss those. You can read the entire note later. There are many high praises for you."

Tom couldn't wait to read to read the note. He couldn't imagine Steve handing out high praises. Guys, in Tom's experience, would joke about something good that another guy did, but actual praising? He would have to see this.

"Steve regrets you are not around to discuss some ideas. He indicates you were decent with numbers and thinking outside the box. He mentions your great people skills as well as your knack for motivating parties to come agreement. Steve feels he falls short in this area."

Ralph handed Steve's message to Tom. "Do you want to look at the details and give this some consideration before deciding?"

Tom took the message. "I've already made up my mind. It'd be fun to be with Steve again. Besides, I can't say no to The Controller. Do I need to let The Controller know I'll take this assignment or will you?"

"I will advise him, sir."

"I guess we have no idea how long this will last. Do you know when I get started?"

Ralph suggested Tom use his ELV to locate Steve and see where he was in the process. "I will go to The Controller's office and let Him know you have accepted the task."

TOM RETRIEVED HIS ELV from his utility bag, which he made a habit of always carrying with him, and set it to find Steve.

Steve was in a large meeting room. To Tom, there was nothing striking about the room. A conference table with seating for about twenty people sat in the center of the room. From the large windows opposite the door, Tom saw a skyline once very familiar to him. After all, this was the home office of the company where he began his career. Many of the older office buildings had been taken down to make way for new structures, including a new parking garage and an addition to the main building.

Under each of the windows were tables covered with boxes, packets of information, and loose papers. Against the opposite wall was another table with containers of water, drinking glasses, carafes of coffee and hot water, cups and saucers, and empty baskets.

Steve was in a chair at the head of the table. Six other people sat in chairs scattered around the table, three on each side. Their names were on the paper name tags in front of them: Amanda, Zack, Frank, Craig, Sara, Jennifer.

Looked like this was Steve's team for the upcoming negotiations. They were finalizing the presentation materials to the merging company.

Steve leaned back in his chair. "We seem to be at a standstill. Let's take break. Amanda, would you please call the cafeteria and see if they can round up some refreshments for us?"

At the mention of refreshments, Tom remembered the soda and bubblegum stops he and Steve used to make. Some client meetings required road trips that lasted several hours. After the meetings, when they stopped for gas, they'd get extra-large fountain drinks. One time on a lark, Tom bought a piece of bubblegum for each of them. Steve's mood seemed to be down and Tom thought the gum might make him a happy camper. It had seemed to work and the bubblegum became a tradition.

An idea popped into Tom's head. He wanted some of the bubblegum from Kathy to be served with the refreshments. Maybe if Steve had some of the gum during the break, Tom could give it test run during the rest of the meeting. Maybe with the gum, Tom could help Steve get through the standstill the team appeared to be in. From what Tom had seen and heard, although Steve was not screaming at the team, Steve's approach could have been worded in a more motivating manner and using a bit of humor never hurt. Tom was sure he could put his words into Steve's mind, and if Steve would use them, the team's planning would be back on track. But he needed to leave for Earth now. Quickly, Tom contacted Ralph and filled him in on the plan.

After talking to Ralph, Tom verified that all his tools were inside his utility bag. He put the bubblegum from Kathy in the little pouch of visibility dust, tucked the pouch back into the bag, and went to the cloud shuttle where he attached the rope ladder. He went through The Veil and set his sights for the room where Steve was meeting.

When Tom arrived in the meeting room, some of the team had left for the restrooms. Others were standing up and stretching. Steve was in that group. Tom was shocked to see how much weight Steve had put on, but guessed that was a price to be paid for moving up the corporate ladder—many late night dinner meetings with heavy food and less and less time for exercise and a healthy life style.

Seeing no new snacks, Tom stepped outside the room and waited for the refreshments to be delivered. Within minutes, he saw a lady pushing a cart, heading his way. She was dressed in a knee-length black dress, black hose, and black heeled shoes. Tom assumed she was from the wait staff for the corporate dining room. *Peg* was the name on her name badge. Although the door to the meeting room was open, Peg knocked on the door and peeked in. "Okay if I bring in the refreshments?"

While she waited for a response, Tom took several pieces of bubblegum from the visibility dust in his utility bag and placed them on the serving tray.

"Need any help?" Amanda asked.

"No worries." Peg easily rolled the cart into the room. First she took the large tray loaded with fruit, cookies, energy bars, and now the bubblegum and placed it on the refreshment table. Then she lifted bins filled with iced soft drinks and juices from the lower shelf of the cart and set them on the table along with the coffee, tea, and bottled water already on the table. She replenished the coffee and hot water carafes, glasses, cups and saucers, various utensils, and napkins. Peg checked with Amanda to see if anything else was needed.

Amanda shook her head. "Looks like we're good. Thanks."

Steve walked over, eying the bubblegum. "I haven't had bubblegum in years." He took a piece, unwrapped it, put it in his mouth, and began chewing.

Tom needed to be brought up to date on the situation. He also needed to know the players—the team—better. As Steve chewed the gum, Tom suggested he restart the meeting with a little reintroduction exercise, having each team member introduce themselves and explain what their primary responsibilities were as far as the team went.

"Start with Zack," Tom said, then stood back and watched and listened.

Steve sat upright in his chair and scooted closer to the table. "Let's get restarted. I'm sure we all know this, but let's review our primary responsibilities to the team. Zack, would you start, please?"

Looks like this gum actually works. Love it when a plan comes together.

Tom watched and listened as the youngest member of the team spoke. Zack, in some regards, reminded Tom of Steve when they had first met, when Steve was fresh out of college. Most of the team was dressed very casually in t-shirts and jeans, but Zack was in business casual with black pants, long-sleeved black shirt, and black tie. Zack cleared his throat.

Yeah, he's nervous, Tom thought. *Will need to feed something to Steve to calm him down.*

"Basically," Zack said, "I help Amanda place copies of the presentation packets on the table before the meeting starts. If asked, at the beginning of the meeting, I introduce myself. After that, sit down, shut up, and observe." Zack did just that.

Tom wanted Steve to say something to boost Zack's confidence, so he sent a really short message to Steve before the meeting continued to the next person, hoping the gum would work with abbreviated thoughts and that the wording didn't have to be precise.

"Need to build his confidence," Tom said in Steve's ear. "Tell him to feel comfortable to pass any observations and suggestions on to you—in private. You don't want the other company to think you have a mutiny on your hands."

Steve nodded. "Zack, some of us have been doing this for a long time. We tend to do the same thing over and over without thinking about how or why. If you have questions about anything we do or suggestions about a different perspective, let me know. In private, of course. I don't want the other company to think I've got a mutiny on my hands."

The team laughed. Tom scratched his head. Looked like this gum was more potent than he'd imagined. *Hope so, thoughts are much quicker to convey than words.*

Steve turned to Amanda next. She flashed a brilliant smile and flirted with her eyes. "My job is to be your slave. Oh, seriously? To get you to the meetings on time. Make sure you're presentable: tie straight, hair combed, zipper zipped. Distribute presentation packets. Help you keep track of the names and interests of the people working for the other company. When the meetings are held here, make sure lunch and break refreshments are arranged. Is that enough?"

Tom leaned down to Steve's ear. "Respond with some humor, maybe something about that's being too easy for a slave."

Steve rubbed the side of his face. "Sounds way too easy for being a slave; I'll think of some other things, if that's the case. Frank, what about you?"

Frank—a tall, thin man pushing sixty—leaned forward in his chair, placed his folded hands on the table, and stated he was the fact man. "If we need additional information from our vendors and suppliers, I'm to contact them. But that shouldn't be necessary; we've asked them everything. Think I'll use the time to get caught up on some sports stats."

Tom fed some more words to Steve.

Steve told Frank his job should be easy. "You don't need to check on the sport stats for me; I'll stay up-to-date on that on my own. Just the facts, Frank. Just the business facts."

Sitting next to Frank was Craig. He appeared to be staring at the yellow legal pad and mechanical pencil squarely in front of him. "I'm the person responsible for recalculating options and redoing spreadsheets if the client requests them."

Craig was a tough one. Somehow Tom had to come up with a compliment for Steve to make. "Tell Craig something like you always do an excellent job," Tom said in Steve's ear.

"Thanks, Craig," Steve said. "I know I can always depend on you to do an excellent job for us."

Craig smiled. Tom got a warm, fuzzy feeling, the kind he used to get on Earth when he had turned a frown into a smile and made a person feel good about themselves.

Steve nodded at Sara, a young woman under five feet tall. On Earth, Tom had frequently kidded some shorter-than-average people as being vertically challenged. He didn't want to be thought of as inconsiderate or politically incorrect, so he carefully selected people who would get his humor and take it as a friendly remark and not as bullying. For now, he would watch her until he felt capable of judging how she might react if Tom were ever to suggest to Steve that he use the term "vertically challenged." She had chin-length black hair and a captivating twinkle in her eye.

"I was trying to come up with something clever, like slave or the fact man, but couldn't." Sara rubbed her hands and said her primary responsibility during the negotiations would be to work internally with various departments, like accounting and legal, to find out what problems they foresaw if adjustments needed to be made to the current proposal. And more importantly, what options they had for solutions.

Tom thought she needed a fun new title. "Maybe call her Super Sara," he suggested.

"You always get things done with very satisfactory results," Steve said. "I don't know how you do it. Some of the problems I've handed over to you have been pretty darn tough. Maybe you should be called Super Sara."

Sara blushed and nodded. "Super Sara. I like that."

Jennifer, a brunette with long, wavy hair, stood up and slammed a folder on the table. "I have the best job of all. Steve, I get to be your boss. And I'm going to be tough. I'm going to be your timekeeper." She pointed at the watch on her wrist. "Making sure you don't go over your allotted time for your presentations."

Many of the team snickered. Tom did, too. *Steve must still have a problem with overdoing his presentations. Be interesting to look at them.*

"I'll step in and answer questions," Jennifer added, "try to reword your explanations and clear out any bumps the other company's team doesn't understand. And the toughest part of my job responsibilities are to help Amanda keep you socially acceptable, reminding you of names, people's interests, families, and what their primary responsibilities are in their company. Any questions?" Jennifer sat down.

Tom didn't know what to think of Jennifer's self-introduction. Either she was one tough cookie or a good actress. How should Steve respond? A round of applause and an outburst of laugher helped him decide this called for humor on Steve's part.

Again Tom bent to Steve's ear. Then he stood back and waited.

Tom wondered about the power of Kathy's gum. *Are quick suggestions going to be sufficient for Steve to pick up on and phrase on his own? Wish I had time to experiment more with this gum before getting involved in such an important negotiation.*

"Okay, boss lady. Maybe I'll call in sick," Steve said and again the team laughed. Steve pulled his chair closer to the table. "Now that I've been introduced to a whole new team and have a distorted understanding of our responsibilities, where were we before the break?"

No one could remember what the last hang-up was about. Steve suggested they move on to the next item on the agenda.

The meeting moved forward. Tom found it hard to work in various rhythms, sometimes just some rapid thoughts, sometimes he felt the messages were almost instantaneous. Most of the time the conversations were moving so quickly Tom couldn't get exact wording to Steve. Interesting to find out he didn't necessarily have to speak the words. His ideas were getting through.

The team whipped through the rest of the agenda without a hitch and finished sooner than expected. Steve looked at his watch. Before telling his team to go home early, he reminded Zack and Jennifer of the time and location of their first appointment with the client and to meet him and Amanda at the client's office. He thanked his team and encouraged them to enjoy the evening. There would be some long days ahead. The negotiations were to start the next day and had the potential to last several weeks.

Amanda stayed to clean up the meeting room.

"Steve, the limo will be here in the morning to take us to the meeting. Is there anything you need done before I leave?" Amanda asked.

"Check and see if the cafeteria has more bubblegum," Steve said. "If they do, make sure the limo is stocked with a couple of bowls filled with bubblegum."

"I was surprised to see the bubblegum with the refreshments," Amanda said. "I noticed you chewed several pieces. Musta been some magic in it. After the break, you were a totally renewed person. Your ideas were very innovative, you got everyone motivated and participating. You even got Frank and Craig to agree on several points; they never see eye-to-eye."

Tom grinned. He'd always believed that humor helped in building relationships. Did chewing the gum help Steve relax, consequently helping the team feel more at ease? Tom wished he knew more about the gum. It seemed to being doing more than just putting his words in Steve's mouth. Many times he'd still been putting his thoughts into words and Steve was already speaking them. Maybe there was some telepathic power in the gum along with word power.

Steve left and a few minutes later Amanda turned off the lights, shut the door, and locked the door behind her.

Tom stayed in the meeting room overnight and reviewed the paperwork for the next day's presentation. If Steve was like the Steve of old, he could get bogged down. He had always told Steve to have the information in his head to address any questions, but not to overwhelm the audience with too many options. Tom decided to put paper clips on places where he'd suggest changes. Steve would more than likely review the presentation in the morning. Tom would make sure there was bubblegum around, and with a little luck, Steve would chew a piece while he reviewed the presentation.

The next morning, Steve and Amanda met in the meeting room to gather the presentation materials. Tom watched as Steve picked up the piece of bubblegum Tom had set on top of his copy of the presentation. Steve unwrapped the gum and started chewing as he thumbed through the presentation. "Amanda, do you know where these clips came from? Did you put them on here?"

Amanda shrugged. "I have no idea where they would've come from. I was the last one here and know the door was secure when I left. You think someone was looking for confidential information?"

"I don't think so. I've glanced at a few of the points marked and see room for some tweaking."

The phone in the conference room rang. Amanda answered it and told Steve the limo was waiting.

"Thanks, Amanda. Please make sure this part of the presentation is on top. I want to review it on our way and make some changes."

Tom rode along with Steve and Amanda in the limo. He noted the bowl filled with bubblegum. Steve put several pieces in his suit pockets, and popped a fresh piece in his mouth as he flipped through the first pages of the proposal.

Could the gum have unintended effects if it got into the wrong hands? Tom wondered. *Or in this case, the wrong mouths?*

He sent a thought to Steve. "Amanda, I've got my supply of gum here in my pockets. That should do me for the day. Don't want to be stingy, but I don't want anyone else to have any."

Amanda promised she would guard the gum with her life.

Tom listened to Steve and Amanda discuss changes Steve wanted to make to the presentation. About halfway through,

Steve put down the papers and said, "Amanda, this sounds strange. All the points marked seem like places my mentor would have suggested be clarified. I'm sure I've told you about Tom."

"Is he in the picture you have in your office? The picture of you and someone else at a seminar?"

"That's him. I was the service rep for Tom's accounts and viewed him as my mentor. Appointments with our clients often required long road trips. We used the time for fun and business. On the way we reviewed the agenda. After the meeting, we summarized the follow-up that needed to be done. We'd get sodas and bubblegum as a treat when we stopped to fill up the car. When we finished discussing the business details, we'd play trivia.

"The time spent driving to the meetings was invaluable. We had already carefully streamlined our presentation, but along the way looked for ways to make sure it was client-friendly. Tom was an excellent relationship builder. He taught me to deliver what you promise."

Steve reached into his jacket pocket and pulled out a folded, frayed sheet of yellow paper. He unfolded it and read it to himself before handing it to Amanda, suggesting she look it over and make a copy for herself when they returned to the office. He explained it was a summary of things he had learned from Tom over the years. "I call this list 'Tom's Top Ten Guidelines to Business.' But Tom didn't need a written list; his values were genuine and came from his heart."

Tom looked over Amanda's shoulder and read the list. He never thought anything he said was worth writing down. Maybe when Steve retired, he'd write a book about business and include something about Tom; maybe Tom's name would go down in history.

❧❧   ❧❧   ❧❧

Tom's Top Ten Guidelines for Business

Be informed

Make the presentation client friendly

Build strong relationships

Anticipate needs

Be easy to work with (but not a yes man)

Deliver what you promise

Know your competition

Thank everyone

Be on time

Make it a win-win for everyone

Two basic guidelines: Make it Fun and Keep it Simple.

❧❧   ❧❧   ❧❧

WHEN THEY ARRIVED at the meeting site, Steve and Amanda gathered up the presentation materials and quickly exited the limo. It had pulled into a No Parking spot and a traffic officer was nearby. They watched as the limo pulled back into traffic, which was busy, but moving.

The sidewalk from the street to the building was filled with fast-walking pedestrians. Tom realized he didn't miss doing business in the big cities: the sounds of women's heeled shoes clicking in the streets; dozens of conversations coming from all directions, mostly from men dressed in three-piece suits and talking on their cell phones as if they were the most important people in the world; the shabbily dressed people screaming warnings of the end of the world. He couldn't wait to get inside the building and away from the trash on the streets, the annoying pigeons, and the smell of the sewer. He much preferred doing business in smaller cities and towns where he could park right in front of the building and where most buildings were less than five stories high.

He followed Steve and Amanda to where Zack was waiting at the front entrance of a building that looked to be thirty stories tall. The building wasn't flashy, blending in completely with the architecture along the street.

Zack was again all dressed in black, but with a very professional look: brilliantly shined shoes, neatly creased pants, a black shirt with gold cufflinks, a black suit jacket and a black tie, which he was adjusting.

Steve shook his hand and gave him a friendly pat on his shoulder. "Ready for your first meeting?"

Zack nodded. "Sure thing."

Steve opened the door of the building and waved the others in. "It's time for our dog-and-pony show."

That was a phrase I used all the time, Tom thought. *Wonder if that was Steve remembering our days together or the gum?*

Tom stayed with Steve every minute of the day: during the presentations, at lunch, during breaks. He even followed Steve into the restrooms. He wanted to observe Steve's interactions with everyone involved, including the representatives from the other company. After the first day of meetings ended, he hopped into the limo with Steve and Amanda and listened to their remarks.

Steve told Amanda he thought their proposal had been well received and asked Amanda for feedback. She told him he had seemed at ease and had kept everyone's attention. From her perspective, Steve had controlled the meeting.

By the end of the week, the negotiating company's representatives had reviewed most of Steve's proposal. It was a complex agreement. So far they were requesting only a few minor changes. Both sides needed to consult with various departments within their own companies. Steve had Sara working with their company's legal department on some potential changes. He confided to Amanda that he sensed a basic understanding had been established and a final agreement might come more quickly than he'd originally expected.

Tom was optimistic about Steve's evaluation of the week's meetings. He knew how it felt to be so close to a favorable decision. After his last presentation while he'd been on Earth, he'd walked out confident the committee he'd spoken to was in favor of his views and would accept his proposal. Could Steve sense how close he was to negotiating a favorable agreement for his company? It was an exhilarating feeling, but had to be guarded, since outcomes were never final until the papers were signed and the ink was dry.

When the meeting ended the next Friday, Tom slipped into the limo and rode with Steve and Amanda back to their office. Steve took a piece of bubblegum and popped it into his mouth. "This seems to be a bottomless bowl of gum."

Amanda agreed. "Peg is doing a good job of keeping it stocked."

They relaxed for a few minutes. Steve broke the silence. "Amanda, you know I sometimes kid about being a wizard. But I've had an unusual feeling since these negotiations started; I think my mentor has somehow been with me. I've found words and conversation to be easy. The jokes I have thrown in are jokes I heard years ago from Tom."

Amanda laughed. "Steve, your sense of humor has been priceless: very funny, hysterical at times, yet clean and politically correct. Something hard to find these days. And I've never seen you so confident and relaxed in dealing with people."

Tom was surprised to see a green star floating in front of him. He hadn't considered receiving messages while on Earth. *Interesting.* Steve's name was on the outside. He opened it and read the message.

> Tom, don't know how your ideas can be getting to me, but if you're helping me, thanks. We're getting close, and I'd appreciate your continued guidance.

Tom felt gratified. He had been with Steve every minute since he'd arrived on Earth to help with this project. He had seen Steve in action and heard his presentations. The negotiations were coming along nicely, but he had not expected to be given credit for his behind-the-scenes work.

THE LAST MEETING was held in the boardroom at Steve's company. Tom was present to watch Steve and the representatives of the other company sign the final papers. The teams from both companies celebrated the agreement at lunch in a private corporate dining room. Everyone enjoyed their choice of chicken, beef, or pasta with salad and rolls. An assortment of desserts, coffee, tea, soda, and water had been set up on a side table.

After lunch, Tom heard Steve and the head of the other team arranging a golf date. He wondered again about the gum. Steve wasn't chewing any now, so it wasn't Tom suggesting the golf date; it was Steve on his own. Did the gum have a residual effect, like a hangover, except it felt uplifting? Could the gum alter behavior permanently? So much to learn about the gum. But for now, Tom silently congratulated Steve, exhilarated that, hopefully, he had played a part in the success of Steve's negotiations and that The Controller would see Tom's performance as acceptable. He was also glad to see Steve talking to the head of the other team about something other than business.

After the representatives of the other company left, Steve thanked his team. He suggested those who wanted to unwind meet at Paddy's, their hangout across the street. "I'll spring for appetizers and drinks, but I completely understand if you prefer to go home. We've put in some long, hard hours over the past several weeks. I'll be there in about twenty minutes, but want to check my office first."

Steve went to his office and shut the door. He looked at the photo of himself and Tom. "Don't know how you were able to help me out here. I have to admit you taught me well, whether or not you realize it, on those long road trips and watching you in action, not only during meetings, but during your day-by-day actions. Thanks."

Tom was embarrassed by the remark. He had just done what was natural to him and was glad he had been able to pass along some of his knowledge and skills.

"I don't give out kudos for most valuable team member," Steve said, "since every person on the team was essential, but if I did, you'd be it. Why don't you come over to Paddy's with me?"

Steve got up, turned off the lights, and closed the door to his office. Tom followed, remembering how much he had actually enjoyed the planning, negotiating, and building relationships that had gone into his job on Earth. The gratification was even better when the results turned out to be a win-win for everyone.

He'd felt like he was part of the team during this negotiation and wanted to experience their reaction to the successful plan they had put together and made happen. Yes, he would go to Paddy's and silently congratulate the team.

Paddy's was once a neighborhood tavern. It had dark hardwood throughout: the floors, the counter, the tables, and the wobbly chairs. Amber lighting gave the bar a welcoming, friendly feeling. It wasn't a neighborhood tavern any more, though. The surrounding houses, built in the early 1900s, had been torn down to make room for the office buildings now surrounding it. Paddy's still did a great business because it served great burgers—considered the best in town—and the people working in the nearby office buildings provided a steady clientele.

Amanda had a small child and was anxious to get home and see her daughter after all the days with long hours. Zack, Frank, Craig, Sara, and Jennifer congratulated each other and Steve on their success. Zack talked about feeling lucky and testing his luck in Las Vegas. He invited Steve to go with him.

Steve shook his head. "I don't think we got this deal done on luck. We put in hours of preparation and hard work. We had a lot of skill on our side. But it does make me wonder what powerful forces are out there for us to use, forces we don't even know about." He finished his drink. "You guys go to Las Vegas if you feel that lucky, but I want to go home and see the little woman."

Tom thought about Steve's wife, Joan, and how nice it would be to see her again. Although he had spent the entire time with Steve during the negotiations, when Steve went home, Tom stayed at the office, since The Controller's instructions limited contact with people on Earth to those involved with the negotiations. As much as he wanted to see Joan, Tom also wanted to be compliant, although the negotiations were final. His job was complete now and he had to return to Heaven. He was anxious to see what his own *little woman* was up to, even if it was only through his ELV.

Chapter 49

THE TRIP TO IRELAND

A Star from Liz

AFTER THE BUSINESS deal with Steve was completed, Tom returned to Heaven. He met Ralph at the snack shop at St. Andrew's clubhouse.

"Have they remodeled or repaired the pro shop since I've been gone?" Tom asked after they ordered sodas. He also ordered onion rings.

"No, it is the same as it has been since the beginning."

"Is there a new groundskeeper? The fairways look greener."

"Sir, there have been no changes here, I can assure you. Perhaps your perspective is changing again."

"Could be." The surroundings certainly seemed different from his first impression. He wasn't at all prepared to admit that he was becoming more comfortable in Heaven and needed to think about that possibility.

The server brought the sodas and onion rings to the counter. Tom and Ralph took their refreshments and sat at a table near a window. It was early evening. Tom and Ralph were the only spirits in the snack shop. Tom saw a few players still on the course as he tried to put his finger on what looked different, despite what Ralph had said about no changes being made.

Next time he played, maybe he'd see something different. Maybe it was the way the fairway was cut, maybe it was the sand in the hazards. Maybe it *was* his perspective. Tom knew something was different; he just had to figure out what it was. He had to admit that every return through the Brick Wall was getting easier. And on every return from a visit to Earth, there seemed, from his perspective, to be improvement in his heavenly surroundings.

Ralph pulled a stack of papers from a brown envelope. "Since this was a project for The Controller, you need to provide the details of the assignment."

"You mean even in Heaven, which is supposed to be stress-free, there's still paperwork?"

"I am afraid so, sir."

Tom quickly completed the report and signed it. Ralph reviewed it, signed off as Tom's GA, and placed the papers back in the envelope.

Tom stretched back in his chair. "Really does feel like I've been on a business trip. Being around Steve was good, but some of the people he was negotiating with were hard core. Feel like I did on Earth after getting contracts renewed. I need a vacation."

A star approached and danced around Tom's head. Liz's name was on the outside.

Tom eagerly read the message.

Hi Hon,

I sure do miss you and think of you every day. Today is one those days I really, really miss you. Saw Glenn and Teresa last night; they just got back from a vacation in Europe. Now I've got the travel bug. I don't know where I'd want to go and I'd sure miss you—you were the greatest travel buddy in the whole, wide world.

Got any ideas? Wanna go with me?

Love you forever.

"Just like on Earth," Tom said, holding up the star. "Always on the same wavelength. Liz wants to go on vacation and what did I just say? I really need a vacation, even more now that I've heard from Liz."

"Sir, would a round of golf help?"

Tom shook his head. "Wouldn't be the same. Golf might be a good way to relax for a day or two, but I need something more. I want to go to Ireland with Liz."

There was a lull in the conversation before Ralph spoke. "Sir, I have an idea. I need to check a few things before I suggest it. Perhaps you could meet me here tomorrow morning for a cup of coffee?"

Tom agreed.

Now that Tom had the idea in his head, it seemed like time took forever to pass. Finally, it was morning. Once again, Ralph sat across from him at the same table near the window. But this time Tom wasn't looking outside. All his attention was focused on Ralph.

"Sir, The Controller reviewed the results of the assignment He gave you. He was quite impressed. I also checked several obscure details in the SWEEP guidelines. Although The Controller and I do not understand your love of being on Earth, we do understand your intense desire to be with your soulmate. Without going into all the details, you will be allowed to spend some extended time with her."

Tom's mind raced. How much time would he be allowed? What did he and Liz want to do? When he realized he could only watch Liz, it felt like he had a ticket for admission to an amusement park, but couldn't ride the rides. He could watch other kids having fun, but couldn't do it himself. But if Liz was happy, he'd be happy.

"If Liz should decide to go on a vacation," Ralph said, "you may accompany her for up to ten days. You may also find the time useful to create some wonder moments if any opportunities present themselves."

Creating wonder moments was the last thing on Tom's mind; in fact, he was wondering if he wasn't having a wonder moment himself. He'd never anticipated a vacation with Liz would be in the realm of heavenly possibilities.

He owed Ralph a world of gratitude. "Thanks, Ralph. Always knew there was something I liked about you."

Then Tom's thoughts turned to getting Liz to plan a vacation to Ireland.

I'll slip some dream potion into Liz's tea and show up in a dream with that outrageous outfit I picked up at Leona's, the houndstooth shorts and the black-and-gold paisley shirt. She surely won't forget that dream. I'll leave her a hint to go to Ireland. How could she turn that down?

TOM OUTLINED HIS plan to Ralph and then put the plan into action. He visited Liz later in the day and put dream potion into her tea. He waited in their home until Liz entered the dream stage of sleep. When Tom entered Liz's dream, they communicated telepathically.

"Haven't dreamt about you in a while," Liz told him. "Thought you'd forgotten about me."

"I could never forget you. I thought you knew better. I was sent on a full-time assignment and had to stay away while I worked on it. Now the project is wrapped up and I'm back to haunt you."

"You can't haunt me," she said with a smile. "How did your assignment go?"

"It went well. Everyone came to agreeable terms."

Liz's eyes widened. "What are you wearing?"

Tom spun around to show off his new outfit. "What do you think? It's the latest in angel wear."

"Whatever. I thought I taught you better than that—you know you're not supposed to mix patterns. The outfit certainly is unforgettable. But if it's angel wear, who am I to criticize? Please don't show the outfit to my mom. It'd drive her nuts."

"I won't. Got a message you're ready for a vacation; I am too. I'll leave you a hint later. In the morning you'll know where I think we should go."

Tom left the dream and returned through The Veil and his Brick Wall. The Brick Wall was feeling less resistant to Tom each time he passed through the barrier.

THE NEXT DAY, Tom set his ELV and watched Liz tell a coworker, Janet, about the dream and her sudden desire to go to Ireland. Janet told Liz she definitely had to go.

FOR SEVERAL DAYS, Tom watched and listened to Liz on his ELV. She was arranging for a guided tour of Ireland. He made his own preparations as well.

Not much to this. Just my rope ladder, make sure all my gear is in my utility bag.

This is great. Without the physical stuff, I don't need to worry about what to pack or what the weather will be like.

This will be fun, I don't have to find my passport, worry about tickets, or get through security lines. Oops, I do need my trusty medium finder, just in case. Don't have to worry about legroom. Think I'll sit with the pilot. Maybe I'll get a chance to fly the plane.

Tom had always wanted to fly jets. He had his private pilot license before he was old enough to get his driver's license. He couldn't explain his passion for flying, but he was intrigued by it. He had wanted to fly jets, but at the time he thought about it as a possible career, corporate airlines and the military would not accept him because his vision, although normal by most standards, didn't meet the requirements for flying jets. He stuck with renting single engine planes, but that diminished as the price for fuel increased.

❧ ❧ ❧

ON THE FIRST morning of the Ireland tour, Tom used the floating spray. He anticipated it would come in handy when he looked for mediums and possibly scouted out places he wanted Liz to see. Tom boarded the bus and looked over the group gathered there. He floated overhead, testing for potential mediums. The majority of the group had no reaction to his presence. A few glanced around as if they had detected a breeze. He drifted lower, closer to ear and shoulder level, and focused on three people who had reacted when he'd glided by.

One woman waved her hand like she was swatting away a fly. He looked at her name badge. Nicole.

Another woman actually turned her head in his direction. *Okay, she knows I'm here. I'll try her as my messenger.* Her name was Carolyn.

Tom tested her through a telepathic message: *Carolyn, see the lady with the red hair?*

Carolyn turned her head and looked at Liz.

Maybe this is will be easier than I thought.

At the next stop, talk to her, Tom urged.

The third person who responded to Tom's presence was the tour director, Dennis. Tom would use Dennis along the way—if there were things he wanted pointed out to Liz.

When the bus made its next stop, Carolyn invited Liz to sit with her at lunch. Over the course of several days, Liz and Carolyn had many conversations. Tom listened in and heard Liz talk about the previous vacation she and Tom had taken to Ireland. Liz told Carolyn she was a widow. Tom had already filled Carolyn in on that situation. He had also mentioned that Liz's birthday was in a few days and had asked Carolyn to encourage Liz to buy a Claddagh ring as a birthday present for herself.

Chapter 50

GALWAY BAY

TOM WAS WITH Liz every minute of the tour; he wanted to see everything and watch her reactions. He had a warm, fuzzy feeling. He loved seeing her Irish eyes smiling. The two of them had traveled to Ireland about ten years earlier for an anniversary celebration. They'd been to several of the places this tour visited, but he was seeing new places as well. He always enjoyed experiencing the unknown.

The tour bus wasn't filled to capacity with its thirty-five or so tourists. Liz sat alone, but always had a seat by the window. Tom knew she was having a wonderful time, listening to the tour director talk about Ireland's history; its culture; the legends; the sheepies, as he called the flocks of sheep; the landscape; and the weather. Many fellow tourists were of Irish descent. Liz chatted with them about their ancestors and the counties from which they hailed. By listening to her conversations, Tom learned that Liz's great-grandmother had come to the United States alone at the age of sixteen and was from County Donegal. He had not known that and was glad this particular tour had an overnight stay in Donegal.

When the bus approached Galway Bay, Dennis, the tour director, brought the tourists' attention to the weather. Tom had taken a liking to Dennis. The tour director had thick, wavy black hair, a constant twinkle in his eye, and an Irish accent that Tom loved. He was a great story teller, and Tom would have loved the opportunity to spend an evening in a pub listening to his tales. He could tell Dennis had a bit of temper. Dennis's face would turn red and his smile would disappear if shopkeepers, restaurant owners, or local tour guides didn't have arrangements absolutely perfect for his tour group.

Dennis pointed to his right. "Do you people know how lucky you are? See those islands? They're about twenty miles away as the crow flies. I've been doing this tour for over ten years now; never before has there been a day I've gone through here and could see them. They're usually hidden by fog. But today it's a grand sight. You're the luckiest people in the world."

Tom knew it was an incredible day, but hadn't realized how unusual a clear day was. The bay was a brilliant blue and he spotted the islands off in the distance. He hoped the weather would hold out for the next day when the tour group would be at the Cliffs of Moher.

AFTER DINNER ON Galway Bay, Liz took a walk on the beach and ran into Carolyn. They stopped and chatted. Carolyn asked if the ring on Liz's right hand was her birthstone. When Liz told her it was, Carolyn remarked, "Your birthday must be next month. You should buy a nice present for yourself, maybe a Claddagh ring. I think your husband would want you to."

Liz gazed thoughtfully at her birthstone ring. "You know, I had the same idea."

Tom felt like a kid anxious to go to a birthday party and hoping his friend would like the gift he had selected. With Liz, he'd always tried to get her the things she wanted, but she never really asked for much. He had liked to throw in a big surprise if he could think of one. One year it was tickets for a concert.

Another year it was a get-away weekend that included tickets for a play she'd wanted to see. He and Liz had known each other inside and out—they said the same thing at the same time, had the same cravings for meals. He was sure if Liz selected a ring, she would know it was a gift from him. But he needed Carolyn to coax her; Liz seldom purchased anything nonessential for herself.

After her conversation with Carolyn, Liz continued walking along the beach. Tom floated along beside her, wishing he could reach out and hold her hand. It was too dark to look for sea shells, but Liz seemed to enjoy looking towards the horizon and the setting sun. She snapped her camera several times. Tom assumed she was trying to capture the sunset and the array of colors surrounding it. She had always enjoyed the beauty of the setting sun. The temperature was cooling and Liz wrapped her shawl around her tightly as she headed back to the hotel. It was the shawl he had bought for her on their previous trip.

Liz stopped at the bottom of the stairs leading back to the hotel and talked to several people from the tour about the folklore and traditions Dennis had entertained them with earlier in the day. One elderly gentleman was proudly bragging about not believing in banshees, one of the topics of Dennis's storytelling. After all the things Tom had seen since crossing over into Heaven, he wasn't so sure banshees didn't exist. He hadn't seen any and definitely didn't want to encounter one.

Liz took a deep breath of the salty sea breeze before going inside and Tom tried to do the same.

Chapter 51

THE CLIFFS OF MOHER

THE NEXT MORNING the bus headed for the Cliffs of Moher. Despite the slow traffic getting out of Galway putting the tour behind schedule, Dennis seemed to be in a good mood and was still expounding on the unusually spectacular weather. The last time Tom and Liz had visited Ireland, it had been foggy and windy.

Guess I might owe a thousand thanks to Ralph.

Tom had hinted to Ralph that he would appreciate some nice weather so Liz could see the Cliffs of Moher, but he'd had no idea what a magnificent gift it would be. He hadn't asked directly for clear skies. It had been extremely generous of Ralph, checking into the possibility of Tom's taking a vacation, and Tom hadn't wanted to ask for too many favors.

As they approached the Cliffs of Moher, the bus again came to a crawl. The road was uphill, windy, and had lots of traffic. People were out to take advantage of the weather.

Although clear, the temperature was on the cool side with a sea breeze blowing in. First thing Liz did, after watching the introductory film in the welcome center, was to purchase a sweatshirt and a golf hat. Tom watched Liz explore the area. She took photo after photo of the cliffs that rose practically straight up over six hundred feet from the sea. Their gray color was a great contrast to the deep blue shades of the sea.

He followed Liz back to the gift shop where she grabbed a quick lunch—a sandwich on brown bread and a steaming cup of coffee without cream. On their previous visit, he and Liz had both ordered coffee with cream one night after dinner. The cream was real whipped cream. They were surprised, not expecting that kind of cream. But they had enjoyed it and had learned something about cultural differences that evening.

After lunch, Tom followed Liz for one final look at the cliffs before the bus left. Along the way, a young lass with very curly, long black hair was playing a harp. She wore a long green skirt, boots, and a heavy tweed jacket. A wool scarf was wrapped around her neck. An Irish setter was at her feet.

A typical Irish setting, Tom thought. They stopped and listened to a few tunes; some melancholy, others very lively. He loved it.

He received an abundance of messages from Liz throughout the day telling him how much he would have loved this place.

She's right; I do love it. Just wish we were in the same realm.

Chapter 52

A Claddagh Ring

A FEW DAYS later, the tour stopped in Killarney. Killarney was large compared to the villages and towns the tour had visited so far. The streets were wider with more traffic. There was a busy downtown area with office buildings, department stores, hotels, and restaurants. Dennis let everyone know that the city had a hopping night life with music and dancing if any of them wanted to participate. They passed through downtown and headed for one of the largest gift stores in Ireland. Dennis promised the store carried everything they might want that was produced in Ireland: woolen clothing, linens, crystal, pottery, books, and jewelry.

Tom knew Liz would never get around to the jewelry counter without some coaxing, so he left her side momentarily to send a telepathic message to Carolyn, asking her to hustle Liz to the jewelry counter. Carolyn offered to look at rings with Liz and guided Liz to the rings before she could protest. Tom pointed out a certain ring for Carolyn to suggest. Carolyn did and Liz immediately asked to look at the ring and proceeded to try it on.

"I love it," Liz said. "It's perfect. It's exactly the ring Tom would have selected for me."

The ring was in the traditional style, two hands holding a heart with a crown on top of the heart. Actually, if Tom had been there to pay for it, he would have gotten one with dia-monds on the side of the heart, but he knew Liz wouldn't spend that kind of money on herself. He was satisfied that she had purchased it. He would have to be sure and to thank Carolyn.

The clerk found the right size. Liz paid for the ring and walked away from the jewelry counter with a new ring on her finger.

Tom hung around Liz while she browsed around the store. The store was mammoth—three floors of shopping. He couldn't see from one end of the store to the other. It was filled with clothing—tweed jackets, capes, hats, sweaters, and scarves, many of which were hand-knitted. There was a huge assort-ment of crystal, pottery, books by Irish authors, and several books about Ireland. The store had plenty of the typical souve-nir items: pencils, magnets, stuffed animals. Tom watched Liz purchase a few more items, then followed her out of the store and back to the bus. She was still looking at her new ring and smiling. He wished he could give her a big hug. But given their circumstances, her smile was good enough.

Back on the bus Carolyn took her seat. Her travel companion, a young girl about sixteen with thick, long, wavy auburn hair and a few freckles around her eyes and nose, looked at her. "Grandma, you have a stunned look on your face. Are you okay?"

"I'm fine, Kerrie." Carolyn said. "I have this unsettled feel-ing. I never knew that lady before this trip and I just helped her select a ring she thought was perfect. How did I know what she'd like?"

Kerrie shrugged. "You always tell me about Irish lepre-chauns. Maybe it was one of those wee people talking to you."

"It was something talking to me. Makes me wonder."

Tom sent a telepathic *thank you* to Carolyn. Carolyn smiled and Tom hoped that was an indicator that she understood. He went to the front of the bus to ride beside Liz who was admiring her new ring. He had to admire it too.

Chapter 53

SPECIAL BIRTHDAY DESSERT

T HE LAST DAY of the tour was the day before Liz's birthday. She was twenty-nine again. Tom had promised her
on her thirtieth birthday she would always be twenty-nine
to him.

He wanted to do something to make the day special. As he
waited for inspiration, he got a craving for cake.

What are birthdays without cake?

The tour's agenda showed a special farewell dinner was
planned at the castle where they would spend their last night
in Ireland. Tom went ahead to the castle, determined to find a
way to surprise Liz. He was in a hurry when he arrived at the
castle and wasted no time finding the kitchen and dining area.
He would look around the castle later if he had time.

At the entrance to the dining area, he paused to look at the
regular menu and at the daily features written on a chalk board.
No cake was offered.

Gotta get a cake on the menu for dessert tonight.

He looked in the kitchen. No one was there. A quick glance
around the kitchen reminded him of kitchens he'd seen on TV
cooking shows. He didn't generally watch the cooking shows,
but occasionally caught a glimpse of the shows—and their
kitchens—when flipping channels. This kitchen had a large

counter where he assumed prep work was done. Pots and pans hung overhead. A large oven was on the side wall.

Seeing no use in wasting time in the kitchen, Tom went to the main dining room where the staff was setting up tables for the evening dinner. He hoped to find a medium among the staff, a person he could communicate messages to who would also be able to convey those messages to Liz. As he moved around the room, he received no reaction from any of the staff. He thought he detected an aura around one of the lads. *Patrick* was the name embroidered on his white shirt. Patrick was a tall, thin redhead. Despite the aura, Tom didn't notice a reaction when he approached.

I need to use my medium finder.

Tom found his medium finder in his utility bag, pulled it out, and directed it at Patrick. It gave a positive response. Tom hoped the medium finder was accurate; Patrick was his only shot as a medium.

He hovered by Patrick's ear and suggested a special dessert cake for the evening. He suggested that the dessert would be available only for the guests coming in on the tour bus.

Patrick excused himself from his coworkers. "I want to talk to the head chef about tonight's desserts. I won't be long." Tom followed Patrick into the kitchen. Previously empty, now a pleasingly plump lady in her late fifties stood at the counter. Her black hair was pulled back into a bun secured in back of her head. She wore a black dress that buttoned down the front, black hose, and sturdy black work shoes. Her name tag identified her as *Brigid, Head Chef.*

"You're right," Brigid agreed when Patrick presented the idea of a special cake. "Though I don't have enough time to prepare a cake. I'll whip up something special with the flavors of the season for tonight's dessert."

After wiping her hands on the white apron hanging around her neck and tied at the waist, Brigid hugged Patrick.

"I love the idea. A special dessert. 'Tis one of the things I miss about running my bed-and-breakfast, chatting with the guests and listening to the special requests they would sometimes have. But after my children moved away and my husband died, I no longer had the energy to keep up with the B&B. My job here gives me the chance to cook for many people and occasionally I get a chance to meet some of the tourists. Is there any particular reason you requested a special dessert? Is there an anniversary or birthday being celebrated?"

Patrick scratched his head. "You know, Brigid, I really don't know where the idea came from. I think it had something to do with the bus tour guests dining with us tonight. If you're pressed for time, maybe you can make a smaller portion, just enough for the tourists in the private dining room."

Brigid nodded. "That would be grand. The servers will need to tell the tour guests about the additional dessert; today's menu is already printed. Will you please advise the staff?"

"I'll do just that," Patrick said.

"Now shoo." Brigid waved Patrick out the kitchen and started pulling cookbooks from the shelves in back of the kitchen, scanning through them.

Tom left the kitchen, relieved. His request was in good hands and all he could do now was hope for the best. The tour bus had arrived and he wanted to catch up with Liz to see what the birthday girl was doing.

The lobby was empty, but he'd probably find Liz in her room. He went behind the registration desk, checked the log, and found out Liz was in Room 428. He headed that direction. Liz was coming out of the room, camera in hand.

Probably heading out to check the grounds and look around the inside of the castle. He would let her be their guide.

She took the stairs to the lobby, then out the door. She went down more stairs to the walkway around the castle and began taking photos. The exterior of the castle was red brick. There were towers at each of the four corners and windows of various sizes and shapes on all four sides. Liz stopped to smell the yellow flowers on the bushes surrounding the castle.

He followed her back into the castle and meandered about. The lighting in the castle was dim. The woven carpets on the floor and tapestries on the wall featured Celtic designs. He stopped with Liz to read the descriptions. Several alcoves in the halls were decorated with fresh flower arrangements; some had the big lilies with strong fragrances, the kind Tom was highly allergic to on Earth, but now, without allergies, had grown to love. Liz stopped at one alcove that had a life-size suit of armor at the entrance. Beyond that was a small stained glass window. Liz snapped several pictures.

The castle gave Tom a warm, cozy feeling. He let his imagination go and wondered what it would feel like to be a knight coming to the castle to rescue his princess.

Liz looked at her watch. Tom looked at it, too. It was time for dinner. He hoped his dessert plan would work.

SOME PEOPLE FROM the tour group were already seated in the private dining room. While Liz chose a seat with some of her friends, Tom communicated with Patrick, pointing out Liz and asking Patrick if he could be her server for the evening.

Tom stood behind her at the table. One of the men seated to Liz's right complained about the silverware. "I never know what utensil to use."

There were both wine and water glasses. A petite lady with a short reach nearly knocked over one of the glasses as she went for the basket of warm breads. Eileen, a lady Liz had spoken to often over the past few days, noted that the white linen napkins and tablecloth were embroidered with white shamrocks along the edges.

Three choices were on the menu: salmon, chicken, and lamb. All were served with carrots and potatoes. While the tourists waited for their dinners, musicians entertained them, playing fiddles, bag pipes, and drums. Tom enjoyed listening to the conversations and the music, but was more focused on the special dessert.

After the entrées were served and eaten, Patrick cleared the dishes away. He returned to present the regular dessert menu and describe the special dessert of the day, a seasonal truffle. Everyone at the table, including Liz, ordered the special. Minutes later, the wait staff returned with the desserts. They were short one at Liz's table; everyone got their dessert except for Liz. Patrick assured her he would return with her dessert momentarily.

Tom followed Patrick into the kitchen. Patrick got sidetracked by a new employee who was having a problem with an order. By the time Patrick had gotten the problem resolved and went for Liz's dessert, the special truffle was gone. He went to Brigid, explaining that he hadn't been able to carry them all and had left one in the kitchen. Brigid appeared to be baffled. As they were trying to sort it all out, a young boy came into the kitchen. He had dark hair, rosy cheeks, and a few freckles below his eyes and around his nose. There was evidence of a recently eaten treat around his mouth.

"Danny, did you just eat a piece of a dessert left on the counter?" Brigid asked the lad.

Danny hung his head. "I'm sorry, Grandma." The boy hugged her. "It was your best ever."

Brigid shook her head, gently pushing the boy away. "You and I will talk about it later. Now go wash your face."

"My grandson's spending the night with me," she explained to Patrick. "His dad and I went out to the car to get his things. I never thought Danny would eat something without asking. He knows better."

Tom was disappointed, but could hardly get mad at these charming people. They were being so helpful. It had been a last minute idea and he'd initially thought the chances were slim that anything would come of it.

Tom sent another message to Patrick. *Think of an alternative. I'm sure she'd really like a dessert with some fruit. Does Brigid have any fruit she can create into a nice dessert?*

Patrick asked and Brigid smiled. "I can do something nice. We'll call it a passion fruit plate."

Patrick went to tell Liz her dessert would be out soon. Tom gave Patrick another message on his way back to the kitchen. *Let the lady know this is a very special dessert, created just for her.*

When Tom saw the dessert, he thought it looked delicious and thought Liz would love it.

Patrick presented the fruit plate to Liz. He said, "This is a special dessert."

"Yes, I ordered the dessert of the day," Liz said. "This looks different than the desserts the others had. But it does look delicious."

"Unfortunately, we ran out of today's dessert," he explained. "The chef apologizes, but she created this special fruit dessert."

Tom sent a message to Patrick. *Tell her again that it's very special and was created just for her.* Tom really hoped Liz would realize that it was special for her. Sometimes she had to be hit over the head.

"'Tis special. Just for you," Patrick said.

Liz beamed. She took a taste. "This is the best ever. Thank you. It's heavenly."

Tom was bursting with delight; he couldn't believe the last-minute plan had come together.

Patrick returned to the kitchen. Tom followed and thanked Patrick for his help. *Please thank the chef, too.*

In the kitchen, Brigid was sitting on a stool, fanning herself. Patrick reported that the lady who was served the special was beaming. "Also, I think I'm supposed to pass on thanks to you, from wherever the idea came from."

Brigid said, "Patrick, you look like you've seen a ghost."

"I didn't see one, but I think I heard one. Not in words exactly, but I got a strange sensation. I'm clocking out for the day. I have an unusual urge to go to Mass. You think I still have time to get to St. Michael's?"

Brigid nodded.

As Patrick left the kitchen, Tom heard him murmur, "Makes me wonder."

Tom returned to the private dining room. He watched Liz interact with the group who had become good friends over the past several days. They took pictures, exchanged contact information, and bid each other farewell.

He was glad the trip had gone so well. But he was tired. The day had been exhausting, working through telepathic messages and mediums. But it had all been grand.

Chapter 54

JOHNNY AND TEEN CENTER

FTER HIS VACATION and return to Heaven, Tom had the residual relaxed feeling he'd had after vacations he had taken on Earth. He excitedly shared stories and gave details to his new friends, mainly Ralph, Willie, St. Andrew, and Kyle. The main difference between this vacation and ones he had taken on Earth was that he had no photos to show. But after a few days, as on Earth, the relaxation feeling faded and things got back to normal.

Was Heaven becoming his new norm? He'd loved the vacation, but he wasn't ready to admit, even to himself, that Heaven was feeling more and more like home. But Heaven was missing one important part, his soulmate.

Once he'd settled back into his routine, Tom made it a point to check out the teen center. *Might as well take advantage of Johnny's invitation to tour the facility.*

Tom found Ralph and asked for directions to the center.

"Mind if I join you?" Ralph asked.

"Why? Am I coming apart?"

Ralph looked puzzled. "I do not understand, sir."

Tom grinned. "It's part of a routine Liz and I used to go through. You know—if something is coming apart, you might want to join it back together. We thought it was funny."

Ralph tilted his head, frowned, and squinted.

Tom shrugged. "Never mind. Sure. Come along. I can fill you in with more details of my trip along the way."

Tom and Ralph reached the center. Several sports fields, tennis courts, and a swimming pool were outside the large white building. The building was three stories tall, the exterior walls covered with art work. Ralph explained that the art work had been done by students, mostly students who had expressed their artistic ability by decorating walls and bridges and signs with obscenities while they had been on Earth. Here they were learning a positive way to use their talents.

At midday the recreation area was deserted.

Tom looked around. "Seems weird there's no one here. It's a beautiful day. Is the center closed?"

"No, it's open today. Johnny provides these teen spirits with a different outlook on life," Ralph said. "Many of them were exposed to sports in their neighborhoods on Earth, but did not have access to such well-maintained facilities. Many participated in street games when they should have been in school. In Johnny's program, the spirits aspire to more successful lives when they reenter Earth. They focus on skills they need to develop, such as the discipline to study. Johnny can tell you more."

Tom and Ralph went to a side door; it was locked.

"Let's check the front door," Ralph said.

Tom tugged at the door. "Why would a door need to be locked in Heaven?"

"This is a prep school for reentry to Earth. It attempts to prepare the spirits for the reality of Earth. Many schools on Earth now are locked when classes are in session. Consequently, the center has locked doors and security checks. There are regular drills for attempted break-ins or bomb threats. Occasionally a knife fight will break out in the halls."

Tom was shocked. "How do spirits get knives in Heaven?"

"It really is a play, sir. Some of the spirits interested in performing arts careers participate in the center's drama department. Students enact skits common to situations that occur in Earth schools."

Tom and Ralph walked around to the front and found the door open. The guard showed them to the main office. A female spirit was seated behind a counter situated a few steps from the office door. She pointed to a sign-in log on the counter, handed them pens, and instructed Tom and Ralph to sign in as visitors. They did and asked to meet Johnny.

Three more desks were arranged in the office and three more spirits were busy with various tasks. One was filing papers in a cabinet located at the back of the office, one spirit was on a communication device, and a third spirit was arranging papers on a cork poster board.

While they waited, Tom stepped to the door and looked down the hallway.

"Yeah. This sure looks and smells like a high school on Earth," Tom said. "All those lockers, a long stretch of classrooms with closed doors, and funny little windows on the sides. The smell of barely edible food coming from the cafeteria. The scent of various perfumes and colognes blended together. Heaven isn't really so different from Earth, is it?"

"You tell me, sir. You have recently returned from a vacation on Earth. You are working on a pass so you may have easy access between the realms. Are Heaven and Earth so different?"

Why did I ever ask that question? I meant it more as a passing comment, not a question I'd have to answer. I don't know. I really need more time to figure things out.

Before Ralph pushed further for a response, Johnny entered the office.

"Good to see you, Johnny." Tom held out his hand and Johnny took it.

Really good. Dodged answering my own question for now. Hopefully, Ralph won't press for an answer later.

Johnny led Tom and Ralph through the halls and they looked into some of the classrooms.

"These spirits are determined to have good life experiences upon their reentry," Johnny explained. "We emphasize the three R's—reading, 'riting, 'rithmetic—for their fundamentals and as a means to learn how to learn. We focus on basics to provide tools for a happy and successful life: responsibility, self-respect, interpersonal skills, trustworthiness, team building, mentoring, parenting. We help the spirits develop skills to find, interview for, and keep a job. The whole nine yards."

Johnny paused as they reached the school's theater. "Tom, I think you might recognize the guys on stage. I believe they testified at your hearing. Matthew, Mark, Luke, and John teach music. Despite their appearances and where you met them on Earth, they actually are quite gifted musicians. They have cleaned up their acts, too. They gave up their tattered clothes and now wear t-shirts, jeans, and footwear of some sort. They still have long hair, but it's neatly trimmed.

"Most of the student spirits are aware that the guys used to live on the streets. But the students also know the musicians used no drugs and did not put themselves in harm's way. The guys tell the young spirits about the hardship of hunger and living in the elements without permanent shelter."

Tom looked in and saw Matthew, Mark, Luke, and John casually sitting on the floor of the elevated stage. A class of approximately twenty students sat on the stage floor with them, forming a circle. The students held various instruments. They currently weren't playing, but listening to their instructors review some new techniques. Luke noticed Tom and nodded. Not wanting to disrupt the class, Tom nodded in response.

The school's theater seated about two hundred spirits, with a center section and seating along both sides. The stairs from the entrance down to the stage were carpeted in red, matching the upholstery on the seats. The stage floor was wooden and the three sets of red velvet curtains were drawn back.

"I'm amazed at how so many of the spirits I met at your testimony have become involved with the kids," Johnny continued. "All the teens are familiar with the Earth Life Planning Center. Although Sharon is busy with her own plan, she takes time to work with the kids. Leona has come to repair scars from stab and gunshot wounds. She's taken off tattoos and made suggestions for appropriate wardrobe choices."

"Wouldn't that be done soon after their arrival?" Tom asked.

Johnny explained that many of the spirits wanted to keep their tattoos, piercings, and scars because on Earth those markings were their identities and they were proud to have their shells reflect that identity. "But several, after learning of the school and the opportunity to reenter Earth for a better life, have requested removal of the markings. They want to get rid of the reminders and focus on living a clean new life on Earth, instead of dwelling on their past."

Tom and Ralph continued with Johnny to see more of the facility. They moved on, pausing at a beverage machine. Johnny selected three bottled waters, kept one, and handed the others to Tom and Ralph. He drank most of the bottle before continuing. "Willie plays golf with the students, fostering good sportsmanship. Some of the students planning for reentry are looking into Kathy's medical program either as patients or researchers. Greg teaches classes in financial responsibility. He also provides opportunities for the students to get financial experience through his required-to-pay program and often hires them for jobs at the bank. Clare comes by occasionally with ice cream and always reminds them in a friendly way to stay away from drugs and alcohol. When she can, Clare's mother, Meg, teaches a parenting skills class."

"It is astonishing how one spirit can bring together so many others, even in Heaven." Ralph winked at Tom. "Is Heaven really so different than Earth?"

That's a relief; he's not going to press me for an answer.

The ring of a bell signaled the end of class. The halls filled with a horde of students.

Tom thanked Johnny for the tour and offered to help with the teens. "I could play the role of the mean boss."

"That you could." Johnny grinned. "If these kids need it when they reenter, I hope there's someone like you to get them on the right path."

Tom didn't feel he deserved credit for turning Johnny's life around. Johnny had done that on his own by making a good decision and working hard. But if he'd planted even a small seed in Johnny's mind all those years ago, Tom was glad and was very impressed by the good work Johnny was doing now.

After Tom and Ralph left the building, Ralph paused for a moment.

"I do not want to get too emotional, sir. Despite the pranks you like to pull and the way you word things sometimes, your Earth friends are right. You really are a friend to all. I am proud to be your guardian angel."

"Thanks, guess I couldn't have done it without you."

Tom liked the fact that Ralph was proud of him, but felt uncomfortable receiving compliments one-on-one. He changed the subject as quickly as he could. "Let's go find us a golf course to play."

Chapter 55

A CHRISTMAS SURPRISE

IT WAS CHRISTMAS time. Tom had promised his father-in-law, Rayme, he would go with him to look for Christmas trees. He ran into Rayme every time he went to the bank. He sometimes wished he hadn't told Rayme about Greg's invitation—come into the bank and they would fill his pockets with free samples. Tom's concern was Rayme might become an unwelcome customer.

Last time they'd been at the bank, Tom and Rayme had set a date to get Christmas trees. Rayme wanted one for his small apartment. Tom and Ralph also planned to pick up trees for Johnny's facility and for Kathy's center. Although they didn't need to pay for the trees, Tom thought it would be quite an experience to have Rayme along. His father-in-law thought everything was a rip-off and always wanted to bargain for the best deal. On Earth, Tom had watched Rayme haggle over the price of Christmas trees and used cars. Every year around Thanksgiving, Liz had filled Tom in on the lowest prices Rayme had found for turkeys.

The male spirit who managed the Christmas tree lot had set up the perfect scene for a winter Christmas, so the experience of selecting a Christmas tree was similar to a winter Christmas on Earth.

The front of the lot was filled with trees already cut and ready for customers to take away. Beyond the cut trees was a tree farm where spirits could select and cut their own trees.

The lot manager looked to be in his early sixties, judging by his shell. He had on a heavyweight black-and-red flannel shirt, work gloves, brown work boots, jeans, and a black-and-red checkered hat with flaps to cover his ears.

Christmas music was playing in the background and hot beverages were available.

"How much would you give for this tree?" Rayme asked Tom. Tom looked at his father-in-law and didn't like what he saw. Rayme had a twinkle in his eyes and a smile on his face that, over the years, Tom had come to recognize as Rayme's signal that he was scheming something. That something usually meant trouble.

"Five bucks." Tom threw out a number he thought even his father-in-law might consider a deal.

"Nah." Rayme crinkled his nose in disapproval. "Way too much. Look how crooked it is."

Tom shrugged. "Just get an artificial tree. You know I'm allergic to the smell of pine."

"Forget about the pine allergy. Doesn't matter now. You're dead, remember?"

Tom ignored the comment. Rayme was right; his prior Earth allergies were no longer an issue. But there'd been a time on Earth when he had lost his temper with Rayme. Tom had allowed his father-in-law to smoke in his car. Rayme had bought a pine-scented air freshener to put in Tom's car to cover up the smoke smell left in his car. Tom hadn't been aware of the air freshener initially, but in a matter of minutes, his eyes swelled and began to water. He sneezed incessantly. It may have been the aggravation of the allergies, but he let Rayme know—in not the kindest way—that he did not appreciate the pine air freshener, in spite of the good intentions.

Tom selected another tree for Rayme's scrutiny. Rayme shook it to see how many needles would fall off. Very few did. He shook it again. None fell this time. After another careful inspection, Rayme shrugged. "Think I can get it for three?"

Tom waited.

"Hey, I'll give you three bucks for this tree," Rayme offered the spirit responsible for the tree farm.

On Earth, Tom had often been embarrassed when his father-in-law haggled over prices. He felt uncomfortable now as it seemed his father-in-law was bargaining too hard. Rayme had already made two offers on what was, essentially, a free tree. Tom was relieved when he saw a star message headed his way.

He'd gotten many red, gold, or blue stars because of the Christmas season. He had received more Christmas greetings in Heaven than he ever had on Earth. He guessed it was because the stars could get to him with a mere thought. Cards took effort—people had to take time to buy, address, and mail them. He'd never bothered with cards, but Liz had made sure they kept in touch with friends.

Tom was surprised to see the star was purple with orange edges, the type of star sent when someone was ticked. The name 'Bob' was flaming on the outside. Bob had been one of Tom's coworkers.

"This is from one of the guys I worked with. He's upset about something and I should check it out," Tom told Ralph and Rayme. "Here's twenty bucks."

Tom handed Rayme a bill, some of the never-know-when-you'll-need-it money he'd picked up during his visit to the bank, and winked at the tree farm attendant. "Let him pay for the tree. He likes to think he got a bargain."

"Ralph, keep an eye on him." Tom pleaded. "Don't let him get too carried away."

He turned back to his father-in-law. "Don't forget we need trees for Kathy and Johnny, too. See what kinda deal you can get for all three. Get some decorations and lights thrown in. I know you'll drive a hard bargain."

Tom grabbed his ELV and set the screen on Bob.

Bob was at lunch with Sandra and Roger, other people Tom had worked with. The remaining bits of food on their plates told Tom that Roger must have chosen the lunch place, a pub that served lunch, mostly burgers and a few salads. Roger was tall and thin and could eat whatever he wanted. He always went with burgers and onion rings or fries. Tom and Bob both had to work to keep weight off and typically ate low-carb foods. When Roger was with them, however, they'd forego the salads for burgers and fries.

"Looks like Roger's influence won out again," Tom muttered. There were remnants of a bun on Sandra's plate. Bob asked if anyone wanted the last onion ring. Neither Roger nor Sandra did. Bob grabbed it. After finishing the onion ring, he wiped the grease from his white mustache.

They were dressed casually.

Where's their Christmas spirit? They always wear festive ties and sweaters around Christmas. Today should be the last work day before Christmas. From the looks on their faces, they're not happy campers. Wonder what's going on?

Tom headed to Earth. On his way, he tried to listen to their conversation, but the signal from his ELV faded in and out.

He'd heard there was a new version of the ELV, the ELV II. *Should upgrade to the new version. Maybe Santa will bring me one. Hmm, I haven't seen Santa here. What am I thinking? Santa's at the North Pole. Wonder if he'll ever be here or will he live on Earth forever?*

The ELV signal returned.

"Everybody packed up?" Bob asked.

"Everything from my office is boxed up," Sandra said, "and all the manuals are packed."

"Good," Roger said, "you wanna help me? I've been on the phone all morning and haven't even got started."

Sandra agreed to help Roger and asked Bob how his office was coming along.

Bob said he had a few personal items left on his desk, including a picture of Tom and him from a reward ceremony earlier in the year.

"Things haven't been the same without Tom," Roger said. "Now we have to deal with this move. This work stuff really isn't fun anymore."

Bob turned sideways in his chair and crossed his legs. "You know, I'm pissed at Tom for leaving. He still owes me a buck from our last bet."

"You guys always had a bet going. What was this one for—a flight time or how long a meeting would last?" Sandra asked. "Was it for football? Tom always lost those bets."

"He owes you a buck?" Roger raised an eyebrow. "I can't believe he didn't pay up. He always paid, but usually with some lame excuse for why he didn't win."

"We had a bet going—when the manager who laid Tom and me off from our previous jobs would get axed."

"That jerk got fired the day Tom died," Sandra said. "There's no way Tom could've paid you."

"Doesn't matter. The bet was whether he would be fired before or after a specified date. I said before and he was fired earlier than the date we had chosen. So I won. Tom still owes me a buck. Liz offered to pay, but I want the dollar from Tom. Until I get it from him, I can say he owes me." Bob lifted a hand to signal the waitress. "Ready to rock? We need to take down the computers and move Tom's desk."

Bob's remark about Tom's not paying off a bet bothered Tom. He thought of himself as a gracious loser, although he did win more often than not. When he lost, he paid off his losses quickly. Roger was right, however. Tom always had reasons why, technically, he should have won. Now he would be remembered for nonpayment of a loss.

Tom checked and confirmed he had a dollar with him. Since Greg had told him about the you-never-know-when-you'll-need-it money the bank offered, Tom made sure he always had some currency with him. *I'll leave this dollar somewhere in the office where Bob will find it with a hint it came from me. That should shut him up about how I owe him a dollar.*

Tom left to scope out the best spot to leave a dollar where Bob would find it. The entire office suite was in disarray. He considered leaving the dollar in Bob's office or in the office where the files and office machines were, but decided the best place would be in the office Tom had shared with Roger. His old desk was still against the wall, but had already been cleaned out. Only the computer was on his former desk.

He took out a dollar bill. He covered it with visibility dust, then decided he wanted to put his initials on it. He found a pen on the floor, wrote his initials on the bill, and for good measure, added the date. He wanted there to be no question that the dollar had been dropped behind the desk *after* he died. Tom put the dollar between the back of the desk and the wall. He knew the desk would be moved to undo the wires from the computer. He shifted the desk a few times to make sure the dollar would float to the floor when the desk was pushed away.

Tom heard the group returning. As he waited to see their reactions when they discovered the dollar, he poked around the files to see what was happening with his old clients. He listened in on phone conversations and heard familiar voices coming through the phone. He had considered most of his clients to be friends. It was bittersweet to hear them again. They called with Christmas cheer, no work issues today.

Funny, I never thought I'd say this. I really do miss this work stuff.

Bob walked into the small office Tom had shared with Roger.

"Ready to take this thing apart?" he asked, pointing to the computer.

Sandra came to help. When they moved the desk away from the wall to get to the computer wires, the dollar bill floated to the floor. The three looked at each other in disbelief.

"How could a dollar possibly get there?" Sandra asked.

"Probably fell down behind the desk months ago," Bob said.

Roger shook his head. "No, I had to reconnect the computer just after Tom died. I would have seen it."

"I can't believe it." Bob picked up the dollar and turned it over in his hand. "Look. This even has Tom's initials on it. And today's date."

"Let me see." Sandra grabbed the dollar from Bob. She and Roger looked it over and saw the initials and date.

Tom loved the bewildered looks on their faces.

"Guess I can't complain now about the buck he owes me," Bob said with a wry grin.

"Look at it this way," Roger said. "Now you've got an even better story to tell. The guys won't believe this one. We definitely need to get together for some adult beverages after work."

Bob studied the dollar in his hand. "Things that make you go *hmm*," he said.

Tom thought of one more thing he could do. He had seen the office fart machine earlier when he'd been looking through the files. It was a Secret Santa gag gift from an office Christmas party years ago. The guys had shared it and found it good for a laugh when they needed to lighten up on stressful days. Time to put it to good use.

Usually the machine made the appropriate sound when someone sat on it, but Tom's shell wasn't heavy enough to set the machine off. He looked around and found a heavy reference manual to set on the gadget. The fart machine went off.

Bob, Roger, and Sandra looked at each other.

"Did someone else come in?" Bob asked Sandra.

"I didn't hear anyone and I thought everyone else was gone. Buttons told me before we left for lunch that he had an appointment to review the plans for the new office and would be gone the rest of the day."

Tom remembered that David Buttons was the young man hired to manage the office.

The three looked in the other offices, but saw no one.

Boy, do they look stumped! Tom smirked. *Gottcha!*

The three looked at each other. Roger looked a little green. "Makes me wonder."

Tom decided his coworkers had had enough excitement for one day. He left the office and headed to the nearby coffee shop, a place where he and Bob and Sandra and Roger had held many informal meetings. Distracted by memories of work on Earth, the return to Heaven seemed to go quickly. His Brick Wall was hardly noticeable; what once had been his nemesis now felt like it had been shredded into mere strips.

Chapter 56

AWARDING THE PASS

ENCHANTED HOLLOWS HAD become one of Tom's favorite courses in Heaven. Willie had shown it to Tom on their initial tour. It was the course where players designed holes for the others in the group. About once a week or so, Tom and Willie played the course. They were teeing off the eighteenth hole when Tom's Spirits Only Communication System alerted him to a call from Mary, Queen of Scots.

"Tom, I wanted to let you know Ralph, St. Andrew, and I are reviewing your progress on the SWEEP pass."

Am I behind schedule? Are they going to revoke the SWEEP?

Tom swallowed. "Is there a problem?"

"St. Andrew and Ralph are with me now at the clubhouse. We could put you on speaker, but would prefer to meet. Can you be here in a few moments?"

"I'm just now teeing off eighteen at Enchanted Hollows. Okay if I finish the round and meet you after that? Shouldn't be too long, depending on what Willie sets me up for. He's designed some real challenging holes today."

Mary agreed and Tom returned his communication device to his utility bag.

"Willie, don't be too tough on me. I need to finish quickly. Queen Mary, St. Andrew, and Ralph want to meet at St. Andrew's clubhouse to discuss the SWEEP pass."

"Tommy boy, are you sure you want to play the last hole? Getting the pass is all I hear you talk about, except for golf and Liz. We can leave now; I'll take you to St. Andrew's in my flying golf cart to get you there faster."

Tom had second thoughts about requesting a short delay in the meeting. Willie was right; the Sweep pass was extremely important to him. He assumed it was a routine review. But if it was bad news, he could wait to hear it. He'd much rather finish the round than hear bad news.

Willie did his part to get Tom to the clubhouse as quickly as possible. The hole he designed to end the round was an easy par three. They played quickly. Willie waved Tom into his cart after they finished. "I'll just drop you off so you can get down to business. I'll leave the clubs you used today with Kyle."

Willie had barely come to a full stop before he started urging Tom to get out. Before Tom could thank Willie for the fun day and the ride, Willie was gone.

"Glad you could meet us, sir." Ralph greeted Tom as he walked into the clubhouse at St. Andrew's Gate.

St. Andrew shook Tom's hand. "Tom, we apologize for the delay, but we are pleased to let you know you have completed your requirements for the SWEEP. We need your signature on the application and then The Controller's signature is needed. Depending on The Controller's schedule, we should have the paperwork complete before the end of the day."

Tom was surprised. "I don't want to question your counting or your decision, but I thought I had a long way to go. I only recall one, maybe two, direct requests for my help. One request came from The Controller; I didn't think that would count."

"Sir, we have watched your excursions to Earth," Ralph explained. "You do not wait for specific requests for help. You listen to people. You watch them. You know their needs and do not hesitate to make them smile or bring them joy or make them wonder. You are true to your soul, regardless of whether you are in Heaven or on Earth."

St. Andrew added his congratulations, but also had a question. "Tom, you always know what the score is when you play golf, why not during the SWEEP?"

"As I said, I thought I only received only one real request from Earth and that was from Sandra. The other responses to stars came as a natural response, more for fun than as way to make people wonder."

"Whatever the reason, you more than met the requirements," Queen Mary said.

Tom shrugged. "I always did like to exceed expectations."

Ralph nodded. "Yes, I heard 'exceeds expectations' every time you had a performance review at work."

Queen Mary excused herself to drop Tom's application off at The Controller's office for signature. "I have several errands to take care of after that. Hopefully, the application will be ready when I'm through with my to-do list. Why don't you guys play golf and I'll meet you here when you're done."

Tom had just finished playing eighteen holes and a bite to eat sounded good. He suggested an early lunch followed by playing another round with Ralph and St. Andrew. St. Andrew declined, indicating he had too much work to do around the pro shop. After lunch, Tom and Ralph went to the first tee. As they finished the fifth hole, Ralph's spirit communication device signaled an incoming call. He answered the call, then walked out of earshot from Tom. He didn't say anything about the call to Tom after he got back and Tom didn't ask.

After the ninth hole—or at the turn, as golfers refer to the end of nine holes—Queen Mary was waiting for them in a golf cart. She told them she'd finished her errands sooner than she'd expected and had news about the pass. She suggested they come with her to the clubhouse.

Without arguing, Tom got into the cart, beckoning to Ralph. "Let's go." They followed Mary in her cart.

Tom was more nervous than he'd ever been, wondering if The Controller had signed off on the pass. He'd know the final verdict in just a few minutes.

When they reached the clubhouse, Tom wondered if a tournament was starting. An unusual number of spirits were milling about.

St. Andrew met Tom, Ralph, and Mary at the entrance. "Think you'll like what's going on in there." He patted Tom on the back and ushered him inside to one of the private dining rooms.

The room was set up for a celebration. There were balloons, a table with wrapped packages, and a table with appetizers and beverages.

Ralph whispered to Tom. "In case you haven't guessed it, sir, we were so confident The Controller would approve your pass, Mary's 'to-do' list included contacting the spirits close to you and inviting them to join us in celebration."

It took a few moments for Tom to realize what Ralph had told just him. "Wait a minute. I got the pass?" He was filled with a sense of euphoria. He high-fived Ralph and Saint Andrew and Queen Mary. He wasn't sure a high-five was appropriate for a queen and gave her a hug, too. Then decided to hug St. Andrew and Ralph as well. "I have the pass. I never thought it would really happen. I have the pass!"

He was awed by the number of spirits who had gathered to celebrate his achievement. The spirits from the testimony, his relatives, and the friends he had known on Earth and were now in Heaven, along with several new friends he had made since coming to Heaven, filled the clubhouse.

Mary, Queen of Scots, presented the pass to Tom amid rounds of applause. He took the pass and hugged it. It was about the size of a credit card or a key to a hotel room. But it wasn't plastic, it was gold. Scattered around the card were stars fashioned from rubies, emeralds, and sapphires. An engraving in the center of the pass personalized it:

Tom Malone

Has Earned

A Fareway Through Heaven.

Mary also had another gift for him. "The Controller regrets He could not be here, but asked me to give you this one-iron. He only has one request: if you figure out how to hit with it, you teach Him."

Ralph gave Tom a new, state-of-the-art ELV. "The ELV II has enhanced audio and visual performance. I hope you enjoy it."

"Thanks. I wasn't expecting that. But I've wanted one ever since I heard a new version was out." Tom grinned, shrugged his shoulders, and hugged the ELV II. "I love it." The new version of the ELV was smaller and lighter than his old one. He immediately started tinkering around with it to see if there were other new features.

St. Andrew and Mary, Queen of Scots, presented Tom with a new set of golf clubs.

"Tom, given your propensity to change clubs frequently, these clubs can be altered whenever you like, to your specifications," St. Andrew explained.

"Neat." Tom took the seven iron and looked it over. "The grip feels good." He waggled the club a few times. "The shaft feels perfect." He took a couple half swings, then several full swings. He examined the driver, then took several swings with it.

"Bet this will add a few yards to my shots. Can't wait to try them out." He rubbed his hands together in excitement. "Thanks, you guys. I never expected this."

Tom received many other gifts, including a magic carpet and a copy of *The Restless Soul's Guide to Exploring the Universe.* Tom was thrilled by the gifts: he'd never expected anything from anyone. But what pleased him more than anything, with the exception of earning the pass, was the number of spirits who took the time to celebrate the day with him. He felt very fortunate he had so many friends, both old and new.

As the day began winding down, Tom asked for everyone's attention. "I want to thank each of you for being here with me. You are great friends and companions. I have to admit when I first got here, I was a doubting Thomas. Then I began to wonder. Now I know a few things, at least. I have more lessons to learn, but it should be quite an adventure."

❧❧ ❧❧ ❧❧

SECTION EIGHT

A DAY OF REST

❧❧ ❧❧ ❧❧

Chapter 57

PREPARATION FOR THE SEVENTH DAY

O N THE SEVENTH Day, all of Heaven rested.

On the Saturday after Tom earned the pass, Ralph invited Tom to play golf as a celebration. They met at the course near St. Andrew's Gate and played the golf course there, Paradise Greens at Angels Ridge.

It was early in the day when they met and Ralph suggested they sit down and have some breakfast before they teed off. They ordered at the counter and went to the corner table to wait for their sausage and eggs.

Ralph began speaking. "Sir, I have been remiss in one of my duties as your guardian angel. In all this time you have been in Heaven, I have yet to talk to you about the Seventh Day, which is tomorrow. I am sure on Earth you heard Sunday, the Seventh Day, is a day of rest. On Earth, so it is in Heaven."

Tom put a napkin on his lap as their waitress served their breakfast. He asked for a refill for his coffee and continued listening intently to Ralph.

"While The Controller appreciates the traditions held in official places of worship, He does not expect physical or spiritual entities to spend the entire day honoring Him formally. He finds gratitude in watching all creatures enjoy the gifts He has provided."

"So, will we enjoy His gift of golf tomorrow?" Tom took a bite of his sausage.

"Sir, I won't be playing with you tomorrow, but I have arranged a tee time for you. I am sure you'll find the threesome I paired you with quite delightful."

"You mean you're not playing? I thought you were supposed to watch over me all the time."

Kyle announced from the check-in counter that it was time for Ralph and Tom to tee-off. As they picked up their clubs and headed to the first tee, Ralph continued. "Sir, that is the keyword—watch. You have been off on your own, looking for alone time or playing golf or traveling to Earth. I may not always be at your side, but I am always watching.

"You have earned a SWEEP pass; I do not have to be with you every second. If you need me, I will be at your side immediately. But tomorrow, I would like some time of my own and I think you will enjoy your round tomorrow."

After they finished their rounds, Tom asked, "So what is it you're doing tomorrow, if I may ask?"

"Sir, it has been many years since I had time for myself and I would like an opportunity to visit my friends."

"Friends? You have friends?" Tom asked.

Ralph glared at Tom and bit his lip.

Although he had intended the remark to be friendly and made in jest, Tom realized by the look on Ralph's face, it had hurt Ralph.

"I didn't mean to hurt your feelings. I was kidding," Tom said. "You're a very friendly angel. Of course you have friends."

Ralph smiled. "Gotcha. I was kidding too, sir, with that sad look. It is hard to get one over on you." Ralph laughed so hard he had to hold his stomach.

Tom's face flushed with heat. He very seldom got one pulled over on him. "That was a good one, Ralph, I have to admit." He gave Ralph a high-five. "Let's meet at Gramps' for ice cream tomorrow after I play golf and you visit with your buddies."

"I would like to do so, sir. I will meet you there. Shall we go inside the clubhouse now? If any of the three gentlemen you are paired with for tomorrow are there, I want to introduce you."

Tom and Ralph went into the pro shop at Paradise Greens. Both St. Andrew and Kyle were behind the check-in counter, checking spirits in for their tee times and making tee times for later. Ralph asked St. Andrew to check Tom's tee time for the next day and confirm that Tom would be paired with Sam, Harvey, and Bobby.

St. Andrew looked at his log and confirmed their tee time. "You'll like these guys, Tom. They were all great players while on Earth. I'm sure you'll recognize them. If you need any advice, these guys can give you some great tips."

Tom didn't inquire about the last names of the players, but had a hunch who he might be playing with tomorrow. On Earth, he had tended to get overly excited when he had an opportunity to play some of the best courses in the country and usually didn't score well. He expected that would be the case tomorrow. The course, Paradise Greens, was very familiar to him now, but playing with some of the greatest players in the history of golf—that was another story.

He'd rarely met anyone who played golf who wasn't a terrific person. And he had no qualms about meeting new spirits, highly recognized or unknown. But he felt an excitement building inside him about the opportunity he'd have tomorrow in meeting some of the legends of golf. He knew he couldn't control the excitement he felt and just hoped he wouldn't embarrass himself too badly with poorly hit shots.

୧ଓ ୧ଓ ୧ଓ

Chapter 58

A Round of Golf

U PON ARRIVAL AT Paradise Greens the next day, Tom immediately saw three faces he recognized from books and documentaries on the history of golf. Sam, Harvey, and Bobby were highly respected players, some of the most celebrated instructors and innovators in the history of golf. Tom introduced himself.

All three of these gentlemen spirits had on hats reflecting the styles of their times. All were neatly dressed. Tom had always been impressed by the care taken with clothing worn by tour players on Earth: neatly pressed trousers, highly shined shoes, and spotless shirts.

In the shells they had selected, Tom would have guessed them to be in their late thirties, younger than their ages when they passed over, but a few years older than what was considered the prime physical age for men on Earth.

"This maybe a personal question," Tom said, "and you don't need to answer, but I'm curious as to why your shells are at the ages you have chosen?"

They all agreed that they preferred the more sensible course management strategies and controlled ball-striking that came with maturity to the strength and ability to hit the longer shots of their youth, the shots that could also spray golf balls all over.

It was their understanding that if they had chosen shells depicting a younger age, they would have lost the mental skills that came with maturity.

During the round, the foursome tested out each other's clubs. The three older spirits were amazed at how much farther they could hit the ball with the latest technology they found in Tom's clubs.

"No wonder the courses on Earth now are so long," Bobby said after he saw the distance he got from Tom's driver. "These clubs make it much easier to hit than the stiff-shafted clubs used in my day."

Tom tried to hit a feather ball and ended up taking a five putt. But his sand shots impressed the older spirits. Harvey showed Tom a few tips on getting a better reading of the greens and lining up putts. Sam gave Tom some pointers about adjusting his grip.

The round was one Tom knew he would never forget. The foursome was very jovial, telling jokes, ribbing each other on the occasional poor shots, applauding the frequent great shots. The round was strictly by the rules—no mulligans, no gimmie putts. Tom scored eighty-one, his typical score on Earth, but was okay with that. He wished he could run home to tell Liz about it; she'd be the perfect audience. For now, that story would have to wait.

Chapter 59

A Day in the Park

AFTER COMPLETING HIS round, Tom had some time to wander before he was scheduled to meet Ralph at Gramps' ice cream shop. He had no destination in mind and was perfectly content in seeing where his roving would take him. On Earth, he and Liz often took off on road trips just to see what they might find. They had accidently run across some beautiful landscapes, checked out greasy spoon cafes, and discovered some small historical monuments where they learned many new things. He hoped this afternoon would bring similar discoveries.

A street sign indicated the town plaza was straight ahead. He arrived at the plaza and saw many outdoor cafes. Young spirits, students, couples, and groups of friends were seated around tables covered with white tablecloths. The patrons were sipping various beverages: coffees, teas, or wines. The coffee sent out a very tempting aroma, but Tom's mind and taste were currently set for some cool ice cream and he didn't stop for an *au lait*.

Tom heard many languages being spoken, but he only understood English. Maybe it wasn't too late to learn German, a language he'd always wanted to learn.

He strolled past booths of fresh produce, colorful handmade scarves and sweaters, and one-of-a-kind jewelry. A pretzel stand was at one of the corner entrances to the plaza. Tom realized he was a bit hungry and wanted something to hold him over until he got to Gramps'. He ordered a pretzel dripping with butter and covered in cinnamon and sugar. He got a diet cola to wash it down. He took a bite. *Yum.* It was the best ever. He enjoyed the tasty treat as he continued his exploration before he headed to Gramps'.

Tom heard music and headed its direction. He found himself at a huge park where a concert band was performing an upbeat march. He wanted to listen to the band, but he saw so much going on, he decided to take a quick stroll around the park before he sat down and focused on the musical performances.

The park had large open, grassy areas where spirit families had spread out blankets for picnic lunches. There were trees and fragrant flower gardens. He saw a pond with several spirits on the edge. Some spirits had fishing gear while young spirits fed bread crumbs to the ducks in the pond. Colorful kites floated above his head. Tom saw paths for dog walkers, joggers, and bike riders. He caught tempting whiffs of food being grilled.

He heard delightful screams from the younger spirits. "Push me higher," screamed a young spirit from the swing set on the playground. "Tag, you're it," cried another young spirit from the group of spirits chasing each other. And then there was the proverbial, "Don't get hurt," warning from mom spirits, as if the young spirits could get hurt in this environment.

Tom stopped on a path at the edge of the park. He was nearly hit by a young spirit who looked to be about seven years old. The spirit was attempting to stay balanced on a bike. Tom jumped onto the green grass, moving out of the way. He spotted a bench a few feet away. He sat down, leaned back, and crossed his legs, right ankle on top of his left knee. After taking the last swig of the soda he'd gotten at the pretzel stand, he stretched his arms over the back of the bench.

He took a quick glance at his watch. He had about thirty minutes or so before he and Ralph would meet at Gramps'. The sounds, scents, and sights surrounding Tom delighted him; he couldn't wait to share it with Liz. He felt the bench move as a spirit who looked to be about twenty years older than Tom took a seat.

"That grandson of mine is gonna kill me," the gentleman spirit panted. He had thick salt-and-pepper hair and a matching mustache. His sleeveless gray t-shirt was drenched in sweat. He pulled a handkerchief from his shorts pocket and wiped the perspiration from his face and neck.

Seems like an odd thing to say since we're in Heaven and all. Tom didn't say this out loud, not sure how a stranger would react to his comment, but he did introduce himself. "Hi, I'm Tom."

The spirit nodded. "Sorry about the lad who almost knocked you off your feet. He's my grandson. Alex is just learning to ride a bike. He was in a wheelchair on Earth, but when I helped him select a new shell, we asked Leona to design one that would not require a wheelchair. He's so thrilled now, being able to experience things he wasn't able to do in his previous life on Earth."

Tom looked back at Alex wobbling up and down the path on the bike.

The older spirit chuckled as Alex almost took another spill. "Alex was teased by the kids on Earth, but there is no bullying here, physically or emotionally, which is great for the kids. And if accidents occur, there are no broken bones or injuries to contend with. I'm Gabe, by the way."

Tom grinned. "Gabe, nice to meet you. Is there some sort of festival going on? Seems like a lot of activity."

Gabe shrugged. "Nothing out of the ordinary. This is pretty much a typical Sunday. Spirits who have most of their loved ones on this side usually stay here for the day of rest. As on Earth, individuals get busy with daily activities and schedules during the week."

Alex came back to Gabe and parked his bike. "Pops, will you watch this? I'm going to get some peanuts from Granny to feed to the squirrels."

"What do spirits do during the week to keep so busy?" Tom asked after Alex ran off.

"It depends." Gabe named some activities: working—if they were so inclined—preparing for reentry lives, learning something they didn't have time for on Earth, taking up new hobbies.

"Then on the day of rest," Gabe continued, "you'll still see activity, but of a much different type. Some adventurous spirits, mostly couples, use the day to explore other parts of the universe, including the moon and other planets, either out of curiosity or as places to consider for a reentry life. Spirits who left numerous relatives and friends on Earth come to parks where ELVs are available for every spirit to use. They like to watch their Earth friends enjoy the day of rest."

"Really?" Tom had assumed all spirits had an ELV.

"Yeah, some of these spirits have been here for centuries and have no interest in Earth now. Some will still occasionally look in on 'the old neighborhood,' but when and if their neighborhoods start deteriorating, they lose interest in looking at Earth on a regular basis. So the ELVs here are mainly for entertainment."

"Interesting." Tom had never thought about that.

Gabe continued. "Some spirits take advantage of their pain-free existence and return to Earth for the day. Grandpas have been known to guide the swing of a bat and listen to the cheers for a Little League grand slam. Uncles dive into streams and hook fish on fishing poles to see the smiles of their loved ones when they catch their first fish. Dads balance bikes. Moms find lost toys. Grandmas help bake awesome cookies."

Tom nodded. He hadn't ever thought about all the things that could be possible in Heaven. Every day he was learning more and more; it seemed as if the possibilities were endless.

After Alex finished feeding the squirrels, he returned to the family blanket and asked a spirit for a cookie. Tom assumed the spirit was his mom. She handed him an oatmeal cookie and spoke a few words to him. Alex skipped awkwardly over to Gabe.

"Pops, Mom says to tell you it's time to eat." Alex grabbed Gabe's hand and tugged.

Gabe stood and stretched his back. "Tom, why don't you join us? My Helen makes the best fried chicken you'll ever taste. We'll have warm homemade biscuits with honey and crumbly-topped apple pie for dessert. There's more than enough and you'd surely be welcomed."

Tom thanked Gabe for the invitation and explained that he needed to meet a friend. He stood and shook Gabe's hand, thanking Gabe for the conversation. "Can you tell me how to get to Gramps' Ice Cream Shoppe?" Tom asked.

Gabe gave him directions and Tom took off.

Chapter 60

GRAMPS' ICE CREAM SHOPPE

GRAMPS' ICE CREAM Shoppe was evidently a popular hangout, judging by the multitude of spirits milling about. A design of a multi-flavored ice cream sundae adorned the window of the front door. Black-and-white awnings over the windows matched the black-and-white tile floor inside.

It reminded Tom of a neighborhood ice cream shop he and Liz had frequented many years ago. That shop had served a national brand of ice cream, but had had a local, friendly brand of service that was blue-ribbon.

Immediately upon opening the door, Tom caught a whiff of waffle cones. Everything inside the store was spotless and shined to a gleam—the floor, the windows, the tables, the chairs, and even the glass below the counter where he could see the tubs of ice cream and trays of toppings and where little spirits could easily leave fingerprints or nose prints as they pressed against the glass.

Behind the counter facing the front door, Tom saw a gentleman spirit, probably in his late fifties, a spirit who had to be Gramps. The spirit's face had the most jubilant look Tom had ever seen, and his blue eyes actually twinkled. His smile was a mile long—well, maybe not a mile—but it was very captivating and contagious. All the customers lit up when the gentleman greeted them with his friendly welcome, "How's everything with you today?"

There were about six customers in line ahead of Tom. Tom heard each and every customer being greeted, "How's everything with you today?" Not an unusual welcome, but something about its lilting rhythm and the voice of the spirit made Tom curious. Was it a voice from his past?

While he waited, he did some spirit-watching around the shop. At a corner table in front of the shop, he saw a couple of spirit teens sharing a banana split. Tom couldn't count how many scoops of ice cream it had, but there were many more than the typical vanilla, strawberry, and chocolate. It was covered with peanuts, crushed pineapple, marshmallows, strawberries, chocolate syrup, and other toppings Tom didn't recognize. A mountain of whipped cream covered the ice cream, all topped off with a cherry. And of course, what would a banana split be without the sliced bananas on the sides. The spirits, a boy and a girl, each had a long red spoon. They took bites, taking turns feeding each other. Their heads were close together and Tom heard quiet giggles coming from them.

Along the right side of the shop were about twenty tables with chairs. The wrought iron tables near the windows seated two spirits; the tables near the counter had chairs for four.

A second spirit worked behind the side counter, scooping ice cream into cones and dishes. He thought he recognized the spirit. She might be Meg, the mother of the little girl spirit, Clare, both of whom had testified at his SWEEP hearing. He wanted to get a closer look before he said anything.

When it was Tom's turn at the counter, the gentleman spirit greeted Tom with the same welcome he had repeated with prior customers. "How's everything with you today?"

"My day is great. How's everything with you?" Tom asked.

"Everything is perfect with me. Absolutely perfect," the spirit responded.

Yep. That's the answer I'm looking for.

"I have to ask. Did you work in an ice cream store on Sunnyside Drive?" Tom waited expectantly.

The spirit nodded. "I did; that was a great neighborhood."

"I don't want to hold up the line," Tom said, "but I thought I recognized you. My wife and I stopped in for ice cream nearly every night during the summer."

"I thought you looked familiar. If I remember right, you'd like coconut ice cream in a sugar cone."

"What a great memory." Tom was astounded. "Another question, do you have a granddaughter, Clare? She was the one who told me I should be sure to come to Gramps' sometime."

While filling a cone with two scoops of coconut ice cream, Gramps nodded at the back of the store. "She's here today. That's her, wiping off some of the tables. Sundays get busy around here and Clare and her mom come in to help me out."

Tom glanced in the direction Gramps had nodded. He saw a teenage spirit with long blond hair, but not the six-year old girl he remembered. "I don't see her," he said as he took the cone Gramps handed him.

Gramps asked Tom how old she had been the last time he'd seen her.

"About six," Tom said.

"That explains it," Gramps said. "Clare has lived through many lives, and takes on as many shells as she has taken on lives. I never know what to expect from her. But her mom is pretty predictable. Do you know Meg?"

The lady behind the side counter looked up and smiled at Tom. "Just a sec, let me finish this order." She finished dishing up an order for a family of five, wiped her hands on her black apron, came around the counter and hugged Tom. "Daddy, this is Tom, a man we've talked about many times. He was the stranger who gave up his seat on the plane so Clare and I could come and see you several years ago. And he is the spirit we gave testimony for when he was seeking the SWEEP pass. Will you be okay at the counter for a little bit? Things look like they have slowed down. I want to take Tom back to see Clare. She'll be so thrilled."

Gramps thanked Tom for what he had done for his girls and said it was great to see him. He turned to the front counter where a group of seven- and eight-year-old spirits were deciding what toppings they were going to have on their ice cream.

"Clare, there's someone here who would like to see you," Meg announced as she and Tom walked to the back of the shop. Clare turned and ran to Tom and gave him a big hug, nearly spilling his ice cream cone. He never expected such an enthusiastic welcome.

Before Tom was able to strike up a conversation, he felt a pat on his shoulder. He saw Ralph or someone who looked like Ralph. He had never imagined Ralph could look so down to Earth. Ralph was wearing a white baseball cap—backwards. He had on a neon blue t-shirt, loose-fitting, knee-length shorts, and flip-flops. The shirt and shorts were covered with dirt.

"I am ready for the ice cream you promised." Ralph took off his cap and ran his fingers through his mussed-up hair. Tom patted his head and messed it up even more.

"What have you been up to? You . . . you . . . look so different," Tom said.

"Been playing a little football. Quite exhilarating. You should try it sometime," Ralph said.

Tom grinned. "Looks like you're ready for some ice cream. Pick your poison."

"Excuse me, sir?"

"Sorry. You're still not used to Earth slang. What flavor would you like? I have a hunch Gramps has any flavor imaginable."

"Heavenly hash, please."

"I shoulda guessed."

"Looks like you ran into some old friends." Ralph wiped his dirty hands on his shorts before shaking hands with Meg and Clare. "Good to see you again."

Tom returned to the counter, ordered a heavenly hash cone, and brought it back to where Ralph was still talking with Meg and Clare.

"Thank, you, sir." As soon as Ralph took the cone, he took a lick. "Heavenly."

After another bite, Ralph continued. "Sir, after Clare's testimony you commented what a waste it was for someone so young to die. I have not had a chance to talk to you about some of the reasons. Maybe Clare will tell her story. Clare, do you have time to share the stories of your lives?"

"Be glad to, but I need to keep an eye on the counter and give Gramps a hand if the shop gets busy."

Clare pulled out a chair at the table she had been cleaning and sat down. She put the cleaning cloth she had been using on the table and invited Tom and Ralph to sit with her. Meg sat down with them as well.

"I plan to return to Earth for a multitude of lives," Clare began. "In each life I'll die because of someone driving under the influence. It might be drugs; it might be alcohol. When I prepare for a reentry life, one of my requirements is to be born into a family who will either create or support programs to broaden awareness of the grief an intoxicated driver can create."

She paused a moment, as if searching for the right words. "I am a teacher of sorts. Not a classroom teacher, but a real example of the horrific consequences of driving under the influence."

Clare paused and blinked her eyes. "In one of my prior lives, I was driving some friends home after a party. I'd been drinking. I was speeding when I turned onto my best friend's street and lost control of the car. The car jumped the curb and hit some boys walking home from a football game. One of them was the younger brother of my best friend. He was killed."

Clare stood up and said she needed some water and asked if anyone else did. They all did. She went to the cooler behind the counter and came back with four bottles of water. She sat down and continued. "I never got over the pain I caused my friend and her family. I still feel guilty for shortening her brother's life. Although everyone has forgiven me, I haven't been able to forgive myself."

Before Tom could ask any questions, Clare nodded toward the counter. "Looks like Gramps is busy. I better help."

Tom watched her walk away. "Wow. I thought the Seventh Day was a day of rest and relaxation. Pretty heavy stuff Clare put out there." He sighed and thought about how horrible he would feel if he'd accidently hit someone with an automobile. He thought about the strength Clare showed and wondered if he would be capable of doing the same.

Ralph pointed out a customer entering the shop. "Sir, I see your father-in-law walking in. Last time I saw him he was haggling over the price of a Christmas tree. I thought he and the gentleman spirit at the tree lot were going to get into a brawl. I imagined a headline in the local newspaper, *The Harksville Herald*, Scuffle Breaks Out Over Price of Free Christmas Trees."

Tom laughed. "He's gotten over that bargaining thing. When I explained to him that he doesn't have to pay for things, he decided he liked the free concept even better. But you should see his place. He grabs everything he sees and takes it home. He has stuff scattered all over his house. He says you never know when they'll start charging for things, so he'll get it while it's free. He wants to be stocked up when the rest of family arrives."

Although Tom had seen his father-in-law enter the ice cream shop, he did his best to act surprised when Rayme snuck up on him. Most spirits who didn't know Rayme wouldn't pick up on it, but Tom detected by the sparkle in his gray-blue eyes and the smirk on his clean-shaven face, that Rayme had some scheme going on in the back of his mind. Rayme was a world-class practical joker; he loved harmless pranks.

"Seeing it's Sunday, wanna come over for some Polish sausage?" Rayme asked.

Tom and Liz had always visited Rayme on Sundays and serving Polish sausage for the family was a tradition. His father-in-law had been a cook in the Navy and still cooked enough to feed a ship.

"How many pounds of sausage are you cooking up?" Tom asked.

Before Rayme responded, four stars zipped toward Tom. One was orange and purple; the others were blue.

Tom grabbed the purple-and-orange star. "Better see what these are about."

The orange-and-purple star had the name Tony on the outside. Tony was married to Liz's sister, Donna. Liz's entire family was extremely close and Tom found it simpler to refer to all of them as 'in-laws' rather than trying to explain who was related by marriage. Inside, the message read:

I'm really pissed at you. Playing cards with the guys isn't the same without your sense of humor and the crazy games you made up.

The three blue stars were covered with Xs and Os, the kind kids put on cards signifying hugs and kisses. Only their initials were printed on the outside.

K's star had a picture of a rocket on the inside and a message:

Wish there was a satellite so we could talk to you.

The star with the initial M read:

Miss you.

The last star had the initial L on the outside and was simply covered with Xs and Os inside.

After reviewing the messages, Tom pulled his ELV II from his pocket. "Let me take a look at what's going on."

Rayme was impressed. "You have one of those, you lucky dog. I always wanted one."

When Tom located his brother-in-law and his nieces, he showed the image to Rayme. The family was in their backyard, looking at the clouds.

"Really miss them." A tear rolled down Rayme's face. "I don't even know the littlest one."

"She's a lot like you, loves her mashed potatoes and gravy."

"Wanna have some fun? Come with me," Rayme insisted. "I have an idea how we can see them even better."

What's he getting me into this time? Tom wondered.

Tom said good-bye to Ralph, Meg, Clare, and Gramps. "Hope to see you later."

Chapter 61

THE CLOUD MACHINE

RAYME'S SCHEMES USUALLY mean trouble. *I need to stay on guard and protect my pass.*

Rayme took Tom to an amusement park a few blocks away from the ice cream shop. The small park had a few rides: ferris wheel, merry-go round, roller coaster, and a small train. Rayme guided Tom past the rides to an area in back of the park that reminded Tom of a junkyard. Scattered around haphazardly were parts from cars, planes, engines, various tools, cans of partially used paints and oils. In the middle of this mess, Tom saw a tall, thin blond spirit with a blue denim cap in one hand, scratching his head with the other. He had on a blue-and-gray flannel shirt, denim overalls, and well-worn brown work boots. All of his clothing was covered with grease stains. Rayme introduced Tom to Gus.

Tom held out his hand to shake Gus's. Gus wiped his hand on his overalls before putting it out to shake Tom's. There was dirt under Gus's nails and his knuckles were in need of a good scrubbing. *A real working man,* Tom thought.

"Gus fixes stuff," Rayme said. "He's been working on a beat-up cloud machine. He says when he gets it working, he's going to give it to me. I've been testing it for him. I'm getting pretty good at having the machine make different formations with the clouds people see from Earth."

Gus and Rayme told Tom how the cloud machine could be hooked up to an airplane and used to shape clouds over Earth. Rayme complained that Gus wouldn't let him shape clouds on his own because he didn't have a pilot's license.

"Tom has a license. Can he get a plane?" Rayme looked like a hopeful puppy.

"And why do we need a plane?" Tom asked.

"I thought it would be fun to fly with the cloud machine and make some special cloud formations for the little girls," Rayme said.

Tom sighed. He had his doubts. Surely this wouldn't be permissible.

"Let me think." Gus scratched his head. "Tom, aren't you the one I saw in the paper, the guy who just got through the SWEEP process?"

Tom nodded. "I didn't see it in the paper, though it might have been. I did just get a pass."

Gus grinned. "Okay, Tommy, I'll make you a deal."

Rayme's eyes lit up.

"Since you have a pilot's license and a pass, I'll let you and Rayme take the cloud machine out for a real test. Worst-case scenario, the cloud machine won't make the exact formations you want. Here's my card. Take it to the Wright Brothers' Flying School to get a plane. Ask for Amelia. Tell her I sent you. And tell her to lend you a decent plane!"

Tom felt nauseous. *How many times have I let Rayme talk me into one of his crazy schemes?* He thought about other crazy things he had tried, like the lightning bolts with Ralph, but he had felt safe with Ralph. After all, Ralph was his guardian angel and it was his duty to protect Tom. On Earth, Rayme was quite a prankster and one of the very few people who could pull a joke over on Tom. His adventures were harmless, but Tom always wondered where Rayme's ideas would end up.

Before they left, Rayme insisted that the cloud machine be fully loaded with cloud vapor and asked Gus to throw in some rainbow mix.

Always asking for more, Tom thought.

Tom thanked Gus for the special favors and hustled Rayme out the door before he could ask for something else.

He was relieved to run into Ralph on the way to the flying school. He told Ralph what they were doing, hoping Ralph would put the kibosh on the plan. But Ralph said it sounded like quite an adventure and told Tom to fly safe. He also reminded Tom that the plane could not be landed on Earth, especially since Rayme did not have clearance to actually be on Earth. Tom was relieved Rayme was a witness to the conversation and heard the rules.

Great. Oh well, it might be fun. I haven't flown in years. And it should be quite an experience flying from Heaven to Earth. I bet there's not too many spirits who have taken that route.

Tom and Rayme found the flying school. It was a large airplane hangar which could house about a dozen or so small planes. The overhead door was open and they went inside. Everything in the school was spotless, including the floor. Shelves lined both sides of the hangar from the front to the back and reached from the floor to the ceiling. The shelves were full and neatly arranged with what Tom assumed to be maintenance tools, repair manuals, and parts. The planes sparkled. Tom remembered from his flying time on Earth that after taking a plane out, mechanical systems needed to be checked out and the exterior cleaned. Dirt and smudges could cause problems for the next flight.

Rayme asked to speak to Amelia. She came out to see them right away. Amelia looked every bit the confident female spirit. She was average height, had perfect posture, and shoulder-length curly hair. She was dressed in a leather jacket, leather pants, and leather boots. She found a plane for Tom to take to Earth for the remainder of the day.

Orville, her partner, had flight googles pushed up off his face, resting on the top of his head. He had a gray mustache and wore a long-sleeved white shirt with the sleeves rolled up to his elbows. Amelia and Orville helped Tom hook the cloud machine to the plane.

Before taking off, Orville helped Tom with a flight plan. There wouldn't be much air traffic so that wouldn't be a problem, but Tom wanted a map of some sort in case he got lost, and Orville wanted to cover some basics for the plane. First, the plane absolutely could not be landed on Earth. Second, he and Tom had to check Mother Nature's hotline to see if weather conditions scheduled for the midwest where Tom and Rayme wanted to take the plane were compatible with some small, white puffy cloud formations. If Mother Nature had thunderstorms or tornadoes planned, white puffy clouds would not be appropriate. Mother Nature's hotline reported no restrictions for the day.

Tom wondered if the trip to Earth from Heaven was made very often, but he let his imagination soar as if he were the first to set out on the route. He trusted his skills as a pilot. He just wanted to be sure Rayme kept his hands off of the controls.

"Okay. Let's give this thing a whirl," Tom shouted over the noise of the plane. He reviewed the flight plan and headed down where the clouds they made could be seen from Earth.

Tom set his ELV II to his sister-in-law's home where Donna—Liz's sister—and her husband—Tony—lived with their three young daughters. Before handing the ELV II to Rayme, Tom turned up its volume to hear any remarks the family might make.

Donna's family lived on a lake and Donna couldn't resist buying unusual toys for her daughters to have in the backyard. Tom looked down at their yard and noticed a trampoline that hadn't been there on his last visit when he was still living on Earth.

As the plane neared the backyard, Tom saw his sister-in-law outside with the family. Tom heard the girls tell her about some cloud formations they had seen earlier. They told her that Daddy said it looked like Grandpa was showing Uncle Tom how to use a cloud machine. Tom saw a puzzled look on Donna's face and Tony shrugged. "It's something my mom told me about when I was little."

"I'm going to make a loop with the plane," Tom said. "While I do that, show me how this cloud machine works."

"Ready when you are, Captain." Rayme saluted. He had the cloud machine's control panel on his lap. He typed in something.

"That's all there is to it? I thought you had to have special training," Tom teased as he pulled back on the controls to slow the plane down while Rayme formed the clouds he wanted.

"I do have to be a good speller," Rayme said. "I'm making a dolphin for Blue Eyes."

"That was your nickname for the oldest one, right?"

"Yeah, she has the bluest eyes I've ever seen."

Tom glanced at the plane's control panel occasionally. Since they had no authority to land the plane on Earth and there was no air traffic in the vicinity, he enjoyed watching the family from above. From the grin on Rayme's face he knew he was creating some fun for his father-in-law as well.

"And the middle sister?"

"I call her Smiley because she always has a smile on her face. I'll make a duck for her."

"What about the youngest one?"

"Hmm. I'll probably call her Princess. Look at the gold sparkly shoes she's wearing. I think I'll make a shoe with rainbow edges for her."

Tom and Rayme saw and heard the reactions through the ELV II.

The girls were jumping up and down and clapping. Princess was already in Daddy's arms and Smiley wanted Tony to hold her, too.

Blue Eyes was holding Donna's hand. "Look, Mommy. I see a dolphin cloud."

"That cloud looks like a duck." Smiley pointed. "Quack, quack."

"Look, Mommy. I think I see a shoe with rainbows around the edges. They look like my princess shoes." Princess clapped some more.

Donna said she saw a cloud that looked like a monkey and monkeys were her favorite animals.

Tony thought one of the clouds looked like a shamrock. "Looks like they really have the cloud machine working now."

"When we were watching the clouds earlier," Blue Eyes said, "when Mommy was still in the house, I wished there was a satellite so we could talk to Uncle Tom. I wonder if there really is?"

"You might just be right," Donna said. "Maybe there is a satellite. Makes you wonder."

The day was coming to a close. Tom turned the plane back on course for Heaven. The Day of Rest had turned into a Day of Adventure.

かん かん かん

Chapter 62

COFFEE WITH MATTHEW, MARK, LUKE AND JOHN

AFTER THE DAY of Rest had proven to be so enjoyable, Tom began the next day ready to seek new adventures. During his time in Heaven so far, his focus had been on the Sweep. He hadn't talked to Ralph about working. He had seen other spirits working, but at this point, he wasn't ready to think about it. He had become more adjusted to being in Heaven and wanted to learn more about his new surroundings and he still missed Earth. Not that he'd shirk any responsibilities, but for now, he'd relax.

At the park on the previous day, he had seen a flyer advertising a coffee shop. What had caught his attention was the picture of Matthew, Mark, Luke, and John on the flyer. Apparently their group, Spare Change, performed there on occasion.

I could go for a good cup of coffee. He tried to remember the name of the coffee shop. *Harmony something or other. Yeah, that's it, Harmony's Hangout. Think I'll try to find the place and see if the guys from Spare Change are there. They might be good for some chitchat.*

It was still early and Heaven's streets were not crowded yet. Tom saw a spirit jogging towards him and asked the runner if he could give him directions to Harmony's Hangout. The runner paused and stretched his legs. The spirit wasn't exactly sure, but told Tom the approximate location. It was a few blocks off Main Street on one of the few streets in Heaven that was not gold. Tom walked along Main Street, fascinated by new sights, sounds, and aromas.

He came to an intersection with a cobblestone street on his left. He turned and wandered through a maze of narrow alleys and winding passageways, more reminiscent of a European town or village than anything he'd seen so far. He heard church bells chiming; a sound he had always loved when he had traveled in Europe. Signs hung over the entrance of each shop, identifying the business. The stores were mostly two stories tall. Tom assumed they were used like many of the structures in small European villages, with a shop on street level and the upper floor used for extra inventory and as the family home. Large storefront windows displayed the wares offered within. There were pubs, coffeehouses, tea shops, music stores, and book boutiques. He paused for a moment in front of a pastry shop showcasing masterfully decorated cookies and cakes. At the moment Tom wasn't hungry, but the scents of cinnamon rolls and a variety of breads baking were intoxicating.

I'll have to remember this place. The cookies look scrumptious.

The aroma of brewing coffee led him to Harmony's Hangout. The interior of Harmony's was softly lit. A fire burned in a fireplace to the right of the entrance, giving a warm welcome. The tables were small and intimate, mostly with seats for two to four, but many of the tables had been pulled together with larger groups gathered around them.

Several faces looked familiar, but Tom couldn't put names to most of them. He did know most of the spirits had been musicians on Earth and music went back a long, long time. He could identify a few of the more popular spirits from his era. As he passed by, he recognized various songs. The music was softly playing, none overpowering the other, and nothing interfering with the conversations.

Oh my gosh. I'm in the presence of some of the greatest musicians ever. Wouldn't one of those infomercial companies on Earth love to get their hands on the collection of music they could gather here?

Tom attempted to hide his awe while walking to the back corner where he spotted Matthew, Mark, Luke, and John. Today they looked more like they had during their days on the streets, not cleaned up as they had been at Johnny's school. They wore tattered clothing, a couple were barefoot, one had worn-out socks with holes in the toes, and the last was wearing sandals.

"Hi, guys," Tom said when he reached their table.

John rose and shook Tom's hand. "Good to see ya, man."

Matthew moved over to make room for Tom. "Sit down and join us."

Mark stood and asked, "What are you drinking?"

Tom wanted to review the menu before making a selection. "Think I'll check out the blend of the day and look over their goodies. The pastry shop down the street left me with a craving for something sweet."

Luke walked to the counter with Tom and Mark. Luke introduced him to the manager. "Tom, this is Harmony. She keeps this hangout under control. She plays about every instrument conceivable. Her true passion is folk music. You need to hear her play sometime."

Harmony, a tall young spirit with long, straight light-brown hair, blushed and smiled.

Tom did a double take. "I think I know you. Didn't you used to go to Froggy's?" Froggy's was the hangout he and his buddies used to go to after work. On occasion, some local musicians would drop in for an informal session. Tom had loved

Harmony's voice and guitar playing. He was particularly a fan of her folk music.

"Yeah, I was there the afternoon you died."

"Are you still singing? I'd love to hear you sometime."

"I'll be performing later tonight. Hope you can make it."

"Tom is a good friend of ours," Luke said. "Treat him right. Whatever he wants, it's on us."

Tom chuckled. He knew the guys didn't have to shell out any money for the coffee and muffin, but it was a nice gesture on their part.

Tom ordered a large latte and a cherry muffin. *I think this is the first time I've ever ordered a latte without requesting nonfat, decaf. One advantage of being in Heaven is I don't have to worry about calories, weight control, cholesterol, blood sugar, blood pressure, and all that fun stuff.*

When Tom returned to the table he found another spirit had joined Spare Change. He was sitting facing the table—with the back of his chair facing the table. His legs were wrapped around the legs of the chair. Tom put his coffee and muffin on the table and reached out to shake hands with the newcomer.

"Hi, I'm Tom."

The newcomer had delicate hands, but an extremely firm handshake. "Hi, Tom. Glad to meet you. I'm Mozart."

Tom tried to hide a sense of shock. "You've got to be kidding me. You look a little different than the statues of you in Vienna." Tom smiled. He was still a bit surprised how many spirits he was actually encountering, names from throughout history. He always tried to remain cool about it. It was fascinating to meet new spirits, famous or not.

"Yeah." Mozart's long, gray hair was pulled back in a ponytail. The ponytail hung over his right shoulder and he was fidgeting with its ends with his fingers. With a slight shake of his head, he flipped the ponytail back over his shoulder. "Couldn't wait to get away from the white, wiggie hairstyle they like to put on me in pictures."

There was one question Tom just had to ask. "I was on a walking tour in Vienna and the guide showed us the bishop's house where you were supposedly thrown down the stairs. Any truth to that rumor?"

"Won't confirm or deny."

"What about those all-night parties you and some of your contemporaries had? Word in Vienna has it the music got pretty loud and your neighbors were annoyed."

"Yeah, a bunch of us used to jam all night. Sometimes we did get a bit rowdy and the neighbors complained. Bet they're sorry now. Don't see any movies made about their lives or that any of them ended up with their names and faces plastered all over Vienna."

Tom felt a strong twinge. He knew that twinge—it hit him in the gut when Liz was in a difficult situation.

Without even looking at his ELV II, he jumped from his chair. "Really enjoyed talking to you guys, but I gotta go. Something major's going on with my wife. I need to see what it is and how I can help her."

Matthew gave him a silver flute. "Play some really, really high notes. It may help grab the attention of a medium if you need one." Tom had seen Matthew play the flute sideways. He wasn't sure he could play it at all, but put it into his utility bag just in case.

Luke had a peach rose on the lapel of his tattered jacket. He unpinned it and handed it to Tom. "Here you go. She probably won't be expecting flowers."

Mark took the scarf from his neck and held it out. "Don't know how, but this might come in handy."

"Have a song in your heart," John advised.

Even Mozart offered encouragement. "Go for it, man."

As Tom left the coffee shop, he heard Matthew, Mark, Luke, and John humming a familiar tune. It was one of Tom's favorites, one he'd often requested they play when they lived on the streets of Earth.

SECTION NINE

EVERLASTING LOVE

Chapter 63

ALWAYS AND FOREVER

W ITH HIS ELV II, it was easy to find Liz.

It looked like Liz had lost some weight, but she was, and always would be, the most beautiful woman in the world to him. She was in their bedroom, fumbling around in a dresser drawer where she kept an assortment of important items. Some were valuable—their passports, for example. Given their style of impulsive travel, it was easier to keep passports at home rather than in a safety deposit box. Some items in the drawer were significant for their sentimental value, like the wind-up plastic ladybug with heart-shaped dots Tom had given to her one Valentine's Day.

"I know it's here somewhere," Tom heard her cry out to the empty room as she threw things around. She saw the ladybug and paused for a moment. She gently held it to her heart, then kissed it. She looked at the picture of him on the dresser and whispered, "You always could put a smile on my face." She put down the ladybug and resumed her frantic search with tears in her eyes.

Tom watched as she pulled a golden, business-size envelope from a red box. The box was a deep-maroon velvet jewelry box. The material was old and worn. Tom knew it had belonged to her dad. She checked the contents and sighed heavily as she put the envelope in her pocket. Tom recognized it as the envelope where they kept the key to their safety deposit box.

Liz went downstairs, grabbed her jacket and purse, and went to the garage. After hitting the garage door opener and waiting for the door to completely open, Liz touched his car, the white SUV they had owned for about five years.

"Wish I could keep you. You helped make some fantastic memories with all the road trips we put you through. But between the taxes, the insurance, and your decrease in value, I need to let you go."

Always thought she was a little touched in the head. Now, she's talking to my car. Can't be too crazy, though; her reasons make sense. By letting go, I hope she doesn't mean me too. I want to keep riding around with her. I've got to stop her if she's thinking about letting me go.

Tom felt the twinge growing. *This isn't going to be easy for either of us. I've got to be with her.* He checked his utility bag and its contents. He didn't know what he might need. He had his visibility and invisibility dusts, his medium finder, his rope ladder, his floating spray, and his communication devices. He couldn't think of anything else. For about half a second he thought about notifying Ralph, but reminded himself he had the pass. *I can travel to Earth and I'm going for it.*

He went to The Veil. It looked and felt flimsy, not at all like The Brick Wall he'd experienced on his first encounter with it.

Although the situation on Earth with Liz was urgent, he wanted to relish his victory over The Veil.

"I'm going to use you to my advantage," he told The Veil. He tore several long pieces from The Veil and tied them together to form a swing rope, tucking a few extra pieces into his utility bag. *I'm through with the rope ladder.* He pushed back and used The Veil rope to swing down to Earth. He easily slid down with one hand while holding onto the ELV II so he could watch Liz with the other. Despite his growing concern about Liz, he felt triumphant. He had conquered his enemy.

He watched as she stopped at the bank and requested access to the safety deposit box. She pulled some papers from the box, returned the box to its spot on the shelf, and notified the attendant she was finished.

When she got back in the car, she said, "Next stop, DMV."

It helped that Liz had the quirky behavior of talking to herself every now and then. *Makes it easier to know her thoughts. I wonder why the DMV?*

Tom headed for the motor vehicle department. He wanted to get there before she did. He would probably need a good medium to work with. From the strength of the twinge he felt, he knew something major had Liz stressed.

His entry into the DMV office was smooth. The guys from Spare Change had told him that playing really, really high notes on the flute might help him locate a medium, so Tom moved around the office, playing the flute.

This DMV office was a small branch office. It did not handle driving tests, but could handle registration renewals and license renewals that did not require a driving test, and title changes. Near the front door was a take-a-number machine; above that was a brochure holder with instructions for the documents and forms needed for various transactions. Along the front and side walls were folding chairs for waiting customers. In the center of the room was the work area. A counter with two phones on it was in front for customers who had questions that could be handled with an automated system. On either side of the counter were about ten work stations for DMV personnel to sit and talk to the customers. On the outside of the counter were chairs for the customers to sit while transacting their business. Inside the area surrounded by the counter were about six desks and chairs for the additional workers. Also in this area were filing cabinets, book shelves, and various office machines.

Among the workers inside the counter area, Tom saw a heavy-set lady munching a donut, a bespeckled skinny guy not looking up from his desk, and a young girl giving the impression she was on a very important phone call. A gray-haired guard stood stiffly near the door, posturing himself so the tattoos on his arm could be seen.

None of these people so much as looked up as Tom went by. He was disappointed, but he could try again, using his medium finder. Before he could retrieve the medium finder from his utility bag, a lady with dark brown hair came in through the back door. She wore black capris and a brightly colored, diagonally striped top. The name on her employee identification was Hope.

Something about her caught his attention. She had a glow around her, a radiance like the illumination Faith had pointed out when she helped select a medium to get the peach rose to Liz.

That's it. It's the glow on her face.

Hope looked his direction and smiled.

She knows I'm here in this office.

When Liz arrived, she took a number from the machine at the front door. She looked around and took a seat. Tom glided toward Liz and hovered over her head. Hope nodded.

Tom received a telepathic message from Hope. *What number does she have?*

He looked over Liz's shoulder and read the number. He was not sure he could get the message to Hope. By the time he raised his head to send a telepathic response, Tom had already received a telepathic message from Hope. *I'll make sure I'm the one to help her.*

When Liz's number came up, she took a seat on the other side of the counter from Hope's desk. Liz took some papers from an envelope. "My husband died and I need to sell his car soon. I thought I should change the title on the vehicle to my name only so there'll be no delays when I find a buyer. I think I have everything here you need."

Hope reviewed the paperwork. "Looks like the only thing I need is the odometer reading."

"The car's right out front. I'll get the mileage."

When Liz left to get the reading, Tom and Hope used her absence for a quick telepathic conversation. The gist of the message was that he wanted to keep riding around with Liz. Was there anything that could be done to keep his name on the title? Removing his name made their separation feel so final and he wasn't ready for that.

Liz returned to Hope's station. "Surprised you didn't have to take the next number. Thanks for waiting."

Hope assured her it was no problem. "Your husband, he was pretty young?"

"He was fifty-four."

"He had brown eyes?"

"Yes."

"A little over six foot?"

"Yeah."

Tom heard a tone in Liz's voice, like she was questioning where all this accurate information was coming from. He felt he should feed Hope some information only Liz would know and rapidly fired some private details to Hope. He hoped it would give Hope more to go on than his physical description.

"He wore glasses?"

"Did you know him?" Liz asked.

"No, but he's standing right behind you. Do you feel him?" Hope asked.

Liz nodded.

"He says you're just like him. He says you sleep on your left side. He says you sleep with one of his shirts, a yellow one. He says he wants to keep riding around with you."

Hope paused, then made a suggestion. "You know you don't have to take his name off the title. Even with both names on the title, in this state, you can sell a vehicle with just one signature."

Liz picked up the papers and thanked Hope. There were tears in her eyes.

Tom's spirit soared. But he had one last item to take care of. With another telepathic message, he asked Hope if she could detain Liz for a few moments. Hope replied with a short nod.

Tom dashed to the car, searching through his utility bag. He couldn't remember if he had put the pieces from The Veil and the scarf and peach rose from Spare Change into the visibility dust. He gave them all a quick shake in the dust, just to be sure, then placed the gifts in clear view on the passenger seat and tied the remnants of The Veil to the antenna of the car. He went back inside the DMV, put his hand over his heart as thank you gesture to Hope, and followed Liz out to the car.

She got the message. She understood.

He was elated that Liz had kept his name on the title, but he also was glad she had decided to sell the car. He knew that time would come soon, but for now, he could prepare for it. Selling the car didn't mean she would be getting rid of him. If she held on to his car, she'd be wasting money on insurance and taxes. Knowing Liz as well as he did, he had confidence in her decision making and he guessed she would use the money from selling the car for a travel adventure.

Good for her.

Liz returned to the car. The pieces of the frayed Veil were on the antenna. Liz grabbed them and threw them around her neck.

The peach-colored rose was on the passenger seat along with the scarf that Spare Change had given Tom. Liz reached over to the glove compartment, took out a photo of Tom, and taped it to the dashboard. He noticed the photo had sticky tabs on the back of it, one on each corner, the kind of tabs Liz liked to use in scrapbooks and photo albums.

Looks like she's found another use for them. I like it.

Tom recognized the photo; Liz had taken it on their way to Death Valley over a Fourth of July weekend. There had been very little traffic on the road that day. Not many people would attempt to go to Death Valley on one of the hottest days of the year. Liz had taken the photo while Tom was driving. With the light traffic, he had taken his eyes off the road long enough for Liz to snap the picture. He had a very big grin on his face.

One of our strange adventures.

Liz picked up the rose and held it to her nose. She took the scarf off the seat and threw it around her neck along with the pieces from The Veil.

She looked at the picture. "So you want to keep riding around with me. Are you ready for this?"

Tom did a fist pump. He felt like she had just said "Yes" when he held out an engagement ring. He had never proposed and she had never said "Yes." It was always understood between them that they were meant to be together forever.

The pieces from The Veil diminished ever so gradually until they became one fine thread, sparkling in the sunlight. The Veil which had separated them now connected them. One tiny gold thread with the amazing strength to hold together two entities, two restless souls—one in the physical realm, one in the spiritual realm—with the power of true love, always and forever.

ACKNOWLEDGEMENTS

THERE ARE SO many people I owe profound gratitude to for their influence and support in making this idea for a story come to reality.

Mom, you instilled in me at an early age a passion for reading and a love for books.

Dad, you told me to set my goals high; that I could be or do anything I wanted.

Audrey, without your relentless encouragement the first word of this endeavor would never have been written. You encouraged me to get started and stuck with me through the long haul. Getting me involved in a writers' group was a god send. And your circle of writing friends helped me in so many ways. Your persistent belief in me can never be repaid. Thank you.

Vonda and Leon, our weekly meetings were priceless. You helped me find the perfect words and better phrasing. Not only that, you knew my story and its meaning. There were times you understood my meaning better than I did and helped me express it.

Thanks to my wonderful family—Jerry, Sue and Rosie—for their parts in reading the early, early version of this story and making highly useful suggestions. Thanks for the wonderful memories and stories we shared that have become part of this story. Your reminders to keep plugging away were definitely appreciated.

I am blessed with many friends who shared many memories and stories that have been woven into this story. I'm sure you know who you are. And believe me, I will never forget you.

Many friends followed the progress of this project. They frequently inquired about the how the "book" was coming. They often asked just at the point when I had "writer's block" or when I was frustrated with the chapter I was working on. But their interest gave me a jump start and I beseeched them, as a favor to me, to continue asking on a regular basis for updates. Many thanks.

Several early readers of what I thought was the final version of the story, gave me suggestions to give the story more depth. They also gave me encouragement that the story was worthy of seeking publication. Thank you, Carol, Jacci, Brad.

Louisa, my editor, took a leap of faith in taking on my story. She gave clarity to my thoughts, added depth to my characters, and suggested many descriptive passages to bring the story to life. Thanks for your confidence and patience.

With Louisa's guidance, I found the artist whose cover design I found amazing. To me, it reflects the story beautifully and reflects the care of the artist. Thanks, Brandon.

And, Tom, what can I say? You played so many roles. You are my inspiration, my cheerleader, my strength, my role model, and the one who keeps me laughing. Many, many thanks—always and forever!

About the Author

MARY FISCHER was born and raised in the Midwest, the heartland of the country. She currently lives in the Truckee Meadows of Northern Nevada, surrounded by the beauty of the mountains. After retiring, Mary became involved in various volunteer activities. She has been a hospice volunteer for over twelve years, visiting patients and providing respite care for their families. She has served as a group grief facilitator for children who have faced the loss of a loved one. In addition, she has been involved in reading programs in schools, mentoring programs, and youth golf programs.

Mary loves to travel and experience new sights, different cultures, and the marvels of the world. She enjoys golf and spending time with friends. Her greatest pleasure is spending time with the family with which she has been blessed.